WHAT REMAINS

ERRYN LEE

HISTORIUM PRESS

Visit Historium Press at
www.historiumpress.com

Library of Congress Cataloging-in-Publication Data on file
Copyright Registration on file

Deluxe Edition: 978-1-964700-30-4
Hardcover ISBN: 978-1-964700-29-8
Paperback ISBN: 978-1-964700-28-1
E-Book ISBN: 978-1-964700-31-1

To my firstborn, Tyleia, because she was adamant
that her name had to come first.

To my youngest, Sianne, who occasionally pretended interest in
her mother's odd desire to write.

When you find that thing that drives you, pursue it,
until you can make it happen.

I love you both to the moon and back.

Prologue: When the Sky Falls

Herculaneum, AD. 79

Once, Thalia had doubted the existence of Hell.

She had never believed in the pleasant fields of Elysium, where the good dead went, nor the left-hand road that led to Hades, the cold and joyless halls guarded by the hound, Cerberus. But the old Jewish slave who had nursed her as a child had told her tales of *Gehinnom*, a place of fire and brimstone, of eternal torment where a child who didn't obey her parents might end up. The stories had given her nightmares and her sister had laughed and mocked her. Hell, she had said, was not real.

Her sister was wrong. Thalia walked through it, heard it, breathed its scalding breath, and felt it surge and shudder beneath her feet. It beat down on her head like a crazed drummer, pummeling her with tiny shards of fury. And, like Orpheus struggling his way into the underworld to find and claim his lover, she continued, pressed forward into the blinding ash and darkness. She pulled his heavy cloak more tightly over her head to fend off the hail of light rock that pattered down upon her. Thalia inhaled the smell of him, the salt and metal and musk of him, in the weave. It strengthened her.

Had she not known this square so well, Thalia doubted she would have ever found her way. The thick cloud of ash was disorienting. The Corinthian columns that lined the small forum emerged from gloom to tower over her head, much like the column of ash that had erupted from the mountain early that morning, creating an ominous grey wall that went up, up and up until it finally branched out, like the pines that lined the coast road, their spindly branches reaching out their crone-like hands, always inland, away from the sea. Then the ash began to fall. Powdery at first, like snow, then heavier, stinging missiles of pumice that did little damage but were incessant and noisy. They quickly built up, burying the streets and covering the roof tiles. It had been hours now since there had been enough light to see either mountain or cloud.

Many had fled then, creating a traffic jam that blocked the gates, as every man with a cart or wagon or wheelbarrow loaded with possessions, accompanied by white-faced wives, wailing children and frightened slaves, sought to escape. There were few people now. Thalia had seen a handful huddled beside buildings, underneath overhanging tiles, or pushing towards the port or the empty coastal gates. Some slipped surreptitiously in and out of doorways. She ignored them all, filled with her own driving purpose.

The ground beneath her heaved, and the earth roared. Her feet disappeared into the ash and pumice as though she had stepped in quicksand. Thalia threw out a flailing hand, seeking something to steady her. It closed around the foot of a statue, and before her eyes, the ash formed a crested neck and forward ears of a horse. Pulling herself closer to man and beast, sheltering for a moment in their marble shade, she forced herself to breathe low and shallow beneath the scarf wrapped around her face. The caustic ash burnt her throat and seared her lungs, despite the wrapping. She had stood here, just hours ago, watching the Praetorian Guards drag him away. She had wanted to run to him then but his expression forbade it and she had other things to protect.

Not now, though. Now, Thalia cradled in her arms the earthen jug that held every coin they owned, the heavy gold pendant he had given her, even the long strand of pearls her father had gifted her that had been her mother's. She only hoped it would be enough. Enough to pay whatever fine or bribe was required to release him. To free him before it was too late.

A glance upward showed the statue's hand pointing in the direction she must go. A crash above her head caused a deluge of roof tiles, flinging shards in all directions. Only the protection of the statue prevented her injury. A steaming boulder, hurled by the giants somewhere above, came to rest not far from her feet. Not waiting for another near miss, Thalia pushed herself off the marble statue. Dragging her feet from beneath the sea of debris, she lurched forward. Pumice crunched and shifted beneath her feet as she followed in the direction the Praetorians had taken him.

As she reached the alleyway she kept one hand on the wall. In the lee of the buildings, there was less debris, though the roofs on either side groaned with the weight of it. Hampered by the deeper shade of darkness, Thalia left her hand on the wall, letting it guide her along the alleyway. Her gaze lifted to the roofline searching the gloom, seeking the telltale sign of the *carcer.*

There.

From two heavy chains dangled the omega-shaped rings used to bind the hands of criminals and rebellious slaves.

The doorway was ajar. Inside a faint light gave off an insipid orange haze in this world of grey. Holding the jug closer to her chest, Thalia stepped cautiously. Shrouded by darkness, she peered into the dim interior. A narrow room set with a single bench seat preceded three cells, walls of brick fronted by heavy iron bars. Two were empty, doors ajar. A man, a Praetorian guard by the cloak, hand resting on his sword, obscured her view of the third cell. Thalia stepped further into the doorway. She knew she simply had to enter the room, to offer them the contents of the jug she still held against her chest in exchange for his release. Then they could flee. Together. But something held her in the shadows. A sense that something was terribly wrong. The Praetorian shifted, revealing the obscured cell. In the poor light, it was hard to make out the two figures further within.

She studied the shapes, eyes straining. Two men. One was restrained, arms above his head, secured in chains dangling from a beam in the ceiling. She recognised the breadth of those shoulders, the strength in the arms. The second shape faced the first, a whip clenched in one fist. As she watched, the man lashed out, striking the first man in the face with the whip before knocking the feet from under him, leaving him hanging from his wrists. He leaned close, the words he spoke lost in the thunder of rock on the roof.

While she hovered, still in the doorway, bright white light illuminated mountain, cloud and town. Jagged sheets of lightning cast their glow through the doorway, through the high window, through even the gaps beneath eaves and between bricks, invading the furthest reaches of the space before her. Bringing each figure into startling clarity. The light drew both men's gazes towards the doorway.

Her husband saw her first; his eyes widened. His lips formed words.

She wanted to go to him.

The second man shifted his body, his head turned to face her. His nose was twisted and splayed as though it had been badly broken but the face was horrifyingly familiar. A jolt of fear stole her breath and arched through her body as the man's lips began to turn up at the ends. In doing so, they pressed the corpulent flesh of his cheeks, creasing his leonine eyes into narrow slits that gleamed with what could only be described as joyful recognition.

As the light in the sky faded, leaving its impression burned into her eyelids, her heart seemed to falter and then race. Every muscle tightened. Fear became horror.

The words formed by her husband's lips became clear.

Run.

Chapter One: A Body in the Latrine

Ercolano, 2022

'You are not wanted here.'

I had been standing precariously on a footstool, one foot on tippy toes, the other raised and extended to help balance as I reached to grasp the cardboard box on the high shelf and the sound of the voice made me wobble precariously. The words were spoken in Italian. Steadying myself with one hand I hesitated for a moment, decided not to reply, and hooked the edge of the box I had been reaching for with my fingernail, tugging it gently towards me. With each movement a rivulet of dust spiralled down towards me.

'I could think of a dozen projects more worthy of the investment.'

My mother was wrong. Ignoring something would not make it go away. The dangling overhead fluoro flickered in an emphatic pulse to punctuate the scornful voice. I felt my jaw clench restraining the urge to point out that the short man with his gleaming bald head actually had no say in how the Herculaneum Project and *National Geographic* invested their funds and it was they, not he, who had paid for my presence here. But, in truth, I feared he was right. I had been commissioned to undertake new studies on the old remains that had been discovered in the bowels of the archaeological park.

Although he didn't pay my wage, Direttore Franko Cyrano was the superintendent in charge of the Ancient site and he could easily make my presence here far more difficult. Wary of letting him read my frustration I concentrated on tipping the box towards me, and the trickle became a waterfall of dust threatening to engulf me. I turned my face to protect my eyes as particles settled on my nose and eyelashes. I tried not to breathe.

My nose itched.

I restrained a sneeze.

I stepped carefully backward and downward, the toes of my boot reaching for the ancient stone floor. Only when I had two boots firmly on solid ground did I turn and look down at him. Down, because, even without the assistance of the rickety footstool, my modest height saw me tower over the supercilious little man. He glared at me from beneath beetled brows. The top of his bald head gleamed beneath the overhead light.

Did he oil it? I wondered, disrespectfully. A healthy dose of cold-pressed extra virgin olive oil perhaps? The short Italian reminded me so strongly of the Princess Bride's Vizini that I found it hard to take his appearance, or his rages seriously and found myself itching for a vial of Iocane powder. If only Australia was truly the substance's origin, I could have brought some with me from home.

In an attempt to curb my swiftly growing impatience, I glanced away from him at the storeroom shelves filled with boxes labelled *Skull fragments, Scapulas, Left femurs, Pelvic bones*. Over three hundred disarticulated skeletons were stored in the poorly lit and even more poorly ventilated space. An arched roof and a black and white mosaic of octopi and frolicking dolphins revealed the space had once, nearly two thousand years earlier, performed a role as a change room for an ancient bath complex. Once men and women had removed their clothes and belongings and left slaves to guard them while they wandered next door to bath in a series of hot, tepid and cold pools. Now the room contained the discarded bones of the people themselves, sorted, categorised and catalogued. I let my gaze rest on the label of the dusty box in my arms. *Right femurs*, it read, and for a moment I entertained the thought of reaching for one and clubbing the short man with it. The thought almost made me smile.

'Direttore, you need to understand, each of these bones has been touched so many times, by so many different people, almost always with bare skin. Any DNA harvested will be corrupted with cells shed from dozens of hands. If I could just find something untouched... Surely there has been something that hasn't been examined?'

He scowled up at me. 'Thousands of Euros...'

A scuffing sound in the doorway drew our focus. The short redhead that bobbed in the doorway made no apologies. 'I thought I'd find you here, Vittoria. Just checking to make sure you didn't want to join the Prof and I for dinner?'

Holly's British tone was crisp and she made no effort to include the short man in her inquiry. 'Cannavacciuolo, your favourite.'

It was, though I found I had little appetite. I smiled at the younger woman. 'Thanks, Holly. But, no. I have a few results to run through before I go anywhere.'

She nodded, 'Well, don't stay too late.'

I knew my lips twitched into a grin at the scowl she cast at the disgruntled site director.

I reached for a box labelled *Vertebrae*, pulled it from a high shelf, dislodging an avalanche of dust that drifted lazily in the stale air. Trying not to sneeze from a sinus full of inhaled dust, I held the box before me as a shield and walked directly at Direttore Cyrano, daring him to remain in the doorway.

Wisely, he chose to avoid the joust and stepped back, still frowning furiously. I paused in the doorway and spoke in English. 'You do realise that every time I run one of these tests, the bone is completely destroyed?' I glanced back at the wall of boxed bones. 'I assume you want some of them left?' I ignored the gaping expression and stepped out into the marginally brighter light of the old open topped reception room. The sky above turned shades of amber and aubergine with the last light of evening.

'I'm sure you don't mind turning off the light, Direttore?'

'If you don't find something soon Doctor Benino…' He let the threat linger wordless.

He didn't need to finish it. I had to find something worth my time and the investment *National Geo* had made in me. The thought of going back to Australia with nothing to show for my months of work was… inconceivable.

Ω

The urgent peeping of a moped horn gave me scant warning that I was about to be struck. Fortunately, the rider was more reactive than a daydreaming forensic anthropologist and with a fishtailing movement the bright yellow machine sped past leaving a wisp of blue-black smoke and the smell of burnt rubber. The gusset of wind that accompanied the swinging vehicle tugged at me and was accompanied by a masculine voice hurling invective muffled thanks to his bike helmet.

'*Vai a infilare la testa in un buco.*' I shouted at his rapidly disappearing tail light, steadying the paper cups balanced precariously in my hands as a trail of hot liquid made its way toward my elbow. They, and the paper bag filled with fluffy, sugary pastry ensured I could not add any global sign language to my retort.

A passing teen gave me a slanted look, and shook his head in disgust, no doubt for my phrasing of the insult.

'What on earth was that?' My sister's voice sounded in my ear.

'Italian moped drivers,' I snapped. 'They all think it's MotoGP.'

She laughed. 'No, I mean that thing you said. What was that you called him?'

I flushed, glad she couldn't see my face. 'Just something I picked up off my latest step mother.'

I paused in an alleyway safely out of reach of the next Valentino Rossi, placing the coffees safely on the top of an ancient wall, something Caligula might have brushed past once long ago, pulled the phone from my pocket and propped it up against the coffee cup, allowing me to mop the spilt coffee on my pants with napkins entirely too small for the purpose. Clare's face appeared on the phone screen.

We didn't look like sisters. Her head barely reached my shoulders, her hair was long, straight and honey blond where mine was thick, dark and curly at the slightest hint of humidity. Her eyes were hazel, mine were a shade off black. I could see the lines in her face were etched deeper. Was her face rounder, puffier than usual? She was eight years my senior but looked almost as old as my mother.

Worried she might read the thought in my eyes I pulled a sugar dusted donut treat from the paper bag and waved it before my face.

'Bombolini. Tastes like deep fried heaven,' I said before biting into the fluffy sweet dough. 'I'll bring some back for you.'

'Great,' she said, her tone laced with irony. 'Put me into a sugar coma and shut down my kidneys.'

'You know I'd give you one of mine.'

'No.' Her tone was abrupt and serious. She must have seen my expression because she changed the topic. 'You said you had a job offer.'

'Hmm,' I murmured non-committedly. I had almost forgotten the offer, it was so unlike anything I would actually do. Not if I had any other option. 'Yep, nothing I'd ever take up. Working in a war zone is not really my style. You know I like my bones clean and old.'

'Good. You've worked too long and hard for this and given up too much, to give up easily. You had better find something soon to impress old Vizini and make you famous.'

I nodded, though I could do without the fame. Herculaneum was a dream job and I loved working on the ancient site but most of the exciting discoveries had been unearthed decades earlier and I had begun to suspect that even with new technologies its secrets had already been told.

'And if I'm going to do that I'd better get going. Take care of yourself and tell Kate to 'break a leg,' just don't let her actually do it.'

'You could tell her yourself. She'd love to hear from you.'

I smiled and nodded but made no commitment.

'I love you, Tori.'

I smiled at her insistence on the words being spoken aloud. 'Love you too, Clare-bear.'

Slipping the phone snuggly in my pants pocket, only slightly damp and scented of coffee, I checked twice before stepping from the relative safety of the cement bollard, which was all that separated street from pavement, to cross the road.

By Australian standards the streets of Ercolano were ancient, narrow, crosshatched paving stones edged by a metre or so of pedestrian walk, but with no polite white lines or raised curb to protect unwary pedestrians from the traffic. The buildings were old and tired, graffito layers defacing most surfaces, with external air conditioners rattling and whining even this early in the morning, as Italian housewives gathered to buy the bread and coffee that were staples. I loved all of it.

With my coffee in hand, it was a short walk to the gates of the archaeological park. Already a short line of tourists queued at the arched ticket gate with its ubiquitous line of date palms and pencil pines, to await its opening. I flashed my staff badge and walked straight through.

As had become my custom, I paused at the wrought iron fence that overlooked the site. Down below, cut from the side of the hill the buried city awaited. Above it, on the opposite side of what looked like an excavated mine, the rest of the newer, but still ancient town of Ercolano continued as though oblivious of the ancient town below. Behind it all, the peak of the volcano soared, a bluish summit looming ominously and silently in the distance. As always, the sight of Herculaneum lifted me, despite the ongoing worries that kept gnawing at me. Shaking them off, I hurried down through the cement walled tunnel into the bowels of the ancient city, emerging on the ancient shoreline with its infamous 'boatsheds' opening to the left and right.

Stairs rose before me, taking me past the terrace of Marcus Nonius Balbus, a quick detour along a cobbled lane past the bakery of Publius Falco. Following the sound of tapping brought me to one of the insula where restoration work was taking place. A familiar form leaned against the brickwork of a freshly restored wall, gesticulating angrily at some flaw I could not see. Damn it, Cyrano was the last person I wanted to encounter this morning. I scowled internally since my emotions were still raw from yesterday's haranguing, but my movement caught his eye and he swung around and glared at me.

'You are late, Dottore Benino.' He spoke in Italian.

I shook my head. There was little point telling him that after his stern scolding of last night, I hadn't left my office or my microscope until 3am in a futile search for anything that might justify my position here, and with barely three hours sleep I had needed a coffee before I started again.

'*Bongiorno, Direttore.*' I made the effort to be conciliatory. '*Hai visto*, Professore Dalton?'

Direttore Franko Cyrano considered me for a minute. I had long suspected that if I hadn't spoken Italian as well as I did, he would not give me the time of day, not even to criticise. I was told that sometimes visiting archaeologists could spend an entire sabbatical at the site without ever hearing him speak a word of English.

His grudging reply roughly translated to 'Scraping shit in Sector VII as usual.'

I dismissed the Italian's scorn for Professor Dalton's work with the sewers. The fact was, the study had uncovered fascinating details on the diet and health of the ancient people of the region. Or perhaps it wasn't scorn, but jealousy, and the little man was piqued because the interest the study generated had prompted several television documentaries and Dalton had, alongside his innumerable academic articles, logged far more hours than Vizini in popular media. I nodded my thanks, spinning on my heel and slipping through a narrow alleyway, ancient walls looming on either side.

Muffled voices with a distinct British intonation tipped me off to their location and I slipped through a narrow doorway.

'An Earl Grey and an English Breakfast as ordered.'

Professor Andrew Dalton straightened from where he had been stooped over a second form, kneeling in the dirt of their excavation. He accepted the paper cup with a wry smile.

'And good morning to you as well, Victoria. I do wish you wouldn't insist on calling this swill *English Breakfast.*' His clipped British enunciation and stolid disregard for anything not served in a floral china teacup made me smile.

Still, despite his apparent disregard, he took a sip and sighed, passing the second cup to the young woman, the same plumply pretty research student who had intervened yesterday, crouched on the floor.

I passed him the paper bag and his blue eyes twinkled.

'Bombolini?'

Not waiting for an answer, he opened the bag and inhaled.

'Are you sure you don't want to marry me, Victoria?' he asked... a familiar joke.

'I doubt your wife would approve, Andrew.'

He smiled while chewing, his moustache already dusted with icing sugar. Reluctantly he passed the bag to Holly, who took a crisp round pastry and then passed the last one to me. I took a seat on the rim of the low wall beside where she was working, savouring the sweet treat and ignoring the look of disgust Dalton directed at me for my disregard of the setting, but the low wall was thick and sturdy and I doubted my negligible weight would cause it any hardship.

'Do excuse me ladies, I have an appointment with our benefactors.' He brushed the sugar from his upper lip, doffed an imaginary bowler hat and made for the doorway, pausing to give passing instruction. 'Make sure you strain the material carefully, Holly, we do not want to miss anything.' He glanced from the girl on the floor to me, still perched on the wall sipping my coffee. 'Don't you have discoveries to make, Victoria?'

I grimaced as he slipped out of sight.

'Still nothing?' Blue eyes commiserated with me.

I shook my head. 'Three hundred skeletons to study. But if it hasn't already been tested a dozen times, it has been corrupted by poor storage.'

So far I had no clue as to how to make old discoveries new again.

'What about you?' I asked to shift the focus.

Holly had finished her tea and returned to scraping and scooping rubble from the low walled trough I sat along. With practised movements, she emptied the pan load of detritus on the sieve and wooden board beside her and began to sort through it, randomly selecting small, indistinguishable shards of what I could not imagine, to place them in evidence bags.

'Oh, you know the saying, same shite, different day. We take it literally here.'

I smiled. The casual profanity seemed too colloquial for her proper English manner. 'What are you looking for?'

'Well, the Professor wants to prove a theory that the eruption has been misdated. I am looking for seed evidence in faeces, pomegranate seeds particularly, to prove without a doubt that the eruption occurred in October, not August.'

'And I'm guessing pomegranates weren't ripe in August.'

She nodded and pulled a face. 'But it's hard, they are so small and people threw so much rubbish down the *foricae* here.'

As she spoke, she casually plucked a white shard of bone and was about to flick it into her growing discard pile.

'Stop!'

Holly shot me a startled glance, frozen mid-movement.

'May I see that?'

She frowned and held the fragment towards me. I didn't take it immediately, instead slipped on a pair of gloves kept in my back pocket. When I took her offering, I let it lay on my palm and reverently nudging it with a forefinger. I was immediately grateful for the slightly startling burr of warmth I sensed from it. The odd but familiar sensation removed any doubt I might have held at what I was holding; the proximal phalanx of a human thumb. I gestured for an evidence bag and Holly obligingly held it open for me. As Dalton's assistant she was well-schooled in unquestioning obedience. Almost.

'It's just a bone, Tori. We find them all the time, all kitchen scraps end up in the sewers.'

But I was on my knees now, and I could hear my pulse in my temple. Ignoring the rocks beneath my knees, I bent over the low wall and with her brush and the smallest trowel I could find I began to shift the ancient soil where her last scoop came from. More telltale white lumps emerged. I forced myself to breathe and straighten. Letting my gaze drift upwards from where the earth was disturbed, further up the trough a roughly dome-shaped mass barely hidden by the ancient ash and tephra around it took shape, and I shuffled sideways. I forced myself to stop as my hand started shaking, but by then the shape was clear. The ash broke away more easily than it should have, as though what lay below had been waiting for this chance to be exposed, to escape. Already I could make out the gentle inconsistencies of the temporal bone, tracing downward as it depressed into the sphenoid before cresting upwards to the zygomatic bone. White bone, grey ash.

'Is that what I think it is?' Holly asked, breathlessly. She had given up any pretence of sifting through the ash beside her and stepped up beside me, bobbing ever so slightly on her heels as she did when she uncovered anything particularly interesting. With the way her glossy red-gold hair fell over her shoulders, I had often mentally compared her with a cocker spaniel, eager to please. Had she a tail it would have been wagging madly now. She had her phone out, capturing the footage and I realised this was her way of ensuring that when Direttore Cyrano found out that we'd done this, without first seeking his blessing, at least we'll have evidence that we followed the rest of protocol. I considered stopping, informing the park director of the find and formally requesting permission to excavate but then recalled his sneer that morning and it galvanised me. Tucking a wayward curl of dark hair behind my ear, I composed my face for the camera, ignoring the pebble that was digging painfully into my knee.

'These are, without doubt, human remains.' I reached with the brush to sweep away some of the loose debris, exposing more of the skull.

Holly stepped up beside me, the phone lens angled to view over my shoulder.

'The skull looks to be damaged.' I brushed more volcanic dust from around the off-white bone.

Shifting to improve the camera's view, I reached out to gently pry the braincase from its two-thousand-year-old bed. As my fingers touched it, a feeling of heat danced through my skin. I jerked back the offending digits as though burnt. It was the same heated sensation I noticed with the phalange but magnified so that I couldn't ignore it. I had felt the sensation before with human remains, not often, but it unsettled me, creating a feeling of connection that I could not account for, let alone try to explain.

Holly cleared her throat and I realised she was still filming. I flicked my fingers to shake off the sensation but it was still there when I touched the bone again. This time I was ready. The bones gave off a subtle but unmistakable feeling of menace. Beneath my fingers, I could feel a spider web of old healed fractures. I let them speak to me.

'These injuries are old. Here, you can see the skull has sustained significant damage, likely as the result of a blow to the face that would have shattered the nasal bone, and the infraorbital foramen and likely sent hairline fractures up into the frontonasal suture and glabella.'

Holly's disparaging sniff told me I had missed my audience. *National Geographic*'s target demographic was not the same group of academics I usually lectured. I considered the damage in layman's terms, the sort I would use to explain to my mother, who always expressed interest, but could not quite hide her dismay at her daughter's confusing and distasteful career. A doctor of medicine she could boast about to her friends, someone who dealt daily with the dead, however…

I forced my attention back to the bones and imagined I was explaining the find to my teenage niece, Kate.

'This fellow's nose had been broken, so badly that it likely changed his entire face shape, blackening both eyes for weeks and giving the victim chronic migraines for months. He probably ended up looking like a prize-fighter or football player after a grudge match.'

'How do you know the injury is old?' Holly prompted.

I ran a finger across the cracks, ignoring the ill feeling it gave me. 'You can see how the surface has smoothed. That means the injury had healed long before his death.'

Holly shuffled forward to zoom in on where I was pointing. 'You've said 'He' twice now. How can you be sure?'

'See the more pronounced line of the brow and the rounding of the orbital cavity. A female would be less pronounced and more angular.' I considered changing the wording to 'eye socket' but refused. *Nat Geo*'s watchers had to learn something.

'How did he die?'

I glanced up at Holly and the camera, unable to resist a smile. I turned the skull in my hands, careful to support the jaw bone with my fingers and exposed the bowl-shaped indent I had felt beneath my fingers, complete with jagged edges.

'I can't say for certain until we retrieve all the remains and get them back to the lab for analysis. But if you look closely…' I let my finger brush across the area. 'See the bits that look like spider webbing? That's a skull fracture, and see the way the bone had caved in here? Something hit the victim hard enough to cave in his skull.'

'Something... Or someone?' Holly prompted.

'Or someone, with something.' I smiled. 'I can tell you the injury occurred perimortem, no healing has smoothed the edges. It could be the cause of death.'

Holly's face was an open grin as she asked the next question. She already knew the answer. 'Could the damage have been sustained during the eruption?'

'It could. We have seen other bodies with similar injuries, skulls crushed by falling rocks. But that's not the case with these remains. He definitely didn't end up here on his own.'

I watched as Holly stepped back and panned around the room. It was a small, narrow space open to the air above and without windows, not unusual in Roman structures. A great stone slab leaned against one wall, tall and narrow and oddly carved. Around the room, a low stone wall blocked off a foot or more of the space and a slight channel had been deliberately carved out of the stone that ran before it. I watched Holly zoom in on the next section, complete with keyhole shape cutouts in the seat. As Holly began to pan back towards me I put the skull down gently, relieved this meant the annoying buzz of millenia old anger faded as I did so. Brushing off my knees I faced Holly and the camera.

'No self-respecting Roman would crawl inside a toilet to die. The most likely scenario suggests that someone hit him on the back of the head and stuffed his body inside the lavatory channel. Someone strong…' I added, shifting to show how thick the slab was that had been moved to accommodate the body.

'Given the location and the fact that he was found beneath the slab of the seats, it seems highly likely that he was murdered. We'll finish exhuming the remains and take them back to the lab for analysis. But first…' I hesitated to develop the drama, 'We'll have to rule out the possibility that he was alive when he was shoved in there.'

Holly shuddered dramatically. 'Left alive, shoved in a loo? How very prep school.'

I shared a grin with her, knowing we would have to cut that section of film.

A bright flash of light infused the room, creating a negative impression of the skull on my eyelids and nearly making me drop it on the stone floor.

Fumbling to secure my grip, I turned on Dalton. He was pulling the camera down from his face, the broad lens staring at me like a single cyclopean eye. Somehow I managed to swallow the curse on the tip of my tongue, avert my gaze from the apparatus in his hand and remind myself that I was in fact safe and strong and in control.

'Jesus, Andrew! You nearly made me drop it.' I raised the skull still cradled, hot and thrumming in my hands, though I was no longer certain if it was the bone or the projection of my own visceral reaction. As he raised the camera again I turned away, averting my face, obscuring the shot.

'Put it away, please Andrew?'

Holly was staring at me curiously. How could I explain the visible tremour that one flash of white light had caused? The heartbeat pounding in my ears had nothing now to do with the thrill of discovery and everything to do with the trauma in my childhood I had hoped long buried. I forced my attention back to the skull. The roaring in my ears, the racing of my heart. I closed my eyes, counted to five, focused on my breaths. *Safe. Strong. In control.*

'Can you please put that away?' I thought my voice sounded steady.

The very sight of the black box set my heart racing like a panicked hare. An ill-timed flash from a camera could trigger chills and tremors the likes of which I had read victims of war suffer from. I knew it to be classic symptoms of post traumatic stress but I was hardly willing to share why cameras made me nervous and most simply assumed I was camera shy. Thankfully most modern tourists arrived equipped with iphone cameras and selfie sticks which caused me no visceral alarm.

I could not tell her about the man behind the camera lens and the assault that had left a teenager pregnant and traumatised. Instead, I turned and placed the skull carefully back in its bed. *Safe. Strong. In control.* I intoned the familiar mantra in my head and felt it steady me.

Unperturbed by my reaction, Dalton smiled benignly at me, the offending camera slung inoffensively now over his shoulder, dangling from his hip. It was the same look certain male university professors curated for their favourite students. I was grateful to see a couple of evidence bags tucked under his arm.

'I told you not everything found in a drain is rubbish, you know.'

I glanced once more around the room, a body hidden in a toilet shaft was just the sort of mystery I might have dreamed of but never imagined finding. Then a sombre thought invaded.

'I should tell Franko.'

Ω

I had been sitting on the stool beside my laptop for some time, impatiently awaiting the return of results I had ordered as though staring at the screen would somehow speed the process. Still, my gaze slipped irresistibly to the skull now perched on the opposite bench, along with its articulated bones laid out in precise order. From this distance, I couldn't feel anything, but that didn't mean I could forget the discomforting feeling it emanated.

He was a healthy specimen. My earlier supposition of his gender, based on the shape of brow ridges and eye sockets, was reinforced by a jaw that was strong and square. With the touch of my pinky fingers alone I could feel the acute angle of the mandible and the definitive mastoid process. As I had suspected, the fracture pattern that radiated from where the nose had once been, did reach the glabella. The evidence of healing, knitted bone that felt ridgelike beneath my fingers, gave me an estimate of a five-year gap between injury and death. Remarkably, all his teeth were intact, though one of his front teeth had a jagged break that clearly predated death, and wear was minimal, suggesting whoever he was he had lived with a plentiful and varied diet. I estimated his age to be between 35-40 years. I shifted the skull and exposed its occipital region and the craterous indent at the base of his skull. It was the type of blunt force trauma that, had he been alive at the time, would have resulted in immeasurable and catastrophic disturbance to his brain.

The phone to the left of my hand vibrated. I nearly unsettled the coffee I had nestled, cooling, in the other. The screen flickered. Not the test results I was after. A photo, sent by my mother in Australia. A happy scene. A brown-haired girl in an expensive private school uniform, complete with boater hat, laughing with some friends. Kate was my older sister Clare's only child. Clare smiled proprietorially in the background. The photo was my mother's way of reminding me of what I was missing. I should be at home, married, giving her more grandbabies. I swiped the screen to dismiss the image and shifted focus immediately, picked up and studiously sipped my coffee, now stone cold. As though participating in a conspiracy, a second image, this from my sister, showed her daughter mid-stage, her long hair tied back in a queue behind her head. She wore period costume and was captured mid-soliloquy, a plaster skull in one hand, as she performed the role of *Hamlet*.

'Alas, poor Yorick.' Holly's voice came from the doorway. She entered without waiting for invitation. 'Who's the Thespian?' she asked.

'My niece, Kate.'

'She must be good to snag that role.' Holly offered.

I nodded distractedly, as the much awaited results came in with another electronic ping. I dragged the laptop closer and scanned the data. A glance at the chemical analysis of the first and second molars I had sent for testing, told me what I had already suspected.

'Well, he's definitely not a local,' I offered.

'How do you know?'

'His teeth lack the evidence of localised trauma we have seen in most of the local population.'

'From the '62 earthquake?' She postulated.

I nodded. 'Strontium isotope levels tell us he travelled widely around the Empire. More evidence to support your idea that he was a soldier.'

'A Praetorian,' Holly corrected, glancing across at the sword we had recovered alongside the remains while excavating the drains of the lavatory. Given the usual content of latrines, I understood her excitement. I crossed to the case that now held the weapon. It had laid hidden for nearly 2000 years under 20 metres of volcanic rubble that had buried the town and all its remaining inhabitants on a night in October AD 79, and it had taken Holly several hours of carefully cleaning to reveal both scabbard and hilt.

'The sword is ornate but I'm not sure that is evidence of a Praetorian,' I said, doubting the likelihood that we had stumbled across one of the elite force of Imperial bodyguards and intelligence officers.

She crossed to stand beside me.

'I know. But both the hilt and the scabbard are detailed with a scorpion. And the scorpion was a popular emblem of the Praetorian Guard.' She pointed to the hilt, cleaned of more than a millennia of detritus, just enough to see the hint of the shape. A bottle-shaped body, the hint of a curved tail, a suggestion of pincers.

'But a Praetorian, in Herculaneum, in a toilet?' I knew my tone sounded sceptical.

Holly looked hopeful. 'We know from Pliny's writings that his uncle was in the naval party sent as a rescue mission.'

'But he died at Stabiae, he never made it closer.'

'Pliny the Elder didn't, but that doesn't mean that none of the fleet did.'

I shrugged, unwilling to burst my friend's illusions completely. 'Well. Let's see if anything else says Praetorian.'

I turned to the remains. Further painstaking sifting uncovered nearly all of the bones, each and every vertebra and rib, both scapula, every arm and leg bone; the only parts missing were a couple of minor bones from the fingers.

'Our murder victim appeared to have been disposed of whole.'

The bones were typical of what might be expected if this were, in fact, a warrior. Signs of wear on the joints of both ankles and knees were consistent with a lifestyle that included many miles of marching. The right humerus was larger than his left and parts of each bone where muscles connected showed greater development on the right side than the left, telling her he was likely right-handed. It was evidence of an occupation that involved a great deal of lifting and swinging, much like a modern tennis player, but with a weightier instrument, perhaps a sword. Evidence of old and well-healed breaks could be attributed to brutal military training and wild charges. Both clavicles showed evidence of numerous breaks, rehealed each time. There was a notch along one rib on his right side that I was certain was consistent with an attempted and unsuccessful impaling with another weapon, again, long since healed. Bracing myself against the expected sensation, I reached for the skull.

On impulse, I pulled out my phone, switched to selfie mode and took a snap of myself posed dramatically with the Italian version of poor Yorick, sending it to Clare with the caption, *For Hamlet.*

Holly grinned as I pushed the phone aside and carefully turned the skull to expose the occipital bone at the back. I was particularly gentle because the spiderweb of cracks that extended outwards from a deep indent looked as though they would, with the slightest pressure, crumble and fall to pieces on the laminex tabletop. This was still the most likely cause of death. But something inexplicable made me want to look further.

'Why would someone kill a Praetorian?' I spoke the last thought aloud.

We both glanced at the photos I had pinned to the wall of the location of the find. Altogether, the evidence indicated a traumatic death and the disposal of the body in a convenient place. A body wedged in the toilet would both block the flow and reek to high heaven within a few days of its demise, so it was hardly a permanent solution. Potentially the killer had been interrupted, forced to hide the remains quickly and come back later to retrieve them. Only, there hadn't been a later. I couldn't prove any of that, but it was tantalising evidence that within a day or two of the eruption that buried the city, there had been a murder and this man was its victim. More intriguingly, it was a murder that had nothing to do with opportunity.

In addition to the skeleton and sword we had also uncovered a pair of buckles and a second smaller scabbard, too large for an eating knife; it was more likely to have once held a military-style *pugio*, but this one was empty. Finally, a desiccated leather sack that we had not yet opened. Initial scans said these were coins, confirmation that the murderer was not after money. Although the pugio was missing, the sword might well have fetched a pretty price, sold to the right buyer, but it too had been discarded along with the body. That made it far more personal.

'A sword-carrying warrior, slain for no apparent reason and his body hidden,' I said softly.

It was the ultimate cold case. I found myself smiling broadly. Holly beamed back at me. In a little less than a month in Rome, I had found my first human interest story for *National Geographic* and it was a doozy.

Chapter Two: The Golden Plains

Bosporus Kingdom, AD. 65

The sun had reached its zenith and beat down on the golden plain creating a haze that shimmered and seemed to dance off the nodding seedheads of the wild grasses. Two men rode lightly through it, despite being heavily burdened, a fat fallow deer slumped across the front of the saddle. The sound of their banter carried on the lightest of winds that moved the tips of the grasses and teased the loose hair of man and beast.

Alexartos, the elder of the two, let his reins dangle across his mount's neck, leaving his hands free. One he held out to skim across the tips of the grasses, the other reached forward to pat the damp neck of his horse, feeling the heat and sweat that had built up beneath the long, silvered mane. The tall grey mare had performed well during the hunt, neither nervous nor excited by the twang of the arrow and the flash of metal beside her head. Even now, hefting the blooded carcass, she was calm.

The same could not be said for Goson's mount, the solid bay-coloured stallion that Alexartos had raised from birth and named Azos, meaning steady. Ironically, the horse was prancing and throwing his head as though this were the first time he had carried a boy on his back or game across his shoulders.

'Lean back, relax your grip. You make him nervous, little brother.'

Goson shot him a disparaging look but did as his brother instructed and Azos settled back into a more sedate walk.

Alexartos was hopeful. 'I'm almost hungry enough to eat one of these raw.' He patted the spotted hide of the fat deer draped across the stallion's withers.

Alexartos smiled across at his brother, certain his wife would have a meal waiting. He glanced towards the distant plume of white smoke that they had been aiming for. It marked their home for the season, a small hill beside a wide but shallow stream and a broad swathe of grassland. This close, both Azos and the grey mare had quickened their pace, eager to be back with the herd. As he watched, however, the tendril of white became a mushroom of thicker, dark grey smoke, rising ominously.

Something was wrong.

Despite the heat of the day, Alexartos felt goosebumps rise on his arms. His instinctive forward lean set the grey mare into a loose canter, exactly as she had been trained, swiftly leaving Goson behind.

'Artos, wait! What are you…'

The voice stopped abruptly, Goson had seen the smoke and was soon thundering along at his side.

Fear invaded Alexartos's chest. His heart beat like the drums he and Sarukê had danced to at their wedding less than a year earlier. For all his pride in his horses, she was his real pride, his flame-haired girl. She had come at a high price and now he was awash with concern for her.

α

Goson let out a guttural howl to see their father prone in the dirt, a broken spear protruding from his spine. The game his brother carried was pushed unceremoniously into the dirt as he dismounted, more limp bodies to add to the tally.

Alexartos scanned the area from the height of the grey's back, the urgent need to tend to his father warring with a warrior's concern for ambush and a husband's fear for a wife he could not see. But neither ambush nor wife were immediately evident. He pushed himself from the grey's back, landing heavily. Still wary, he strode to where Goson was bent over their father but had little doubt the older man was dead, the dark stain in the dirt spoke volumes. Close up, their father's eyes were even more sightless than usual, the cloudy film open to the world but without their usual light. He had been scalped.

'Scythians!' He cursed.

The blind old man must have put up quite a fight, given the raiders had bothered to take the grizzly trophy of his scalp. Goson, still crouched in the bloodstained dust beside their father, looked broken but Alexartos knew he had no time for that. Fear and grief could be ignored. *No, must be ignored.* Assured the raiders were long gone, Alexartos scanned the wreckage of their camp. A coldness settled over him. In the mess left by the raiders it was hard to determine what had been taken, a few weapons perhaps, a collection of furs he had tanned and readied for trade. The large cauldron was missing, a heavy weight, that might slow them down. The tent that was their home had collapsed over a burnt frame, extinguishing the fire they had set inside. No doubt the raiders had taken everything of value, even the one he valued most.

The herd of horses he had painstakingly gathered, traded and bartered for were absent from the plains below the hill but the grass was well trampled in the direction they had gone and it would be an easy track to follow.

A glint of reflected sunlight grabbed his attention and proved to be a blade, the knife he had made for his wife and given her at their wedding. It lived in her belt unless it was in her hand. He bent to pick it up. Blood on the blade said she had put it to good use. He would retrieve her from her captors when he had exacted revenge for his father's death.

'Artos?' Goson's voice tugged at him.

It was then Alexartos saw it. As Goson tugged at the collapsed tent something emerged, he recognised it instantly. Sarukê's boot, so intricately embroidered with geometric designs in the thread she had dyed herself in orange and blue. Her long graceful calf was exposed, the curve of her bottom and hip, her long tunic pushed up over her back. A few mere strides and he held his wife in his arms, her clothing wet with blood, the damage to her belly exposed as he pulled Sarukê into his arms. Her sightless eyes, the eyes he had loved watching so much, were the same colour as the endless summer sky, so rare and precious a colour. Her flame hair was dark with blood. As he saw the damage to her hair—they had scalped her like they had his father—something snapped in Alexartos. He could hear Goson's voice, buzzing like a gnat around his head but none of the words made sense. Gently, he carried her, his beautiful young bride, her body feather light and limp, to where their father lay and fell to his knees in the dirt.

Eyes dry, Alexartos stared into the distance, below him the flattened grass led off across the plain, an arrow-straight line disappearing over the far hill. A fly landed on the flayed skin of his wife's scalp. Alexartos stared at it, then back at the line in the grass. Wordless and deaf to the sound of Goson's panicked questions, he laid Sarukê carefully down. With infinite care, Alexartos pulled his wife's tunic down to hide her injuries. Pushing himself to his feet, he shrugged off Goson's touch and turned from her.

Soundless in rage and grief he ran, not at the lanky grey mare, but at Azos, the horse he had ridden into countless battles. Startled by the headlong rush, the grey mare followed, galloping at the stallion's flank. Alexartos was deaf to the distant cries of his brother to come back, to wait for him. All he could hear was the rage.

α

From the endless grass of a distant hillside the Roman *Legatus*, Vespasian, sat astride his horse. His gaze followed the direction of his *Praefectus'* arm. Lepidus' keen sight had picked a disturbance in the distance. On the plain below a herd of horses, being pushed along by seven mounted Scythian tribesmen were making swift—though not unduly hurried—passage across the plain. Along with the herd they were driving before them, each of the riders seemed to be burdened by the evidence of a successful raid. One appeared to be struggling with a particularly large cauldron. There was no evidence they were concerned about reprisal, no backward looks, just laughing banter that carried across the hills.

Vespasian considered the horses. At first glance, he thought they were his stolen cavalry mounts, but as they moved closer it became apparent they were not. The beasts' confirmation and carriage were superior to the paltry military mounts that many of his men had been issued. Still, the herd was large enough to mount an entire *decurion.* Here were horses Vespasian desperately needed to replace the beasts lost when the Roman camp had been raided three nights earlier by Sarmatians. He could not lead a cavalry unit with half his men on foot. The Legatus knew he could fight the approaching tribesmen and claim the horses as prizes of war. He had enough mounted men to do so, but it was a risk he would rather not take if there was any chance of a better resolution. Perhaps they could purchase the animals, instead.

He was about to give the order to descend when Vespasian noticed a trail of dust on the horizon, originating from the direction from which the group had arrived. He held up an arm and the men around him halted. Perhaps the seven were not alone. It was not more Scythian raiders who came into view, instead, a pair of riderless horses broached the hill. Judging from their shape and size, one was a tall grey mare and the other a dark-coloured stallion. As they drew closer, the *Legatus* noted something odd about the darker shape, too much bulk about the stallion's neck made its movements seem laboured. Vespasian watched intently. Attuned to his silences his men watched mutely as the gap between the herd ahead and the two horses behind steadily closed.

Sound carried well in such open spaces and as the Scythians drew closer to the Roman watchers, Vespasian and his men could clearly make out the tone of the easy conversation even though the language was foreign to them. At this distance, they should have noticed the watchers on the hill, but their eyes were on the herd in front and their minds were occupied with conversation. Several of the raiders seemed to be teasing the fellow carrying the unwieldy cauldron and their raucous laughter covered any sound made by the approaching horses. Possibly, Vespasian thought, this was the stallion's herd and he had come to reclaim them. But the stallion never issued the bugle that would call the animals to him and the pair's stride never wavered as the two horses approached the herd. Vespasian was puzzled when the Scythian raider trailing at the back of the group toppled silently off his horse. Being at the rear none of the raiders seemed to notice. When a second Scythian dropped just as soundlessly Vespasian men began to shift uncomfortably. Both figures had simply disappeared into the grass. Then a third man fell but not before giving a sharp yell that carried across to the watchers on the hill. The stallion had not yet reached the herd, but the angle he ran at had shifted and Vespasian could now make out what had been odd about the horse's shape. There, pressed up against the side of the horse's neck, so close they could have been one creature, was a man with a bow in hand.

By now the raiders had swung around, their voices were heightened, perhaps perplexed by their missing numbers. As they did, an arrow shaft sprang from the eye of another of them, this man too disappeared soundlessly into the sea of grass. Vespasian cursed internally. Was it possible his new cavalry horses were going to be snatched from his grip before he had even secured them?

'Is he mad? He's just one man.' Lepidus muttered.

The *Legatus* could see him clearly now, long black hair trailing out behind him, like the tail of the stallion he urged onwards. From the men behind Vespasian came murmurs of appreciation. In a matter of moments, four of the raiders they had been watching had been downed, three remained and none of the rest seemed fully aware of the peril they were in. The watchers on the hill, all experienced warriors, could not help but be impressed. Vespasian maintained his silence, completely absorbed in the action playing out below.

He frowned when, moving as one, the few remaining Scythian riders turned and heeled their mounts into a gallop, angling away from the herd and their lost men, almost towards Vespasian and the watchers. The cauldron was dropped, lost in the grass. The grey mare joined the abandoned herd, which was milling in confusion. The approaching stallion shifted its angle too. The rider could be seen quite clearly now, clothing identified him as a Tauri tribesman. He had shifted from his position by the neck, there was no longer a need to hide. The bow and arrow he had wielded were gone. In his right arm, the warrior hefted a solid hunting spear. Gripping the horse with knees alone the warrior adjusted his body and threw the weapon in a mighty arc that ate the distance between the man and his quarry and came to rest in the lower back of one of the three fleeing Scythians. The man was thrown forward and off his horse by the impact. One of the Scythians roared and, dragging at his mount's neck, halted their headlong retreat, pulling the horse around in an arch to meet his pursuer. His companion followed.

The Tauri on the bay stallion had also pulled his mount to a halt. Even from the hillside, Vespasian could see the animal's sides heaving and the spray of white foam that coated the animal's neck, chest and sides. By now, the two Scythian raiders had wheeled to face him. The Tauri had discarded his bow, his arrows were spent and his spear was still lodged in the last victim. He faced his opponents with only a drawn knife. The biggest of the Scythians laughed and called out what Vespasian assumed was an insult at the barely armed man, who failed to respond. The Scythian pair took the time to arm themselves. No longer chased and facing a man armed only with a knife their response was negligible. One drew a bow and arrow, the other Vespasian recognised instantly as a Roman cavalry sword, he swung it around in a showy display.

'Two denarii on the Tauri.'

'At two against one? They've seen him now, and they're Scythian.'

'Four denarii says the Scythians scalp him.'

Behind him, Vespasian could hear his men calling odds and taking bets on the outcome. He could put a stop to it, he knew, but three things made the life of a legionary bearable–gambling, camp whores and regular meals–and he knew the latter two had been in short supply this campaign.

Below, the two remaining Scythians were bearing down on the single rider. With their heels to their horses' ribs, they hollered wildly, the sound carrying shrill and wild on the wind up to the watchers on the hill. The Scythian archer was pressed close to his horse's neck, bow drawn and prepared to fire, the gap between the men and their enemy swiftly closing. It would be impossible to miss at that range. The arrow flew, straight and true and just as it seemed it would pierce the Tauri's chest the man's bay stallion reared and the arrow shaft ploughed deep into its neck. The stallion screamed, pawing the air before collapsing backwards, carrying his rider with him. Vespasian found himself inexplicably saddened.

In the long grass, the archer circled, searching for his victim. There seemed a strong likelihood the man had been crushed when his horse had fallen. One of his men called for payment of the bet when, in a movement Vespasian found too quick to follow, there were suddenly two riders on the back of the archer's horse. Before the watchers on the hill could make sense of what happened, the man in front, the Scythian archer, toppled. His throat opened by the Tauri's blade.

The Scythian swordsman, without the benefit of Vespasian's superior viewpoint, seemed surprised. His mount's hooves tore up the grass as it wove from side to side, its master clearly undecided as to what action to take. No one on the hill was terribly shocked when an arrow bloomed in the swordsman's throat and, as the last of the Scythian raiders slid gracelessly from the saddle, there was only one man left. The Tauri, armed with the Scythian archer's bow, slid from the back of the borrowed mount and walked across to the felled bay stallion.

α

Alexartos was panting as he crossed to Azos, not with exertion but with the after-effects of the rage that still stirred fruitlessly in him. The stallion lay on the ground, his sides heaving from the headlong gallop, eyes full of pain and trust as his master, companion on a thousand raids and hunts, a million rides, knelt beside him in the grass. A line of thick blood trickled from the arrow stuck through his neck to emerge amongst the long black strands of his mane. The horse groaned and one back leg kicked out half-heartedly as Alexartos palpated the injury to ascertain his next actions. Laying the Scythian's bow on the grass, he pulled his knife.

'There, there, old man. You have done well. Stay still now,' he crooned as he patted the sweat-slick neck and reached across. There was resistance as he sawed with the knife and Azos shuddered. Alexartos knelt, pressing down on the old stallion's neck and he stilled. He pulled downwards on the shaft which resisted for a moment and then slid free, slick with blood to be discarded on the grass. The stallion lay unmoving as the Tauri stood again, casting his eye around for where his enemy had fallen. They had something he wanted. He turned back, and nudged the bay in the ribs with his boot.

'Time to get up, old man. Your women are wandering.'

With a groan the stallion heaved to his belly, then rocked himself back onto his feet and shook, his whole body vibrating. Azos snorted, flaring his nostrils. Blood flowed down the already sweat-dark neck but it was an ebbing flow. Alexartos drove the arrowhead he had cut off into the grass with his boot and struck out towards where Sword Man had been.

The Scythian's horse, well-trained, waited beside the body of his master, reins trailing in the long grass. There was no need to finish the man off, his eyes were already trained on the heavens, and an opportunistic fly had landed on one eyeball. Alexartos leant down, plucked the trailing ends of a long brown and grey scalp from the man's belt and tucked it into his own. Without another thought for the man who had killed his father, Alexartos turned to walk away, paused, stooped to pick up the Roman sword and added it too, to his belt. It was then he became aware of the watchers on the hill. Since they were only watching, he shrugged and turned from them, making the trek back to the Archer. There was no glorious red hair at his belt so Alexartos continued. The rage in him remained but was carefully contained now, at bay. Grief, he refused to acknowledge at all. With long strides, he made his way to the next body.

She was young, dressed in the same open tunic as the rest, the nipples of her barely-budded breasts just hidden. Padded leather pants, still tucked into her boots, were soaked in blood. Her legs kicked feebly as he approached. The soft pointed cap had been lost in her fall and her hair was loose around her head. Very young. Tears had cleaned tracks down her dusty cheeks and her dark eyes were filled with pain as she stared up at him, teeth gritted. His spear had missed her spine but from the angle of it, as she hunched around it as if it were a precious possession she was guarding. Artos knew the injury to be mortal—a gut wound.

For a moment the angry beast inside him uncurled and raised its head, baring teeth. Alexartos considered walking away. He didn't. Instead, he knelt beside the young warrior.

He touched the spear shaft gently. 'This is your death.' He spoke softly. Their tongues, not the same, but similar enough that she understood. She nodded, teeth still clenched. Her eyes slipped to his knife. He drew it, still shiny with the blood of her men and showed it to her.

She nodded and lifted her chin to expose her throat.

Alexartos said a prayer to the goddess of the hunt and laid his knife against her throat. To honour her courage he held her eyes as life and light drained from them. He wiped her blood on her tunic, and in doing so exposed a glimmer of gold, a beautifully wrought golden pendant in the shape of the goddess of the hunt, the one he was named for, Artos. He recognised it instantly. He had fashioned it for his wife but had allowed her to convince him to trade it, along with a pair of pelts and a dozen bronze arrowheads, for a trio of fine mares for their herd. The Scythian man Alexartos had traded with had given it to his daughter, the dark-haired girl on the ground before him. At that moment he realised the death of his father and bride were his fault. The Scythians had followed him back to his camp and simply waited for the best time to raid. Alexartos spat on the ground, jerked the leather strap which snapped and tied it too to his belt.

It was not until the fourth man that he found the fiery red strands he sought. Tucking these reverently into his belt he stopped searching. Catching the grey mare, he leapt lightly onto her back and pushed her head around to face the direction they had come from. A whistle ensured Azos would circle the mares the Scythians had stolen and bring them after him. With his boots pressed to her side, the grey slipped into a ground-eating canter.

Alexartos was aware the watchers had ridden down from the hill and approached, he just didn't care. Let them follow him if they chose.

α

Vespasian rode three horse lengths in front of the rest. They kept a steady pace, behind the herd, almost as if they were stragglers. They followed, no weapons drawn, until the Tauri stopped at the hillside camp. Another young man silently greeted the returned warrior, then stood staring in the direction of the Roman Legatus. The warrior spoke to the younger man, like enough to be his brother, who shrugged. Both men turned their backs and set about digging graves. Vespasian dismounted. His Praefectus followed suit. He halted the rest, and allowed only himself and the five tribunes to approach.

Rather than speaking, they collected rocks which they piled up not far from the rising mound of earth beside the two graves. When there was enough to cover each with a cairn in the style of the plainsmen Vespasian stepped back, his men with him. They watched silently as the two young men gathered first the older man and then the young woman and laid them in the ground, accompanied by an assortment of tools and treasures. In the hands of the beautiful red-haired woman, the Tauri placed the Roman sword, having done so he looked towards Vespasian with one brow raised. Vespasian kept his face studiously blank. The warrior dropped his gaze, reached for his belt and carefully placed the two scalps suspended there into the holes before he began to kick the earth back in.

Vespasian took a step forward to help but was stopped by a stern look from the warrior. So he waited. His men waited.

When the last of the rocks had been placed above the earth, the warrior turned to the younger man and gave a command. The youth set about putting together a collection of belongings. The elder turned finally to Vespasian. He spoke, a string of guttural words the General did not understand. A gesture brought up a dark-skinned young man, whose almond-shaped eyes revealed a plainsman heritage. The translator spoke.

Vespasian nodded acknowledgement of the thanks before meeting the young warrior's stern gaze. 'I want to buy your horses. I have many men in need of mounts.'

The man's eyes narrowed as he considered the line of soldiers, each one mounted. He plainly found the calibre of their horses wanting, as Vespasian did himself, seeing the long legs, fine fetlocks, rounded necks and glowing coats of the herd now grazing under the watchful eye of the bay stallion and the grey mare, not far from the camp.

'But I also want you. Join us and I will make you my *centurio exercitator.* Teach my men to ride and fight as you do. Rome needs warriors like you.'

Vespasian waited while the offer was made. For a moment the warrior's lip curled up disparagingly but he glanced across the still-smouldering camp and the two rock-covered cairns. His dark eyes met Vespasian's, warrior to warrior.

'You fight the Scythians?' He asked through the translator.

Vespasian nodded.

'What is your offer for the horses?'

Vespasian tilted his head, considering. 'I will pay whatever you choose as long as you join us.'

The warrior looked at the youth beside him.

'Your brother too.'

The warrior nodded. Vespasian smiled broadly. The warrior did not. But that hardly mattered.

Chapter Three: A Roman Woman's Purpose

Rome, AD. 71

The old palace blazed with light. It radiated from every niche, surface and wall. Lamps of every size and description from ornate and skillfully worked golden lampstands, like trees with a dozen branches, each blooming with fiery blossoms, to ridiculous winged phallus lamps which were suspended on wires and hung from the ceiling, all contributed to the glory. There were brightly glazed lamps shaped like pigs, bulls, and fish, ones that depicted erotic scenes, others with comic faces, and when it seemed the palace had run out of these there were simple glazed bowls from which multiple wicks floated.

'Why all the lamps?' Thalia murmured, 'Has our new Emperor abandoned the mule trade in favour of investing in olive groves?'

Clementia gave her a stern glance. Thalia ignored it, she knew her voice had been pitched low enough that only her older sister, pressed snuggly beside her on the dining couch, could have heard.

'The Emperor wants everyone to know the evil times have passed,' Clementia lectured softly.

Thalia sniffed. 'I hardly think anyone has forgotten Nero, Galba, Otho and Vitellius.' She touched each finger to her thumb as she counted off the four emperors who had held the Empire briefly in a year of civil wars. But as she looked around the room she realised she was wrong, they had forgotten, or at least they wanted to appear that way. All around senators mixed with soldiers freshly returned from the Judaean provinces, artists and actors rubbed shoulders with wealthy up-and-comers like her father, and gladiators shared goblets with senator's wives and daughters glittering with precious oils and gems and jewels only recently reclaimed from secret hiding places. It seemed that for the first time in years, Rome was breathing freely again. Musicians clustered around the immense columns of the room played stirring romps more in keeping with battlefield army camps than the imperial palace, all with the aim of impressing the man seated on the raised dais.

Emperor Titus Flavius Vespasianus, nursed and nurtured on the battlefield, lauded General of successful conquests in Germania, Britannia and Judaea and now the most powerful figure in the empire, sat upright on the couch, forcing those around him to do likewise rather than reclining as was both good manners and established custom.

Thalia and her sister were seated, adorned in matching sunset-shaded silks, modestly draped in jewellery, at a couch neither too far from the emperor nor close enough to show undue favour over the ranks of wealthy senatorial families. Provocatively, Clementia wore jewellery gifted to her by the Emperor's son, Titus. A sizeable carnelian hanging from a gold chain draped in the centre of her forehead. It matched a pair of carnelian earrings dangling from her ears. They were not gifts worthy of an Emperor's son, for when given he had been a mere soldier in his father's cohorts. Beside her, Thalia restlessly fiddled with her mother's favourite piece, a triple strand of mismatched and misshapen pearls around her throat with more woven through her dark tresses. At least she felt comfortable sitting upright, almost as if it was the usual thing to do. Thalia stifled a smile to see her older sister on a tilt as though there was nothing she would like more than to slip onto one elbow and tuck her feet up beside her. Despite her discomfort, Clementia engaged in diligent coquettish conversation with the ageing senator to her left while Thalia, less comfortable in conversation, let her gaze drift from one scene to another.

They had all gathered tonight to welcome Vespasian, first emperor of the new Flavius dynasty, newly returned to Rome to claim the empire that had been declared his, but also to farewell his golden son, Titus. Her sister would be grateful, Thalia knew, to have her former husband far from the capital. She had caught Clementia looking in his direction many times already this evening, through narrowed eyes. For his part, Titus seemed oblivious. He was a jolly golden godling descended from Olympus, surrounded by beautiful people, the wealthy and the powerful. Just now he had his head close to that of a copper-haired man, both handsome and expensively dressed, who laughed with his head thrown back at something Titus had said.

'Who is that?' Thalia asked.

Clementia's lips pressed together as though she had tasted particularly bitter wine. 'Senator Lucius Valerius Messalinus.'

Thalia's eyes widened. Messalinus was one of the wealthiest and most loathed men in the empire. A distant cousin of the late Emperor Nero, he was despised as a ruthless informer. Thalia watched him curiously, one hand rested companionably on Titus' thigh. A half-dozen women fluttered their eyes at both men.

'Stop it.'

'Stop what?'

'Staring. You are the daughter of the Praetorian Prefect, not some ill-educated Plebeian from the Subura.'

Flushed red, Thalia shifted her gaze and focused instead on the musicians. In the corner a gathering of military men had begun a frantic stomping dance, accompanied by much pushing and shoving and laughter. From the dais Vespasian smothered a less than imperial grin.

'Quartia!'

An elbow dug painfully into her ribs and she narrowed her eyes to glare at her sister. 'It's Thalia!' She refused to be referred to as 'Fourth,' and her sisters had already assumed names based on their father's agnomen, cognomen and praenomen, calling themselves Marcia, Arrencia and Clementia rather than their given denomination Prima, Secunda and Tertia; First, Second and Third. Their father had been singularly unimaginative. Left without options, Thalia had determined that if she must be a number, she would instead number herself amongst the Roman deities known as the *Gratiae*, the Graces, goddesses of beauty, joy and music. The name she had chosen was the name of the third Grace, Thalia-Youth. She had spoken the name many times into her mother's tarnished bronze mirror and was certain it fit her suitably.

But her sister was not looking at her, she was sitting straight upright now and staring across the room. Clementia rose with a grace Thalia could not possibly replicate. Thalia scanned the huddled masses for the source of her sister's alarm until she caught sight of her father's tall frame marching towards them. Clementia's hand groped for her own, pulling her to her feet. Thalia was perplexed, her father rarely stood on ceremony.

Her confusion only lasted until she saw the crimson-edged robes of the man accompanying him. His dark copper hair was unmistakable but he was not laughing now, in fact, he appeared rather uncomfortable. This was not unusual, her father's authority was enough to make the bravest man quake. But he didn't appear afraid, just ill at ease. Thalia rearranged her features to reflect her sister's blank expression with a suitably vapid smile.

Her father smiled broadly on seeing them but his eyes expressed a warning.

'Ah, here they are. You know my third daughter Arrecina Tertia.'

Clementia smiled thinly as Father's guest nodded disinterestedly in her direction. Thalia was certain that her sister's cool disposition masked some strong emotion.

'And this is my youngest daughter Arrecina Quartia.'

Her sister's nails dug into the flesh of her arm in warning. A warning she ignored.

'I am called Thalia.'

Her father rolled his eyes and pursed his lips and Thalia was grateful when he did not contradict her. 'Daughters, this is Senator Lucius Valerius Messalinus, friend to the Emperor's son, Titus.'

He was more than that, Thalia knew. Messalinus, gossip said, had been raised with Vespasian's own sons with the Emperor as his foster-father. She pressed her lips into a smile and kept her eyes dutifully downcast. 'It is an honour to meet you, Senator.'

When the man made no immediate answer she glanced up. Messalinus was not a tall man, perhaps a few fingers taller than she was. His hair was a thick auburn arrangement of curls which displayed both his connection by blood to the late Emperor Nero, but also his care for his own appearance. The artful arrangement of curls was designed to look haphazard, though she imagined it was the work of hours and a very adept hairdresser. He was not ill-looking. In fact, his features were so perfectly aligned and pleasing to the eye that he may well have sent the sculptor Juventius into raptures and had him design a new sculpture of Narcissus inspired by Messalinus. His lashes were longer than her own and framed eyes of deep blue. His aquiline nose was prouder than her own which ended with a pert little stub she found displeasing. His chin was strong and his mouth a pleasing bow that she thought had just tipped a little at one side.

Knowing he studied her just as intently, Thalia raised her chin a little. Clementia's nails dug deeper into her arm, and her father's brows lowered. But Messalinus nodded.

'She might do. Now if you will excuse me, Prefect, our Emperor is gesturing for me.'

Her father nodded, as close to obsequious as she had seen him with anyone short of Vespasian himself. It made him look like an eagle masquerading as a sparrow. As the senator turned away Thalia caught her father's expression of triumph and a shiver ran through her.

α

It was the seventh hour and the midafternoon sun beat mercilessly down on the courtyard beyond her father's study turning the paving stones into hotplates and causing the vines that traced their way across the trellis to hang limply, curled at their edges. The heat haze made the figures painted in fresco on the courtyard walls seem to dance, as though the nymphs and the satyrs that chased them were truly alive. A pair of slaves stood to either side of the backless chair her father sat in, steadily waving fans that stirred the air but did little to ease the stifling heat. A third slave sat upon a stool, a writing table perched on his knees, awaiting her father's response to the letter that had prompted Thalia's summons.

Her father stared at her with the implacable stare that made him so effective as commander of Vespasian's Praetorian guards.

'But Pater, I don't want to marry.' She knew her voice had taken on a childish tone but it couldn't be helped.

Her father stared at her blankly. She changed her approach.

'I mean, I'm not ready. I have so much yet to learn.'

The wrong approach, as it turned out. 'Enough Quartia, I have permitted this bookish foolishness for long enough. It does a woman's mind no good to indulge in fantasy. Besides, what good are all those scrolls you waste my money on if you do not use them to educate your children? Your sister was a mother by your age. A man like Messalinus is sure to give you plenty to keep you busy.'

She considered her father. He had not crossed his arms yet in the manner that said no more conversation, so there was hope.

'But Pater, he's Messalinus! Everyone we know says he is a monster.'

Her father's eyes narrowed and she knew time was running out.

'Lucius Messalinus is a fine man, an impressive politician and a friend of those in power. Of course, he has enemies that malign him.'

Thalia cast a glance at Clementia who, while present, was uncharacteristically silent, as she had been on the matter since their father's announcement. It was a rare thing for her sister not to tender an opinion but Thalia was too distraught to truly notice.

'Besides, since your sister was returned to us we need a new connection to the Flavians.'

Clementia's eyes narrowed but her silence persisted.

'But you're Prefect. You see the Emperor every day. Surely there is no man closer.'

'And I can be replaced in a heartbeat. Don't you think there are thousands of veterans who shared Vespasian's campaigns who would be eager to take my place?'

He was right, she knew, but was not ready to give up. As she opened her mouth he silenced her with a gesture.

'I cannot understand your objections. Is he not rich enough?

'You know he is, Pater.'

'And well connected. He was raised alongside Vespasian's sons.'

'Well, yes, but…'

'And he is not an ancient greybeard, or an errant warrior, always in distant lands like your sister's Titus.'

'No.'

'And I am told he is considered handsome.'

He was, though she was unwilling to admit it.

'Surely all the girls you know would be envious?'

It was true.

'Quartia, this marriage is an opportunity that we cannot afford to miss. Until now Messalinus has not shown the slightest interest in seeking a wife. If we do not act, the prize will go to another family. Probably one of those old families who look down on us.'

Thalia was summoning the courage to list all the reasons that the match was not ideal but as she did so her father crossed his arms and she knew the opportunity for discussion had ended.

'I will send to the augurs to determine the best date for a wedding. Prepare yourself daughter for soon you will fulfil your purpose and become a wife.'

α

'My Father tells me that the Emperor had great plans. That he will turn Emperor Nero's lakehouse and lake into a great permanent amphitheatre that will be the crowning glory of the new Rome. He said that Nero's giant statue will be remodelled into the god Apollo and set before the arena.' Thalia was babbling, she knew. It was unlike her but she was pleased to be able to share this knowledge in conversation with the man she was to marry. His hand secured her elbow, ensuring she did not trip as they descended the steps to the imperial box, where Messalinus' privileged position had ensured a pair of seats.

'I have heard the rumours but I cannot confirm them.'

They slipped beneath the silken shades that covered the Emperor's box. The view of the stadium that doubled as a racetrack was unimpeded from this prime position and she was tempted to step up to the railing to see the sand below. To do so, however, would draw the Emperor's attention and while Vespasian was no Nero, only senators really wanted to attract his attention. Senator Lucius Messalinus seemed unaffected by the close proximity of the Emperor. He raised a hand to acknowledge the older man before turning to direct the slaves that had followed them. Thalia was dismayed to find they were not carrying food or fans but a tiny writing desk and boxes of correspondence. Her future husband seemed oddly ill-at-ease in company. Women watched his every move. Men did too, but with a wary eye, not a desirous one. She wondered how many of them had lost family members or fortunes to his actions under Nero. Still, he was silent rather than taciturn company. He answered her forays into conversation with nods or indeterminate sounds rather than words. But, as her father had made clear, Messalinus was handsome, rich and connected. She told herself to be grateful. He seemed a different man to the laughing demigod she had observed beside Titus at the banquet.

Ignoring the speculative, curious and envious gazes of the women in the box, Thalia fiddled with the excessive amount of jewellery each new morning seemed to present, all gifts from the man by her side. They were gaudy and garish and designed purely for ostentation. Proof that he was rich and powerful and that she was marked as his new property.

'You are very fortunate to capture such an eligible man.'

Thalia glanced at the woman who had appeared beside her. She smiled wanly. Perhaps she was, but she hardly knew him. They had met only once since she had accepted his offer, and the theatre had not been conducive to conversation. Thalia knew him as little now as she had the night of the Emperor's banquet. Refusing to acknowledge what she knew to be a gossip seeking intrusion, she turned her gaze down upon the sand below. While the bestiaries battled enraged bulls and wild cats and criminals were set against each other to fight to the death, Messalinus read, conferred with his secretary and wrote letters and missives, sealing them then and there with wax and sending messenger boys to deliver them.

From time to time, he glanced up, once reaching to caress her hand and bring her fingertips to his lips in a way that caused Thalia's heart to miss a beat and brought an unexpected flush of heat to her cheeks. She could not deny he was handsome.

Slaves arrived with platters of delicacies, from which he nibbled as he read and she watched the guards prepare for the lunchtime executions. The wine was pleasingly cool and of a quality that even she, in her limited knowledge of wines, could appreciate though not name.

As they ate Thalia averted her gaze from the executions taking place in the stadium to watch the gathered crowd.

'I had not imagined the daughter of the Praetorian Prefect would be squeamish,' her future husband observed, she thought she detected a hint of mockery in the tone.

'Hardly. My father taught me that such displays are important as a deterrent to future criminals, but I find little entertainment in the castration of debtors and burning of arsons.'

His eyes lingered on her measuring, scrutiny that made her shiver with uncertain emotion, before turning away, his focus back on his work. For a while, her attention was held by the sight of a naked man, a thief, hands tied behind his back set astride a bull. Leopards were released into the stadium. Thalia listened as spectators called bets on the timing and manner of death. The winners howled in joy as the bull, swinging round to face the charge of the large spotted cat, dislodged the man and subsequently gored him through the chest before trotting a safe distance from the approaching leopard and standing, snorting and pawing threateningly at the earth. The fortunate cat had barely disembowelled the human victim when it was driven off by *venators* armed with spears and nets. Thalia had little expectation that the majestic cat would last many more spectacles.

It was mid-afternoon when Messalinus finally put away his paperwork. The sun beat down on the arena, doing little to dampen the spirit of the crowd. The executions that were the forerunners to the real action were over, the sand stained red from man and beast.

'Who will you back?' Messalinus asked, gesturing at the rotund figure of the bookkeeper hovering by his side.

'I brought no coin.' She smiled apologetically.

Messalinus raised a brow. 'Nor should you.'

He waited, making it clear that the bet was on him. She considered the gladiators milling below, waiting for the signal to begin the melee. Pointing out a round-shielded Hoplomachos who had been paired against rectangular-shielded Thraex, and a net-wielding Retiarius, she watched the obsequious little man jot down notes to record her bet. Her husband-to-be began a lively conversation with a balding Senator to his right and barely looked up until the jingling red-cloaked servants of Charon dragged the few bloodied corpses from the sands with the hooked staffs, leaving only bloodsoaked sand as a sign they had even fought. They were the gladiators who had performed so poorly they had received the *iugular* gesture rather than the *mitte* of remittance that would see them walk from the sands and live to fight another day. Her Retiarius was still amongst the living but the Hoplomachus was dragged unceremoniously from the track.

Only when the anticipated prime bout was set to begin did Messalinus turn his attention to the sands. It was to be a battle between Priscus the Gaul and Varus the Roman, and the crowd thrummed with anticipation. Both fighters were favourites of the crowd and of Vespasian himself.

Messalinus gestured to the round bookie, who could barely contain a jig at his good fortune, and placed a substantial bet on the smaller, lithe and fast-moving Gaul, adding a smaller but still significant amount on the same man at her request. The odds were particularly good since Vespasian himself had betted on the giant, Verus.

'Come.' Messalinus offered his hand, drawing her to the balcony. His hands, she noted, were smooth and soft, but his grip was strong. They stood side by side on the balcony of the Emperor's box, only a few feet separating them from the Emperor as they watched the brutal and lightning swordplay. Thalia found her hand gripping his forearm when Verus knocked the sword from Priscus' fingers and sent it soaring, end over end into the crowd, where miraculously it was caught by a quick fan instead of causing additional bloodshed.

The men, heroes from rival *ludi*, had fought on other occasions and knew their opponent well. Both wore full-faced crested helmets and carried rectangular shields and short swords, though the taller Verus wore only one shin guard while the opposing gladiator had two. They battered each other for many minutes before, in a move too swift for the eye the Roman disarmed the Gaul, kicking his opposition's sword behind him and out of reach. The crowd roared with bloodlust as Verus closed on the now unarmed Priscus, but the battle was not over. Discarding his shield and launching himself into a theatrical roll the Gaul came up standing, one hand gripped around a spear left by a defeated Hoplomarchos. With a grace come from long practice and a weapon familiar to him, Priscus launched the spear. Verus raised his shield but not quickly enough and the projectile lodged in the muscular flesh between the helmet-protected neck and the heavy leather armguard.

Thalia winced. Messalinus gripped the rail and roared, his voice lost in the crowd.

Unable to effectively remove the projectile, nor fight with it in situ the match ended with Verus on his knees, the protruding spear resting on the sand, with his own sword held at his throat. Had he been more grievously injured and not a favourite of the Emperor, Verus would likely have ended his career that day in a spurt of arterial blood. As it was, the victor clasped the man's wrist and pulled him to his feet. The pair walked out, side by side to the adulation of the audience.

In his excitement at the win, Messalinus had gone so far as to pick her up and spin her around, planting her back on the ground with the swiftest of kisses to the left of her mouth that left her blushing and her heart racing. She had no need to hide it though, for he immediately turned to the bookmaker to arrange his winnings. His lips were soft and warm and his breath, she noted, was sweet.

For the first time, she began to wonder what it might feel like to have those lips linger lower, on her naked skin. The thought set a trail of goosebumps along the fine hair of her arms.

α

Thalia's head ached from the six tight locks, curled and coiled and arranged atop her head, leaving only a few dark tendrils to curl about her face. The hairdressing slave had long since collected her money and departed, taking with her the gladiator's spearhead with which she had divided the design and displaced any ill luck she might have carried. Thalia knew that by the time of the ritual 'bedding' she would probably be suffering a violent headache. As if this was not sufficient torture, the bindings around her chest were so tight that they cut into her underarms and left her feeling breathless.

'Can't you loosen them a little?' she begged her sister who was conducting the slaves that buzzed around her.

Clementia considered her critically as she stood in the centre of the rooms wearing only the cloth about her loins and the bandage trying valiantly to tame the overabundant curves of her breasts.

'No.' Was the blunt reply. 'I don't know where you got all that —' She waved her hands in a gesture that followed the general shape of Thalia's generous bust, slender waist and rounded hips. Clementia's own frame was willowy and boyish, her breasts small, having never performed their natural function of nourishing the daughter that perched on the sleeping couch behind them.

'Perhaps you should have eaten less in the last month.'

It was an unjust accusation and Thalia's eyes narrowed. Clementia's divorce and her return to her father's house had made her the oldest female in residence and thus entitled her to command their father's slaves and household. She had used this privilege to halve Thalia's meals over the month preceding the wedding until Thalia had been so hungry she had found it necessary to raid the fruit trees in the gardens, gorging until the juices ran down her chin. Thalia recalled wistfully the years when her sister was absent, living in the house upon the Palatine she had shared with Vespasian's golden-haired son, Titus and their infant daughter.

'Perhaps if you had eaten more, Titus would not have divorced you and sent you back.'

It was petty and she knew it but the expression on Clementia's face almost made the discomfort bearable. Thalia shifted her gaze to consider her reflection in the polished bronze plate one of the slaves held. She would have preferred to check the reflection in the pool in the garden or the impluvium in the atrium, both gave clearer reflections but she knew it would not be permitted. Already a slave stood waiting, folds of cloud-white silk bunched ready for her to step into. The fabric was soft and finely woven and completely without embellishments. Pulled up and secured with gold pins at her shoulders it covered the offending bandage that tried to flatten her chest. A second slave, this one borrowed for the sole purpose of arranging the ornate Gordian knot of the belt that would sit on her waist as a symbol of her innocence and the promise of a virgin bride, waited patiently as the first slave tried to settle the fabric on her hips.

As the first woman stepped back and the second replaced her, Thalia let her gaze slip to the large chest near the doorway. It was the last of her dower goods and yet to be collected and carried up the Via Sacra to the palace on the hill. It was packed not with clothes and ornaments but with the personal library she had begun to accrue in the short years spent as an only child, benignly neglected by her father and raised by a series of slaves, the last of which were purchased to teach her. And teach her they had. Once she had mastered the written word, first in Latin then in Greek, each trip to the macellum or forum was an opportunity to collect yet more scrolls, each one now carefully stored in the chest near the door.

'You look beautiful.'

Thalia smiled in the direction of her sister's daughter, eight-year-old Julia Flavia, whose golden curls, the hereditary gift of her father, floated about her face making her appear like one of the cherubic *puteo* that always accompanied statues of Nero or were found painted or carved onto household shrines.

'Let us hope Lucius Valerius Messalinus thinks so too.' Thalia was determined not to let the child see the combination of fearful anticipation the idea of marriage seemed to evoke in her.

Her sister remained silent.

Chapter Four: Mario Rossi

Rome, 2022

The night air had a brittle quality, a touch of ice so thin it didn't form. As I exhaled the breath came from me in a serpentine mist that betrayed the late hold of winter. After the warmth inside, the chill brought goosebumps to my flesh and I regretted the high neck but sleeveless cashmere top that fit so snuggly and was grateful I had chosen the thicker of the long black trousers I had to go with it. I had never been much of a skirt girl. Placing two hands on the marble balcony I leaned over and breathed out slowly and deliberately, watching the pattern of my breath.

'Your father is delighted to have you back in Rome.'

The voice that came from over my shoulder was as smooth and thick as Italian coffee. Before his death, I had often joked that if Sean Connery offered I would have taken him home in a heartbeat, despite his age, if only just to hear him say my name in that delicious Scottish brogue. Clare had wittily suggested as a forensic anthropologist I should be far more interested in him now.

My companion Massimo was, I thought, close to the Italian equivalent, at least when it came to the sheer luxuriousness of his voice. But, unlike the aged Bond star, Massimo was in his mid to late thirties. My mother would have called him an Italian stallion, the type with an ample supply of dark glossy locks, and rich, swarthy Mediterranean skin. Rippling with muscles and sex appeal.

I made a noncommittal sound to acknowledge his words.

'Have you been away for long?'

Turning back, I studied the man who had followed me onto the balcony. Massimo was handsome, his voice reached something deep inside me and I found him compelling. But when I looked at him I was reminded of a black leopard I had seen at Taronga Zoo. Sleek, beautiful, mesmerising and perilous. I shivered in a way that had little to do with the cold air.

'When I was a child I spent many holidays here. I didn't see much of him then,' I said, waving a hand, disrupting the fog my breath left in the air. 'My father was always a busy man.'

He stepped to the railing beside me, nursing but not drinking from a glass of wine. I drew my gaze back to the view. Lights illuminated the ruins in the distance.

'I sense there is more to the story?'

I shrug. 'I don't know you.'

'Yet.' A smile lifts half of his lip. 'Is that not the purpose of conversation?'

I concede but choose my words carefully, some of the memories were painful. 'I was a difficult teenager, I grew weary of travelling every holidays and missing my life at home so I stopped visiting. But I lived here in Italy for a year when I was sixteen, on a study tour. My older sister chaperoned and my father loaned us a villa in the hills. I had hoped we might fix things then....'

We hadn't. I had rarely seen him in the twelve months I had lived here and we had a devastating row towards the end. Since then I had seen him only three times, though regular deposits in my bank account had kept a roof over my head and food in the fridge while I had spent years at University.

'Italian men often have difficult relationships with their daughters.'

'Do you have daughters?' I ask.

He laughed, the tone rich. When he shook his head I was reminded of *Shrek*'s Prince Charming.

Dinner had been a far smoother event than I had anticipated, as I chewed my nails in the back of the gleaming green Alfa Romeo my father had sent to collect me. My father had been charming and was clearly besotted with his newest acquisition, a wife four years my junior. I liked Guilia, though this was only our second meeting. She was a first-year resident at one of the large hospitals in Rome. She kept us entertained with stories of her blunders, which I suspected were more for making me feel at home than actual errors on her part.

'So, who do you think killed him?'

For a moment I drew a mental blank. Then I recalled recounting our discovery over dinner. I had been a little surprised to find I was not the only dinner guest when my father's driver, arriving exactly on time, delivered me to the villa promptly at seven. My father, Gianni Benino, was a politician, the Italian Minister for Foreign Affairs. He rarely missed the opportunity to dine and schmooze in one convenient setting. The rich, the powerful, the famous, and the influential all got to share the grandeur of my father's not-terribly-modest villa. Tonight's guest was no exception, while I was uncertain who he was exactly, the confidence he oozed spoke of wealth and prominence and a comfort with power that could not be schooled. I chided myself for judging him without giving him a chance. Italy was all about chances.

'I am afraid that is not the sort of thing I can determine from the remains.'

'But isn't that the role of a forensic anthropologist, to solve crimes?' Massimo asked.

I shook my head. It was a common misconception. 'Not really, my job is usually to identify people from the evidence that remains. To give people back their names if I can. Sometimes, it means identifying their cause of death.'

'And you have.' He raised his glass, the wine was purple-black in the pale light.

'His cause of death, perhaps? Blunt force trauma. His name is something else entirely and unless some ancient murderer wrote an account of stuffing a Praetorian down a toilet I suspect he will forever be a John Doe.'

'John Doe?' His left eyebrow rose.

I smiled, 'John Doe is the term Brits, Americans and Aussies use for an unidentified male. I suppose you have an Italian equivalent though I don't know it.'

Masimo's expression grew thoughtful.

'Mario Rossi.' My companion proposed.

'Mario Rossi? Well, it is more inventive than John Doe I am sure.'

'Not really. Mario is the most common praenomen name in Italy, and Rossi the most common cognomen. You are cold.' He observed.

He was gazing down at the arms I had crossed beneath my chest, rippled with goose bumps.

'A little,' I admitted, shifting my arms upwards to cover myself. 'I was in such a hurry this evening that I forgot to bring something warm.'

I was bemused when he shrugged off his jacket and wrapped it around my shoulders. I schooled myself to stillness at his touch and although I wanted to refuse I was even more surprised by how warm it was and how good it smelled as it settled around me.

'Thank you.' I smiled appreciatively.

When he returned the smile I noticed again the dimple in his left cheek that I had watched during dinner.

'An opportunity to be chivalrous to a *bella donna* is always welcome.'

A movement inside the window drew my attention. Guilia beamed, watching us.

'How do you know my father?' I asked, seeking to deflect the increasingly intimate situation.

Massimo took a sip of his wine. 'We work together.'

I nodded. 'In politics.'

He nodded, considering me thoughtfully.

'And what do you do… in politics.'

'Oh, this and that. I work a lot with tourism and liaise a bit with museums and archaeological parks and the like.'

'So you will have visited Pompeii and Herculaneum.'

If his smile turned condescending I couldn't blame him. 'I am sorry,' I proffered the apology before waiting for his response. 'I guess ancient ruins are far less exciting to you when you live in a city surrounded by them.'

For me, it was still a buzz to wander past the Trevi fountain and through the old forum. Although I had toured the Colosseum half a dozen times it still thrilled me to stand beside it, looking up.

'On the contrary, I am proud of my country's heritage. You had heard, of course, that they have discovered more of what they believe is Emperor Nero's private bathhouse. I saw it just last week when I spent some time admiring the paintings in the *grotte* of the *Domus Aurea*.'

'Nero's golden house? I haven't been there yet.'

He set his near-empty glass on the balustrade beside my hand and turned to face me. 'Come with me tomorrow.'

This close, I could smell the spicy scent of the cologne that I also inhaled with each breath from the jacket around my shoulders.

'Thank you. I couldn't.' I tried to find a suitable excuse and settled instead with a vague hand gesture. 'My work you know.'

The dimple returned. 'Yes, I understand how busy work can be. Perhaps another weekend? The next time you come to visit your father. I will show you Nero's palace and take you out to a little restaurant for dinner.'

What was it with Italian men that made them so hard to say no to? For a moment I spared an empathetic thought for my mother, the victim of Italian passion, not at all what I wanted for myself. I forced myself to return his steady gaze and rebuff his offer.

'That sounds lovely…' I started but before I had broached the 'but,' Massimo nodded.

'Excellent. Your father tells me he has invited you next weekend for the opening performance of Tosca at the *Teatro dell'Opera*. I cannot make the performance but I will pick you up the next morning, shall we say around 11?'

He slipped his hand beneath mine and turned us back towards the villa. 'Come inside, it is too cold out here tonight.'

Surprise made me compliant. I was still considering how to politely decline when Massimo announced our plans to my father who smiled broadly and clapped him on the back.

Ω

The ancient boat houses along Herculaneum's long-lost foreshore were the most frequently visited places on the site. Usually, the spot was shunned by researchers because it buzzed with ghoulish tourists, cameras held out, flashes ready to capture glimpses of the hundreds of skeletons that had been found huddled inside them. But for days now the torrential rain had dampened their enthusiasm and glaring warning signs and barricades blocked even the most intrepid voyeurs.

Today it seemed the foreshore had returned, deep puddles occluded access and brimming streams burbled merrily down from the ancient city and the more modern one higher still.

It had almost stopped raining but the sky was bleak and little light made it this far down even on the best of days. Balancing on one of the planks provided I ducked beneath the arched entryway into a deeper darkness, the powerful torch in my hand did little to dispel it. Even though I knew that the greenish bones, scattered like twigs, intertwined and entangled were fibreglass replicas carefully placed by earlier anthropologists, it was still an eerie feeling to crouch in the dark space. Even knowing none of the skulls were real as the empty caverns of their eye sockets absorbed the light and returned only darkness, I fought the urge to shudder.

'You know I hate it here, don't you Tori?' Holly's voice, barely a whisper, was enhanced by the enclosed space.

She assigned herself as my assistant while Dalton was away on a visit home to Cambridge to give a series of lectures. I was grateful for her help as both the pressure and my workload had increased after *my* surprising find and the interest it had engendered in the new excavation thanks to the *National Geographic* coverage. The interest in our 'latrine warrior' had eclipsed the earlier interest in a new find in Pompeii of a man whose head had been crushed by a falling block of stone while trying to escape. Direttore Cyrano had been thrilled that our discovery had received more publicity than that of our sister dig in Pompeii, with its larger site and more famous reputation.

Holly shivered violently, rubbing her hands against the cashmere of her cardigan. I understood how she felt. More people had died here than anywhere else on the site. In fact, it had been believed that most of the ancient inhabitants had escaped until the boat sheds had been discovered.

'Do you think they knew?' She asked.

'That they were going to die?' I had once wondered this myself. 'No.'

I turned and looked towards the lighter grey of the gated opening. Two thousand years earlier the azure shoreline would have been visible, bustling with fishermen and their families, hauling in the catch of the day.

'No. I think they were waiting for it to end, waiting for rescue.'

Holly shivered, hesitated, then leapt a wide puddle, skidding in the slick mud, arms windmilling.

'Careful,' I warned, unnecessarily. Her longer legs allowed her to step across with a small amount more grace.

'Where is all the water coming from?' She asked, her torch skipping over the dark pools.

'I don't know. Seeping through the walls I guess. It looks like a lot of it is coming in through the back here.'

I stepped gingerly over the skeletons, like a bizarre game of Twister, trying to find safe places to step. The pool of water was deeper here and I shone the torch on the rear wall of the shed, tracing a rivulet of water that ran down the wall to a spot where there appeared to be a crack in the vault at about chest height. Using the closed umbrella I carried and compelled by a force I couldn't explain, I reached forward to test the strength of the wall and was unsurprised when, rather than resisting, as stone should, the tip of my umbrella penetrated the space. Swiftly pulling back, I froze, shocked at my own temerity, torch shining on the gap that I had just enlarged. A gap that now burbled merrily with a stream of water.

'That's not good.' Holly murmured.

I shot her a frustrated look. Dalton's assistant could be the queen of understatement. We both remained utterly still, studying the rapidly growing pool that reached towards our gumboots, fearful that the rear wall might subside in a rush of water and debris and flood the tunnel and its living and non-living occupants. I was sure that for several minutes my heart chose not to beat and I may or may not have forgotten to breathe. In time, the joyful fountain slowly eased until it became once more a steady but sluggish flow.

'What do you think? Do we need to move them?' Holly gestured at the scattered fakes.

I shook my head and glanced back at the gloomy light of the shed entrance, where black plastic curtains had been pulled aside to allow their entry. 'No. It has slowed and the forecast was for the rain to stop soon.' I hoped. It had barely let up in a week and I was tired of being damp and cold. 'Come on. When it has dried out some more we will come back and check things over, the wall, that gap...' I gestured at the dark space where my umbrella had punctured what should have been solid stone, 'We will need to let Cyrano know, it will need exploratory work and possibly a work team to shore it up.'

Holly nodded. 'Well then. Shall we get a coffee? My hands are so frozen I can barely grip the torch.'

I could think of nothing I would like more. The tiny cafe across the street from the embarrassingly luxurious villa my father had rented on my behalf had proven to be a popular venue for the team and they regularly drew straws on who would do a coffee run. Imagining my hands wrapped around the hot cup, I grinned.

'Absolutely.'

'And you can tell me what you're going to wear for your date with Massimo of the massive ego.'

With one last glance at the gap in the wall, its flow now reduced to a trickle, I turned and carefully navigated my way back to the dull light of the wet afternoon.

Ω

'You'll never guess!' Holly thrust her way into the room with all the grace of a bull elephant, an impressive achievement given she barely reached my shoulder.

I narrowed my eyes in my best Cyrano impression. Holly rearranged her expression hastily to appear *almost* penitent.

'The hole in the boatshed was a niche all blocked up with volcanic debris. Guess what we found in it?'

She barely waited for my raised eyebrow.

'Bodies!' She filled the silence, I envisioned her tail wagging again.

While not unexpected, the news was still exciting. After so many years as a site under protection, no further excavation allowed, it seemed the city was desperate to throw us new clues.

Ω

'Don't touch anything until the film crew arrives.'

Direttore Cyrano swung to face us, the light nearly blinded me as he turned in our direction. Belatedly, he lifted a hand and dimmed its ferocity. His grin was almost as bright as the beam. He wiped clean hands on the jeans he wore religiously with his knit vest and jacket. All these finds meant publicity and publicity meant investment and all this was good for Cyrano as Direttore.

'I mean it!' He threatened, wagging one finger for good measure, the effect ruined by his Cheshire smile.

Internally I sighed in relief. Although he'd excited by the latrine body, Cyrano had been furious that we hadn't alerted the film crews before beginning the excavation. Despite Holly's phone footage, we had been forced to painstakingly recreate its discovery for the benefit of the cameras. The interest in the press releases had resulted in a marked increase in the site's popularity, sparking a flurry of eager tourists who got in our way and asked an extraordinary volume of inane and repetitive questions. We had almost welcomed the bad weather, at least the rain and mud had put many off.

Unwilling to wait for the crew, I knelt on the duckboard in front of the recess, shining my lamp into the darkness. The water had done a fair portion of our work for us. Two gleaming skulls rested against each other in the mound of volcanic debris. I could easily make out the top of their spinal columns, clavicle, partly exposed scapula and a tangle of humeri, radii and ulnas which suggested the pair had been locked in an embrace at the moment of death. The sight made me ache deep inside. What would it be like to have someone there to hold you at that moment? Someone whose shoulder you could rest your head on when the worst occurred. The irony of envying a pair of skeletons did not elude me.

I itched to touch them but, with Cyrano still hovering, chose discretion as the better part of valour. Instead, I prepared an internal monologue to address the camera and its distant audience. The very fact that that did not set my hands shaking was a testament to the sheer volume of short interviews I had recently done for the *National Geographic* and the Herculaneum project. I could now even manage to keep my gaze settled in the correct part of the lens to ensure it appeared as though I was speaking directly to the viewer. I didn't imagine I would ever feel completely comfortable though.

'Holly? I'm going to need my kit bag, a body bag and have the film crew bring their strongest lights.'

Ω

I had never carried out an entire excavation under the glass eye of the cameras and it was unnerving. But not as unnerving as the discovery that the remains beneath my fingers gave off the same odd warmth and tingling sensation as the latrine body. It had taken all my self-control not to react visibly before the camera. It was the same warmth but not the same tone as the other, and as I slowly and methodically worked through the layers of ash and lapilli I could almost envision the pair. Her hair pinned in plaits about her head, her face turned to rest in the hollow of his shoulder, his own head resting on hers. As I had expected their arms were entangled as he held her locked against him, cradling her in his arms. I was not in the least surprised to find what remained of a smaller skull, resting where it had fallen when its fleshly casing had decomposed, to lodge itself between the bones of her pelvis, as if awaiting rebirth.

'She was pregnant?' Holly murmured over my shoulder.

I shook my head, gently cupping the fragment which rested on the palm of my hand. I shifted to allow the camera to zoom in on the small skull portion.

'No. The child is at least two years old, perhaps even a three-year-old, you can see that the posterior, sphenoid and mastoid fontanelles are all fully closed.' I pointed out each join in the bone as I used the medical terms, treating Holly and through her, the audience, as one of my students. For a change, she didn't chide me for my use of big words.

I passed the skull to Holly who placed it gently between the two larger skulls we had collected. I had decided, without any real evidence besides their physical location and the intuition that came with the tingle, I felt in the bones and could never explain that these were her parents.

'It's possible that DNA might be extracted that might link these three, but so far the DNA extracted from these ancient and heat-impacted bodies has proved of minimal use.'

Untangling the child's bones my vision blurred and made sure to keep my face from the cameras until I had found some measure of restraint. I focused intently on sifting through the ash to find the granular remains of a child's easily decomposed skeleton, locating a collection of fragments that looked child-sized but I had a strong feeling were not a child's. Then, in the ashes beneath the bodies, a glimmer of ash-encrusted metal proved to be a fabulous find, a child-sized gold chain. With the pad of my thumb, I scraped away some of the crusted ash and turned to display the item, a vaguely crescent-shaped pendant, in the palm of my hand for the benefit of the cameras.

'The child was likely a girl.' I spoke for the benefit of the camera. 'This pendant would have been hung about her neck at eight days old when she was given a name by her parents. See how it is a crescent shape, not round like more commonly found bulla?' I sought the lens of the camera, speaking through it to my audience, and imagining them as the students in my class. 'A bulla was a protective pendant given to boys to protect them in childhood. There has been some evidence that girls received a lunula rather than a bulla, crescent-shaped rather than round, for the association of the shape with Demeter, a protector of children.'

My words choked in my throat as I envisioned my sister Clare, curled protectively around the infant Kate, her husband leaning over her, touching the tiny pink cheeks with infinite gentleness.

'It didn't do much to protect her,' said the head cameraman, a genial man by the ironic nickname of Killer.

'No,' I agreed softly. 'It didn't.'

Chapter Five: An Unusual Arrangement

Rome: AD. 71

Thalia stared at the stone phallus and the jar of oil. She tried to ignore the whispers and giggles of the women around them. The broad-shouldered youth in a red cape, a priest of Subegus, grinned as he waggled it in front of her. Recalling the instructions Clementia had given she drew herself upright, breathed deeply and thrust her hand in the jar of oil. It coated her fingers and palm in a viscous golden glove. Touching her wrist to the lip of the jar to stop the drips, she reached towards the generous stone member, which was suggestively pressed towards her, and rubbed it vigorously, oil slicking the smooth surface. The women were laughing now and Thalia's face flushed hot with embarrassment. Gytha, the pale-skinned, fair-haired Britanni girl her father had given her on her twelfth natal day, offered her a clean cloth to dry her hands as the young priest chased the woman about the room with the greased phallus, to much hilarity.

Thalia accepted a small spelt cake from the platter offered by the priestess of Libera, goddess of female fertility. Within the cake were baked seeds of the pomegranate. She took a single bite, for the aim was to find the number of offspring one might produce in the number of seeds spat out from a bite of cake. Thalia wanted children or believed she did, but she had been present when her mother died in childbirth and the much-awaited son with her. There had been so much blood Thalia had been reminded of a sacrifice. So the bite she took was neither too large, nor too small. She chewed carefully, not wanting to crack or inadvertently swallow the seeds. The coarse flour had been well soaked in a heady syrup. The red-cloaked priest and his rock-hard phallus had slipped out the door and the women pressed closer to observe. Thalia met the priestess' open gaze with a growing sense of panic, as careful as she was she had not yet found a seed. Then something hard met her teeth, just one seed, and a small one at that.

Relieved, she leaned forward to spit the seed in the priestess' waiting palm. The woman gave her a reassuring smile, and with a wink shook another couple of seeds from the hem of her sleeve so that three round pink seeds sat in the flesh of her hand.

'Three is a fine number.' Someone observed.

The women agreed.

'Three will free you financially without ruining your figure.'

Three was the number of children that would emancipate a woman from the financial control of her husband or guardian. The number ordained by Augustus, the first Princeps. It was the kindly priestess who, like a hen rounding up wayward chicks, gathered the women and moved them towards the door and out, allowing her husband to enter. Only Clementia and Gytha remained.

Her relief when Messalinus shut the door behind them all was beyond measure. Then she felt the shaking begin in her fingers. She twined them together in front of her as she stood before him, Gaia to his Gaius, holding them in front of the ornate knot he would need to deftly remove to consummate their marriage. Recalling the stiff stone phallus, dripping with oil, she felt her face once more on fire and she dropped her gaze to her fingers and the gordian knot beneath her hand.

Messalinus' single glance at her sister had seen Clementia and the slave slip silently, but not without a long, almost sorrowful look in her direction. Thalia dismissed this as jealousy. For the first time in their lives, the younger sister had eclipsed the elder. Thalia had a powerful and wealthy husband, and Clementia was a divorced woman, with a small child and no current offers. Thalia would live in Nero's golden house on the hill, while her sister returned to her father's modest apartments to wait until life provided another opportunity. Thalia almost felt for her sister.

When he made no move to step closer, Thalia risked lifting her eyes. Her new husband stood three paces back, and stared. His eyes were red at the rims, she had no doubt this was from the copious cups of wine he had consumed. Her cup hadn't needed refilling, though she wished now she had taken the opportunity to drown her fears in the blood-red liquid. For the first time since they had met Messalinus seemed completely uncertain. His hands, she noticed, gripped the folds of his toga, his knuckles white. She hadn't considered that he too might be nervous.

Untangling her fingers and brushing the silken folds of her tunic she forced herself to step toward him. Messalinus seemed startled when she did. She stopped a step away from him. They studied each other in the flickering light of the oil lamps; she was tempted, once again, to reach out and run her fingers through his golden curls but his eyes were stormcloud dark and she had no idea what thoughts hid behind them. And she had never in her life been so forward as to touch a man.

Finally, Messalinus reached out, took both her upper arms in his sure grip and drew her towards him. The fingers of one hand trailed down her upper arm towards the swelling of her breasts. His touch was light and she shivered, odd sensations made an ache in her groin. She wanted something more. He let a palm cup one warm globe, a thumb brushed against the raised nipple.

Thalia had never kissed anyone. She knew from their boasting that many of her peers had practised the art with slaves, either willing or unwilling, most but not all kept it relatively chaste to ensure their virginity was not called to question. There were, of course, many ways to be pleasured that did not involve the loss of the maidenhead. Thalia had never, not once, considered using her father's slaves in that way. They had a far more important purpose; to teach her. But now, she wished that she had, even once, felt a man's lips pressed against her own. Messalinus had kissed her at the games, certainly, but it was the most fleeting of touches, just brushing the corner of her lip, though she was certain if she lifted her hand to her lips she would feel it lingering there. She had no idea what to do with her hands, so she gripped the white silk of her tunic, her heart taking little skittering leaps as she watched his lips, so she saw the odd twisting of his mouth. It was fleeting but she registered it as disgust.

He turned her body so that she faced away from him. Still reeling from the expression, she complied; his hands grasped her hips and drew them back towards him, he thrust his own against her, she felt his frustration in the pinching grip on her hips. What was she doing wrong? She closed her eyes, stilled herself to pliantly allow her body to be moved by him. One hand wrestled with the gordian knot. He groaned in frustration and instead raised the skirts towards her hips, still pushing his weight towards her. And then he stopped. The grip on her hips slackened.

His breath against her neck was ragged and hot and thick with alcohol but after a time of standing there it calmed. Thalia didn't dare to move. He shifted. His lips were warm as he pressed them against her head. Eyes still closed she shivered as he dropped them to brush her ear.

'Sleep well, wife,' he whispered in a voice thick as winter honey.

And then his grip was gone.

She opened her eyes in time to see him slip out onto the balcony that opened out into the darkness.

α

She woke late. Far later than was her habit. Usually, her father's slaves would have woken her, washed her face and hands and feet, dressed her and set food before her to break her fast. Instead, she sat up, blinking in the bright light that spilled in from outside. Perplexed, she gazed about the space until her eyes fell on the slave, Gytha, huddled in a miserable heap near the door.

'Where are my clothes?'

The slave blinked at her in dark-eyed horror and Thalia saw how reddened her eyes were, as though, like her mistress, she had been crying. 'I don't know, Domina.'

'Where are my chests? My books? My toiletries? My breakfast?'

Gytha's eyes grew wider and wilder. Her voice was barely a whisper. 'I don't know Domina, I tried to find them but…' Her voice trailed off as two lines of tears threaded down her cheeks. 'Domina, the slaves here were… unkind.'

Thalia stared at her in consternation. It seemed as likely for the slave to spring a head of snakes as to neglect her duties.

'What do you mean, they were unkind?'

Although Gytha was more than a year her junior, her life experience made her seem years older. Except now. Just now she looked barely older than Thalia's niece, Julia. The slave's head dropped further into her chest. 'They did not help.'

Frustration shot through her already frayed nerves. She was hungry and thirsty, she needed to wash and still dressed in her wedding attire; the white gown and marriage belt.

'Then get up.' Thalia heard the pitch in her voice rising, 'Go out there and find someone who is not unkind.'

Gytha stared at her, owl-like, but long trained to obey, clambered unsteadily to her feet and turned to face the door. It was then the bloom of red, the smear of blood, vibrant in its sunburst pattern was revealed. The tunic itself was torn and a line of darkening bruises around the girl's arms spoke volumes. Thalia understood.

'Stop!' She commanded as the girl's trembling hand met the door. 'Who did this?'

A tearful shrug.

Thalia considered the slave. It was obvious that the girl had been violated, an irony considering her mistress was still intact. Already feeling unsettled, Thalia's emotions teetered between surprise that the slave still had her virtue, anger that someone had violated her property, or embarrassment that the slave had been deflowered when she had remained intact after her wedding night. The girl was clearly distressed and usually Thalia felt an unfashionable amount of empathy for the slave, but today… she swallowed a hysterical giggle that threatened to become an even more embarrassing sob.

The slave hovered, face pale, one hand still on the door.

'Wait. I need your help.' Thalia, frantically trying to gather her scattered emotions, gestured at the belt around her waist, tied back where she could not reach it. 'Help me with this and we will go out there together.'

Relief flooded the girl's features and she hurried to assist. With trembling hands, she battled with the knots until the belt fell, with a dull thud, to the floor. Both young women stared at it, stepping back as though it were a viper that might strike.

Thalia brushed her hands down the loosened front of the white gown. 'Well, then.' She tumbled the cushions off the couch and took up the brightly coloured coverlet she had slept under, wrapping it around her and securing it under her arms. She passed the second piece of cloth, the white sheet that was supposed to collect her first blood and was as pristine now as it had been last night.

'Wrap that around your waist.' She instructed before turning to the door.

The hallway was empty but following the shady memories of her walk to the room she backtracked through the corridors until she reached the peristyle. Dozens of slaves were industriously working to repair the damage last night's festivities had caused. Some were sweeping up glass and pottery from the vessels that were smashed in celebratory inebriation. A dozen currs battled for the food scraps that had been tossed on the tiles or in the gardens. Several men drained what was left of the wine that had burbled through the fountain. A trio of gardeners repaired damage to shrubs and bushes, one with a pail of water shuffled back and forth from the faucet in a hidden niche in the wall, to wash away the vomit that overgorged guests had deposited in garden beds. Over a dozen slaves carried furniture or were on their hands and knees scrubbing the marble floors. Her eyes washed over them, until she found one man, also a slave, judging by his simple tunic, standing overseeing the action, giving terse orders that made the recipients flinch.

Pretending she was not in fact wearing her bedding, she strode across to him, Gytha close behind. He had the grace to look startled to see her.

'Where is my husband?'

He tilted his head just enough to suggest respect. 'Domina, *Salutatio* is finished. The Domine is at the baths and will, from there, go to the Senate house. He will not return before evening.'

The final sentence was uttered with a hesitance that suggested she may not see him then either. Thoughts churned. She wished she could simply turn and ask her sister, but Clementia had returned with her father to the apartment on the Vicus Viminalis. What would Clementia do in this situation, she wondered? Around her the slaves continued their busy work, the only sign they knew the woman was their new mistress was the distance they gave her.

'Very well.' Thalia forced a nod. 'Find the majordomo and send him immediately to my rooms.'

The slave nodded but made no move to comply, clearly weighing his existing instructions against her interference, finally, he gestured to a passing slave and spoke terse instructions before turning back to her and bowing his head.

α

She was seated on the couch when there was a knock upon her door. The firm confidence of it told her it was the man she had sought. Thalia waited for several breaths before she waved to Gytha, who stood beside the door, indicating that it should be opened.

The man who entered stared at her, curious and cautious. He was handsome and about the same age as her new husband, she guessed. He looked familiar. On his head, he wore the odd woven cap of a freedman, a sign he was still new to his freedom and wanted to ensure everyone knew he was more than a slave. She wondered, briefly, what he had done to deserve it. He met her eye with the newly acquired confidence of a manumitted man.

'Your name?' She demanded.

'Valerius Catullus Felix, Domina.' He dipped his eyes for a moment, his name confirmed what she suspected from his familiar appearance. The slave was an acknowledged bastard, likely freed to serve his legitimate half-brother.

'I require my chests and all my belongings to be brought here immediately.'

The man, who had identified himself as Felix, replied. 'I don't know where they are, Domina.'

She narrowed her eyes. 'You are my husband's majordomo are you not? Responsible for his entire household?'

He nodded.

'Then I cannot imagine a full dozen chests could arrive in a household and you do not know what became of them. Find them and have them brought here, immediately.'

Felix pressed his lips together but dipped his head and turned to go, brushing past a recoiling Gytha as he did so.

'Wait.' He stopped and turned back to her, his eyes carefully lowered though she could see his jaws were clenched. 'Send me a woman.'

'What woman, Domina?'

'Any woman. Surely your master has female slaves? Find one, no, two, who can serve as my women until I purchase new slaves. Tell her to bring water to bathe in.'

'Domina, the house has the finest baths in Rome.'

Thalia pursed her lips. 'So I have heard, but until I have clothing to wear I can hardly visit can I?'

He dipped his head and turned for the door.

'And Felix... ' she called before he disappeared from view. 'I have not yet broken my fast and I am hungry, have the kitchen send bread and fruit and wine, well-watered. And ensure that I never have to ask again.'

Her husband's half-brother disappeared from view.

α

It was several days before a commotion in the house revealed the return of her husband and prompted Thalia to put down her scrolls, have Gytha fix her hair, and venture outside the small world of her rooms and balcony.

When she did, there was no sign of Messalinus. A youth sat playing the harp on the edge of the impluvium. All her husband's slaves were handsome but this one, particularly so. A pretty boy with golden hair whose eyes widened a little when he saw her but he did not stop playing. She noticed they were lined with Kohl in Egyptian fashion, making them stand out. They were, she saw, the colour of the sky in summer. His tunic was finely made and dyed in a blue shade that matched his eyes but it was unadorned.

'Are you one of my husband's slaves?'

It was a foolish question, a fact she realised as she spoke but the words had already escaped her lips.

He nodded after a moment, dipping his head in acknowledgement though his fingers never stopped playing. He was good, playing with long, graceful fingers. The music soared about her. He studied her with as much curiosity as she regarded him and it occurred to her in that moment, making her blush in a way that made him smile, that the pretty boy was probably a *catamite* as well as a musician. Many men kept pretty boys for sexual purposes, especially young unmarried men. Clementia had once explained it to her in a way that made perfect sense. A young boy, no matter how pretty, could not be impregnated, thus losing the service of a slave who would likely have to be sold. Thalia had told her how callous she thought the practice.

'You know nothing of the world, Quartia. Go back to your scrolls,' Clementia had sneered.

Thalia was angered at the time, not in the least for her sister's stubborn resistance to using her real name, but because she was not unworldly. She knew of carnal things, she had read the poetry of Sappho and Ovid and Catullus. Still, confronted with a boy who likely had shared her husband's bed as Thalia had not, she was not entirely sure what to do.

'Where is your master?' She finally blurted.

The boy nodded in the direction of the tablinum.

Her husband stood when he saw her, crossing to her and taking her hands in his in a way that made her traitorous heart skip. He pressed a kiss to her forehead, the same way he had on their wedding night. She wanted to lift her lips to intercept it but she was not truly sure how.

'You look well. I apologise for my absence, I have had much business to attend to. Felix tells me you have made yourself at home.'

The tone he used left Thalia uncertain whether it was a compliment or criticism. She glanced at the majordomo who stood silently in the corner.

'One of your slaves raped mine.' The words tumbled artlessly from her lips. It was hardly the statement with which a wife welcomed a husband home. She flushed.

He raised an eyebrow but did not correct her. 'You know this for certain?'

'I do. She was a virgin.' She could hardly have felt more heat in her face, speaking to her husband of virginity when she herself was still intact.

'And is not one now.' He made a sound of displeasure, and clicked his tongue behind his teeth. 'A virgin slave, a rare and valuable commodity. Be assured, my love, I will find out who did this and they will be punished.'

'You will?' she frowned, surprised.

He smiled gently, squeezing one hand.

'I will. Aside from any damage to your woman, whoever it was owes me an *ass*.'

Thalia blinked in confusion.

Messalinus smiled indulgently. 'I do not permit random copulations in my household. If a slave takes a woman he must pay for it. It is an honest transaction that keeps fornication to a minimum, rewarding those who work hard.'

Thalia shook her head slightly in disbelief, but found her mouth opening, again of its own volition. 'Then surely the *ass* should belong to Gytha.'

'Gytha?'

'My slave.'

He smiled. 'Yours, ours, mine. She belongs to you, you belong to me, therefore she is mine, as is the *ass*.' His perfect teeth gleamed.

Thalia suddenly remembered the winnings from the gladiatorial bout that he had never passed on.

'Come now, is that all you want?'

Thalia breathed deeply. 'I have borrowed slaves from my father to serve me in my rooms. I would like to buy some of my own.'

Messalinus crossed back to his desk and his paperwork. 'Of course,' he replied, not lifting his head. 'There will surely be things that you need. I trust given your upbringing that you are a frugal spender and will not run through my money too quickly.' He glanced up briefly with a smile that suggested a jest, standing in the golden hall in Nero's golden house surrounded by material splendour there was little chance she could make a serious dent in his funds.

'Buy what you need. Slaves, scrolls, jewellery… Make sure the accounts are given to Felix and so long as they are reasonable there is no problem. You will no doubt need a new wardrobe to match your new position.' He glanced at her gown, a pale saffron piece of fine linen from her clothes chest. A piece her sister had carefully embroidered with embellishments of flowers. 'See to it that you address that before being seen about in Rome.'

She pulled her gaze from the tiny flowers that dotted the hem, work that was so intricate and perfect it shamed her, knowing her own stitches had suffered at the expense of her reading and writing. Yet, these perfect stitches clearly displeased her husband. He was busy with his papers and did not look up so she considered herself dismissed.

As she reached the door his voice checked her.

'While we are setting ground rules. Be aware that your family are not welcome here unless your father needs to come on official business. You have a new life now and need to part with the old one.'

'I may not see my family?' The shock made her uncharacteristically placid.

'You can visit them, perhaps once a week would be enough, but no more than that. You must act in all ways as depicts your new status, as the wife of a wealthy senator. It would shame me if anyone were to comment on my wife's common background. You cannot help where you come from, and your father has done well for himself and is an important person to the Emperor, still, everyone should better themselves.'

His eyes met hers until she found herself, quite against her inclination, nodding.

When she was back in her room she consoled herself with the memory that he had included scrolls alongside slaves and gems, as items worthy of purchase. She wondered idly, how many scrolls exactly?

Chapter Six: Under the Light of a Thousand Stars

Tetyanivka, 2018

The baby snuffled and hiccuped, wet and heavy and increasingly relaxed on his shoulder as he alternately patted and crooned and rocked. They were far enough from the old farmhouse that the air was clear of smoke and he could no longer hear the raucous noise of the party. His twin sons celebrated their fourth birthday and the entire family had gathered. His wife's family anyway, his own parents were too nervous to travel from the capital. Her mother and father and even her ama, along with her brother and his wife and their three children. As with all family gatherings there was music and laughter and singing and the combined cacophony, along with his brother-in-law's homemade *bouza* had made his head ache, so when two-month-old Melie had become unsettled he had kissed Elirë's flushed cheek and volunteered to walk her outside until she fell asleep. Had it still been safe to drive about Tetyanivka Samir Al'Shani might have taken her in the car and driven until the soothing rhythm of motor and road lulled her to sleep. But these were not those times. As persecution escalated in the disputed eastern Oblasts, he had acted to move his family further from harm, bringing them to the farmhouse, a few miles from the small mountain village where her family were originally from. Now he wandered the hillsides, rocked, patted and sang Elirë's favourite American love ballads until, at last, Melie fell asleep.

He would not stay out much longer. The air in the mountains was clearer and colder than at home, and even in early autumn, when the days were still warm, the nights smelt of snow. As he looked up at the light of a thousand stars, Samir sang Ed Sheeran lyrics into his daughter's milky-scented neck.

A cracking noise startled him, but mercifully didn't wake the baby and his first thought was to wonder who had brought the firecrackers. But the second burst of sound shattered any illusions. It was gunfire, coming from the direction of the farmhouse. Two conflicting emotions shot through him, the desire to run towards the farmhouse and his family and the protective instinct that froze him on the hillside as his baby daughter snuffled softly into his neck.

More shots crackling through the darkness decided him. Still rubbing the baby's back he stepped quickly, just short of running, in the direction of home. He pulled short in the treeline, in the light that spilled from the windows of the old brick house were two motor vehicles and a collection of motorbikes. How had he not heard them? Beside one of the vehicles, an amber glow indicated the inhalations of someone with a cigarette, his shadow clearly outlined the weapon he carried.

Samir had a gun and was considered a reasonable shot, but his weapon, an old SKS was tucked in a trunk inside the farmhouse, with inquisitive four-year-olds he made sure the trunk was always shut and the key kept high out of reach, the gun would be no use to him now.. He hesitated, it was quiet in the house, except for the harsh laughter of men, voices he didn't recognise in a language he did, one that sent a frisson of fear down his spine.

Mercifully, the barn was shrouded in darkness. There were no animals in there, besides the chickens, the farm's only stock, two aged milk cows were in the paddock beyond the house. But his ancient Volvo was parked in there, with more miles on the odometer than could be shown and in the trunk, his father's old World War Two rifle. The old man had thrust it at him, wrapped in a bath towel as they hugged farewell in Donetsk. Samir had never bothered to remove it. Keeping to the shadows Samir stepped carefully to avoid any sound that might alert the watcher, only 15 metres away. His heart thumped so loudly in his skull that he felt sure the man would hear, and the baby's snuffles sounded so loud in his ear that Samir was sure the noise would alert the man until he heard a tinny screeching sound that at first puzzled, then thrilled him. The man nodding his head to the sound of the screeching, listened to music while he stood sentinel outside. With a sigh of relief, Samir slipped into the dark earthy smells of the barn.

He groped his way to where he knew the Volvo waited, put a hand to the driver's side door, and then froze. If he opened the door the internal light would come on, clearly visible from the driveway. But the light in the back was broken. Elirë had tired of reminding him to fix it. Running his hands down the door panel Samir found the rear door handle. He paused to listen, nothing changed, gingerly he opened the rear car door. With the weight of Melie's head supported, he tucked her on the floor, wrapped in his outer jacket. Mercifully, though she made suckling noises she did not wake. He pulled the door shut, lifted the handle and pressed his hip against it until he felt more than heard the muted click. It was a sound he almost missed because at the same time he heard his daughter, Samara, scream.

All thoughts of removing the rifle from the trunk disappeared as more shots rang out, accompanied by his wife's scream. Samir shot across the damp lawn, nearly tripped on the rocky garden edge, and was through the doorway before the sentinel could drop his hand to his weapon. The scene that met his eye was far beyond his scope of belief. Samara was standing by the old hearth, his daughter's dress was torn and one of the men was standing behind her, a knife at her throat and one hand groping her breast. Another man was laughingly holding Elirë back as she tried to reach the body on the floor; her brother, Rustam's. The blood already pooled across the ancient wooden floorboards left little doubt that Rustam was dead. His wife, Saide, her face splattered with his blood, sobbed on the floor beside him. About the room, his twin sons and their cousins crouched wide-eyed with horror.

Elirë's father struck out at the man holding Samara with an arch of his cane but before the blow even landed one of the men pressed their handgun to the back of the old man's head and there was a muffled retort. The impact toppled the old man with his silver hair to the floor at Samara's feet, her eyes wide with terror and distress. Samir's own momentum sent him crashing into the man with the handgun and surprise alone allowed him to wrestle the weapon from his grip and knock him backwards. The man stumbled over Rustam's body, landing half on top of Saide who leapt at him with her bare hands, scratching at his face and grabbing handfuls of hair; her screams had taken on the eerie pitch of the unhinged. Another gunshot and she froze, then, as if in slow motion she crumpled over the body of her husband.

Samir found himself standing less than two feet from the man groping his daughter. Without a moment's hesitation, he raised the muzzle of the gun to the man's temple. The groper's eyes widened for a moment and then he grinned. His mouth was a checkerboard of toothless spaces. It took a moment for Samir to understand why. As he stood there, with the gun pressed to the man's temple, silence descended. Without his sister-in-law's hysteric wailing the room fell quiet, or almost. Elirë was on the floor beside her father and brother sobbing softly, tears ran down her cheeks as she looked, not at the body but at him, and Samara. The man who had tripped was back on his feet, cursing softly in Russian. He had a second gun in his hand, pointed not at Samir, but at the centre of Elirë's back. With a hand at the scruff of her neck he dragged her, unresisting, to her feet. Not taking his eyes off Samir, the man secured his gun between broad white teeth as he dragged a cable tie from a pocket and tied her arms behind her back.

'We might take this one with us.' He spoke in Russian, but here, so close to the border, many did. The lines beside his eyes betrayed a grin Samir couldn't see.

Two other men, their faces obscured by camo-coloured masks and dressed in olive-green fatigues stood at different points in the room, they both had guns trained on Samir. He recognised them as 'Green men', unmarked soldiers, self-styled peacekeepers with Russian accents and weapons, the sort that currently held the neighbouring peninsula of Crimea. In the doorway the lonely sentinel had arrived, the cigarette still hanging from his mouth, his weapon also trained on Samir. At the table, with the as-yet uncut birthday cake, Elirë's grandmother keened quietly as she rocked on the wooden chair.

'This your daughter, eh?' Checker-mouth asked in thick Russian as his hand continued to squeeze and pinch at his daughter's chest.

Samir said nothing, Samara's eyes pleaded silently with him, tears threading their way down her face. She looked so like her mother that he ached to pull the trigger, but the gun at the man's head was the only leverage he had. He cocked the weapon. The man holding his daughter took the knife from her throat and with a swift movement drove it into the wooden table beside them. But he did not release the girl, instead, his hand slipped through the rent in her dress to her underwear, and Samara moaned fearfully.

Samir pushed the pistol harder against the man's temple, the words that followed he spoke in fluent Russian.

'Let her go and I won't blow your head off.'

The man giggled.

'Ah, the hero speaks the mother tongue. I tell you what, put down the gun and I'll let you watch, and if she pleases me I might let you live.'

One of the men behind him guffawed.

Samara whimpered as the man's fingers injured her sensitive flesh.

As Samir squeezed the trigger he met Elirë's eye, apologised for what he knew would be his death, but the explosion that should have kicked back at him was instead a quiet click as the firing pin met an empty chamber. A delayed shot cracked, pain spiralled outwards from just below his knee and his right leg collapsed, dropping him to his knees, an action that amplified the agony in his lower leg. Blinking to clear his eyes of white flashes he met Elirë's tearwashed face. A plume of white smoke drifted from the sentinel's gun. It rested beside her cheek. Defeated, Samir shut his eyes. When he opened them again it was to see the but of a rifle crash into his nose with a sickening crunch that propelled his head back into the heavy wood of the fireplace mantle. As he fought the blackness he heard a voice command.

'Enough of this. Put the *suchka* in the car. Kill the rest.'

Chapter Seven: Bodies in the Boatshed

Ercolano, 2022

'Bravo! Bravissimo!'

The audience surged to their feet as the majestic soprano who had played the lead in Handel's *Agrippina* took the main stage, her bumbling husband Claudio a few steps behind.

I had struggled throughout the performance, not because the opera was in Italian, but because I was distracted by the setting. Tonight's performance, with its small crowd of rich and famous, was held on a stage inside the Colosseum and the golden wash of lighting had only emphasised the surreal but appropriate setting.

Massimo leant close, his breath warm on my neck. 'Did you enjoy the performance?'

It was a pointless question. Massimo had heard me laugh, seen me cry and put his warm hand over mine when I gripped the armrest between us a little too intensely.

'It was *meraviglio, magnifico!*'

He smiled proprietorially, as though I complemented the man rather than the performance.

'Thank you for bringing me.' Despite my initial misgivings I found I actually meant it. 'I have never seen anything so marvellous. Although I do feel a little sorry for Agrippina. Your history has painted her as such a villain.'

He glanced at me, amused by the assertion. 'You pity a woman who killed her husbands and slept with her son?'

I shake my head. 'I pity the woman who has been so smeared by history that others believe that so easily of her.'

He shook his head, bemused. 'It is true, she was not wholly at fault. Agrippina represents a cautionary tale of what becomes of a woman if her men let her gain too much power.'

In shock I gaped at him, open-mouthed, but he had turned already to greet a fellow opera fan and was shaking hands and kissing cheeks. I turned to give myself time to swallow my anger, letting the majesty of the view soak into my psyche until I was able to smile when he reached for my arm, drew me closer and introduced me to an older man and woman I recognised from Italian television but could not identify. The woman wore a diamond choker so broad it could have once graced Catherine the Great. I was grateful that Holly had insisted we shop for a dress for the opera, overriding my decision to attend in pants and a nice top. The sleek velvet dress that cocooned me actually made me feel comfortable amongst the gleaming stars that walked around me. And if Massimo's expression was any guide, he too appreciated the tight black dress.

His hand tightened beneath my elbow and steered me carefully down the perilous temporary staging. Despite my instinctual reaction to be offended at being manhandled, I settled on gratitude because the heels Holly had insisted on were at least an inch too high for me. At least until I turned and was startled to find myself face to face with. or rather looking down on the thinning hair and pink gloss of a familiar scalp, one right on eye-level with the low v frontage of the velvet dress and my unusually exposed cleavage.

Direttore Cyrano.

His eyes flashed with an excitement that seemed completely at odds with his usual expression. Something at once both avaricious and obsequious. But it was a gaze that had nothing to do with the hint of dusky breast at his eye level for his eyes were all for my companion, and though he addressed me his gaze never left Massimo's face. I was uncertain whether to be perturbed or offended.

'Dottore Benino.' He simpered, still not meeting my eye. 'What a pleasure to see you here, and in such esteemed company.' His hand shot out in Massimo's direction.

My companion blinked at the little man for a moment before accepting the outstretched hand on offer. As soon as Massimo's hand was in his grip Cyrano clapped his other hand over it as if he would hold it hostage.

'Massimo Di Mao. An honour to see you again. I trust you enjoyed the performance?'

Massimo eyed the Direttore with a bemused expression and frowned. 'Have we met?'

Cyrano's face fell and I found myself speaking. 'Massimo. This is Direttore Franko Cyrano, he is in charge of the site at Herculaneum, and my boss in a manner of speaking.'

'Ah of course, my apologies Direttore, the light in here is not what it should be. I didn't make the connection.'

Massimo struggled to retract his hand. I could tell that he truly did not recognise the little man.

'It would be a pleasure to have you visit our little site again soon. There have been so many new discoveries. I would be honoured to give you a personal tour.'

A twitch in Massimo's right brow and a corresponding tilt to his lips betrayed Massimo's amusement. 'Ah, you refer to Vittoria's wonderful finds.'

I flushed conscious of his hand, still bolstering my elbow, fingers grazing the curve of my breast.

'Yes, I will have to visit soon. Now If you will excuse us, there is someone I need to speak to. I let his hand exert pressure under my elbow, tug firmly but gently and moved off obligingly, leaving Cyrano in our wake.

'Come, Bella Donna, I will introduce you to Agrippina. Your pity will no doubt amuse her.'

Ω

I had mused over Cyrano's reaction for the remains of the evening and had to remind myself several times to focus on the conversation on offer as we sped towards my father's townhouse in Massimo's sleek silver Maserati. I didn't wait for him to open the door, but found that between the low level of the seating and the tight sheath of the dress I was grateful for the hand he had offered to assist me. I was still pondering my conundrum while dodging away from the arm that settled in the small of my back and exerted pressure to pull me closer.

Safe, strong, in control, I reminded myself, glancing up at the light that spilled from my father's terrace apartment. I shifted away from his hands and his lips and offered an apologetic smile.

'I had a wonderful evening. Thank you so much for taking me. I have never seen the colosseum by night before. It was magnificent.' Tilting my head away, his lips landed warmly against my jaw, his nose brushed my ear. The smell of his cologne was expensive.

'I feel like a wayward teenager again,' I commented, gesturing at the lights aglow above us. 'It seems my father is still up. I should go. Thank you, again! I really enjoyed the opera.'

I slipped from his grip, grateful for the second time that evening for the sleek black dress with its slick fabric, and up the steps without looking back. It was not my father, but Guilia who was waiting, coffee in hand, expression of anticipation clearly evident.

I turned on her. 'Just who is Massimo?'

'Did Gianni not tell you?' She frowned then let her face brighten. 'Massimo is the Minister of Culture and Tourism.' Guilia twinkled, 'That includes Antiquities, you realise? Your father invited him because he hoped it would be a useful connection forwarding your career. And Massimo has been something of a protege of his.'

I felt goosebumps creep across my flesh, my stomach churned.

Ω

'Massimo of the massive bank balance is Minister Di Mao?' Holly's head tipped curiously. 'You didn't tell me that you moved in such exalted circles.'

I managed a frown. In truth, I had no concept of who he was until that night.

I chose to ignore Holly's comment and focused my attention on the articulated remains in front of me. I spoke across the bench as I measured the femur length of the skeleton of the male. One of the three we had discovered in the boathouse. He was particularly tall for Romans of the time, I estimated about 6 foot, taller by a head than the average Roman male. His leg bones were thicker and stronger than even today's standard.

'Look at this.' I pointed out the wearing of the upper femur and hip joints.

Holly rolled her eyes. 'You remember that I am only on loan right? Anthropology is not my field. Tell me what I am supposed to notice and get back to the gossip about Adonis and his actress friend.

I scowled at her. 'The thickness here looks like Poirier's Facet, sometimes called 'horse-riding syndrome.'

'Our guy likes to ride horses, so what?'

'So Romans rarely rode. Like our lavatory warrior, his teeth tell us he was not a local.' I let my hand drift across the skull, measuring the cheekbones, ignoring the warm sensation the bones gave off. 'His skull and cheekbones are broad and a less pronounced nasal bridge suggests he might have some connection to the more Asian provinces.'

Given that Rome was a melting pot of ethnicities this was not a shocking discovery. I packaged a molar to send for DNA testing.

Like the lavatory body, the man's bones showed wear that could be consistent with time served in armies and the damage associated with the lifestyle of a warrior. The right arm and shoulder development of this man was even more pronounced than the other, something often seen in occupations such as blacksmiths, but again that was supposition. I would not make the same mistake as Bisel, who had studied the boatshed bodies before me, assuming detailed identities, even naming bodies, based on bone features that could have any number of possible interpretations.

I turned to the next bench. Beside the male, the woman's remains looked tiny and fragile. At only 5'3" the top of her head would barely have reached his shoulder. Hers was a frame more akin to what I would expect from remains found in Italy.

I heard Holly sigh as I ran my finger across the spider web of fracture marks on her left cheekbone and eye socket suggested a painful break but the edges were smooth and rounded, the injury long healed. Still, I could almost feel the lingering ache in my own cheek while I was touching her. Today, an injury of this type was an indicator of violent assault or domestic violence. Who had beaten her? Why?

'I'm waiting. Don't you know I am living vicariously through your dating experiences?'

I shot a measuring glance at Holly. I suspected that she and Dalton were closer than they appeared but she had not disclosed a relationship and he was a married man so I kept my opinion to myself.

'Right. Well, between shooting me dirty looks and lounging all over Massimo, Agrippina—I think her real name was Gianna— thought my pity for her character was quite hilarious. You know her teeth are in excellent condition.'

Holly cocked her head. 'Gianna's?'

'The victim's. Far better than any I've seen at Herculaneum so far.'

'They ate well here. Mediterranean diet and all that. Loads of variety.'

I nodded, this was Holly's area of expertise, and the reason she spent so much time investigating the ancient sewers.

'I think it's more than that. She has no cavities and almost no wear to her teeth.' This suggested good oral hygiene and a varied diet including, importantly, bread that was ground finely enough to be without too much of the grit that caused the greater wear in the less fortunate. She was young, no older than 25. I was not wholly surprised to find that her teeth too lacked stress marks.

'Whoever she was, I doubted she was anywhere near the bay of Naples when the earthquake occurred.'

Holly was staring at me. In her hand was a tiny partial rib bone. Disturbed by the strength of the feeling I got when in contact with the child's bones I had given Holly the task of articulating the smallest skeleton.

The child's remains were in the poorest condition. The small bones, more flexible and less dense than adult bones were easily corroded and there was much less that remained of her to analyse. Many of the smaller bones were completely absent. While I felt strongly that she was female and the lunula corresponded with my feelings, there was nothing I could do to prove the find definitively.

'Are you sure?' She asked.

'Why?'

'What are the odds that all the remains you found were foreign?'

I considered the question. 'Herculaneum was a tourist hotspot, even in the Ancient World.'

Her nose scrunched up the way it often did when she was thinking.

'Yes, but we are talking about October right? The season is done. The tourists would have gone home. Umm… Tori, is it possible that there was more than one child?'

I glanced at the fragments Holly had been laying out and could see her concern, there appeared to be additional splinters of what might have been ribs and three femur fragments. I managed to stifle a smile. Reaching over I sifted out the non-human bones.

'Animal.' I pointed out. 'Very young children and many animals share some bone similarities that change with age.'

Holly flushed as I sifted through the assortment of bones from the 'not yet identified' pile and found a series of canine teeth and part of a small animal skull and pointed these out to my assistant. 'I suspect the child might have been harbouring a pet.'

I reached to shift the order of a couple of ribs and nudged the tiny mandible. The dental x-rays of the child's jaw, showing the unerupted teeth confirmed my assertion that the child was around three years old. I pulled my fingers back, confronted yet again. Each time I touched them, all three of them, the imagined feeling of warmth and familiarity felt stronger and I fought the urge to reconstruct their features in my mind. It was not as though I could ever tell definitively what their skin tone had been, or their eye or hair colour, nor could I ever put a name to them. Still, I knew that *National Geo* would love a visual representation, so I ordered an MRI of both skulls and requested the results be sent to a colleague in Melbourne who would use computer generated images to reconstruct their faces.

I added teeth from the woman and child to the package to be tested for DNA but because of the heat involved in the eruption, I had little expectation anything usable would be found. Still, technological advances occurred constantly and there was nothing to say one day it could not be useful.

'Could you package all these off for the courier?' I asked, handing Holly the collection of teeth and bone fragments.

'Only if you tell me how it ended.'

I glanced at the remains. We had each body completely catalogued and photographed and, as expected, could find no evidence of cause of death, beyond the one anticipated. I suppressed a shudder.

'Death was probably a result of suffocation caused by the toxic fumes of the pyroclastic that hit the shore and boat sheds shortly after midnight.'

I considered the three skeletons. It would have been a swift if horrific death, though not instantaneous as those exposed to the red-hot cloud who had been waiting on the beach.

Holly snorted. 'Not theirs. Your date.'

'Oh. Well, it was less horrific. A kiss on the cheek when he dropped me at my father's. He was a perfect gentleman.'

Holly stared at me incredulously for a moment, sighed in exasperation. 'You do know how much good dating the Minister for Culture and Tourism, the very man with oversight into every archaeological park in Italy, would do for your career right? Cyrano couldn't get rid of you if he tried.'

When I failed to answer she shuffled out the door.

There was little more I could do to explore these remains until the full array of test results returned. I turned my attention to the items we had recovered in close proximity to the bodies. A small clay lamp, imprinted with the shape of a running horse, had been found in the ash at their feet. Scarce illumination for a night as dark as the one Pliny had reported.

As well as the gold lunula, a number of other metallic items had been unearthed, including a pair of lapis lazuli earrings I imagined hanging from the woman's lobes, and the pugio, an oversized knife. These I had given to Holly, who had been wriggling with excitement at the thought of revealing the secrets held beneath the hardened ash.

A second pendant, tangled in the vertebrae of the female skeleton had caused a sensation. After initial cleaning it had become clear that this was something unique. A voluptuous female figure in gleaming gold. Cyrano contributed an hypothesis that the pendant was Scythian in origin, a female form, particularly curvaceous, likely a regional goddess. This was an intriguing suggestion given what I had learned of the male victim's likely origin. News of that find had spread quickly and my small workspace had seemed crammed with visitors until the project decided that, for its safety, the relic would be moved to the Museo in Napoli.

That left me with the final object, an earthen jug.

The jug was glazed in *buchero*, an iron-rich black slip and etched with human figures. It was the size of a skull and weighed a significant amount, which had proved to be largely the weight of sand. Holly had proposed that the sand had been added to silence the noise of coins jingling inside, and I could not disagree. The coins were largely silver and bronze. A reasonable sum, but not a lot, not when one considered the gold pendant found alongside.

And then there were the dozens of small nacreous spheres we had found in the sand, revealing their iridescence even under dim light. Each unique in shape, flawed pearls, drilled through the centre which suggested they had been suspended on a necklace. They were not unique among finds from the doomed cities, I knew, but they were a delightful find that I suspected would find their way into an exhibit somewhere. After counting twice each, Holly and I concluded there were 173 individual pearls, enough for a three strand rope. These had been carefully bagged and sent to be cleaned and tested. I had never owned so much as a pearl, but Clare and I had taken turns wearing my mother's strands, wrapping the ropes about our necks or dangling them in our hair when we played dress-up as children, only when our mother was absent. The memory made me smile.

Now, I considered the vessel itself. It was a beautiful specimen, but small enough and simple enough to be carried without attracting undue notice. As I tucked my fingers around its handle and lifted I felt an itch between my shoulder blades, like I was being watched. I turned, expecting Holly or Cyrano but found no one there. Noone but the box on the shelf containing the latrine man's remains, the skull eerily positioned so that it appeared to be staring.

I laughed at my own foolishness, but as I examined the jug I could not shake the uncomfortable feeling and gave in to the irrational push. Taking the lid off the box I gently turned the skull around so that its indented occipital lobe faced me rather than the orbital sockets. But as I did so I noticed again the rounded impression made by what I suspected was a murder weapon. There had been nothing that matched in the latrine chamber but that didn't mean that the weapon hadn't been carried away with the murderer. My eyes slipped to the earthen jug. Something like that, for example, would make a rounded impression in the skull. It was certainly solid enough and when it had been filled was heavy enough. Taken by the whimsy of my proposition I brought the skull back to the bench, just as Holly returned. She raised an eyebrow. I shrugged, unable to put my odd fantasy in words without sounding ludicrous. I handed her the skull, turning it so the damage faced towards me. I turned to the table, wrapping my hand around the vessel's handle once more and lifted it towards the skull.

As the vessel neared the skull it was obvious that my supposition was right. Something like the vase could easily have resulted in the impression on the skull. In fact, although further testing would be needed, the corresponding damage to the skull matched the convex wall of the jug almost perfectly. I found I could not put the jug down quickly enough, my hand was shaking and I tucked it deep in my pocket where it would not be seen. I turned back to Holly who was staring at me in wonder.

'Take photographs.' I glanced in the direction of the lab camera. 'Do measurements, send both pieces to be scanned.'

I turned back to the coins on the bench, trying to hide the roiling in my stomach and the pounding in my head. Then I gave up on trying both to focus, and keep my lunch down. I couldn't imagine what was wrong with me, perhaps a migraine.

I picked up my jacket and my kitbag. 'If anyone needs me I'm heading home.' I gestured vaguely towards my temple. 'I have the worst headache and I need to shift it before tomorrow.'

Holly grinned knowingly. 'The Italian Stallion, right?'

Perhaps that was the true cause of my nervous stomach. The Opera had been a delight and Massimo had been a charming and attentive host so, despite my lingering reservations, I had agreed to a second 'date'. Tomorrow he was taking me to see the Domus Aurea, the remains of Emperor Nero's great golden house. But as I forced open tightly clenched fists it finally occurred to me who Massimo reminded me of. And it set a chill up my spine. Holly failed to notice as I fumbled with the door handle and when I let myself outside I inhaled great gulps of air as though I had been held underwater for too long. Massimo looked nothing like him, not really, though both were tall and well built and it was patently unfair to assume that he was anything like the man in my past that I had deliberately not thought of in over a decade. Still, mentally scolding myself did little to relieve the growing anxiety that resulted in a stronger throbbing in my temples.

I considered calling Clare. She always knew what to say to reassure me. But when I did the mental calculations I realised it was barely 4am back home.

Ω

It was well past midnight when I switched the lights on in the lab. The familiar crackle that came with a faulty socket, as usual, made me pull my fingers back quickly. I made sure the door was locked firmly behind me. There would be enough trouble should it become known I was onsite at night. How could I explain the compulsion? Despite the fascination I had felt walking through the subterranean vaults that were once the grandest villa in Rome I had felt distinctly uncomfortable and I hadn't stopped thinking about the jug and the skull and the way they had felt in my hand.

The remains in my office had come to so dominate my thoughts that I could actually envision them in life. As I had wandered the remaining halls of Nero's golden house I had actually imagined them there, the sneering Praetorian, the dark-haired young Roman woman and the tall warrior of Asian origin. The only one missing from the picture was the child. There was no reason I should, no likelihood that any of them had ever been present in Nero's palace, but I simply couldn't shake the impression of them.

Unlocking the door to my lab, I switched on the overhead lights and crossed to the shelf where we stored the evidence when not in use. I pushed the short step stool in place and with one foot on it and the other suspended for better balance, I leant to retrieve the container in which the latrine victim's remains were stored. With care to ensure I didn't overbalance I stepped back to the floor and, kicking the step aside, brought the remains to the central bench and laid them out. Again I felt unsettled by the malevolent feeling the bones gave off.

I worked from reconstructed skull down the body, laying out the vertebrae and working from there to fill in the ribs, then the arm and leg bones until they formed an outline of the man. I had come to agree with Holly that he was likely a Praetorian and it seemed equally likely that he had formed part of the rescue attempt that had come from Misenum, an attempt that, judged on the absence of written evidence, likely failed. Testing of the teeth had conclusively proven that this man had not grown up in the region nor spent much of his life there. Of his death we could be certain. But who had killed him and why had left me sleepless. Or perhaps, more accurately, a nightmare in which I had played out the man's last moment had left me, heart pounding, wide awake and checking my own hands for signs of blood.

I ran my fingers over his radius and ulna, damage to the bones there was evident but old and long healed. His ribs likewise showed evidence of a violent lifestyle, marred with old healed scoring on bones that correlated with the life of a soldier in a time when swords, arrows and daggers were the weapons of choice.

I returned to the skull, cupping it in my hand meant forcing myself to ignore the disturbing feeling it evoked in me. With the jawbone held in place I shifted it to look more closely at the damage. The scans had confirmed my suspicions. The impact to the skull had indeed been made by something similar in shape to the sand-and-valuable-filled jug, but the skull and jug had been found in two different places with no evidence to link them. Nor could I establish any other link between my four bodies other than that, like my murder victim, the two adults in the boat house had not lived in Herculaneum all their lives.

I had decided to conduct another survey of the remains when something caught my notice, beneath my fingers, on the protruding lump that was the mastoid process, a scoring to the bone. Shifting my grip on the skull I turned it over, positioning it under the light of the magnifier.

Sure enough, there, at the base of the skull was an angled slice, an incision that cut into the then-living bone of the mastoid process. A shiver ran through me. The damage was near enough to what would have been the carotid artery. I looked more closely at the mandible and saw evidence of a scrape that could be consistent with the edge of a knife grazing along the jaw until it struck the nearby mastoid process. I had seen similar marks on the skull of the exhumed body of a male prostitute in Sydney who had been killed in the 80's during the gay-hate-crime murders where the perpetrator had grabbed a handful of hair, tipped the head back and sliced so deeply into the victim's throat that not only had they nearly decapitated the young man, they had scored the bone itself.

Placing the jawbone on the bench I moved to grab the lab camera but found the drawer where it was kept empty and cursed my coworkers under my breath. Instead, I grabbed my phone and using the flash took a series of images, measured against a handy paperclip. I would download them in the morning to save with our files. Dropping my phone on the counter I crossed to the evidence boxes that linked to the remains and flipped the lid. The first contained the jug, the pearls, coins, the dagger and the exquisite gold pendant on its chain. I pushed the box to one side, turning instead to the second, the one containing what was left of the scabbard and buckle and the sword and the pouch with its collection of coins. The coins had interested us all. They were proof the murder was not a robbery, they were also, according to the specialist we had sought, almost the exact amount of money as a Praetorian's wage, further confirmation of what other evidence we had on the markings of the sword and scabbard.

It was the sword I sought. Despite the weathering of millennia, I was surprised again by its weight as I lifted it with care from the box, bringing it with me to the skull. It was the only sharp implement that had been in the latrine. I knew the value of weapons in ancient times, they were not something one threw away, and yet this had been discarded with the body. Was it because it was too recognisable? Or was it perhaps the murder weapon? Had the killer knocked the victim unconscious before using his own sword to cut his throat?

A Roman gladius was not as long as the swords of later eras but it was not a small implement, I compared the damage to the jawbone with the angle of the blade, shifting it along its entire length and then turning it in case the alternate edge was a better fit. The evidence was conclusive. The sword, even taking into account its weathered edges, was not a match for the damage.

Placing it back in the evidence box, I closed the lid. I turned to the second box, the evidence from the boat shed, my gaze lingered on the jug, whose rounded centre so closely fitted the damage to the skull. I was considering taking it out once more when my focus shifted to the large dagger. Blades were common in Rome. Men, women, even children wore belt knives and used them for all sorts of purposes from cutting their food to cleaning under their nails. But this was not a common blade. Like the Praetorian's sword it too had a hilt of ivory. The weapon had sustained considerably more wear than the sword, but then the sword had been protected by the granite case of the latrine.

I found myself picking up the now clean weapon, the first time I had done so and was disturbed to find it felt familiar in my hand. On closer inspection of the hilt I could make out the hint of a pattern. On impulse I placed the pugio on the surface of the bench and turned back for the box I had just returned to the shelf and drew out the gladius. I placed it on the bench beside the smaller weapon. Grabbing my phone I took a series of photographs, despite finding my hands trembling.

It was immediately clear that these two weapons matched. If I were a metallurgist I suspected that I would find they were made using the same base metals, using the same technique and likely made by the same hands. I resolved to have Holly scrape samples for analysis tomorrow before Andrew, who had flown back yesterday, claimed her back.

The faded symbols on the hilt of the pugio had the same suggested shape as the scorpion on the gladius, implying that it too was the weapon of a Praetorian.

Was this proof of a second Praetorian? But if it were true, why was he huddled and hiding at the rear of the boathouse, his remains entangled with the woman and child, rather than at the entry or on the beachfront itself? It simply didn't make sense.

Almost reluctantly, I picked up the pugio and felt again the sensation of familiarity. With a sense of dread, I stepped up beside the skull. I knew what I would find before I placed the blade beside the jaw. With the pugio in one hand and my phone in the other, I took a series of snaps that would show that this second weapon, or something very like it, had caused the damage to the skull. As I held the weapon in my right hand I imagined using my left to take hold of the Praetorian's hair to pull it back towards me, leaning over the prone body as I had in my nightmare to press the pugio to the man's throat and slice from left to right, digging the blade in so deeply at the right that it shaved the mandible and jarred against the bone of the mastoid process, almost sticking. In my mind, I could see the bright gush of blood and feel its heat as it washed over my fingers, while the body jerked beneath my left hand and then subsided.

I dropped the pugio on the bench beside the skull and had enough time to lean across the sink before the scalding burn in my throat became gut-wrenching spasms as all that was inside me poured outwards. When the heaving subsided I hung over the sink, a single trail of thick saliva dripping from my chin, making its way towards the mess at the bottom. My throat scalded and my eyes flooded with tears. It took two hands, one on each side of the sink to push me upright. When I did, the room swam as though underwater.

I ran the tap until I had cleared the sink of what I had deposited there, cupping my hand to bring water to my lips and rinsing to clear my mouth of the acrid taste, though no amount of swallowing dislodged the raw burn in my throat.

I wrapped the dagger in a towel, fearing to touch it again, before sealing what I felt were both murder weapons, jug and dagger, in the evidence box together and pushing them back onto the shelf. I should have taken notes, recorded my thoughts and findings but the lingering sense of horror drove me.

Barely conscious of doing so I locked the lab, reset the alarms and stumbled my way, like a drunk, back through the darkness of the site to the road which led to my apartment. I spent so long in the shower that the water ran to cold while I tried desperately to blank my mind, to find the clinical professionalism that was essential to my role. I wondered if I was going mad.

Huddled beneath the light covers, I tossed and turned until sleep finally claimed me and dragged me under and in my dreams I was a child, posing before a camera, revelling in the glamour of the moment, changing pose and expression with each click and whirr, from smiling to pouting, from confident to demure, not realising until too late that the smiling face behind the camera was that of a predator.

Chapter Eight: A Dutiful Wife

Rome AD 71

Messalinus, she decided, wanted a statue not a wife. One he could keep in his golden house. Someone silent.

It was not merely associating with her family that Messalinus frowned on and Thalia swiftly discovered that despite a new wardrobe, life beyond the hill on which Nero's villa sat was closed to her. At first, it seemed a sequence of coincidences that kept her trapped in the villa. Litters would not be available, a guard could not be found to escort her. She was of too high status to walk to Rome, it simply was not done, did she want to humiliate him? There was unrest in the city and her husband considered it unsafe, he valued her too highly to risk her. She was his wife, not a courtesan, why would he expose her to the common rabble of the theatres, circus or games? If she wanted performers they would perform here in the domus before a select group of friends, his, not hers.

Each message was delivered by supercilious Felix.

Messalinus himself remained charming. He solicitously took her hand and placed it on his own when they entered the great domed hall used to entertain their guests. This it seemed was her only practical role. To grace the couch by his side as the hostess of his gatherings. From there he listened placidly as she spoke of her latest acquisition of knowledge. Reclined at the table beside her, he plucked delicacies off the shared platters and placed them on her lips, pickled quail's eggs, a taste she loathed, but she opened her mouth and accepted with grace. It was a gesture of affection, she assured herself.

'I would like to visit Nero's baths tomorrow, if a litter could be arranged.'

For an instant, his lips compressed and a flicker across his brow resembled annoyance, then it shifted, so quickly she could doubt the expression had ever been.

'My dear, the baths here are more conducive to good health and far more luxurious. And a senator's wife, my wife, should not lower herself to bathing publicly.'

His tone was entirely reasonable, and his words were true. Nero's baths, including the great red porphyry caldarium, were far superior even to the most luxurious thermae in Rome.

'Unless of course, you wanted half of Rome to see you naked?' A brow raised as though he was considering whether this truly was her motivation. One of his guests tittered at the veiled joke. Thalia fumed. It was not as though her husband wanted her body for himself, unlike the bathhouse patrons he had never seen her naked.

She forced a smile. 'In truth, I do not go to bathe. Gaius Licinius Mucianus is going to be speaking about the natural history of the East and I would love to listen.'

'Then invite him to attend us. I am sure such a learned man could teach us all something of the East.' His gestures encompassed their audience of his friends, allies and sycophants. 'Though in our last conversation I found the man tediously boring. He is more likely to put us all to sleep.'

An obese senator in garum-stained toga brayed his laughter from an adjacent couch. Thalia let a passing slave boy fill her wine goblet while others brought in a succession of dishes that made up the main course. The fat senator ogled both boys, and dishes appreciatively. Messalinus scowled as the man let a hand the size of a ham bone rest on a pair of youthful buttocks while selecting a morsel. Thalia found herself wondering what her husband might charge a senator for the use of his slaves. The thought made her blush.

She was startled when Messalinus took her hand, turned it over and pressed a gentle kiss to her wrist and she was frustrated to feel her traitorous heart respond to his touch.

'My wife adores the written word. I swear she is the most well read woman in the Empire. Certainly, she has spent near half my fortune on scraps of parchment and tutors. I thought a wife more interested in books than baubles would save me money. Who knew how much scrolls cost?'

His audience laughed again and she flushed. His hand lingered, running idly up the inside of her wrist leaving her with goosebumps before turning to pluck an olive from the tray, tossing it in the air before catching it between his teeth. He winked at her as his perfect teeth closed down on the flesh.

'I swear she would prefer to nestle on a couch with a hairy Greek tutor or a new copy of Aristophanes than she would with me.'

More laughter accompanied his jest.

Thalia said nothing. She chewed on her anger and swallowed it, the way any dutiful Roman wife did.

'Did you hear,' said the fat senator, 'that Titus is on his way back to Rome?'

Thalia might have kissed the man for changing the subject but that she felt Messalinus startle beside her, like he had been shot by Jupiter's bolt.

'And that he is bringing that Jewish harlot back with him. They say Vespasian had forced him to leave her in the East but clearly the affair continued. Perhaps he intends to force his father to accept their marriage.'

When Titus had divorced Clementia all assumed he had a new wife in mind. Every patrician woman in Rome had been hopeful. But to marry Berenice, the Jewish Queen? It would be like Caesar and Cleopatra all over again. Romans would never accept her. She noticed then that Messalinus was shaking.

Was he stifling laughter as some of the senators were, or had he taken ill?

Thalia pressed a hand to his muscled shoulder; he flinched, his flesh was flushed, warm to the touch. But before she could express concern, her husband stood abruptly and stalked wordlessly from the room. Senators and sycophants stared open-mouthed after him.

'You must forgive my husband. We ate last night with Senator Cornelius Gracchus and I fear the oysters may not have been their freshest.'

She saw the men glance at the dish on the inlaid ebony and ivory tripod table before them.

'I can assure you, Messalinus would never serve anything less than the freshest.' Although she hated their slimy texture, Thalia took up one of the shells and swallowed its contents. The fat senator happily followed suit before turning to find one of the evasive slave boys. The nearest was wide-eyed with trepidation.

'Do you know when Titus Flavius is expected to return?' She asked, deftly guiding the conversation. Clementia would be interested to hear the news, and likely be grateful to be out of the city.

Messalinus did not return. Felix remained close by, measuring and memorising her words no doubt to repeat later.

When she returned to her rooms, escorted by the resolute Felix, she noticed that all the lamps inside Messalinus' suite of rooms were darkened. Outside the door, in a miserable heap, a small boy sat weeping soundlessly. As they passed he glanced up at her in abject misery. In the pale light of Felix's lamp, his cheeks were damp. The boy's odd silvery-coloured eyes were pale and arresting, brimming with tears and rimmed with red. One cheek bore the unmistakable red imprint of a hand.

In her room that evening, as Gytha ran a comb through her dark curls, Thalia considered the evening, wondering at Messalinus' odd reaction. Replaying conversations in her head, she could find nothing to warrant her husband's odd behaviour. He had jested about her preference for curling up with a book or a Greek scholar rather than her husband. Did he mean that? Did he actually believe that she would prefer her scrolls to a chance to perform her marital duties?

α

Thalia sat perched on the low bench in the courtyard, the soft fletchings of the feathered stylus resting on her bottom lip, forgotten in her reverie. It was the seventh hour and the midafternoon sun beat mercilessly down on the courtyard, turning the paving stones into hotplates and causing the vines that traced their way across the trellis to hang limply, curling at their edges. The heat haze made the figures painted in fresco on the walls seem to dance, as though the nymphs and the satyrs that chased them were truly alive. Cicadas chirred in the shade of the one massive tree, an ancient pot-bound resident, which must have been selected specifically for this courtyard by Nero's architects. It was rumoured it had once stood in the centre of the forum. In defiance of the Roman summer, the olive spread its shade across the small courtyard. Beneath its tough leathery leaves and wisened branches, the young woman sat, transfixed, a humming insect with its armour like carapace and large beady black eyes clung to the knotty bole not far from her head. Thalia was not watching it. Instead, she was studying the fresco. To one side, half hidden by vines, a nymph had been captured, a pair of furry-legged satyrs with lascivious expressions held her while a third was positioned behind her, in flagrante delicto, his expression gleeful.

The emperor Nero had been famed for his creative tastes and the Domus Aurea, her new home, was lavish in ways that put her to shame, as did many of the sculptures and artworks that graced every wall and niche. Heroic nudes were not uncommon but the lewd scenes and amoral shapes made her blush and avert her gaze. Most times. Still a virgin, Thalia could not help taking the occasional glance at a particularly informative fresco and pondering whether such a thing was actually possible. She pulled her gaze away, only a little flushed, and considered the quill in her fingers, ink long since dried.

The blank parchment before Thalia was a letter to her sister, or should have been, had she been able to work out quite what to write, but short of describing the statues and frescoes there was little to tell, and to do so would be very little short of obscene. On the bench beside her were an armful of scrolls, some quite rare and unique, all funded by Messalinus' seemingly unlimited generosity. But they had failed to capture her restless mind. Gytha sat cross-legged in the shade beside her, embroidering tiny gemstones onto a pair of silken sandals she would wear tonight. She had rarely left Thalia's side after the first night and her assault at the hands of the male slaves of the villa, reluctant to pad Messalinus' purse at her own expense. The girl seemed settled but she startled easily. Yesterday, when one of the male slaves had entered the rooms unannounced Gytha had dropped a crystal bottle of oriental perfume, probably worth more than the slave was. It had shattered into a thousand shards and Thalia's rooms still reeked of the heady scent.

Beside a listlessly burbling fountain, the old slave woman, Clulia, whom Felix had brought to help with her immediate needs sat weaving, humming softly. Pausing only when she let her gaze fall on Gytha, then her eyes took on a deep sadness.

'She is broken,' the old woman murmured. Thalia thought she was speaking to herself as the old often did, until she continued. 'You need to send her back to your family.'

'She belongs to me,' Thalia replied.

'And if you value her at all you will send her away from here, the others too.' The slave spoke softly, gesturing with her chin to the three Greek slave girls she had purchased playing knucklebones in the corner, waiting for instructions that had not been forthcoming. 'They are too pretty. Only harm will come to them. There are too many men in the villa and too few women and those of us that survive are old and used before our time. If you care for her; spare her. Buy boys, ugly ones with clever hands.'

Thalia was puzzled by the woman's advice. It was rare for a slave to speak her mind and the woman had been virtually silent since Felix delivered her. It had made her study the old woman closely and realised that she could see the familial resemblance between Felix and the old slave.

'You are Felix's mother.'

The crone nodded.

Thalia tilted her head, considered the beautifully painted rape depicted on the wall then turned her gaze to the wizened crone.

'Clulia? Does my husband make use of the slave women?'

The old woman looked up from her weaving, giving Thalia an appraising glance.

'The Domine does not lower himself with slave women.' Then she added, 'He is nothing like his father.'

Thalia mulled on the woman's words. The old woman had just revealed something, she was just not sure what. She wanted to know more but knew she must tread carefully, the slave had far deeper loyalty to her husband than she did her new mistress.

'Tell me about my husband.' Thalia deliberately used the peremptory tone of a mistress, the one she had learned to use to commend obedience from childhood.

The old woman's eyes narrowed and her lips pursed.

'Please?' She used the word so seldom, if ever, granted slaves. 'I want to understand him and I am failing. You have served his family for many years. Help me.'

The old woman kept her eyes on the small portable loom before her but she clearly considered the matter. 'He was a sweet boy, once.'

Thalia felt the frown between her brows but held her tongue.

Old Clulia shook her head at the memory but to Thalia's surprise, spoke anyway. 'I was born a slave here, more years ago than I care to remember.'

Thalia nodded, home born slaves, *verna*, were always considered the most valuable and loyal.

'When I was of age the old Domine, your husband's father, took me to his bed.' The old woman glanced from the girl on the floor to the nymphs in the fresco. 'I was young and pretty like Gytha then. The old Domine had a wife he did not like, but she was wealthy and well-connected, important to secure influence. He also had a healthy appetite and filled the villa we lived in then with many pretty serving girls. He took them all in turn.' Clulia glanced at her new mistress and added carefully... 'As was his right with property.'

Thalia nodded. The slave said nothing new or shocking.

'If a slave fell pregnant the Domina ensured she was sold, she would not tolerate any home-bred slaves. I was a particular favourite though, and when I became round with child she tried to sell me; the Domine would not part with me. It caused a terrible row between them and in the end the Domine had her beaten, fairly badly for defying him.'

Thalia felt the old woman's eyes on her once more and she evaded the look afraid that if she met her gaze the old woman would think twice about speaking so.

'He was not a brutal man, but he could not allow his wife to defy him, you understand? It became a competition between them. She became spiteful and angry. He evaded her bed unless guilt forced him to share her couch in the quest for an heir. I think he even contemplated freeing one of his slaveborn bastards and adopting the boy so as to negate the need to visit her. For her part the Domina found excuses to sell any slave that took his fancy, failing that she had them flogged so severely that many were left disfigured and thus undesirable.

Felix's mother ran an absent-minded hand along a crack in her face as she spoke. Until that moment Thalia had thought merely a sign of advanced age. Now she realised the silvered line was a scar, one that ran from in her hairline, across her cheek and ended with her lips, narrowly missing her eye.

'And then the gods took pity on her and she fell pregnant. I too was pregnant at the time and although she argued bitterly for an Aegyptian wetnurse, the old Domine insisted a *verna* made the best nurse. So, when the young master, little Lucius was born he was put to my breast with Felix. Never together mind, not when the Domina might see. I kept Felix well out of view and out of mind, though the boys grew up together.'

Thalia nodded again. It explained her husband's closeness with the Majordomo whom Thalia had suspected was his bastard brother. The old woman's voice fell so soft that Thalia was forced to strain to listen.

'It was only a few months later that she told him she was again with child, demanded he sell all his women or she would leave, and take both his sons. It was folly. All know that a man owns his sons. He did nothing. In time the child was born, another boy, just as she had promised. I think he was so pleased he even considered selling us then to appease her, but the Emperor Claudius made him proconsul and sent him to administer Africa. He wanted to take young Lucius and Felix and I with him but she refused, arguing the heir should never leave Rome. In retaliation, he took the infant Gaius instead.

The youngest boy grew up in the military camps and on the battlefield. Messalinus grew up in his mother's skirts. She kept him with her always and doted on him. The boy could do no wrong. As soon as the Domine sailed, the Domina had her revenge. She sold almost every female slave, most to brothels in the harbour district. I feared my fate, and Felix's, but she kept me and a handful of other women who the old Domine had favoured. We were given menial jobs like scrubbing the chamber pots and forced us to serve any of the slave men who desired us for the price of a coin apiece. Each week she would count the coins in front of us, or have the boy do it. He was given the coins as a reward.'

That was until the day she caught him with a naked slave girl. He must have been ten or eleven years old. Felix said it was innocent, they were just playing but Domina was furious. Perhaps she feared he was following his father's footsteps, and she had the boy flogged. It seemed the Domina had lost her mind. Little Messalinus was so startled he barely made a sound, in shock I guess, and that made her even angrier.'

For a while there was silence, except the whir and clatter of the shuttle and heddle stick.

'When the old Domine returned a month later, the boy still wore the stripes on his back. When he discovered what had happened he had his wife beaten severely. Then he sent her to the Vestals. You know how they care for those who are declared mad? I believe he paid them well to keep her guarded and out of sight. Only young Lucius grieved for her.'

Clulia was silent for a long time, her gnarled fingers never stilled at the loom.

Thalia found herself looking at Gytha as she sat on the floor, still sewing the tiny precious beads in precise patterns on the silk. Her own father had used their slaves on occasion, she had no doubt, especially after her mother's death, but she could never recall knowing about it specifically.

'What happened to her?' Thalia asked.

The old slave frowned. 'She died shortly afterward. Never recovered from the beating.'

'And his father?'

'The Old Domine? He backed the wrong Emperor after Nero died and when his man was killed, the old Domine felt it wiser to keep far from Rome and prove his loyalty to the new Emperor through his military service.'

'And Gaius?' She spoke the name hesitantly. She had never heard her husband mention a brother.

'With the 14th legion in Batavia.'

Thalia considered the old woman's words. From the anticlimactic first night, Messalinus had not once entered her space, never once pressed himself upon her. Was her husband so scarred from his early experiences that he was afraid to touch her? It certainly explained his seemingly callous attitude towards her, even accounted for the odd incident with Gytha and the coins.

She glanced at the fresco once more. The nymph's face was averted so Thalia could not be certain if the delicate creature welcomed or abhorred the attention of the generously endowed satyr. She thought about her handsome and distant husband and felt pity for an abused and orphaned child. At first, his neglect had hurt and confused her. Now it occurred to Thalia to wonder if perhaps he was waiting for her to show him she was ready.

α

'Take me to my husband.' Thalia spoke the words she had practised all afternoon.

Since the odd banquet when Messalinus had left without a word, Thalia wondered if something had, in fact, been amiss with the oysters. Her husband had become even more a stranger. He disappeared, away from the villa for days at a time and came back reeling and drunken, eyes bruised and red-rimmed. The one meal they had shared saw him silent and ashen, he had barely acknowledged her. The household was tense and Felix kept all from the door, except for

Messalinus' boys. She replayed Cluvia's words in her head, felt pity for the boy who had been the pawn of his parents and had been left physically and emotionally scarred. She could save him with her love, she was sure of it.

The Freedman had the nerve to frown at her, glancing over her scandalous attire. It was the same expression that her father might have used, had she been a child playing dress-ups. It only hardened her resolve.

'Must I repeat myself?'

'The Domine gave instructions that he is not to be disturbed.' Felix was truculent.

So was she.

She had waited for an evening that her husband had remained at home and gathered her women around her. They oiled her body with precious scents, wove flowers and pearls in her hair, and hung rubies around her neck like pomegranate seeds, letting them fall in the deep crevasse between the plump white cushioning of her breasts. She let one of the giggling Greek slaves anoint her nipples with an ointment that made them blush, the touch of the brush raising them to erect peaks, and they gowned her in a tunic so sheer she could see the colour of the nipples and the dark brush of hair between her hips. They had gowned her in a *stola* of cerulean silk and summoned Felix.

She followed the still muttering Major Domo's heels as he swept through the maze that was Nero's golden house, catching glimpses of artworks, adorned in the gold leaf for which the villa had attained its name, as they slipped through corridors she had never been down.

He halted at the doorway, frowning at her.

Thalia frowned back. Her hand trembled as she held the gown closed before her, her long hair trailing behind her, like a virgin at her wedding.

He opened the door a crack and in fear that she might lose her courage Thalia pushed past him and into the space that was solely her husband's. The room was darkened. Dozens of flickering lamps did little to dispel the night. She hesitated, her courage momentarily flickering as she oriented herself. The sleeping couch had its tall back towards her, whatever wood it was carved from was gilt in gold leaf and shimmered dully in the candlelight. It faced towards the open balcony.

Thalia felt Felix's hands grab her elbow, even as she heard the moaning sound coming from the space before her. A panting of breathing, punctuated with low groans caused an ache beneath her ribs. Shaking off his clinging fingers she advanced, heedless, until she stood before the couch and looked down upon him.

It was like looking on a stranger. Messalinus was thin and his muscles seemed wasted with ill use. His lips were dry and cracked. Her husband's red-gold hair was tousled dark with sweat. His skin was flushed with exertion and his eyes stared towards the ceiling, glazed and unfocused. His limbs were shaking. The golden boy, Aeneas, was seated cross-legged by his feet, dressed only in a loincloth, his head bowed over his harp, soft music washed over the scene but did little to cover the sound from the couch.

An expression of horror must have somehow escaped her lips, Aeneas looked up at her. Her husband remained oblivious, unseeing.

'How long has he been like this?' she asked.

She went to drop beside him, taking the clenched hand in her own, but Felix caught her elbow again in a crushing grip and pulled her back from the bed.

'You must leave. He would not want you here.'

She stared at him uncomprehending as another mindless groan erupted from Messalinus' lips, even Aeneas flinched. Her husband's body contorted, arms flailing.

Thalia fought against the arms that held her. 'Tell me you have called the physicians.'

Felix nodded. 'He has been bled to reduce the melancholy humours but to no effect.'

For the first time, she noticed the bowl at Aeneas' feet, a silver scalpel emerged from the red-black pool that filled to near the rim. A trickle of dark blood still oozed from the slice on Messalinus' inner elbow, staining the ivory-coloured velvet of the couch's plush cushions.

Felix tugged at her again, fingers digging into her wrists, and pulled her back towards the door and her waiting women.

'No. I should be here.'

He shook his head, more adamantly this time and continued to pull her towards the door, pushing her into the arms of her waiting women.

'Go. I will send news.'

She let them pull her away.

α

When it became clear that Messalinus would live, but that the fever had stolen his sight, her husband had slipped into a deep depression and none of the bloodletting dictated by the dozens of physicians to ease the imbalance of humours in his blood had helped. When he was lucid he raged, the sounds of smashing pottery, the clatter of hurled metal vases, the shatter of glass were followed with the wailing of slaveboys and finally, by wretched sobbing. Thalia had wanted to go to him but Felix was adamant. Her husband could not see her and would not see her.

Even his slaves were expelled. They lurked outside the door like a pack of beaten hounds. Thalia might have pitied them, had she not seen in herself their likeness.

In the end, it had been Emperor Vespasian, who had descended on the villa on his way back from hunting in the countryside who presented a solution. The bluff soldier had visibly shuddered before entering the halls of Nero's golden villa. He had stood in the doorway to her husband's darkened rooms and tutted. Thalia was certain Messalinus only feigned sleep but she could hardly say such a thing to the Emperor of Rome. She drew him away, offering refreshments in the Eastern atrium.

'It is trying to see him like that. Did the physicians I sent arrive?'

She nodded, and thanked him. They had drained her husband of yet more of his blood, until the veins showed blue bruises beneath his skin but she said nothing of that.

'Did you know that your husband fostered with me? He was raised and tutored alongside Britannicus, Nero and my sons. He was like a brother to them.'

Again she nodded, it was one of the reasons her father had valued the match so highly.

'My son, Titus, is returning from Jerusalem. He makes a slow journey, they say, weighted down with prizes of war. Even brings a Jewish Queen back with him.'

The Emperor's snort of disgust at news of his son's mistress could only be due to her race, Thalia assumed, because Vespasian himself kept a mistress about the palace, a former slave who had once served Nero's family and now greeted his guests as though she were an Empress. The Emperor sat in a curule chair rather than reclining when the slaves had appeared with wine and delicacies, so Thalia sat also. She could only imagine the havoc the unexpected visit had caused in the *culina*.

'I have a villa by the sea in Baiae. Messalinus has been there once, he and Titus ran the beaches, naked as slaves until they were as brown as one.'

The Emperor glanced in the direction of Messalinus' rooms. 'Tell him I command that he go there, the sea air works wonders for the blood. I will send Titus to visit when he returns, that should cheer him also.'

The offer, put to him by Felix, who was the only person, aside from Aeneas, who was allowed to pass the threshold, prompted the first sign of life from her husband. Plans were immediately laid. Thalia, filled with hope, and looking forward to the change in view, had been bitterly disappointed when she was informed, through Felix, that she had been forbidden to attend him. She was, instead, to remain and oversee his estates and interests.

Thalia told herself it made perfect sense and only showed how much he trusted her. But as she watched the household empty of her husband's favourite pieces and saw wagon after wagon haul away her husband and his belongings, she found herself wondering. If the mosaics had not been cemented in and the frescoes painted directly on the walls, might he have taken them too and left her in a completely empty house?

α

Thus followed the year Thalia came to think of as the silent year. From her near-empty villa on the hill, she watched Rome empty for the summer. The prolonged heat kept many in the country until late in the Autumn. Vespasian himself returned to the East to lay siege to Jerusalem and all social events stalled. The only thing that seemed to progress was the work on the walls of the Emperor's grand amphitheatre. When the missive came announcing that Messalinus was on the via Sacra and would shortly arrive. Thalia found she could scarcely recall her husband's features.

He arrived in a grand litter born by a matching team of negroid slaves, oiled until they shone and gleaming with sweat after the climb to the villa. Golden Titus rode at the side of the litter and was swift to dismount and assist in Messalinus' descent as the slaves knelt in the dust and steadied the vehicle. Her husband's hand remained on his friend's arm as her former brother-in-law led him towards the great entrance, past the rows of slaves attending his arrival. Thalia was pleased to see that the time by the sea had done wonders. Messalinus strode upright and confidently, his hand resting on his friend's arm looked almost casual though she had little doubt it assisted in his balance. His eyes were no longer reddened and lacked the cloudiness that came with age blindness. It almost appeared, as he let his eyes drift across the scene that perhaps his sight had returned. Thalia felt her heart lift but there was no hint of recognition in his face as his gaze passed the spot she stood, waiting.

She stepped forward, allowing her feet to scuff on the fine gravel beneath her feet. Messalinus' focus shifted in her direction but though his face turned towards her there was no recognition in the blank gaze.

'Welcome home, Messalinus. Well met, Prefect Titus.'

He smiled, reaching out a well-manicured hand in her direction. The one, she noted, that did not rest on Titus' arm. She tried to dampen the stirring of jealousy this caused, reminding herself to be grateful that Messalinus had flourished under his friend's dutiful care.

'Arrecina Quartia, my wife. It is good to be home, to be back in Rome.'

She fought the tightening of her lips at his use of her other name but reminded herself that though he could not see, Titus could. So she forged a smile instead, one that took in both of them.

'It is good to see you both looking so well.'

They did, their hair lightened by the sun, their skin darkened. Both men looked the picture of health and either could pose for a sculptor without shame.

'It is all down to Titus' good care. For a soldier, he has made a wondrous nursemaid.'

She found a genuine smile for the Emperor's son. 'You have my thanks, dear Titus. Now please, come inside and get settled. I will have refreshments brought to the western triclinium; you must be starving.'

The rumble of her husband's stomach echoed her words and Titus laughed, a bluff chortle.

Messalinus' hand squeezed her wrist, though fleetingly. His hand, resting on her own, was light as the touch of a butterfly. 'I thank you, wife. But I would have a platter brought to my room. I am tired and would rather rest than be exposed to the eye of the curious. I am not yet fully skilled at feeding myself without upsetting platters and goblets.'

'Of course, I will see to it.'

He squeezed her wrist once more before releasing it and letting his foster brother, Titus, guide him to his chambers.

Chapter Nine: Sharks in the Water

Naples, 2023

The coastline of Naples spread before us like a painting in watercolour. A ribbon of white and cream-coloured buildings interspersed with brighter shades, in the background the looming blue-green double peak of Vesuvius and between us and it, miles of sparkling blue, dotted with sailing boats. I had sent a full half dozen shots of the scene to Clare in hope of making her envious, though I knew travel was not really something she aspired to. She had responded with a benign *'That's lovely. Enjoy your day.'* We had just finished a light Mediterranean luncheon of salads, cold meats and fresh vegetables along with several glasses of fine wine, which Massimo himself served, despite the hovering wait staff. After the second glass, I placed my hand over the glass each time he offered a refill. Massimo's other guest, Fumio Gallocchio, was more content to oblige, both with the meal and the wine.

Fumio was a short, barrel-chested man with a mane of silver hair, a prominent Latin nose and a heavily whiskered chin. I had begun to imagine that Massimo had invited him purely to make himself appear even more striking when the older man admitted he was an underwater archaeologist.

'You study shipwrecks?' I asked.

He nodded, smiling, taking yet another refill of his wine glass. 'I also study shipwrecks.'

In the end, he too pushed back from the table, and stood, wandering away from the table and to the railing overlooking the pristine blue. Seeing me watching, Gallochio waved me over, then leaned out overlooking the gap between the twin hulls.

Our vessel was not the largest yacht in the bay. At a little short of 30 metres or, as Massimo informed me, 100 nautical feet, it was dwarfed by the size of some of our neighbours on the bay. But it was sleek and powerful, the sort of luxury vessel that probably cost as much to rent for a week as it had cost to buy my apartment at home. The name, *Salacia*, was painted near the bow. Salacia was, I knew, the goddess of salt water.

As Massimo folded his napkin and stood, gesturing to the waiting staff, I stood. Their response was immediate and the remaining meal and all its accoutrements were swept from the table. Curious, I moved toward Fumio, Massimo at my side, like a faithful black labrador or a particularly attentive prison guard. I mentally nudged my thoughts back in the direction of labrador in an effort to be fair.

A glance at his face showed he was aware of what I was about to see but contained a boyish enthusiasm at the secret he had kept. Since rebuffing his kiss at the villa of Nero, he had made no further move and I respected that. His patience impressed me and made me doubt all the stories my mother and the media told me about Italian men. For the first time I had begun to wonder if I was fair to tar all men with the same brush.

Once my hands were on the railings at the side of the immense yacht, the older gentleman leaned over the rail and pointed out and down. I followed his lead. The sky was so clear that the water was nearly transparent, an azure film rippled with silver, acting like a window to open the world beneath. Below the vessel was a scene I could not immediately decode. A stretch of black and white in geometric patterns spread across the seafloor. Shaking my head I refocused. It was undeniable. Beneath me was a Roman mosaic that stretched almost the length of the boat, made of black-edged hexagonal shapes, black triangles, and circles containing yet more circles, each created with the use of tiny tesserae. I shot a startled glance at Gallocchio who was grinning indulgently.

'Below us is the atrium of one of the villas of Portus Julius. In this villa alone we have uncovered over 20 rooms.'

I listened, but my focus was already back on the unearthly scene below.

'Portus Julius was a spa town where many of the patricians would holiday for the benefit of bathing in the hot springs.'

I nodded, aware that the Campi Flegrei, the 'fields of fire' as the Romans had known the region, neighbouring Napoli, Herculaneum and Pompeii, had been littered with volcanic heated springs. As I watched, a small, sandy-coloured stingray disinterred itself from the sediment on the seafloor, glided across the mosaic's surface, its undulating movements unearthing more of the design.

'Was it lost during the eruption?' I asked.

He shook his white mane. 'No, it subsided sometime in the 4th century. There are records that Hadrian visited the town during the latter parts of his illness to take the healing waters.'

I sniffed. Given Emperor Hadrian's premature death it clearly hadn't helped. But then sharing baths, even hot ones, with hundreds of others carrying varying conditions from which they sought relief and healing was, in my mind, a good way to cross-contaminate.

'Would you like to dive?' Massimo spoke from over my shoulder.

'Really?'

His smile broadened, flashing his perfect teeth. 'It is part of the archaeological park but I have special permission for us to dive, if you'd like.'

He gestured at the two men standing by carrying what looked like wetsuits and snorkelling gear. 'It is shallow enough to snorkel, The depth here varies between one and four metres.'

I smiled at him, for the first time today it was genuine. With the beauty of the day, the benign company of our chaperone, and the opportunity for a rare dive on a site of archaeological significance, the strain of my discoveries of the last days, and the nightmares it had evoked were fading away. I had not wanted to be here. I had made excuses of my work until Massimo had his office call Cyrano and request my presence directly. Had he been able to do so I thought the little man might have tied me up and delivered me to the dock with an apple between my teeth. Even my father had pressured me, through Guilia, to make his good friend happy and benefit from the association.

Massimo immediately began stripping his shirt, revealing the well-formed body beneath. I know my mother would have been making comparisons to the statue of Adonis right about then and I felt my cheeks colour. He clearly had no inhibitions as he shucked off his chino shorts leaving only a pair of black Speedos. I was inclined to make an internal comment about men who wore speedos but I had noted that most Italian men favoured them over the board shorts more common at home in Australia and there was no question that Massimo had the physique to pull it off.

'Is there somewhere I might change?'

I was, as instructed, wearing my brand new one-piece beneath the peasant top and denim shorts I wore, but was reluctant to simply strip while so many watched on.

Massimo simply smiled. He made a shooing gesture towards the man holding out the wetsuit towards me. 'Take Signorina Benino to my cabin. We will move *Salacia* to the dive site while you change.'

And so, as the engines roared back to life, throbbing with power, I followed my guide beneath the deck.

Massimo's cabin turned out to be the entire front of the vessel, a room almost as large as my apartment with a bed considerably larger, laden with deep red pillows on a gold and crimson cover. A pair of deep leather armchairs took my top, shorts, small handbag and sandals. Out the small porthole windows, the pale turquoise sky and azure waters alternated as we dipped through waves sent up by the vessel's motion.

With some tugging I managed to manoeuvre myself into the wetsuit, using the neoprene cuff attached to the zip to pull it up and into position. In the full-length mirror panel opposite the bed I deftly tugged my loose hair into a plait more useful in containing the mass underwater. The wetsuit emphasised my curves and made my reflection sleek and streamlined in a way that almost caused a blush. I recalled the enthusiastic encouragement of Holly and Guilia and my resolution to be open to new experiences. I was safe. I was strong. I was in control. Shaking my head to dispel my doubts, I pushed open the cabin door and followed my guide back out to the deck which had by now fallen still once more as we reached our destination. I took a moment to appreciate the view of Vesuvius towering over the white and pastel cities across the bay.

Surprisingly, Gallocchio was still dressed in his ill-fitting suit, comfortably seated on a deck chair beneath a broad umbrella, a laptop balanced on his knees.

'You are not diving?' I asked.

'Not today. Massimo knows almost as much about the site as I do, he will guide you.'

Not for the first time I wondered whether the wealthy playboy actually did any of the work he was paid to do, surely the Italian parliament had to sit some time?

To his credit, although he smiled broadly, Massimo did not leer at the figure-hugging shape of the wetsuit.

Instead, he held out a pair of goggles and snorkel and gestured to the unwieldy flippers. He seemed just as comfortable in the gear as he had in the tuxedo he had worn during our outing to the Opera and the more casual attire of our subsequent trip beneath the city and into the dark spaces of Nero's golden house.

Just as he had done then, keeping any touch purely supportive as he had helped me to my seat in the private box at the Opera and aided me in clambering down the stairs that led into the bowels of Rome, Massimo's touch, when it came was sure and gentle as he helped steady me as we sat on the edge of the yacht.

Ready? His lips formed the word from beneath the goggles that framed his face.

I nodded, the soft rubber of the snorkel tucked between my teeth.

'The area we are diving today is the nymphaeum of Claudius. It is filled with statues. Most of them are replicas, replaced when the originals were moved to the Naples Museum. You might recognise some of them. When you have had enough tug my arm and we will go back up. You have snorkelled before?' he asked.

I nodded, spitting out the rubber between my teeth to answer the question. 'Yes, I did a lot of diving in Tasmania.'

I recalled the cold waters of Tasmania, the sleekly gliding seals that had frolicked in the waters around us, and the exquisitely coloured but fragile-looking leafy sea dragons that drifted on the current. The last time I had dived there we had needed to hurry back to the dive boat when a particularly curious great white arrived, sending my heart into panicked thumps. I glanced at the turquoise water beneath us. 'There are no sharks?'

'There are sharks, but no recorded attacks in these waters in the past hundred years. You are perfectly safe with me, Vittoria.' His voice was warmed honey and I allowed it to soothe away any residual concerns. With the rubber gripped once more within my teeth I followed his lead, dropping back into the surreal world below.

Ω

'What have you done?'

I had not heard him entering and I jumped at the abrupt and caustic tone. I force myself to calmly put down the camera and resolutely, and a little angrily, take my time looking up from the workbench, where I had just been photographing the child's remains for my files. Direttore Franko Cyrano looked uncharacteristically flustered.

'I beg your pardon?' I challenged, realising belatedly that after weeks of having spoken to me in English he had spoken in heavily accented Italian.

'I said, what have you done?' He repeated.

I ran through the events of the day in my mind but was unable to pinpoint any action that might have caused Cyrano this level of consternation… Nothing. Nothing at work at least but in my mind an alarm sounded.

'I'm not sure what you're talking about, Direttore. Perhaps with a little more detail, I might be able to explain.'

His face was infused with an unusual combination of puce and scarlet that extended to his bald scalp and which I attributed to building ire.

'They threatened our funding!'

I blinked. No wonder he was so distraught.

'Who did?'

'The *Ministero per i Beni e le Attività Culturali*. They threatened to close the entire excavation and it is all your fault, so I repeat. What did you do?'

I forced my mouth shut for one thing. By now Cyrano's irate tone had drawn a circle of witnesses, all of whom heard the last pronouncement and were displaying an array of reactions of shock, concern and horror.

'The Ministry of Cultural Heritage threatened us?'

'*Si.*'

'Why me?' I forced the words, even though I knew.

'That is what I want to know. Why have I been told that either I withdraw your accreditation and permission to work on this site or the Ministry will revoke both their contribution to our funding and our charter.'

The strength in my legs evaporated abruptly. Fortunately, my grip on the table sustained me. All eyes were on me, speculating what I had done to so threaten the entire project.

'That's not fair…' I stammered.

Cyrano's eyes were slits behind his stylish tinted spectacles. 'Fair?' The little man repeated, his chest puffed out like a peacock. 'I myself took the call from the Minister of Cultural Heritage. Minister Di Maio was most insistent. Your position here in Ercolano is cancelled and you are encouraged to leave Italy as soon as possible lest your visa be withdrawn.'

'Minister Di Maio insisted?' The familiar name nearly made me retch. I forced the words onto my tongue. 'Massimo called you?' My hand found its way to the still-raw bruises around my neck, covered by my trademark turtleneck. I sat heavily on the stool behind me and was grateful for Holly's abrupt presence and reassuring arm around my shoulders.

'Massimo the magnificent prick?'

I nodded dazedly, still trying to process the shocking pronouncement.

Holly gripped me in a hug as she glared at the Direttore.

'What did Minister Di Maio accuse her of exactly?'

Cyrano frowned. 'He did not say, merely elaborated on what would happen if her presence here was not rectified.'

Holly stared down at me in horrified concern, her eyes brushed on the bruises she alone had noticed. I shook my head in warning, pushing myself to my feet. 'Give me a moment. Let me pack this up and I will make some calls.' I didn't want to say I would call my father, it was just the kind of thing Cyrano would scorn me more for. I forced myself to sound more confident than I was. 'I am sure it is some mistake.'

Holly nodded. 'Yes, mistaken identity or something.'

Andrew was there now too. 'I will talk to the consulate and see what can be done.'

I nodded, distantly grateful, but with little expectation of his success. The political system in Italy bore little in common with British, American or Australian law.

Almost by rote I carefully repacked the remains of the child in the tiny box into which the few fragments that represented her short life fitted. I picked up my kit bag, reached for the camera still sitting on the bench and retrieved my backpack. With Holly's arm still around my shoulder I made my way through the sea of faces and out onto the plaza. With Holly on one side and Andrew on the other, I was gently escorted from the park, my face hot with humiliation and my mind distracted by the feeling of loss that had washed over me as I closed the lid on the small girl's remains.

It took me half an hour to raise my father on the phone. His voice was terse and shadowed.

I felt like a schoolgirl again as I sketched the short conversation I had with Cyrano, with the entire excavation team as witnesses. There was a hollow buzzing silence on my father's end.

'And what is it you want from me, Vittoria? '

I fought to keep the terseness from my voice. 'I thought you might be able to help me. Reverse the decision. Talk to Massimo.'

Again the long silence.

'Vittoria, you assaulted the man. A good friend of mine and a very important person in his own right. Do you have any understanding of the difficult position that has put your stepmother and me in?

Now it was my turn for silence as a sickening ache formed in my stomach.

'What did you say?'

A terse exhalation. 'Massimo told us how you assaulted him.'

'I assaulted him?' I echoed distantly as though hearing my own voice from across the Colosseum.

Ω

I had been foolish, I could admit it in hindsight, after the magical experience of the dive we had returned to Massimo's yacht. Fumio was gone, having been taken by dingy back to the mainland. Massimo's staff had prepared a three-course meal on the deck and thirsty from our underwater exertions I had indulged a little too freely in the fine wine that had been provided. I was not entirely sure how much I had imbibed because the server had simply kept refilling. The sky had changed from azure to lavender to violet and the stars that lit the sky were echoed by the lights from the shore and their reflections on the water. It seemed surreal.

I was ashamed to admit I did not know when I had come to be lying on the bed in the cabin I had changed in. I had some memory of stifling a yawn over the delicate serve of *torta setteveli* and being offered and refusing the chance to lie down. He had been all concern at the time. I do not claim he had drugged me. I had had too much sun and, lulled by the cool water, had not had enough to drink before relaxing my inhibitions and consuming all too many glasses of red. But when I woke his hands were all over me and his lips were on my neck, one hand buried in my hair.

When he met my lips with his own the feeling was as intoxicating as the wine. I was reminded whimsically of learning about Romeo and Juliet in school as a teen and the accusation Juliet charged her ill-fated lover of 'kissing by the book'. If Massimo kissed by the book it was not because he read it, but because he wrote it. It was only that in my economy of clothing I had neglected to pack underwear and was still wearing my swimsuit that I had the time to sift my senses enough to know that while a little snogging with this dark Italian man was not altogether unpleasant, I was not at all inclined to further intimacy. I pushed him away, murmuring apologies. Massimo took it with good grace, helping me up from the bed with a steady hand. But as I scanned the room for my bag he let his fingers wander, pulling me back towards him, placing his lips with increasing and unlistening ardour on my own, his hand kneading at my breast with forceful determination. My head was clamouring with warning signals and my legs insisted I try to run. But they had locked and frozen.

I clearly recalled pushing him away, telling him I wanted to leave, and feeling increasingly panicked at the knowledge that I could not simply walk away because the steady rocking of the vessel told me we were still at anchor in the bay.

In response his lips became more demanding, his fingers forceful. I could still feel them on my body. When I pushed away once more his kiss became so bruising that our teeth knocked painfully together and as I pushed at him with both hands he abandoned my breasts to wrap a hand around my throat, fingers closing as he pressed against me, pushing me back into the wall, his continued interest clear and determined as it thrust against me. It evoked memories I had buried so deeply I had almost forgotten them, and my entire body began to shake. Short of breath and able to scream only in the deep recesses of my mind, I had done the only thing I could think of. With every bit of strength and the extra force gained from adrenaline, I lifted my knee and rammed it between his legs.

Ω

Had I assaulted him?

Yes.

The memory left me trembling as I let my body fall backwards against my bed, the phone held loosely against my ear.

'Yes. You are fortunate we are friends and Massimo chose not to press charges. Vittoria…' he sighed. 'It is time for you to go home. I am tired of being responsible for cleaning up your messes. You are not a child any more.'

I found myself sitting on the edge of the immense bed, my hand trembling so badly I could barely hold the phone. His voice seemed to echo through my head.

'I will have my office book your ticket for Sunday. Vittoria, are you listening? It is time for you to grow up and take responsibility for your actions.'

'Your friend Massimo,' I spat the word, 'tried to rape me.'

Another long silence.

'I thought we had this conversation long ago.' My father's voice rang with disappointment. 'You cannot lead men on and expect to simply walk away. I will pay for your rooms until Sunday. Go home, Vittoria.'

The line went dead.

With the breathtaking pain in my chest and stomach consuming everything that was left of me I forced myself unsteadily to my feet and walked into the bathroom, barely taking the time to strip my clothes before stepping into the shower. I never heard the metallic clink in my pocket as my pants dropped to the marble-tiled floor, so I forgot entirely that earlier in the day—before Cyrano had arrived— I had slipped the lunula still in the small ziplock bag, into my pocket to take it to Holly for cleaning. The water was scalding at first but I didn't care. It rained over me at volcanic temperature. I scrubbed my body with soap until there was nothing left of the bar, until my skin was red and nearly raw. When the water went cold, I stood there still.

Chapter Ten: Welcome to the Globe

Rome, 2023

I rang for a taxi. Shoved all my belongings haphazardly into my suitcases and dragged them, my precious kitbag, laptop and camera bag and the cherry red paper bag with Clare's birthday gift of Ferragamo boots—still in their box—down the stairs, past a blinking concierge and into the street. By 5 pm I was sitting in the departures lounge at Rome's International Airport.

I didn't contact my mother.

I did send a brief email to Holly. I was devastated at being forced to leave the project in the lurch even though I knew Cyrano would relish taking over my investigation. I let her know I had arrived safely at the airport; I failed to mention any destination. I doubted she would come after me.

I sat, numbed, in the thinly upholstered chair of the airport lounge for hours. Battling feelings of loss and anger, torn with indecision. I contemplated confronting my father, even Massimo, but when I thought about it my hands started shaking again and I had to wait until it passed. I even considered reporting it to the police but everything I had heard of the Italian police force reminded me of bad crime dramas featuring the Mafia. Instead, I studied the terminal screens, considering destinations. Flights to Australia flickered up on the screen, announced boarding, admitted delays, announced departures. I remained paralysed. So I was surprised when my phone, on silent, buzzed in my pocket at nearly 10 pm. There was only one more flight to Sydney before the terminal closed business for the evening. I had not yet bought a ticket.

'You know we will do everything we can, I have connections you know.' Dalton's voice was thick with concern when I picked up the phone on its eighth call.

'I know.' Despondency laced my voice.

'Are you really ready to return to Australia?'

'No. But I don't really have a choice.' I didn't elaborate.

'Actually, you do.'

My laugh was edged with bitterness. 'I don't.'

'I have a friend in the United Nations. He needs forensic anthropologists to aid in an investigation and he wants them from as far away from Europe as he can find them.'

I let the words wash over me. Not really concentrating as I stared out the floor-to-ceiling windows at the Boeing 747 taxiing down the runway as another set down wheels to land with a bouncing lurch. Beyond them, complete darkness. I recalled the job offer I had received some months after my arrival in Italy, the one I had dismissed out of hand because I *had* my dream job.

'Tori, are you still there? He's building a team to work in Ukraine, cataloguing evidence of war crimes. I know it is not what you prefer but you are the best person I could think of.'

I could hear the lighter burr of Holly's voice prompting in the background.

'At least until we have worked out how to get you back here.'

'The Ukraine,' I repeated, my thoughts whirring. I thumbed through my phone to the email offer I had received months earlier.

'Just Ukraine,' Andrew corrected in a pedantic tone that almost made me smile.

'War crimes in Ukraine,' I repeated, clicking to open the email, rereading the offer.

'Yes. If you were interested I could speak to him.'

Was I interested? Not really. The word Sydney flashed onto the screen with the word *imbarcando:* boarding. I hadn't yet bought a ticket.

'Your 'him,'' I asked, hearing the wary hope in my voice. Had I been sitting on the alternative to a disgraced return all this time? 'Would that be Dr Bruce Habermann?'

'You know him?'

I inhaled deeply, let out the breath slowly as I contemplated. I had heard Habermann lecture about his work both on the Twin Towers and in Bosnia. The stories he told, both fascinating and horrifying, confirmed my decision to focus on the archaeological aspects of anthropology rather than the more modern crime scenes. It was Habermann's name at the bottom of the job offer.

'Not well,' I answered glancing again at the sign advertising the Sydney flight. 'When do they want people?'

'When is the next flight?'

'Isn't Ukraine an active warzone?'

'Zelenskyy has it more or less under control.' He attempted reassurance. 'Russia has largely retreated to the borders. There is very little fighting there now. I'm not even sure the rest of the world noticed.' His expression was dry.

They had. I had seen the Colossseum bathed in yellow and blue lights and recalled our own Opera House in the same cheerful colours. Financial sanctions had been enacted, borders had opened to accept refugees, tanks and weapons supplied. But despite urging no country had become actively involved for fear of triggering a nuclear war.

'And the Russians are really going to let people walk in and investigate the war crimes they committed?'

'It is the United Nations, Victoria. Russia still wants their invasion… forgive me, their liberation of the territory to look legitimate, they cannot afford to offend the United Nations.'

I sniffed. 'As I recall, Ukraine is not part of the United Nations.'

'You're thinking about NATO. Ukraine has been a UN member since 1945.'

I held my phone in front of me and swiped the screen, typing in a quick query.

There were several International Airports in Ukraine. But there were no commercial flights to any of them. No domestic airline flew into warzones, no matter what Dalton or the Russians termed the occupation.

'How would I get to Ukraine?' I mused aloud.

I could hear the muffled buzz of conversation and imagined his hand over the base of the phone. The voices cleared abruptly.

'You would need to fly into Moldova or Poland. Belarus is closer but they support Russia. You'd need to meet with UN representatives in the airport, cross the border and travel with a UN convoy from there.'

I swiped my screen, keyed in a few more words. Answers flashed up.

'I could be in Moldova tomorrow afternoon.' The words sounded odd in my ears. A night sleeping in airport chairs was not appealing. 'Could you arrange it with Dr Habermann by then?'

'Really?' He sounded surprised. It was warranted.

'Really.' I spoke the word around the thumbnail I was chewing.

He chuckled. 'Send me your flight details and I will have someone meet you at the airport.'

The aching pit in my chest did not dissipate but it seemed to shallow a little. I would not have to tell my mother I was coming home; entering an active warzone was safer than admitting I had failed.

'Victoria. When you are ready you can tell us what happened.' His voice oozed concern.

I spat out a fragment of nail. 'I know.'

Ω

'Ukraine! You can't be serious! You do know there is a war going on over there. Honestly Tori, you spend too much of your life buried in the past, you need to get your mind back into the present and take a good long look around you.'

I might have argued the injustice of her accusations, only this was Clare, and her words so closely echoed my own that it only felt distantly amusing to hear her parroting my own thoughts. When Clare was furious she looked just like Mum, except rounder in the face as a consequence of years of dialysis and anti-rejection drugs. From the flash in her hazel eyes to the way her mouth tightened and clipped her words, she channelled our mother. I considered telling her that, but figured I was in enough trouble already.

She must have seen the tilt of my lip because her eyes narrowed and then narrowed some more.

'What happened? Why this sudden change of plans?'

'Nothing.' I lie, 'I told you about the offer ages ago.' I ached to tell her but fear that she would judge me held me back, even though I know... *I know* she would never do so. 'It's just a change, an opportunity I couldn't pass up.'

'Italy was just a change, Tori. Herculaneum was your opportunity, your dream job, remember? The reason you packed up and left us all behind.'

Her words cut deeper than I dared let her see.

'I haven't forgotten that, Clare. Things are just not working out here.'

I made a show of checking my watch wondering what had possessed me to make this call. She would not make me cry in an airport, even one as busy and impersonal as Rome's. I scanned the thinning crowds and looked towards the flickering overhead screen, checking the departure times once again. Clare was silent but even through the laptop, she was studying my face, the way she had when we were children and she suspected I had gotten myself in trouble. She was usually right. A tiny line formed between her two evenly tweezed brows.

'What happened,' she repeated, only now it wasn't a question.

I could feel my throat constricting as though even my body rebelled against considering the previous twenty-four hours, let alone speaking about it. The memory of my father's scathing tone still lingered. 'There was a man…'

She was silent. She had learned that trick from Mum, I was always compelled to fill the silence.

'He was a friend of my father's. A politician with more power than I realised.'

Her eyes lingered on mine and I forced myself to hold them steadily, easing the words through my teeth. 'I wasn't interested, but he wouldn't take no for an answer.'

I waited for her to say it. To tell me I needed to come home where she could protect me, the way she always had.

'I hope you showed him what no looks like.'

I clenched my jaw and tears threatened. It had been her solution before. Self-defence classes, she had taken them with me. I forced myself to remember that I was a grown woman and sitting in a busy airport terminal. It helped.

'I did. And he didn't…' I wasn't going to say it here. The little old Italian lady sitting opposite had her head tilted as though listening intently, I had no way of knowing if she understood English and no inclination of being the next point of gossip in some Sicilian sewing circle. 'But he showed me what happens when a woman says no.'

She nodded, though her expression of concern lingered.

'Tell me you reported him to the police?'

I frowned. I had considered that but had dismissed the inclination. He had not actually succeeded and I was a foreign woman and he an obviously rich and well-connected native in a society that was still highly patriarchal. I had little doubt who they would have believed and besides, he had ensured I would have no chance to do so.

'He knows people who uninvited me from participating in the dig.'

'Oh Tori.'

I shrugged. 'I need you to keep it from Mum as long as you can. She won't talk to my father so she needn't know what happened. And when she does find out about where I'm going I need you to convince her that I will be okay.'

'Will you?'

I scowl at her through the screen. 'Of course I will. I'm not going on a tourist visa. I'll be working with the United Nations. You don't think they'd allow people in if it was that dangerous do you?'

'I repeat my earlier question. You do know there is a war? That people are being killed, every day.'

I sensed the win. 'Precisely. I'm needed there, Clare. It's what I do.'

'It's not what you do. You like your bones old and dry, even I know that. It will be horrific.'

I nod. It is as though her doubt tightened, hardened something in me that needed firming. 'It will. But I can be useful there.'

'You could come back home.'

Something in her voice made me stop and stare at her. My Clare would never say that. I leaned closer to the screen and stared at her face. There were dark rings beneath her eyes, like bruises. She had tried to cover them with powder but I could tell. And her face was pale and puffy. Even her lips seemed bleached of colour. Suddenly I could make out the whirr and beep of a machine.

'Are you alright, Clare?'

Did I imagine the sideways glance, as though she were avoiding the question?

'I am dialysing, Tori. And the neighbours had a party last night that was so loud and so late… I couldn't sleep. And your niece has decided she is a teenager with all that entails. Should I go on?'

She sounded exhausted. What time was it in Australia, had I even stopped to notice? I shook my head, I'd been so consumed with my own drama I hadn't even stopped to check on her. How long had it been since we had last spoken?

'Should I come home, Clare?' I let the question fall and a silence lingered for almost too long.

She frowned at me. 'Stop it Tori. And stop looking at me like that. David is taking care of me.' Her voice had strengthened. 'Home would be safer than Ukraine and you still have a job waiting for you at the University. But are you *really* ready to come home?'

I felt my emotions waver. Clare rallied, her head was higher, her eyes fierce with concern, for me I realised, not for herself. If Clare said she was fine, then she was fine. *And she had said it, hadn't she?* I tried to recall the exact words of our conversation. I searched her face a moment longer before answering. She raised a challenging eyebrow. Was I ready to go home? I found my head shaking. As usual, speaking to Clare has toughened my resolve. 'No. I want to be here until something in my universe aligns and I can get back to where I need to be.'

She searched my eyes and found whatever she was looking for, nodding.

'Promise you will stay safe. And if I don't get a message at least every second day I will call Interpol, or whatever it is they have over there!' She threatened.

I nod. 'I have to go, they have just called boarding. I love you.'

'You never asked about Kate.' Her voice held motherly censure.

'I don't need to. She has the toughest Mumma bear around, nothing is going to mess with that kid. Besides, Mum sends twice daily updates.'

Clare shakes her head, but I am shutting my screen, ready to stuff the laptop in my carry on bag.

'I'll tell her you send your love.'

I hear the words just before the screen clicks shut. I wedge the laptop in the bag and straighten in my chair, back still kinked from an uncomfortable night in the terminal. With my phone and my ticket in hand I stand and join the line. The old woman one step ahead of me gives me a look of sympathy but says nothing.

Ω

Despite the fact that the distance between Rome and the UN headquarters in Kyiv was only as far as Melbourne to Brisbane up the east coast of Australia, the trek was neither easy nor short but blessedly so tiring that I had little time to wallow in my misery. After a cancellation, I had to wait 24 hours for the flight to Chişinău, Moldova, though the flight itself was less than three hours. If I never saw an airport lounge again I thought it would still be too soon. I don't think anyone has flown near Ukraine without a high level of tension since Malaysian Airlines Flight 17 was shot down in 2014. I knew many of the nearly a hundred forensic experts who had been flown to the empty field and the 50 square kilometres preceding it to scavenge through its scattered fragments of plane, passenger and cargo, though only after the Russians had had access to the area for 17 days prior. I had seen photographs of the work they had done and been grateful I had not been able to travel at the time. As a result, while flying into Chişinău Airport I had many reservations about what I was doing.

I had been involved in crime scenes before, but never mass graves, never war crimes and my entire being fought against it. My option, however, was to turn tail for home, admitting to myself and worse, my mother, that I had failed. With such high-powered enemies, I doubted National Geographic would ever approach me again and my access to the buried cities of the Campi Flegrei would be as tourist only, assuming the Italian government even allowed my reentry into the country.

When the tyres of the Boeing 777 hit the tarmac I was not the only one who said a silent prayer of gratitude. The woman beside me closed her eyes for a full three minutes as she murmured prayers over the chain of beads wrapped around her wrist, the *misbaha*, Muslim prayer beads. Across the aisle, a middle-aged businessman crossed himself in the more familiar sign of the cross. That he did so with his thumb and first two fingers, tucking the third and fourth fingers into his palm revealed a likely Orthodox connection. But the gesture itself was familiar, reflecting the Catholic faith, the faith of my mother and father. I knew from my Google-based research that there would be far more followers of the orthodox religions in the region than followers of Islam. I also knew that in Kharkiv and neighbouring Donetsk, east of the capital Kyiv, particularly in the areas impacted by war crimes, the population of Islamic adherents was larger and often victimised. Most had been expelled from the region in the 1940s as part of an ethnic cleansing regime though small pockets of the Islamic community remained, like tenacious weeds in the rocky hillsides.

Periods of religious tolerance and intolerance along with shifting power plays and avaricious neighbours had long seen the area brutalised by warfare. A few years earlier, when the Russian 'annexation' of Crimea went largely unchallenged, Putin set his sights on a greater prize and the much-disputed invasion of Ukraine began. Despite global condemnation and widespread sanctions, only the Ukrainian army stood as David to Russia's Goliath, cheered by the global community waving flags of blue and yellow, but ultimately expected to fail. Somehow, the Ukrainians had held on and even managed to gradually push back the Russian incursion. Although the Russians still held Crimea and tracts of Eastern Ukraine, active warfare was limited and the UN deemed it safe to push for an investigation of alleged war crimes.

Entering the terminal I was grateful to see a handwritten sign with my name on it and recognised the craggy chin of Dr Bruce Habermann. He waved, great whole arm movements as he recognised me. I started to offer a hand when he crushed me in a bear hug. Habermann, I knew from internet stalking, was of Jewish-German descent, his family having fled Germany to America at the start of the hostilities in the 1930s. He was as far from the mental image you might have of a Jewish scholar as one could get. To look at him though, one might instead think he was a Viking and I could easily imagine him as a berserker. His frame was immense, tall and broad at the shoulders and as he pressed me against him I fitted neatly beneath his chin, the handwritten cardboard crushed between us. His once-red hair still showed a hint of faded orange and was as full and thick as my own, tied back with a piece of rawhide at the back of his neck. Peeking from beneath the collar of his shirt faded green-blue tattoo ink hinted at an adventurous past.

'How was the flight?'

I wondered briefly what Dalton had told him.

'Not bad. A bit tired, airport terminal seats don't make great beds,' I offered.

'I'd say you could sleep in the car on the way but the roads aren't great in these parts.' He looked me over, I imagined he was adding notes to some internal personnel profile. 'Now, just put your stuff down and we'll get you some breakfast, but first...'

He turned the sign around to reveal a second and third name scrawled on the back. In minutes I was being introduced to Dorian Muller and Leon Graff, a pair of Swiss autopsy technicians with whom I had unknowingly shared a flight. Both spoke flawless, if heavily accented, English.

Breakfast consisted of McDonald's hotcakes liberally coated in additional tubs of maple syrup procured by our indefatigable leader and loaded with soft-serve ice cream. Was there anywere in the world the franchise didn't reach? It came with cups of substandard but boiling hot and very welcome coffee. Unfortunately, it also accompanied my stress of luggage being lost somewhere between Rome and Chişinău, which I was assured I would get back in time.

'Don't worry. One of the other women will no doubt lend you something. You women share clothes all the time right?'

I grimaced but nodded obligingly, pleased that I always kept at least one pair of clothes in my hand luggage. If I had to wash out my undies by night, so be it.

'I was surprised when Andrew told me you were interested in the position. Pleased, but surprised.'

I was flattered by the implication that he knew of me. I summoned a half-truth. 'I was in Italy working on a dig but I found the situation didn't suit me. I was planning on a flight home when he mentioned the work here. It felt like something I could do.'

He nodded over the polystyrene edges of his coffee cup.

'And are you here to stay for a while or just to help out?'

'I'm not sure.' I spoke honestly. I was grateful when he nodded and let this pass.

Soon we were on the highway, sitting high up in Habermann's 90's Landcruiser and within minutes of closing his eyes Muller was asleep, snoring softly, while his countryman buried his nose in a book. I envied them both. Travel had never been my friend, and even on the long straight stretches of Australian roads travel sickness often assailed me. I had taken tablets but still had to keep my eyes firmly on the road ahead. In better years the trip would have taken around four hours but years of civil unrest in Ukraine had meant that the roads had deteriorated badly once we left the cities and despite the four-wheel drive it was rough going and jarring both on the backside and the nerves. There were sections when bomb craters had removed the road entirely and we needed to go off-road.

As we neared Kharkiv the situation slowed further with regular roadblocks and checkpoints, where at each we all had to step out of the vehicle as soldiers from one side or the other went through the vehicle, including all our possessions and were presented with our paperwork. Eventually, each time we were waved through, a little more worn and frustrated than before. Between stops, Habermann filled me in on the situation in the region and prepared me for what I might find.

Kharkiv had been heavily damaged by shelling but despite being the focus of Russian aggression for over 6 months the city itself had not fallen.

'The brunt of the damage and loss of life occurred in Izyum. We will be based there. Since the Russian retreat in September, we have been involved in exhuming mass graves outside the city. We've also excavated a number of graveyards where Russian forces had 'reburied' civilians amongst the existing graves.'

He spoke without taking his eyes from the road, turning the wheel and lurching over the verge to follow the armoured vehicle ahead of us across a puckered field to avoid another crater. We bounced around, grabbing onto seats and handles, grateful for our seatbelts until Habermann rediscovered the road.

'The remains in the mass graves have often been burned to hamper investigation so we also rely on reported burials by friends and relatives, who risked their lives to seek out and bury the remains of civilians killed during the invasion and in the months thereafter. These,' Habermann said, 'provide us with the best evidence because they haven't been tampered with.'

'We work for the International Criminal Court, under the protection of the United Nations. While the local forces will not hamper our investigations they will not aid it either, and those who inform to us need to do so with extreme caution since many of their neighbours are Russian sympathisers. In truth, it is hard to tell one side from the other at times and many Ukrainians have chosen to fight for Russia, though you won't hear that on the NBC or BBC, and much of the region still remains under Russian control. Something not likely to change in a hurry. Everything we do needs to be done with extreme care because we don't get a second chance. This means your record keeping and processes must be impeccable because we hope they will all end up in court.'

He stopped talking for a moment and looked over at me, narrowly missing a pothole that could have swallowed the entire vehicle.

'You realise that if you do this you could be called in at any time to testify before the ICC?'

I nodded.

'Good. Because a face like yours would be a bonus to us. I saw the segment on the discovery of the body of the praetorian you found in the toilet. A shitty way to go.'

I faked a smile at the well-worn joke.

'That's where I recognised your face from!' Graff leaned forward now, studying me in the rear vision mirror. I had noticed the puzzled looks he had given me earlier. 'So, how did he really die, and who stuffed him in the toilet?'

I shrugged my shoulders and settled for silence as he and Muller, not waiting for my response, went on to debate not only the merits of my performance but also the possible motives and means for the murder I would now never get to solve. I listened with half an ear as I studied the evidence of a far less peaceful takeover than the one the Russians pretended, visible in the scarred walls, broken buildings and an overabundance of burnt-out Russian-type military vehicles. My attention was caught by the white-columned frontage of a blue-painted church above which rose two towers replete with arched windows, gold domes and coptic-style gold crosses. The blue paint smudged with smoke but mercifully it stood whole.

'A miracle it wasn't hit,' Graff spoke over my shoulder, crossing himself as he did so.

'Ah, home sweet home,' he said as Habermann swung into a park in front of a large faded brick building, boasting four stories overlooking a fenced-off complex. Behind it, the evening stars were starting to make their appearance in an indigo sky. My stomach rumbled.

'Welcome to Honcharova Kvartira,' Habermann offered as he clambered down from the Landcruiser, tossing Graff and the still-blinking Muller their bags. 'The Mars Hotel was nicer, but it's closed just now.' He gestured towards a blackened, open-fronted building down the road that was little more than rubble. I clutched my knapsack and my kit as though afraid to lose all I had left and looked from the ruined hotel to the squat square building we had pulled up before. Several windows were boarded over and the outside was riddled with bullet holes but it appeared whole.

'We call it the Globe.' Habermann smiled at me. 'Not like Shakespeare's theatre, but because we share it with people from all over the globe. Even fugitives from Australia.' He winked. 'Come, let's find you a roommate.'

He was right, the building was awash with accents, many I recognised, some I didn't. I was relieved to find my roommate to be a grandmotherly Scottish anthropologist with a brogue as broad as her hips and rosy apple cheeks. Like Habermann before her, Morag scooped me into a hug which pressed me against her ample bust before releasing me to consider our shared space. I quickly determined that she would be a good 'roomie'. Her things were carefully stored in her suitcase, except for a colourful knitted blanket, a pair of pink embroidered pillows and a trio of silver frames holding an astonishing array of friendly-looking faces all with round pink cheeks.

Habermann paused at the door. 'Morag will make you feel at home, but I can't see you sharing clothes. I'll see if I can't talk to one of the younger broads.'

'Any chance the kitchen is still open?' I asked as another rumble beset my midline.

'I think we missed dinner.' He foraged through the pockets of his army-style vest and pulled out two slightly scrunched choc-chip muesli bars and a small apple, all of which he chucked in my direction. 'That might keep you going until breakfast.'

I stared at the bounty dubiously as Habermann disappeared down the hallway and the hallway lights flickered and dimmed.

'Come back in Lass. I am sure we can find something more filling than that.' And with the suggestion, Morag busied herself over her suitcase pulling out a small single propane-fueled burner, a teapot, and a square tin that, it turned out, contained the thickest, moistest fruitcake I had ever tasted, so full of nuts that my jaw was aching before I had finished plucking up the crumbs from my lap.

With a mug of black tea and a slab of cake under my belt, I found myself tired enough to crawl into the narrow single bed and actually sleep, but not before a short, mostly cold shower, cleaning my teeth, washing my underwear and hanging it in the shower cubicle to dry.

Ω

Over breakfast and a cup of tea, courtesy of Morag's twice-used teabags, my Scottish roommate grilled me on my experience. It seemed she had decided that I would join her team while I learned the ropes.

'So, ye'll not faint then, at the whiff of the corpses?'

I shook my head. I was not a fan of the odour of the deceased but I had a strong stomach and the smell had never yet made me faint or throw up.

'Good. Ye'll not know how many wee lassies I've had, doctors like you even, who have keeled over at the stench of an exhumed body. Some laddies too.'

I knew this to be true and every time we brought in an exhumed corpse to the university back home the technicians would lay bets on which student or doctor would lose their breakfast or equilibrium first.

She led me through the front gates of what had been part of the Central Izyum Hospital, the fenced compound across the street, flashing her credentials to the door guards, men with AK-47s who had set up guard points outside the gate mirroring uniformed UN soldiers a few feet inside the gate. The once lush gardens were straggly and overgrown but still a beautiful sight in a warzone. We entered one of the larger buildings and tracked our way down two flights of stairs to the basement morgue. A room nearly as large as an aircraft hanger and filled with metal-topped benches, each with its own washbasin. At one end of the room, five large freezer containers hummed noisily, run by large portable generators brought by the UN. A low gateway led to what appeared to be a loading bay for small trucks. A partitioned-off section was labelled with clear warning signs suggesting that behind them was the X-ray station.

Already more than a dozen people were at work, teams clearly visible. A pair of technicians would bring a body out of the chiller rooms and sign it over to a pair of radiologists who would shift it behind the partitions and conduct whatever scans were available there. It would reemerge to be signed over to a forensic anthropologist working alongside a student or two and a pathologist.

'Over here, Lass, you can have the bay beside mine. The last lassie found she couldn't stomach the work for long, was in tears and shaking out the back before the first shift was through. I couldn't talk her back in. Back with her parents in England by now, I suspect.'

I suspected I could listen to Morag talk all day but swiftly discovered her warning was timely.

The smell was bad, worse than anything I had encountered in my career to date. It lingered in the air despite the great roaring air purifiers that cycled the air in the basement out into the world and pulled clean fresh air back in. I had never worked in such a large space with so many remains before and the combined odour seemed to sit in the back of your throat. I knew in a week I would barely notice it, but until then I tried to breathe shallowly. My first body was that of an old man, shrunken and dehydrated enough to almost look like an Egyptian mummy. Morag offered me a crash refresher course in odontology and showed me how to correctly fill in the reams of forms that accompanied each body and corresponded with their dental records. To make my first job easy my poor chap had very few teeth remaining and clear signs of where he had lost a couple to what must have been incredibly painful abscesses. The ones that remained were well-worn with age and stippled with cavities.

He also had ligature marks, permanently impressed on the bare flesh of his wrists. I removed fibres of rope to add to my samples. Finally, a bullet hole in his forehead from where some soldier had executed him at point-blank range.

'Why would someone even see the poor old man as a threat?' I murmured to myself.

'They probably didn't, Lass. He was probably just in the way, or saw something he shouldna.'

With the help of a medical student from Greece, I removed his tired paisley pyjamas and sent them off to be cleaned as I continued my examination. They had, I noticed, a neatly hand-stitched monogram on the pocket that once clean might identify the body, either by initial or perhaps by having some equally ancient old woman identify her own stitchwork. Unable to identify any other injuries, not that any more were needed with a bullet to the braincase, I started with measuring the lengths of his femurs. I sliced through the hardened skin of his chest to access the bone tips I would need, to send along with the single tooth I removed for testing and to confirm the age estimate I had given, which was in fact much younger than he looked, but at sixty, far too old still to be in a war zone in his pyjamas.

I sensed Morag watching me as I worked but was so intent on my job that I didn't look up until I had finished both the examination and the paperwork. She greeted my gaze with a smile. 'You'll do.' I found it to be high praise.

Chapter Eleven: A Satyr in the Gardens

Rome AD 72

It was the sound that drew her. A sound that viscerally reminded her of finding Messalinus an *anni* earlier, panting and sweating on his sleeping couch, lost to the grip of the fever that would claim his sight and take him from her. It came from the trees overhanging her husband's balcony.

She had considered going to him that evening. Having even called her women to her to prepare her, but recollections of her last foray to his rooms made her dismiss them again. Restlessness had driven her to walk the gardens. The moon was bright enough that the poplars that lined the marble gallery cast dark shadows and made the white marble railings shine like moonbeams. The villa was silent, shrouded in darkness. The sound, punctuated with gasps and whimpers made her hurry forward, careless of her step, to the foot of the balcony.

At first, she couldn't comprehend what she saw. It seemed like a body made of entirely too many limbs, something monstrous and dangerous. It writhed and jerked rhythmically, but not in the way Messalinus had when ill. Rather, it was like a man on horseback, moving with the stride of the beast beneath him. Only, there was no beast. Not truly. The moon was so bright that her husband's face was illuminated, perfect marble features, eyes wide, staring blindly, mouth open in panting. His neck arched either in ecstasy or pulled by the hand that gripped the red gold curls and pulled them backwards, much like a rider would grasp a handful of mane on a runaway horse. The beautiful, agonised features of her husband.

Behind him, Titus' hair gleamed white gold in the moonlight, his eyes closed as he pulled Messalinus closer, rocking in time with him as both of them moaned and panted.

Thalia stood frozen in the dark shadow of a cypress pine. For in that moment, she understood. Titus had clearly claimed exactly what she had been longing for.

She might have slipped away, unnoticed, but for the pebble that crunched beneath her sandal and she turned to disappear into the darkness. All three of them froze. In the darkness a nightbird cried its melancholy sonata, and, spurred by the sound, Thalia turned to flee. A crunch and crash of the brush behind her said she was being followed. She pulled the hem of her tunic up to her knees as she fled. A glance behind showed Titus had leapt the railing she had just stepped away from, as she turned back she discovered her mistake. A moon-drenched statue of a scantily clad maiden, ironically paused in the act of flight, a pair of satyrs strung out behind, reached out one hand as though grasping for help. It was the hand that clipped her cheek, knocking her staggering sideways, causing a bright halo of light to explode across the left side of her face as a still-naked Titus grabbed her from behind and one hand wrapped in her hair in a bizarre parody of what she had just witnessed with her husband. Then he was pulling her back, kicking and flailing but still stunned to silence towards the balcony.

Soundless, he tossed her over the marble rail to fall at the feet of her husband. Messalinus, poised on the balls of his feet, alert and wary and completely naked above her, his flagging phallus, lit with pale light, descending into the dark hair of his pubic region. From her position at Messalinus' feet, she watched Titus leap effortlessly back over the ledge, coming to stand, his bare feet a palm's length from her face. He reached over her to cup Messalinus' face in one hand.

'Who is it?' Her husband demanded, brushing away the caress.

'Some slave gi…' his lover started to reply as she raised her face and the moonlight fell over his shoulder, '*Futeo!* Titus swore.

'What? Titus! What is it?' Messalinus' eyes were wide but blind, fortunate not to see the horror and disgust in her expression.

'It's… her.' Her normally articulate former brother-in-law managed.

'Her who?'

'Your wife.'

Her husband's expression was so horrified Thalia could not help a snort of hysterical laughter and once begun, she found she was unable to stop.

'Get her inside,' Messalinus hissed.

When Titus reached for her Thalia threw herself backwards, evading his grip, so he herded her, arms out as though corralling a horse, back through the open doorway and into the relative darkness of her husband's chamber. Messalinus followed cautiously, one hand out in front of him in case he collided with an obstacle.

One by one, as if by some sinister magic, the lamps about the room flared into light, filling the room with dull ambience and revealing the pair of slave boys moving about with tapers sheltered from errant breezes by their palms. Thalia could see through her right eye that the space had been cleared of almost every item that might cause impediment to her husband, leaving only the sleeping couches, arranged in a triad in the centre of the room. Around the space, eyes blinked in the semi-darkness. Slaves. Boys. All boys. Titus was grinning as he backed her towards the triad of couches until her calf brushed the back of one and she was forced to sit. When she looked towards the door Titus wagged a finger and shook his head.

'That would not be a wise choice,' he said.

As there was little to convince her otherwise, Thalia sat. Her face throbbed from the impact with the statue and she gingerly used her tongue to check that her teeth had not cracked. But the movement caused too much pain in her cheek. Likely that was what she had heard crack. Certainly, her eye was swollen beyond use.

Messalinus entered the room with a slow but steady step. She could almost hear him counting the steps in his mind.

Titus cleared his throat to give him direction and Messalinus cocked his head, checked his stride and stepped unerringly up beside his golden lover.

Side by side, even with the use of only one eye, she could appreciate their beauty, the blond head beside the red-gold. Titus was slightly taller and although his shoulders were broader from years swinging a sword, his waist was narrow and his hips were sculpted. The muscles in his legs bulged, making his flaccid member, so proud and engorged earlier, seem puny and vulnerable.

He chuckled to see her looking. Thalia looked away.

One of the slaves helped Messalinus into a tunic of dark-coloured silk, belted it about his waist, and then stepped back into the background. Her husband stepped lightly to the left until his leg bumped the couch and he put out a hand to guide him. He sat in the military style made popular by Vespasian, his back straight. Unlike the Emperor who sat with two feet firmly on the floor, Messalinus tucked one bare foot behind the other.

Thalia was silent, if she remained so she would not have to face his direct blank stare. She found she could not look at him. Inside she berated herself for not being more worldly. How had she not noticed the relationship between them that went beyond comradely affection? Her cheeks burned when she thought of her wedding feast, sitting to one side of her husband, while his true lover sat on the other. How many had known? How many had sniggered? When she considered her clumsy and ultimately futile attempts to seduce him she wished that Hades might open his gates beneath her feet and swallow her.

Titus watched her with the hint of a smile.

'Stop it.'

Thalia jumped when Messalinus spoke.

'Stop what?' Titus drawled slowly.

'Stop smiling. This is not amusing.'

How aware he was of his lover.

Titus grinned and then rearranged his features, even though Messalinus could not truly know what expression his face held.

'I want a divorce. I want to return to my father's house.'

The words spilled from her lips before she was aware of them.

Messalinus' glance seemed to pin her, but not quite, his gaze drifting ever so slightly off beyond her left shoulder. It was disconcerting how emotionless his face was.

'No.'

She stared at him, uncomprehending. 'What do you mean, no?'

'There will be no divorce. You will remain here. You were bought and paid for and you are as much use to me now as you were the day I purchased you. More perhaps.' The expression on Messalinus' face was thoughtful. 'No,' he said, thumbing his chin. 'We must work this to our advantage. It might be pleasant to do away with all the pretence.'

Thalia realised her mouth was open, prompting another smug smile from Titus.

'How could I possibly be of use to you? You are a *cinaedus*.' She almost recoiled to hear the filthy term in her mouth. The word for a man who was used like 'a woman by other men. A glance about the room full of pretty young slave boys assured her he was not always the receiver but that was of little concern. Using boys for sexual pleasure was considered acceptable, a man might even keep a young lover, so long as the boy was not a Roman citizen and so long as he was discarded as he approached manhood.

But this was something else. What they had been doing was both shocking and sickening. A Roman man did not let himself be used by another citizen, bent over and violated by another man. Such a thing was a disgrace, to be used like a woman. A thousand thoughts marched with hobnailed boots through her still reeling mind. The fact he had not married until so late, the look of disgust she had caught when he had touched her that first night, the way he had shunned her bed. The close relationship between Messalinus and his foster-brother, the way they were almost always touching in some way. She could not keep the thoughts from her face. Titus' lip moved in amusement.

It was all well for him. He was not the one being taken. Golden Titus played the man's role. Messalinus' dominant left hand shot out unerringly, colliding with the cheek she had already injured and knocking her from the couch to the floor.

With her head ringing and a dull roar in her ears, a counterpoint to the other roar, one of pain that had taken over the entire left side of her body, she was somehow aware of Titus moving to position himself between them.

'Messalinus, if you kill her they will interrogate the household slaves and that would not be a pleasing experience for either of us.'

'I'm not going to kill her.' Her husband's voice dripped with scorn and seemed to echo around the room both in and outside of her head. 'But I will not have my wife using such filthy language.'

Thalia allowed her face to rest against the chill of the tiles as she waited for the room to stop spinning and the lights to fade. Titus reached out and stroked Messalinus' back, as she watched the tension bleed out of her husband.

'Why not divorce her? Send her home to Arrecinus Clemens. Let it be her shame. It will disgrace him to have both his daughters rejected.'

Her husband exhaled. 'Titus, you are beautiful and brutal but you are not terribly smart. If I sent her home, what would stop her from speaking against us?'

'I wouldn't.' She forced the word out through broken lips, a trail of saliva followed them. Titus' face formed a picture of disgust, much like hers had earlier.

Messalinus shook his head. 'Here, as my wife, I can command her loyalty. As my wife, she cannot testify against me. We married by ancient rite so divorce would be near impossible anyway.'

He reached out to take Titus' hand. 'And that's a good thing. If I didn't have a wife I would have to remarry. It is not like I have a handy Jewess to parade around the palace to irritate my father. Besides, I have found having a wife suits me. My father no longer harries me and I am not hunted like a white hind by hopeful fathers every time I attend functions.'

Thalia did not have to imagine Titus' smirk, they were both staring down at her.

'Did my sister know?'

The moment she spoke, Thalia regretted it. The thought had been one that flickered through her mind and should not have passed her lips.

Titus tilted his head, considering her. 'She never warned you?'

Thalia shook her head before thinking, setting her vision spinning again.

'She may have suspected something but I doubt she ever knew for certain. I did my duty by her, we had a child. I find my pleasures in many places.' He smiled again, this one the almost charming one. Thalia considered the Jewish Queen Berenice, who had given up her country to return to Rome with her conqueror lover, who let his countrymen scorn and denigrate her. Was this why men who loved men were considered so shameful? Because they lowered themselves to be treated as women? A treacherous thought rose in her. What was so bad about being a woman? Was it really so demeaning to be bedded as a woman? Women were essential, they created life. Thalia found herself staring at her husband in horrified consternation. 'What about children?'

The words escaped before she could rein them in.

It was Titus who rattled off a laugh at the curl of Messalinus' lip. 'I told you you should have taken the elder to wife. You could have adopted Julia as yours and married the child off to an heir of your choice. Or married some fat matron and let her drop a cuckoo in your nest the way Augustus did.'

Messalinus was silent, considering, a wry smile twisted his lips. 'Are you suggesting I do as the Greeks do and lend you my wife for the begetting of a whelp. It couldn't be as bad as riding that skinny cow you married.'

Thalia did not know which wore the more shocked expression, for Titus' mask was a mirror of the one on her own face. Then as the shock faded one side of his mouth twitched and he looked at her considering. She lurched back. 'I am not livestock to be bred!'

'To the contrary, my dear,' Messalinus murmured. 'If you want a child that is exactly what you are.'

She froze. 'You wouldn't.'

One of his eyebrows arched upwards and his head tilted in consideration.

'No.' She threw out a hand as though to ward off the idea, though a futile gesture he could not see. Titus seemed torn by offence and amusement at her reaction. He stepped closer, letting his fingers run across the line of her shoulders as he leaned close, his breath in her ear. 'Are you certain? I was able to please your sister.'

Messalinus sniffed, a disparaging sound that told her he was not serious. 'Don't play with her Titus. I have no desire for children. And for the moment my father is happy to wait. He and Gaius are too busy trouncing barbarians in Batavia to worry about heirs right now.'

Thalia's thoughts spun. A child would have given her life purpose, someone to love and be loved by. Already any illusion of finding that in her husband had been shattered, and even this lesser hope, he had snatched away. Still, the thought of his touch made her skin crawl. As though he heard her thoughts he turned to her.

'Be grateful, you are the envy of many women. This life and the privileges you have been offered, all the while still able to make offerings at the temple of the virgin huntress, Artemis. Why, it is almost like being a vestal.'

Except, she thought but this time managed not to say, that the vestals had legal control over their lives, where she had Felix to oversee her every action and purchase.

Above her, Messalinus clicked his fingers and no fewer than three boys responded to his summons.

'Make her a pallet in the corner for a bed. One of you, report to her rooms and inform her women that the Domina was summoned by her master and that she will not return tonight. In fact, tell the kitchens to bring a platter here for the Domina to break her fast.'

'What are you saying, Messalinus? I don't want her here.'

Her husband caressed his lover's face. 'Titus, if her watching bothers you, blacken her other eye and she will not be able to see you. And if she speaks, well… we can always stop her mouth.'

A pair of slave boys gripped her beneath her arms and pulled her, not ungently, towards a distant corner of the room where a few meagre blankets, no doubt their own pallets, had been arranged. Wallowing in her own helplessness, Thalia turned her face towards the wall. Titus and Messalinus were still speaking but the shaking had overtaken her entire body and she pulled the threadbare blankets around herself to try to stop the cold that had taken over. Thalia found she was unable to even cry.

α

Thalia followed Felix back to her room. It was a completely different space to return to. All her possessions remained untouched, a platter of bread, cheese and olives lay under cheesecloth on a tripod table, awaiting her pleasure. But the room was completely and utterly silent. In fact, as she slipped back through her memory of the walk here she could not recall hearing a single female voice. None of the half-dozen or so slaves that would usually be in attendance were visible. Gytha was nowhere to be seen, even old Clulia was missing. Anger reflected from the majordomo's eyes as he informed her that she was to stay in her rooms unless accompanied by one of his men.

With her vision restricted still in her left eye Thalia felt disoriented as she walked through the space, as quiet as her family tomb. Felix did not wait to be dismissed, disappearing as soon as she entered the rooms, leaving her completely and utterly alone. She ate, a little, soaking the bread in wine to soften it and sucking it through gritted teeth. She could not open her mouth wide enough for the olives, but she crumbled the cheese and ate it in tiny increments. Thereafter she slept, not waking until the dark of night. No lamps had been lit and the room was plunged into darkness, the only light streaming in from the balcony, another cursed moonlit night. Thalia relieved herself in the pot beneath her bed and curled up, spending the next hours willing herself to sleep. In the end, she did walk, slipping out of the doorway onto the balcony, despite Felix's orders there was no guard. The cool night air took some of the maddening ache from her cheek and the moon lit the tears that ran down her cheeks. They were not, she discovered, tears of heartbreak but of the anguish of humiliation and helplessness.

It was not only her lack of vision that contracted her world to a suite of rooms, it was the fact that, without seemingly being instructed, the entire household abruptly ceased to see her or hear her voice.

No one spoke to her. Not one of the slaves acknowledged her appearance, though they slipped silently in and out of her rooms to bring or remove platters of food or remove and return the pot that sat under her sleeping couch. Still, there were small signs of kindness. Meals of soft broth and finely ground bread, easily torn and dunked, were accompanied by a small pot of pungent ointment that reeked of herbs and honey. Thalia applied it with gingerly gratitude rubbing it in small gentle circles and was pleasantly surprised to find it did numb the ache.

On the third day, a slender, pretty slave boy of perhaps ten or eleven presented himself to her rooms and set about the actions of tidying and setting the room to rights. When at last he came to stand, hesitantly before her, Thalia considered him beneath still-swollen lids. The boy had pale creamy skin but sloe eyes and tight curls that suggested African descent. She recognised him as the same silver-eyed boy who had been weeping outside Messalinus' rooms on the evening, she now realised, her husband had been told his lover Titus was returning with a mistress. His eyes narrowed as he considered her appearance, the tangled hair, crumpled tunic and bruises and she noted pity in his eyes.

To be pitied by a slave, she didn't know whether to laugh or cry.

'Domina, may I brush your hair?'

Thalia considered refusal, but she missed the quiet presence of Gytha, the simple reassurance of human touch, she nodded, closing her eyes as the boy first ran his fingers through her hair to deftly remove the tangles before setting about brushing it with long steady strokes. She winced when his brush neared the damage to her cheek and his touch became gentle though still sure. The lad was clearly no stranger to the chore and she could not imagine how that might be, given Messalinus' hair was not lengthy. Finally, the boy began to confidently twist and weave the strands into intricate swirls and knots. When he stepped back, again shyly, she ran her fingers over the arrangement with surprise.

'Thank you.' She spoke the word that she couldn't remember using with any of her former slaves, but by this stage, she was so grateful for simple human touch and the child had proven more than skilled.

The boy's face coloured.

'You have done this before?'

He nodded, not looking at her. 'My mother was an *ornatrix*, she worked at *lupanar* in the port district.'

Perhaps she had once been a hairdresser, but if she worked at a brothel among the 'she wolves' it was not her sole use or talent. Thalia considered the boy, no doubt born of the lupanar. A shewolf's cub. That might explain the boy's colouring. The whores of the lupanar came in all colours and races.

When she asked what had happened to her women the boy shut his mouth and no amount of gentle coaxing would convince him to open it.

The wolfling, whose name she discovered to be Kaeso, was the one bright light in her world. Though he rarely spoke he was a peaceful companion, as skilled she discovered, with pastes and paints and lotions as he was with hair. He did not replace the quiet chatter of her women but he was gentle company. Each day she set herself a challenge to draw words from him.

Her missing women did not return. Not even old Clulia.

α

It was the festival of Floralia before she saw her husband again. Messalinus was seated in a curule chair by the open window of his smaller tablinum. Around the generous office space busts of his ancestors stared down upon her, expressions supercilious. The gentle breeze tousled his curls, which it seemed, in honour of Flora, were crowned with a garland of summer roses. He was as beautiful and treacherous as a summer storm. He appeared to be watching the scene out the window, turning only when Felix cleared his throat to indicate their presence.

He smiled. It chilled her, lingering like an unwanted guest in the corner of his mouth.

'I have a gift for you.'

Thalia frowned. One of Messalinus' boys approached. Like all Messalinus' boys he was beautiful, his features perfectly symmetrical, his hair pale gold, his eyelashes long and dark, hiding eyes that were almost violet they were so dark. One of the few tidbits she had gathered from Kaeso was that her husband discarded his 'boys' as soon as they became blemished with adolescent spots or their voices broke. This had been the fate of Aeneus, the golden musician, who had not returned with his master from the seaside. She suspected Kaeso both feared and longed for this moment though he was some years yet from adolescence. The new boy kept his eyes down as he approached, bearing with him a small ivory carved box. As he moved she noticed the tinkle of tiny bells, chains of them wound around his ankles and his wrists, ringing merrily as he stepped towards her. Messalinus' new favourite stopped before her, bells falling silent, and opened the lid to reveal fine golden chains, dangling with colourful gems and dozens of tiny crocus shapes, each enamelled in pastel shades. As she lifted one of them they tinkled merrily.

When she had been a child, Thalia's father had taken her to watch a troop of dancing girls in the palace, slaves from the distant reaches of the empire with smooth dark skin; they had spun and gyrated, twisting their supple bodies into the most extraordinary positions, wringing their hands as they moved. Each movement accompanied by the gentle chiming of bells. Thalia had wanted nothing more than a set of chains not much different from the ones in her hands, but that was long before she had truly understood the reality of slaves. She no longer envied those girls with their smooth skin and supple bodies, nor did she wish for the tinkling chains of their slavery.

Thalia glanced from the beautiful gold and bejewelled chains to the base metal ones secured around the boy's extremities.

'I am not a slave. I do not wear chains.'

The lurking smirk became a smile, a cold one. 'You are not, which is why I had a goldsmith prepare these.'

Without looking she dropped the pretty shackles back with a musical chime and set the lid back down.

He raised one eyebrow, his gaze now closer to where she stood, though disturbingly off-centre. 'Why must everything be a battle with you? When I came to an agreement with your father it was because he promised you to be a quiet bookish thing. A woman who would not cause me bother with tantrums and selfishness. And yet, you spurn my gifts and treat me with disdain.'

She stared at him openly, free to do so without his knowledge.

'You want me chained so my comings and goings become part of your soundscape.'

'Indeed, and why should I not? If you were in my position would you not like to know the whereabouts of those who serve you.'

'I do not serve you.'

'But you do. As my wife, you serve my interests. Come. Sit.' He offered waving a hand at the same couch she had been backed into nearly two weeks earlier. 'Titus and Felix tell me you have injured yourself grievously and it has left you disfigured.'

Thalia's expression wavered between astonishment and disbelief that he would claim mischance and ignorance of the slow-fading bruises and the lingering headaches they had left her with. It was only then she noticed the presence of another in the room. A movement near the doorway revealed itself to be the domus' smith, a man with hulking shoulders, rough-hewn features and a charred leather apron covering his chest. He was accompanied by the Praetorian, Petronius. The man had been assigned to guard her husband by his lover and had been a near-constant shadow, a shadow that seemed to crawl with malevolence. While the Praetorian smirked, his amber-coloured eyes reminded her of the lion's in the arena, predatory and cold. The smith's face was bleak as he looked at her.

'So, clearly we will not be holding any banquets in the near future. But, as soon as that ghastly face has recovered we will begin afresh. Titus cannot always be beside me and it would be inappropriate for Ganymede to sit by my side at a banquet.' The general wave of a hand included the new blonde catamite in his statement. 'I may live in Nero's palace but I am no Nero. Felix tells me that you ran my household admirably in my absence so I have decided to put you to honest labour. You will be my eyes in places I cannot go. You will report on those things I cannot see and be my ears where I cannot hear.'

He held a hand out and violet-eyed Ganymede was instantly by his side, one arm placed under Messalinus' hand to help him stand. The boy led her husband unerringly towards her. When he reached out a hand Thalia shifted back but her husband's hand was quicker, wrapping his fingers through her hair and tightening his grip. Slowly, he exerted pressure pulling her closer to him so that her face was pulled so close he could drop his chin and inhale the scent of her hair. Messalinus' second hand ran down her shoulder and gripped her upper arm, not hard enough to hurt but enough to warn that he could, should he desire to do so. He pulled her closer, his fingers still clenched in her hair so that her head was forced against his shoulder, his other arm pulled her body up against his.

She recalled the way he had done the same to Titus, dragging Titus' mouth down to his own and meeting it with his passionate kisses. She felt short of breath, what air she could gain came in short ragged gasps and her stomach rebelled, only by clenching her teeth, an action that caused pain to her still tender cheek and by swallowing rapidly did she avoid losing her meagre breakfast.

He forced her to stillness, her head against his shoulder, breathing in the male musk of him. How could she have ever felt attracted to him, to have desired his touch?

'You are my beloved wife.' He whispered the words against her temple, his warm breath moving the pieces of hair that had escaped Kaeso's braid. The endearment made her shiver. 'But beyond that, you are mine. I do not relinquish what is mine, nor do I let insults go unpunished.'

He pushed her back from him, holding her at arm's length, his unseeing gaze slipped over her.

'Ganymede, remove your chains.'

Although his master could not see, the new golden boy blinked at his master in confusion. 'Domine?'

Messalinus' voice dropped an octave and the threat in it was clear. 'I said, remove the bells.'

Thalia watched the boy begin to shake, the movement translated into a euphony of tinkling from the chains in question.

'D-d-d-dominus… I cannot.'

There was no less menace in the voice when Messalinus spoke again, repeating his demand.

'D-d-dominus, they were soldered on. I cannot remove them.'

One sculpted eyebrow rose on her husband's face, 'Erastus?' The burly smith shifted in his spot beside the smirking Praetorian.

'Dominus. I am here.' His voice sounded like the wheeze of one of his bellows.

'Erastus, my wife's bracelets were made with clasps were they not.'

'I believe so, Dominus. Though the work is not mine.'

'How difficult would it be to have those clasps removed? My wife is worried she might lose my gift.' Messalinus' head tilted in the direction of the smith's voice.

'It would not be hard Dominus, but to solder the chains near such delicate skin could cause unsightly burns.'

Messalinus shook his head, frowning. 'Now that would be a shame. It has been such a long time since I have seen my wife, Erastus. But I recall she has fair skin. Am I correct, Erastus? Does my wife have fair skin?'

The man's eyes widened fearfully, uncertain which answer would see him risk more. 'Y-y-yes, Dominus. Your wife has fair skin.'

The smith's gaze was apologetic and pitying and to her surprise, Thalia found she could not bear the thought of a slave's pity.

Messalinus nodded, turning his soulless gaze back upon her. 'I thought so. I would hate for anything to blemish that skin, especially given you have already proven so accident-prone. Would you?'

She shook her head in silent seething fury, then recalling his blindness, uttered the words. 'I would not.' She turned to the boy. 'Ganymede, if you would be so kind as to help me fasten my husband's gift?'

The chains tinkled merrily as the boy secured them about both wrists and at both ankles. Messalinus smiled to hear the sound.

'See,' he said as he sat back down, 'That wasn't all so hard, was it? Erastus, you are dismissed.' The slave fled as fast as a man of such bulk would allow.

'Now, sit.'

She did, bells tinkling merrily with the slightest movement.

'Let us speak of more pleasant things. Emperor Vespasian has nominated me for Consul next year.'

Thalia forced her jaw to stay tightly closed despite her shock. Messalinus was blind. It was unheard of for a consul to be disabled in any way. Did Vespasian know about his son and her husband or was he as ignorant as she had been and was merely acknowledging a man who had long supported the Flavian cause?

'As Consul, it is expected that my wife will make all manner of public appearances with me, and host dinners by my side. Our first appearance will be at the feast of Bona Dei.'

Thalia considered this, she weighed her words carefully. 'I will need my women returned. They will be needed for all manner of jobs in preparation for such events. I would not want to let you down.'

Messalinus rubbed his thumb along the line of his jaw thoughtfully.

'I have enjoyed the lack of women's giggling and gossiping. There is, I assure you, nothing that a woman can do that a boy or a man cannot do better. The makeup of our household will continue as it is and if additional slaves are needed you will inform Felix and he will ensure suitable candidates are purchased.'

'Gytha was my personal property, a gift from my father.'

He tutted softly. 'We spoke of this long ago. What is yours is mine to administer.' He paused. 'What is it that you think I did with her, sold her to the lupanar? How cruel you must think me. But not to worry, I believe Titus took the woman to serve his daughter.'

Relief and anger seared through her but the close watchfulness of both Felix and the Praetorian, Petronius, made her keep her expression closed and guarded.

Chapter Twelve: Bodies in the Fall

Tetyanivka, 2023

I had been warned that it was the site of a grisly mass murder. What I found instead was a field knee-high with seeding grasses and buzzing with insect life, the sky a cloudless blue. It was late spring and the day was warm. My newest lab assistants, twin boys with blond hair and blue eyes and a thick Texan drawl were recent arrivals and first year med students. Tim was breathing heavily under the weight of an assortment of shovels and digging tools but his eyes glowed with the excitement of being out in the field and on assignment. His identical twin, Jon, a heavy knapsack on his back loaded with the other equipment we would need, was busy flashing flirtatious glances at shy Genevieve, a young forensic pathologist. None of them seemed in the least bit bothered by the fact that behind them two UN soldiers, their uniform embellished with a small pin that boasted a French flag, their hands on their weapons, eyed the forest dubiously. Two more of our party worked beside the old refrigerated truck parked near the farmhouse, setting up the tent and unpacking our equipment. Another pair of UN guards waited with them, doing little to assist this process, which all-in-all was probably best.

When Dr Habermann had sent me out of the city to investigate a crime that had occurred in a distant hillside village and told me that I would be met by the farmer who claimed to have buried ten family members said to have been slaughtered by a branch of Russia's 'peaceful enforcers', I had been both excited and terrified. Habermann trusted me to lead the investigation but the region was still infected with Russian sympathisers and from time to time Russian troops from the occupied regions of the Donetsk Oblast.

Despite the narrow winding roads and the deep potholes, the scenery on our journey had been picturesque and there was little visible sign of the brutal war that had torn lives apart and resulted in the deaths of untold thousands. We had pulled in some way past a small village, where early-blooming wildflowers, thick grasses and reaching vines grew up around the blackened remains of a farmhouse. From the dirt road, I could spy the blue-green ribbon of the Siverskyi Donets River and beyond it the patchwork quilt of early spring fields. The farmer I had expected was absent. Instead, the tall broad-shouldered man in front of me was standing, his back to the arriving vehicles, staring towards the remaining building, a barn with a sagging roof. Through the open door, I thought I spotted the square shape of a decrepit Volvo. When he turned I admitted to being surprised. He was younger than I had imagined, perhaps in his early forties. Despite eyes shadowed with old grief, he was well-groomed, his jaw just dusted with dark stubble. His skin was swarthy but without the lines and signs of a life spent in the paddocks. Instead of the ragged overalls I had expected, he was well-dressed in a black button-up shirt, neatly rolled to his elbows, a pair of jeans and boots ready for hiking.

He had met my gaze for a moment then looked over my head towards our UN escort, exchanged a few short words in fluent French with the soldiers that accompanied us, who answered in kind, and without so much as an introduction, turned to stride out across the paddock, a confident tread that seemed to hide the barest hint of a hitch in his step. He did not wait, instead, we scurried after him, struggling over the low fence, across the overgrown meadow and towards the shadows of the green and gold forest behind, draped in its spring gown.

It was not until I was fully halfway across the meadow that I froze mid-stride. I had done the unthinkable, stepping without a moment of thought for what was beneath my feet. I had seen too many children on crutches, men on benches with folded-up pant legs, and skeletal remains with tibias and fibulas flayed and shredded or missing entirely to not know better. I internally cursed myself, then shifted the blame to the soldiers trailing along behind whose sole job it was to keep me safe and prevent my headlong flights of foolishness. Aware of the remains of my small troop approaching quickly from behind I consoled myself with the reminder that I was walking in the tall man's footsteps and therefore, given he was still walking, should be safe. I resolved immediately to follow more precisely and lengthened my gate to match his own long purposeful stride.

Ahead, the broad-shouldered man leading our small party had reached the far end of the meadow. He ducked beneath a low-hanging branch of a verdant spruce tree, the motion upset the rhythm he had established and his gait hitched a little, revealing once more the limp that I had noticed earlier but he seemed determined to hide. Following him into the blessedly cool shade, I hoped he was not leading us on a wild goose chase.

In front of me, our guide hesitated for a moment and, so intent on following his precise footfalls and listening intently for any click, I very nearly ploughed unceremoniously into his back. I was startled when he dropped back on his haunches and launched himself, skidding smoothly down a bare rock face, one hand held out for balance. The drop was not far but I hesitated at the top until he met my gaze with a raised, almost cynical eyebrow. No offer of assistance, no gentlemanly hand to steady me? I felt a tendril of annoyance drift to the surface. Frowning, I edged closer and crouched, my knapsack of precious instruments held protectively in front of me, letting gravity pull me downwards. Copying his style with my left arm held aloft to help keep balance, I skidded down the bare surface, my heart increasing pace. Hitting the soft earth below I stood, knee-deep in a pile of last season's leaves, and could not help a triumphant grin that I had not overbalanced and made a fool of myself. For a moment I thought I saw a flicker of brief amusement in his expression before I turned to retrieve the blanket-wrapped package of tools from Tim before he tossed down the heavy knapsack and slid down the surface with a barely suppressed holler of youthful exuberance. Jon followed, landed safely, immediately thrusting his bag in his brother's direction, prepared to catch Genevieve who shot him an appreciative smile. The two soldiers followed with more care and less noise.

Brushing dirt and a confetti of leaves from my palms I turned back to our guide, any sign of humour I had perhaps imagined wiped clear from his expression. He pointed out a rectangular shape, drawing an invisible line in the air between three tall saplings and an outcrop of rock. The ground beneath was invisible beneath a deep layer of last season's fallen leaves.

'That is where I buried them.' His voice was deep and sombre and his words were in perfect, though heavily accented English.

I nodded, gesturing for the twins. Tim stepped up beside me, unravelling the blanket to reveal a pair of shovels, Jon was already setting out the flags that would map the extent of our initial excavation. I turned to our host. 'I am sorry, I never got your name.' I was ready to reach for and shake his hand but he never offered it.

His eyes were so dark they were almost black.

'Samir Abraimov Al'Shani.'

I clenched my fingers forcing my fist into a ball so that it was less obvious that I had awkwardly reached for his hand. 'Mr Al'Shani, thank you for guiding us here. Please know we will treat the grave with the utmost respect.' I wondered if he would grasp my meaning; he clearly spoke English but how much? A question I reconsidered when he stared at me, not blanky, but impassively. He did not move.

'Mr Al'Shani, I need you to leave.'

Still, his dark eyes bored into mine. I slowed my speech. 'Mr Al'Shani, you need to go now.' I pointed in the direction we came from.

'No.'

The thread of annoyance I felt earlier thickened a little and despite reminding myself that the man had lost his family I found his manner frustrating and felt my brow furrow.

'Sir, the report I have said the remains have been buried for about five years now.'

He nodded. 'Five years, two months and eleven days.' His English was excellent and I detected a hint of a British accent, schooled in England at some point, I imagined.

I pursed my lips, catching my top lip between my teeth and glancing at the UN soldiers, who shrugged.

I had never unearthed a mass grave with family members standing beside me. 'Mr Al'Shani, please, I don't think you understand. Some of the remains will be decomposed, but not all of them. It is not a sight you want to see.'

He nodded, gravely, but did not move. When he spoke his words were precise and contained but his tone was a raw and gaping wound. 'I don't think you understand. I dug this hole, I carried them here in my arms, I buried them. I will not leave.'

I forced my mouth shut and turned to Tim. 'Set out three bags to start with, we will see how we go from there.' The section he had motioned to me was not a broad space, and I doubted there were actually the number of remains Dr Habermann had cited when he had told me about the scene. I took one of the shovels in hand and used it to scrape the cushion of leaves back carefully to bare earth then stopped and met the gaze of Samir Al'Shani.

'Mr Al'Shani.' I met his dark glare. 'Samir, please? You can stay but you must stand over there,' I gestured with my free hand to the rock face the UN soldiers were leaning against, a patch of sunlight spilling through to light the leaves around their feet with golden fire. 'When we begin you cannot come any closer, not under any circumstances,' I spoke as much for the soldiers as for our host. 'This is a war crime investigation. Nothing can be allowed to corrupt the evidence.'

From his expression, I knew he understood perfectly and he nodded and stepped towards the soldiers then turned back, folding his arms across his chest. Only the tick of a muscle in his jaw betrayed the stress he must have been under. I sighed, met Genevieve's questioning gaze and shrugged.

Ω

Exposing the remains had not taken long, the grave was shallow and Jon had hit rock not terribly far beneath the surface. This was pleasing, ensuring that we would not lose any pieces of evidence. Genevieve stood ready, camera in hand, to document every step of the excavation should it be called as evidence.

As the bodies swiftly emerged it was all I could do to keep looking back at the man who had carried them here and buried them. The twins were unable to resist, darting glances at him, despite the harsh warning glares I sent in their direction. The doubt I had experienced on seeing the extent of the space Samir indicated as the grave of some ten people was abruptly shattered. Jon looked at me in confusion, glancing at the first three body bags Tim had set out. Limited on space as we were, the plan had been to remove the first three before rolling out any more bags.

I shook my head and kept my voice low. 'Put whatever you find in a bag, any bag. We will reassemble and assess back at the tent.'

They nodded, faces now bare of any excitement at their first foray into the field. Tim looked decidedly green. I passed him a telltale white bag with a circular opening. 'Whatever you do. Don't contaminate the evidence.'

I was impressed by Genevieve's fortitude and grateful for the effect it had on the young men, forced to step up to match her. I pushed up from my knees, wiped the dirt from my hands onto my cargo pants and arranged my expression. As I had instructed, Al'Shani waited beside the two UN peacekeepers. I was grateful that the backs of my three assistants largely blocked the view of what they were photographing and carefully and methodically removed piece by piece from the ground. I forced myself to look the man in the eye, my own body further blocking his view.

'Grenade or Rocket Launcher?' I forced myself to ask.

'I don't know.'

I was oddly relieved to hear he had not been present at the time though it was little consolation knowing he must have returned to find them.

'The farmhouse. Was that where it happened?'

He nodded.

I looked at one of the UN guards. 'I am going to have to check the farmhouse.'

They looked at me blankly, despite the fact I had been reassured that one spoke English.

Al'Shani took pity, translating for me. They conversed in rapid French before one adjusted his weapon and stepped forward. I turned back to our host.

'I need you to show me where it happened.'

He nodded but didn't move, his eyes still on the grave. 'They burnt it down.'

I considered the remains I had just seen, which were not wholly consistent with cremation in a fire. I was by now, very familiar with the type of trauma caused by explosives. 'Yes, but afterwards, right? After you removed the remains?'

His eyes flicked to mine, a hint of a nod.

'I need to search for anything you missed.'

He closed his eyes, shook himself and turned from the grave. With far less effort than it took me, who had to cling to trees for support, he ascended the slope. I felt vindicated when the soldier had even more difficulty than I did in his ascent. I halted at the meadow, gesturing to our non-English-speaking guard.

'Tell him to go first.'

I would not defy protocol a second time.

The farmhouse had collapsed in on itself so it took some effort to remove the larger beams of burnt timber. Our Peacemaker added a shoulder and soon both men were well coated in soot by the time we reached the area Al'Shani had indicated. The roof had clearly been thatch so there was limited debris. The walls were interlocked logs but their thick clay coating kept them from burning except where damage from the explosion was evident, but exposure to air and water had done their damage. It was clear however that the damage from whatever the explosive device had been was considerable.

A stone-walled fireplace centred us where Samir indicated he found the bodies. I did not expect to find shell casings, since the Russians had clearly returned to 'clean up' but given the state of the remains I did hope to find further evidence of bone shards. While the men stood back I sifted methodically through the ashes. It did not take long before I found what I sought. Carefully slipping my find into a small ziplock bag that I labelled with a permanent marker.

Samir cleared his throat. Intent on my search I hadn't noticed how close he had come until I was staring up at him from my hands and knees, the angle making his tall frame even more impressive.

'Let me help, please?'

I pursed my lips, not replying immediately.

'Show me what you're looking for and I'll be another set of eyes.'

I considered the liquid anguish and determination in those eyes. Against my better inclinations, I nodded. Reluctantly I showed him the fingernail-sized, ivory-coloured fragment I had found. 'Anything that looks like this, larger or smaller, locate but do not touch.' I pinned him with my most serious authoritative gaze, the one I used on students who talked during a lecture. 'If you do touch anything the scene will be considered contaminated and I won't be able to use any of it as evidence. Do you understand?' To my surprise, his lip wavered in what might almost be considered a smile. He nodded.

We worked, side by side, sifting through the remnants of what must have been his life, pausing from time to time as I considered and discarded or added evidence to my little bag. As instructed Al'Shani would alert me when he thought he had found something. It had probably been an hour since I had added the last piece to my bag when I finally voiced the question that kept running through my head.

'Why you? Why here?'

Al'Shani glanced up from where he was crouched.

'I mean, yours seems to have been the only place attacked.' I recalled our drive through the quaint village near the river. The land on the opposite side was occupied by Russia, but the village could have been photographed and put on postcards.

'I wondered that myself. They also burnt down the monastery at Sviatohirsk but the village wasn't targeted. In the end, I just assumed that someone in the village had an issue with Tatars.'

'Tatars?' The word was familiar but I failed to understand the context. 'Like Huns or Mongols?'

His lip raised a little in a half smile. 'Hardly. My wife's family fled Crimea in 2014, they were Crimean Tatars, an ethnic group with links to Türkiye. Our people have long experienced persecution at the hands of the Russians. Perhaps one of the Orthodox families in the village didn't like having Muslims living so close by.'

'Your family was Muslim?'

He shrugged. 'In an ethnic sense. My own family do not practise their faith. I value my roots but I am not a religious man. Elirë, though? My wife was a believer.'

The sound of voices beyond the farmhouse forced me to lift my head. I could see the rest of our party returning across the field. The sun was far to the west and the sky was gaining the bruised hue of late afternoon. Tim was clearly winning on the wooing stakes for he shared the burden of the first stretcher and body bag with Genevieve. Jon followed behind having commandeered our second peacekeeper into sharing lifting duties.

I stretched my aching back and walked to meet them.

'You're finished?'

Genevieve grimaced. 'No. But these were closest to the surface. I think it is about five sets of remains.' Her gaze slipped to the two bags, very little to show for her tally.

'Take them to the tent and we can begin.'

Chapter Thirteen: A Disputed Identity

Tetyanivka, 2023

Beneath the shade of the tent the mid-morning air was hot. The twins had propped up each side of the tent with blackened timbers from the farmhouse in order to allow a wisp of breeze and the slight clearing of the air but it did little to dispel the heat or the fuge of death. Our makeshift tables currently held four sets of remains, the previous three having been preliminarily sorted, assessed and bagged for return to the morgue back in the city. If what Al'Shani had reported was true, there were three sets still to retrieve. Most of what was on the tables had been pared back to bare bones but flesh remained on those who had been buried deeper below the surface. The pair of UN soldiers set to protect the tent, were standing outside despite the heat of the afternoon sun and the layers of protective clothing and body armour. They had preferred that option to the cloying aroma of death that had turned one of them pale and set another to divulging the contents of his lunch. The remaining soldiers accompanied the rest of my party in the cool shadows of the copse of trees beyond the distant fenceline. Three foldable tables were set out under the tent. Genevieve was examining the fractured remains of a well-charred skeleton. I had already articulated what remained of the bones, and this amounted to about half of the usual total. I couldn't help but study the profile of the man hovering in the entrance, neither within, nor without. He was facing the dirt road which led to the farmhouse. A muscle in his jaw twitched intermittently, the only sign of an elevated stress level. A trickle of sweat wound its way from beneath the dark hair of his brow, along a strong cheekbone, over cheeks with a shadow of regrowth, over the clenched jaw and down his well-tanned neck to soak into the black button up shirt.

I forced my gaze back to study the blackened tibia of a woman who had been about my age at the time of her death when the man in the doorway spoke.

'We have company.'

A glance over his shoulder showed this to be true. A vehicle, travelling quickly, was raising a cloud of pale dust. From the corner of my eye, I saw our UN guards shift position, their hands moving to rest on weapons, their stance more erect, their bodies stretching to assume more space.

The vehicle was a black SUV, not much different from one I might find at home on a station in Australia, kitted out with floodlights, additional aerials and a custom cage on the back to lean on while hunting feral pigs, deer or culling kangaroos. But the weaponry on the back of this vehicle was no hunting shotgun, instead, it sported a pair of machine guns, manned by a figure in full combat gear, goggled against the rising dust, his lower face covered with a mask. All four seats in the vehicle were similarly occupied. Samir Al'Shani, shifted uncomfortably.

My hope they might just be a passing patrol was shattered when they decelerated slightly to slip through the gateway and pulled up in front of the shattered farmhouse, a cloud of dust obscured them for some moments. I scanned the vehicle for any indication of Ukrainian signage and was forced to admit there were likely Russians. My heart began to pound and a fine sheen of sweat that had nothing to do with the warm weather broke out on my brow. Slipping off my gloves and tucking them in my pocket I stepped up behind Al'Shani, whose expression when he glanced at me was unreadable. When the car doors opened and the men spilled out he moved to position himself slightly ahead of me. I barely noticed, intent on the man who I had taken for the group's leader, whose swaggering walk belied the weight of weapons on his person. The man's eyes skipped over the UN soldiers, his lips curling derisively, they slipped past me and settled on Samir Al'Shani. He opened with a stream of words I couldn't follow. While Russian and Ukrainian languages are related I was certain that the man's consonants rang with the harsher tone of the Russian accent. I had picked up a few words here and there in both Ukrainian and Russian, enough to order a drink, but the tone of the phrase akin to 'who is in charge here' was known to me despite the words being foreign.

I pushed forward to place myself beside Al'Shani, who had not, at that point, opened his mouth.

'I am Doctor Victoria Benino, with the *Ob'yednani Natsiyi*, the United Nations. And you are?'

I resisted the urge to shiver and step back when he turned his full gaze on me.

'How can I help you?' I asked when no reply was forthcoming.

'Show me your identification.' It was a demand, not a request, his English rough but understandable. We complied, well accustomed to the procedure. As the swaggering commander gestured to one of the others to step forward to check our identity, each of us showed our passports and verification documents issued by the United Nations. None of us released our grip on them. He stopped when he studied Al'Shani's, tearing it from the man's hands and passing it to his superior, who studied it closely, eyes narrowed as he scrutinised the man it had been taken from. He was not alone, a sharp eyed soldier, standing towards the back, his face obscured, was studying Al'Shani intently. His eyes narrowed.

'Demir Binici?'

I tried not to blink or frown as the man I knew as Samir Al'Shani nodded his head in acceptance of a different name. A frisson of fear steeled my spine as I wondered who it was exactly that I had spent the previous 36 hours with, Al'Shani, Benici or someone else entirely?

'This says you are a citizen of Turkey.'

'Türkiye.' He corrected with an easy smile.

'Why are you in our country, Demir Binici?'

From behind I noted that Al'Shani's jaw tightened at the suggestion that Ukraine, even the disputed Donetsk Oblast belonged to Russian forces, even if the one who addressed us bore no badge of the Russian army. When he spoke there was a subtle shift in his accent, one I took to be Turkish.

'I was visiting family in Dnipro when I heard the scientists,' he shrugged in our direction, 'were in need of translators. I speak some French, and Russian as well as English and a little Dutch.'

There was silence for a minute as the man shifted his gaze from the passport to Al'Shani/Benici's face.

'The pay is good,' said the man who had guided us to the bodies.

'Mr Binici's assistance has been very useful, even if he did get our team lost guiding us here. None of the Peacekeepers speak English, you see.' I lied, hoping my childhood drama classes would aid in the deception. Clearly, I was not in Samir/Demir's league.

The soldier closed our guide's papers, tapping the corner of his passport against the palm of his hand before slowly holding it out. Samir/Demir was casual in his movements as he reached out to grasp it.

Before he could take it a third soldier stepped up behind the first, speaking in hushed tones, a rapid staccato of guttural Russian.

The first man paused in the act of offering the papers, Samir's fingers closed on the other corner, leaving them suspended between the two, one heavily armed and the other, weaponless.

'My sergeant says he has seen you before.'

Our guide tipped his head, frowning slightly. From my angle, I could see the tension in his neck and shoulders, but I doubted the Russian could see it. He appeared to consider the man who had stepped up.

'I spent some time at the University in Simferopol about ten years ago. Were you ever there?

His voice was calm, even friendly.

'Captain, if you don't mind,' I interjected. 'We have a lot to do. I have an investigation to finish, and I am keen to get back to Kharkiv.'

My second lie was a careful one. It felt diplomatic to omit that we were part of the team exposing mass graves at Izyum. I had no idea if these men had been party to the violent attacks on civilians at Izyum but there was no need to connect myself with that investigation.

When the man's cold grey eyes met mine I gestured at scattered bones on the makeshift table we were using to sort the remains. This lot was charred black and heavily damaged. I was immensely grateful to see that Genevieve had covered the less burnt remains, the ones still clinging with flesh and dirt.

'They are burnt.' The man observed brusquely.

'Well, yes. We were told the house had been burnt and there were bodies inside. We were sent to investigate a possible war crime, but so far this just looks like an ordinary house fire. Tragic, but not concerning. We will be finished soon, I would think.'

I did not think I imagined the sharp sidelong look the sergeant who had challenged Samir/Demir gave the farmhouse, nor his surprise when I mentioned bodies.

By now the Captain's nose was crinkling as the odour of freshly unearthed remains, strong and pungent, assailed his senses.

'You are welcome to stay and add to our guard.' I shifted out of the way, gesturing he should step inside the shade of the tent. 'Protocol would require that I record all your names, but I can't see that as a problem. Genevieve, can you grab a pen?'

The man shifted, scuffing steel-shod feet in the dirt.

Although I doubted they understood a word the French peacekeepers shifted their stance, appearing relaxed but vigilant, hands resting comfortably on their weapons. I prayed silently to the God of my parents that the twins would not emerge from the forest with the next load of body parts.

It would seem luck was with us. The one I had come to think of as Sharp-Eyes shot another glance at Samir/Demir before muttering softly in Russian. The Captain seemed to consider the words before nodding but made no aggressive moves. 'Very good. We will leave you to finish your investigation. Keep a watchful guard, this area is not completely free of local insurgents.'

Pretending to be gulled into believing they were with the Ukrainian forces, I nodded as the man turned.

'Captain?' I called.

He hesitated, looking back over his shoulder.

'My guide will need his papers. Without it, we will never get through the roadblocks into Kharkiv.'

The man glanced at the bundle of papers in his hand, tossing them negligently into the dirt at Samir/Demir's feet as he turned back and strode toward the armoured car, his men following closely.

When they pulled out onto the dirt track I felt our guide shifting beside me and heard his low-voiced thanks. I did not look at him, instead, I waved cheerily in the direction of the departing vehicle. 'I think you would be wise to leave us now.'

I felt his nod as I turned to Genevieve. 'Wait ten minutes then slip down to the gravesite. Tell the boys to bag everything they can find. We are leaving in an hour and I don't want anything left. Make sure they obscure the grave before they return. Photograph everything.'

Hopefully, if we did need to return we would find it untouched. I turned back to Al'Shani, or Benici, or whoever he was. 'Please let the Peacekeepers know our intentions, then I think it is best you leave straight away. I trust you have a way back to wherever it is you really came from?' I didn't think it was the ancient Volvo in the dilapidated shed.

He nodded, glancing over at the tables with their covered remains.

'Take care of them.' It wasn't a question.

'Of course, we will. I trust Doctor Habermann has a way to contact you when we need to, Mr Binici?' I let my tone carry the challenge.

'Al'Shani.' He met my eye directly and corrected.

'I am sorry for your loss. We will do all we can to return your family to you and ensure the prosecution of those responsible.' I knew I sounded cold and far too pithy for the man who had buried his family and stood between me and the Russians but it was all I could offer.

I stretched out a hand and this time he took it in his. I really shouldn't have been surprised at the strength in his grip. I was startled by the warm tingle though. I had never felt it in anyone living.

Chapter Fourteen: A Servant of Rome

Rome, AD 74

Alexartos stood in the forum. Despite the hustle and bustle of the masses who had come to worship or petition the gods, to shop in the forums, to eat or drink in the *popinae* or *tabernae*, to watch the comings and goings as the law courts or in the Senate or simply to be seen, very few invaded the space that Alexartos occupied. In fact, they shied away, apologising and dropping their gaze should they get too close. He did not carry his sword, such a thing was not permitted in the heart of the empire but his clothing unapologetically declared: warrior. His tunic was dusty from travel and stained from saltwater from his crossing. His *caligae* were standard military issue. His leather breastplate was purposeful rather than decorative and marred from fulfilling its purpose. He stood in the shadow of the sculpture of Augustus and his four horses. The sculptor clearly knew horses, for he had even depicted the veins in their legs and the curl of the hair beneath their fetlock. Alexartos was almost tempted to reach out and brush his hands against the nearest beast, but that he knew such an action, even more than the travel-stained clothing, would identify him as a foreigner. Instead, he whistled at the boy sitting cross-legged in the shade, a charcoal stick in his hands, drawing a series of gladiators fighting, on the marble of the plinth the sculpture stood on. Alexartos could see the boy's art was not the first to be set there.

The boy looked up at him, wide-eyed. The scamp looked half-starved. Alexartos showed a glint of bronze between his fingers, making it disappear as soon as the boy's eyes recognised the offer.

'Take me to General Vespasian.'

'You mean Emperor Vespasian?'

Alexartos shrugged and nodded at the correction. Emperor or General made little difference to him. He had a report to give.

'Two *asses*.' The boy offered, shrewdly doubling the coin Alexartos had shown him. When he received a nod the boy dropped the charcoal stick, leaving it for the next artist, and brushed off some of the dust. With a glance to make sure his benefactor was following he shot off into the crowd. Alexartos followed.

α

Despite the missing military attire, Vespasian stood out immediately to Alexartos. His bearing was military, despite the glowing white toga with its broad swathe of red. He sat on the golden curule chair almost like he would a horse, his legs braced widely at the knee. Alexartos knew the moment his General saw him because the man stood immediately, strode through the mass of men huddled around him and crossed the space between them. Alexartos offered his forearm but the General gripped him in a brief but solid hug.

'Artos! It is good to see you. Look at you, still covered in dust. Didn't anyone show you to the bathhouse before sending you in here? Never mind. Clearly, you have news.'

Vespasian's arm braced his shoulder and pulled Alexartos along beside him, steering away from the waiting senators and out toward the gardens.

'General, I was sent with news from Judaea.'

Vespasian tutted. 'Princeps now, Artos.'

'Apologies, Princeps.'

Vespasian took a seat beside a fanciful fountain. A beast with a shape that was half horse, half fish, spouted water out its flaring nostrils.

'Princeps, I am sent to inform you that the mountain fort has fallen.'

Vespasian beamed. 'Excellent news. That will take the heart out of any further resistance. I guess you bring slaves and plunder? Have they been sent to the markets yet?'

Alexartos clenched his jaw and did not answer for a moment. His mind, far away on a red dirt mesa, high up above the plains below with its army of red-cloaked soldiers and siege machines. Above his head the endless blue sky and flies, clouds of them.

'Plunder, yes. Not much considering what the siege cost.'

'No matter, the sale of slaves will make up for it.'

Alexartos shook his head, half to shake the images from it, half in denial. 'We captured four. Two died on the way.'

The Princeps frowned. 'You lost two thousand slaves on the way?'

'No, Princeps. We lost two slaves.'

His General stared at him blankly.

'They took their lives, every man, woman and child on the mountain. We found four left alive.

The Emperor of Rome was silent. It was not hard to follow his thoughts. Hebrews did not kill themselves. It was against their faith. It made them excellent slaves because, unlike some other barbaric tribes, they would not take their lives and deprive their owners of a valuable asset. Vespasian himself had made a large fortune on the slaves he had taken in Jerusalem, hundreds of thousands of them. Finally, the Princeps nodded.

'I find I respect them for their choice. It was almost Roman of them.' The new Emperor's brows furrowed with a thought. 'Artos?'

'Yes, Princeps.'

'It seems wrong that some were enslaved when the rest went to meet their god. Find the ones that were left. Send them to meet the others.'

Alexartos' lips tightened fractionally but after considering his General's serious expression, he nodded.

'It was an expensive campaign. I was sorry to hear of the loss of your brother.'

Alexartos said nothing for a few moments, it was a pain too raw to think about. He acknowledged his General's comment with a short nod. 'Lucius Silva and his men have turned back to aid in establishing the new Roman colonies in Jerusalem.'

Vespasian nodded.

'Are there any messages you would have me take?'

The man in the white toga frowned.

'I will head back tomorrow, unless there is somewhere you would rather send me.' He offered in hope that returning to the dull duty of enforcing Roman law and custom in the devastated region was no longer where his General wanted him.

'No...'

Alexartos stared at the General.

'Artos, I would have you serve Rome here for a while. Enjoy the benefits of all you have fought for over the last ten years. I'll make you a procurator of the Praetorians. You can serve under Titus and Clemens, both good men, they will find you a position worthy of your experience.'

Stay in Rome? The seething stinking capital of the Empire. Rome, where the closest he might get to a horse was in the stands at the circus. The idea was repugnant to him. But Vespasian was his General, his Emperor. He pressed his fist to his chest and dropped his head in acquiescence. The Emperor clapped him firmly on the back, a blow which might have felled a lesser man.

'Excellent. Go, find my baths. Tell my steward you have my permission to bathe and have him find you clothing suitable to join us for dinner. You will share my couch and you can regale the prissy senators of Rome with stories of our conquests.'

Vespasian was grinning broadly at the thought. Alexartos had no choice.

α

Thalia considered her reflection. Kaeso had expertly twined her mother's pearls through her dark curls, more pearls, perfectly round and interspersed with emeralds and lapis lazuli traced her neck, leaving her with the impression of some dark goddess of the seas, Selucia perhaps, as she stared at the reflection in the mirror. It was the finest she owned, a perfectly polished surface, only the slightest of distortions marred her features, if she held her head just so it completely obfuscated what small swelling and bruising remained on her cheek. This most recent gift was the result of having failed to disclose a rumour she had heard about the dealings of one of Messalinus' rivals.

In the two years since the incident on the balcony, Thalia had, as her husband demanded, made herself useful to him, mingling with the wives of the wealthy and influential men of Rome, visiting their homes, inviting them to the Domus Aurea, sharing wine and food and baths and entertainments. And, most importantly, listening to their gossip. It had not taken long before they had associated the Consul's young Equite wife with passing on gossip. Never openly welcomed amongst them, her position as Consul's wife had ensured her invitation and grudging acceptance. But when Messalinus began to act on the tidbits she had shared with him in order to undercut business rivals or defame his political opponents with specious court cases, prosecuted by his clients, even the way they looked at her had changed. Although they could not turn their backs on the Consul's wife, they were far more careful with their words in her presence. Clearly, they failed to understand that she was not the only spy in their homes, that the burly guards who attended her, the litter bearers, even the pretty boy slaves who attended her person reported directly to Messalinus. She had been relieved when her husband had handed the Consulship to the next man and invitations had ebbed. Tonight was her first banquet in a sennight.

Thalia handed the mirror to Kaeso.

'Are you unhappy with the style, Domina?'

She met the boy's worried expression. 'No, Kaeso, you have very adept fingers. All the women I meet are envious of your talents. I could sell you in a heartbeat and the bidding war would be furious.'

She saw the boy's expression cloud then clear to an impassive mask.

'Forgive me, Kaeso, I spoke in jest.'

It was not appropriate to thank or apologise to a slave but the boy had proven himself far more loyal than she deserved. It was Kaeso who had provided the cool compresses that eased the swelling around her eyes the evening her sister, heavily pregnant with her latest husband's second son, had refused to acknowledge or speak to her after Messalinus had undermined a lucrative trade deal her husband, Publius Virgilius Maro, had invested in. This had left the man so close to penury that without a loan from Messalinus he could not afford to continue in the senate and now he was a very reluctant but indebted client. It was information Thalia had reluctantly shared, knowing that the slave beside her had also heard the tidbit, a boastful discussion of the house Maro had intended on buying when the shipment of marble he had invested in to supply the ever-inflated needs of Vespasian's building projects arrived from Libya. Still, Clementia had not forgiven her.

Her father, Messalinus' co-consul, had looked at her with grave disappointment and he could no longer hide the curl of his lip that implied disgust when he sat beside her husband, his fellow Consul. Neither her father, nor her sister understood. *How could they?* Failure to disclose such information would have resulted in punishment, either like the bruise she wore tonight, or in some other twisted manner. Once he had punished her by taking Kaeso back into his bed for a month. She had been forced to watch the boy grow thin and pale and silent and was able to do nothing to save him. She preferred to wear the bruises.

Tonight's banquet, at which Vespasian was guest of honour was hosted by Tiberius Plautius Silvanus Aelianus, an ageing hero of Rome, twice consul, urban prefect, pontifex and feted general whose provision of grain during the great famine a decade earlier saved many in Rome from starvation. Aelianus was a good man and his wife Aemilia was one of the few who would speak kindly to her and include her in conversation when the women of Rome would have cut her completely. It was for Aemilia that she wore her current bruise, having failed to betray a rumour overhead about the woman's discrete and short-lived affair with the Emperor.

Thalia tipped back her head and let Kaeso begin applying the fine powders that would conceal the bruise and the collection of purpled fingerprints his pet Praetorian had left on both her upper arms. She was grateful that the bruise was not on her left cheek, which had taken a long time to heal after cracking under Messalinus' hand. Since that day, her husband had never laid a hand on her, he had his pet Praetorian do it for him. Petronius seemed to have no qualms about inflicting whatever punishment her husband devised, whether it was burning priceless scrolls, administering a beating or retrieving Kaeso to warm Messalinus' bed. Once, after he had administered a beating, Thalia had been certain she felt the press of an erection against her when he 'helped' her up to return her to her room. The man made her skin crawl although she was fairly certain Messalinus would have killed him for overstepping orders and forcing himself on her. He did not tolerate anyone taking that which he considered his.

When Kaeso put down his brushes and turned to retrieve the *palla* that would match her gown, Thalia critically considered the now near-invisible bruises before turning to the boy who held out the sea-green head covering she had chosen.

α

Until he saw the woman in the green, Alexartos thought he was the most uncomfortable person at the Emperor's dinner. Alexartos hated reclining to eat and had only been comfortable that night on the occasions Vespasian forgot himself and raised from his elbow to sit upright, gesturing garrulously as he recounted some battle or another. Then it was the other guests who looked uncomfortable, forced to sit as he did. Oddly, the woman in green seemed most comfortable when sitting too, at least until Vespasian remembered himself and slumped back down to his elbow.

Alexartos was not entirely sure what drew his eyes back to her. She sat in near silence. From time to time, when Titus was too busy, she reached out to take something from the shared platter and place it between her husband's lips or on his upright palm, her mouth moving softly to tell him what each morsel was. The matching jewellery on each wrist tinkled musically with each movement she made. He didn't think a single bite passed her lips. The man, ex-consul Messalinus, puzzled Alexartos. He was clearly blind. Although his eyes followed the voices of those he conversed with there was a blankness to them that revealed the truth. That in itself was unusual, for Rome seemed to scorn any evidence of disability or imperfection. Still, Vespasian's golden son clearly had great affection for the man, and the gold head and red-gold head were positioned so close at times it was hard to tell they were two distinct beings. Titus too, fed the man with his own hand and ensured his wine goblet was kept full and near at hand. When their heads came together the dark-haired woman would look anywhere but at her husband, her expression so blank it might have been sculpted, and by a poor sculptor who could not quite capture real human expression. Artos pictured the sculpture, a sea nymph, he imagined, judging by the shade of her gown and the pearls strung through her hair.

In truth, he could not work out what it was that drew him. Aside from the blank expression, she would not have been the muse for a sculptor, not in Rome at least. Her shape was rounded with curves that were generous and better befitted an earth mother figure in his homelands, than the slender goddesses of Vespasian's Rome. Her clothing was of obvious quality in costly shades and rich silks. The jewels that decked her were expensive and tasteful but unlike other women who constantly touched their adornments to draw attention, her neck may as well have been bare. She had a pleasant, symmetrical face, with well-manicured brows and eyes so dark they seemed an abyss. He was sure that her left cheek was bruised, but she kept it turned away, both from her husband and her Emperor so he couldn't certain. She spoke only when spoken to. None of the women that he saw engaged her in conversation, or so much as glanced in her direction. Not even the pretty wife of their host, seated beside her husband and Vespasian, acknowledged her presence or departure.

She left the festivities as early as was decent, revealing matching anklets that chimed in concert with her wrists as she moved. He didn't think her husband even noticed.

Chapter Fifteen: The Trouble with Twins

Izyum, 2023

I was grateful for the business of the morgue around me to distract me from replaying the sensation in my hand when Al'Shani held it. Back in Izyum, Genevieve was quickly reclaimed by my colleagues but I was allowed to keep the twins to help me sort through the remains in the bags.

Laying out what we had on the benches in the old morgue we quickly discovered that it was indeed likely that, as Al'Shani had stated, there was something of at least ten bodies here. Starting with the skulls each on their own bench we began the painstaking process of trying to piece the remnants together. Two of the remains were elderly. A male adult had been riddled with at least a half dozen bullets, I was not yet sure which had killed him. Two women had been shot at point blank range in the back of the head, execution style. One had fibres of rope in the remaining tissue of her wrists, it tangled with the prayer beads that had been bound there. Tim took several close-up photographs before we moved on. The bodies were burnt from their close proximity to an explosion, some more badly charred than others. We had many parts of bodies that we needed to identify before determining which set of remains they fit with. Some fitted neatly together but we soon discovered a problem. The body of a small boy, perhaps four years of age, had two left feet which, despite the popular adage about poor dancing, was categorically impossible. There were remains of three other juveniles, but none matched our spare left foot, one already having one, the other being too old.

We stood around the bench looking down at the feet, neither wearing shoes, both badly decomposed. One matched the kneebone and femur of a hip bone that had been wearing a pair of blue trousers, still with a handful of marbles in the pocket. The other did not. In addition, we had a torso that had been draped in fabric Tim insisted was a spiderman shirt. Both Tim and Jon were staring at the bench across the room where the paperwork, which included the statement made by Al'Shani about who he had buried. None of us had opened the front cover, not being willing to let the findings prejudice us in the arrangement of the bodies, preferring to work with the puzzle we had and no preconceived assumptions.

'No,' I said. 'Not until we have done all we can.'

It was hard, walking away from that bench, leaving the two left feet sitting there. As we kept working it became apparent that it was not merely two feet. An assortment of duplicate parts had accumulated on the bench with the feet. There was little doubt that we were looking at two children of remarkably similar age and size.

Many hours later I was forced to concede both success and defeat. We had successfully proven there were at least ten bodies and for each one we were able to identify unique parts. We had removed teeth and bone samples from each corpse and sent them to be measured and tested. What clothing had been salvaged had been sent to be cleaned, except that associated with bench six. We had secured samples for DNA testing for the remains on all of the ten benches. These would be cross-referenced with samples Al'Shani had already given. Dental records had been checked to give us a few names but we still had three benches to consider, one empty, one with a jumble of duplicate parts and one with a collection of those pieces too damaged to link definitively with anything we had sorted so far.

Finally, unable to do more I nodded at Tim, who shot across the room with an energy I could not even imagine summoning. Jon and

I watched as he slipped through the sheets and let out a holler, shooting a fist in the air. 'Twins!'

'Identical or fraternal?' I asked.

His expression fell. 'Identical.'

Damn. DNA testing could not help us with our mystery.

'Any mention of what they were wearing?'

He scanned back through the information. We watched his focus skip and jump across the pages. Finally, he shook his head. 'Only that they were boys. It was their fourth birthday party when it happened.'

We were silent for a time, digesting the information, fully aware of the small body parts on the table before us. I racked my brain for any other way but in the end, admitted to myself that I would have to speak with Al'Shani. I could not say why I never considered sending either Tim or Jon to do the job.

I found my hand in my pocket, as I often did now when I was thinking, gently rubbing my fingers over the lunula that I still swore I would return to Herculaneum at some point. I could hardly send it by post though. Especially not from here. As I touched the now familiar shape my eyes fell on the short chain of beads I recognised as a *misbaha*, Islamic prayer beads, they had been wrapped around the bones of the right wrist and hand of one of the female victims. Dental records confirmed this to be Elirë, Samir's wife. We had removed a bullet from her skull that had been administered execution style. The bullet fragments were evidence that would be used in court. My eyes slid back to the beads. Perhaps I could return this small token, once I had it cleaned. That would give me time to think about how I would begin the conversation.

Ω

Habermann agreed that Al'Shani would need to be interviewed and given the likelihood of our lines being tapped, it was agreed that I was the best person to send. I could travel by UN convoy to the outskirts of the city. From there the recently reinstated Metro system would take me to the city. I was given permission to take the *misbaha* and return it to him.

'Are you able to keep a straight face when you interview him? There is no need for the poor man to know the details and it's best if he learns nothing that would alter his testimony in any way.'

I narrowed my eyes at the suggestion I was unable to hide my thoughts. Habermann sighed.

'I was able to convince the Russians that we were no threat.' I omitted the fact that I had been forced to hastily leave the tent after they had departed to throw up and it had been several hours before I had stopped shaking.

He considered me sceptically.

Ω

The outskirts of the city of Kharkiv had sustained the most damage during the Russian bombardment. In many places the buildings, blackened piles of rubble still stood much as they had immediately after the attack. In others, efforts had been made to clear the piles of mangled metal and cement and great empty spaces were left. Typically, my UN escorts spoke little English so the hours it took to reach the city were ones of silent contemplation of the horrors that the people of Ukraine had suffered.

Not as many had died in Kharkiv as in Izyum but the damage was still sobering.

The people were sober too. Some looked at me, hedged in by my two armed UN escorts with curiosity, others with suspicion, many faces were blank and empty.

I was to meet Samir Al'Shani at the Universytet Metro Station so my guards had determined that using the newly restored metro was a wise choice. Underground travel was safer than risking building collapse above ground. And besides, many of the streets of Kharkiv were still obstructed by the rubble.

No one had warned me about the Metro.

Each time we emerged from the flickering darkness and slowed into a new station my jaw dropped even further and the amusement of my escorts grew, white smiles beamed out of their dark faces. The design of each station was a unique architectural marvel that left me itching to hop out and explore, but when my fingers touched my phone to take photos my guards shook their heads. Despite their grandeur, it was clear that the metro had been used as a bomb shelter during the worst of the bombings and was still in use by many as a temporary home. The squalor of these emergency accommodations was at stark odds with the surroundings.

When we hopped from the brightly painted yellow and blue train I was greeted by an avenue of white marble-lined pillars, lit by immense chandeliers hung from cupolas that dotted the length of the station. Unable to resist I defied the clear warnings given by my guards and lifted my phone as though checking a map and took a series of quick snaps to record the scene. One of these I immediately sent to my mother in lieu of the dozens of messages I had failed to send over the months I had been in Ukraine. I accompanied it with the briefest of messages assuring her I was still alive. Then, ignoring the dozens of unread messages on the phone I tucked it back in the satchel, held tight against my chest. Kharkiv, like many cities in Europe, was a hotbed of petty theft and pickpocketing was rife, especially now so many of the inhabitants were homeless. Foreigners were always a good mark and I knew my gaping was a clear indicator I was not a local. Armed though they were, I did not trust my guards would keep me safe from the swift fingers of a pickpocket. I resumed gaping openly as commuters bustled past, up the stairway and out into the brighter light of day.

I let my gaze drift over the scene and nearly skipped past a well-dressed figure in a pair of khaki chinos and a white button-up shirt, rolled to his elbows. He was leaning against one of the marble pillars, an open newspaper spread before him. But as he meticulously folded the paper and tucked it under an arm, I recognised him. He looked so neat and handsome that I had the irrational desire to pull my phone back out to check my appearance. I had little doubt bouncing over rough roads for hours before being shuffled down into the metro had done little for it. I had not even really considered wearing something other than my trademark attire, today's turtleneck a pale mauve over my well-worn black pants. Nervously touching my hair, I was grateful it had remained more or less in place and was more Lara Croft than Medusa. With a momentary consideration for my latent vanity, I tucked a few flyaway strands behind my ear and patted down the bubbles that had escaped my braid and reminded myself that my track record with handsome men was abysmal.

He was crossing towards me now with a nod to my guards and an open-handed gesture that implied he was no threat. As he neared I was met with my usual social paralysis. Do I kiss his cheek in the European fashion, offer to shake hands, or simply say 'hello'? His brief smile suggested he had read my mind.

'Dr Benino.' He did not reach out a hand, instead flashing his identification for my guards. The shift of his head gestured towards the stairs. 'This way.'

'Thank you for meeting me here.' I offered a depreciating smile and fell in step beside him, the UN soldiers taking up position behind. He took the stairs two at a time, his long legs making it look effortless. I spared a brief glance at the station behind me before following.

We emerged into a wide cobbled space. It was empty but for a half dozen military vehicles and a few heavily armed soldiers sporting the Ukraine flag as a reminder that the war for Ukraine was far from over. He strode across the space towards a leafy park. I followed, letting his silence set the scene for a conversation I was not entirely comfortable having. The shady park was a welcome respite from the swiftly approaching summer. Sheltered by the trees and surrounded by green lawns and park benches it was hard to imagine that we were in a city, let alone a warzone. The park looked largely untouched by the fighting. Had it been in Australia, I would have expected to see couples holding hands on park benches and families on picnic rugs. There were people, but they hurried purposefully or lingered, casting nervous glances.

I was startled to hear a trumpeting sound followed by a guttural roar I recognised from holidaying in Africa. It was completely out of place here.

Al'Shani smiled, 'The Kharkiv Zoo is through there.' He gestured to a well-worn path but led us in another direction. We crossed a narrow street and continued down a cobbled pavement. A line of glossy green trees ended startlingly with four or five blackened and shattered husks, the building behind them missing, only a mountain of wreckage, including a collection of burnt-out car carcasses remained. The next building resembled a mechano kit, blacked bricks gave way to a jumble of metal jutting out at angles, like badly set braces. There were windows missing from the building on the opposite side of the street, some gaping like empty eye sockets, still boarded or covered in plastic, the apartments still liveable. Rubble reached the roadway and we skirted around it, cement blocks, powdered bricks and twisted metal invaded an open space, a children's playground. Although the brightly painted equipment was free of damage it was empty. Parents no longer trusted in their children's safety. I imagined small faces pressed against the glass in surrounding buildings, looking wistfully at the swings.

Al'Shani stopped outside the next building, pushed a key to a common entry and ushered us inside. The UN soldiers stepped closer to me, their hands moving to their weapons as though they suspected Al'Shani of nefarious purposes. He led us up several flights of stairs before stopping at a red-painted door. When he opened it and moved to usher me inside, one of the soldiers held out a hand, said a few words in what I took as an African dialect and gestured for us both to move to one side.

Al'Shani shrugged, gesturing for the men to enter. One did, obviously doing a quick check of the space beyond the door before returning with a nod.

'After you,' he said, his hand settled on the small of my back, barely touching as he guided me through the doorway. I had barely registered the touch and the warm tingle that came with it when he turned to face our escorts. A flurry of words was exchanged and, rather than follow, the pair settled themselves, taking up positions on either side of the doorway.

'My apartment is not large. And I'd rather not have armed men in there.' He eyed the guns they carried distastefully and spoke in English.

'I'm sorry,' I replied. 'We have rules and I am not allowed to travel without them.'

Al'Shani shrugged. 'They are happy to wait outside.'

Chapter Sixteen: The Professor of Linguistics

Kharkiv, 2023

I considered the space that opened before me. A small apartment, a single open space with a curving metal staircase to a loft above. The external wall was bare red brick, a bookshelf loaded with books boasting titles in several languages, including a ubiquitous copy of Homer's *Iliad*, in Greek I noticed, took up the narrow space between two bare arched windows. Beneath each sat a radiator. The floor was made up of mismatched and discoloured tiles, adding to the industrial feel a number of exposed pipes ran overhead and the lights were too-bright fluoros. A faded cream-coloured lounge took up one wall, a Turkish carpet hanging behind it. A round plush red ottoman and a glass topped table were the only other items of furniture, along with the four matched grey chairs. It was a tidy space, everything appeared to have its place, with one exception. On one end of the lounge a neat pile of sheets and a patchwork quilt, not unlike Morag's, implied the lounge doubled as a bed.

A familiar soft toy figure, Bluey the Australian cartoon dog, perched on top of the pile.

'When my parents lost their home in Donetsk they moved to an apartment in Kharkiv. They lost it in the bombing so they have taken up residence on my couch until they find a new apartment. Sadly, they are not the only ones looking and of late there are many fewer apartments.'

I nodded, glancing out the window at the shattered building across the way, wondering idly where he had hidden his parents for the day.

'Coffee?' He asked.

I turned from the window. 'Please.'

Al'Shani began opening cupboards and extracting items. I eyed the bicycle perched above the cupboards, raising a curious eyebrow.

'When the metro was shut, cycling was the only way to get around.'

Standing in the man's home I became acutely aware of my purpose in meeting him, patting my knapsack to reassure myself as I pondered how to start a difficult conversation, when it occurred to me to wonder what he had actually said to the guards, and how he had known what language to say it in.

'What language do they speak?'

He glanced at me.

'The guards,' I clarified. 'You spoke to them, they answered.'

'Chadian Arabic. They are from Eastern Chad.'

'Chad. You speak French, Russian, English, and what was it… Chadian Arabic?'

A half smile as he sat. 'It is a *lingua franca*, a bastardisation of French and Arabic common in Northern Africa. I speak nine languages well, and another four or so, enough to get by.

'What are the others?'

'Along with Ukrainian? English, French, Russian, Spanish, Italian, German, Arabic and Turkish. It's not so hard, many of the romance languages are similar, and once you know Arabic many of the Middle Eastern dialects are easily picked up.'

I shook my head, he didn't even appear to be boasting. 'And the ones you speak a little of?

'A little Hindi, Mandarin Chinese, enough Latin to transcribe a text and a touch of Aussie, mate.'

The last he shifted into a decent Australian twang. I found myself smiling.

'Why? Are you a natural polyglot or just a world wanderer?'

He added several spoonfuls of dark grounds to the water in the copper pot, stirring slowly and carefully before looking towards me, and considered me for a long moment before answering. 'I am a Professor of Linguistics at the National University in Kyiv.'

I didn't know quite how to respond. My farmer, who had buried his family in a field in a village south of Kharkiv, who had worked beside me in the farmhouse to find fragments of their bones, was a linguistics expert?

'As Professor Al'Shani, or Demici?'

He raised a dark eyebrow, his lips compressed. 'You have a good memory for names,' he observed. 'Demir Benici is my cousin. When I fled Ukraine I stayed with them in Türkiye for many years. Demir and I are the same age and look similar so he loaned me his documents should I ever require them. One of the Russians looked familiar, I didn't want to leave him my name.'

I recalled the fellow who had seemed to recognise Al'Shani. I wanted to ask the obvious question but he turned from me and took two cups from a high cupboard, filled them with water from a bottle in the fridge and set them atop the glass table. They clinked as he set them down.

The rich aroma of quality coffee made me glance up. Decent coffee seemed to be an anathema in a warzone.

'Wherever did you find real coffee?' I blurted.

Al'Shani was standing by the gas stovetop, a long handled copper pot, dark foam simmered at its rim. This he scooped off effortlessly, depositing a spoon of it in each of the waiting cups.

'I could tell you, but then I'd have to kill you. The black market is no joking matter in Kharkiv.'

Immediately, I painted a mental picture of balaclava-clad men in leathers running a black market from a dark corner of the chandeliered splendour of the metro station. Privately amused by my imaginings I crossed to the arched window.

Out the window, I could see the skeleton of the apartment building across the road. The outer wall was missing and several apartments were open to the elements, still partly furnished. A few floors were missing entirely. I wondered what had become of the families who had lived there. Had they joined the huddling masses who had existed in the Metro tunnels, left homeless by the bombs? In the street below, a sparse but steady flow of Kharkivan locals bustle past, clumping occasionally, briefly, looking nervously over their shoulders before moving on, automatically creating space between them. One older woman, hair wisps of silver, crowned in fabric flowers had set up a stall out of wooden boxes on the street corner and called out to interest passers-by in whatever she was selling. A few stopped, but most ignored her.

'Sugar?'

'No.'

His brow became quizzical. 'Have you ever had Turkish coffee?'

I shook my head. He immediately reached for a pot of sugar and added three generous spoonfuls to the burbling liquid, stirring it carefully. Al'Shani brought the spoon to his lips, blew on it before tasting, then added another spoon of sugar, giving the mixture one last stir before pouring the thick dark liquid into the waiting cups. The smell was enough to make my mouth water.

'Please, have a seat.' He gestured to the grey chairs.

I pulled out one of the chairs and sat. My knapsack cradled in my lap. On the table an old aluminium can, decorated with coloured paddle pop sticks and stuffed with pencils and crayons in varying sizes, sat above a pile of colouring books. On the floor beneath the table a cane basket overflowed with rolls of brightly coloured wool, stuck with knitting needles. Like Bluey, an odd hint that Al'Shani didn't live alone.

Without spilling a drop, though both cups were brimming, he brought the platter to the table and set it before me.

When I reached to take a cup he held out a warning finger. Crossing back to the cupboards he pulled out a cake tin and a plate, which he piled with squares of what looked like thick golden cake. These two were placed on the table between us before he sat across from me. The sweet honey scent of the cake mingled with the richer aroma of the dark brew.

'Stop!' Al'Shani warned as I reached for the cup once more.

I froze my hand, mid-gesture.

'This is *cesve*. A favourite in our country. We borrowed it from the Ottomans and as with Turkish coffee there is an art to drinking *cesve*. Listen carefully.'

I did as he gently explained the complex process of appreciating the rich near-black liquid. I followed his instruction to the letter, watching him sip first the water, then careful not to disturb the grounds, lifting the rich liquid to his lips.

It was piping hot, exactly as I liked my coffee, rich, earthy and bittersweet and it seemed to infuse directly into my veins. I sighed deeply as I set the cup down.

Al'Shani smiled, before a serious expression filtered through. 'Now. What can I do for you, Ms Benino?'

'Victoria please, although my friends call me Tori.'

Friends? Really? Who was I kidding? Co-workers with whom I was comfortable would perhaps come closer. My fault really, I felt guilty about the dozen or more messages from Holly that I had failed to answer.

He seemed to consider this.

'Vittoria,' he repeated, with a husky intonation on the 'r', clearly determining that whatever we were, we were not friends. I was not sure why this disappointed me. He pronounced the name in a similar way to my father, but with enough altered inflection that this did not bother me. 'What can I do for you, Vittoria?'

His gaze was so intense that I hesitated, before remembering the beads in my satchel. My hand went to my knapsack and I rustled through it, one-handed, locating the handkerchief I had wrapped them in. I brought it out and held it towards him. Al'Shani eyed the offering warily, reluctant to take it, so I unfolded the first layer of cloth, revealing the gleaming carnelian beads beneath. I saw the breath leave him and his fingers flex then clench. I placed the misbaha on the table between us and dropped my hands back into my lap, watching him intently. His eyes had taken on the liquid darkness I had noted in our earlier meeting. I took a sip of coffee to give him some measure of privacy for his thoughts. Finally, he reached across and picked them up between finger and thumb, revolving his hand so they fell over his fingers and nestled in and around the palm of his hand, much like we had found them in his wife's grip. He clenched his hand around them and closed his eyes, breathing deeply for a minute.

'They were Elirë's,' he finally spoke, pronouncing the name differently from the way I had heard it in my head as I read it in the file. 'They were my wife's.'

'I know,' I spoke. 'Elirë.' I tried to capture his intonation. 'It is a beautiful name.'

His smile was fleeting. 'She was a beautiful woman.'

His gaze fastened on mine. 'You knew they were hers.'

I nodded. I could hardly explain how intimately I was acquainted with the bones of his family. 'I thought you might want them back. Early, I mean. You will have to sign for them of course...' I was rambling. His gaze never shifted.

'Then you have identified her remains.'

I nodded again. 'Yes. We have identified all of them except...' I forced myself to hold his gaze. 'Except the twins.'

He nodded.

'Because of their identical DNA, we cannot tell them apart. I need to know more about them to be able to correctly determine who is who. I need you to tell me about them.'

I fought to keep my face as still and blank as I could as I listened intently while Al'Shani spoke of his children. I could not let him see that the news that Irek had lost one of his two front teeth when three was irrelevant as there was too little left there to identify anyway. Nor when he mentioned how Artur had broken his left arm falling off the barn roof while chasing cats. And I kept particularly still when he recounted Artur's habit of keeping marbles in his pockets on the off chance he could encourage anyone to play a match with him. I only permitted myself the flicker of a smile when he mentioned that Irek always, *always*, wore his favourite Spiderman shirt and that on the evening before their birthday, Eirie had to wash it and dry it over the fireplace as he slept.

When he finished speaking nearly an hour later we had finished the coffee as well as two plates of the sweet amber cake he called *babka*. The second round of coffee was just dregs in the bottom of the porcelain cup. We were both silent once more and I let my eyes drift to the window. I wanted so badly to ask him how he had done it. How he had found, collected and carried the mangled remains across the field, dug a hole and gone back for more... Knowing the state of the remains I could not imagine the fortitude it must have taken to carry limbs and pieces rather than bodies across that field. But I couldn't ask. I couldn't comprehend and part of me really didn't want to.

Already it was almost impossible some days to deal with the remains I was assigned, not knowing their names or faces, not until they had been stripped to bare white bones and all their humanity stripped clean. In the same way, our humanity was stripped bare as we worked and clearly, the humanity of those who committed the atrocities in the first place was missing.

I was startled when his fingers brushed my own.

'Where did you go just then?'

My eyes were blurred and I turned from him to blink them clear. He left his hand beside my own, not quite touching.

'I'm sorry. I didn't mean to upset you. It must be very hard to do what you do and remain untouched.'

I summoned a smile. He stood, taking the plate and cups back to the sink and leaving them there. 'What time does your train leave?'

A glance at my watch showed it was later than I thought. 'In two hours.'

'And you have all the answers you need now?' he asked.

I nodded, suspecting strongly that he knew just which pieces of information I had banked for reference and which I had discarded, he struck me as someone who read faces well.

'Then allow me to walk you back to the station.' He stood, offering me a hand.

He frowned when I took it. I wondered if he felt the now familiar warmth between us too. He clenched a fist when I removed my hand and I pretended to ignore it.

'Thank you for the coffee. I haven't had a decent cup since I left Italy.'

He nodded, pointing out the way to the door, as though in the small space I might have forgotten where the exit was. The soldiers straightened as I walked through the door, the smell of cigarettes lingered in the hallway. When we exited the building the old woman from the corner glanced up at me. Al'Shani crossed to her, greeting her warmly as I stood awkwardly on the bottom step. After a moment he rifled through her boxes as she talked to him softly. They were ribbons, I realised, most the width of my hand and each meticulously embroidered with designs. I had seen many like them in this country. As he sifted through the collection the old woman looked over at me. Her eyes were a startling blue, complementing the patriotic yellows and blues of her costume.

Al'Shani straightened, folded two ribbons around his fist and handed her a couple of crumpled notes. She smiled a gap-toothed smile, said something I could not interpret and patted his hand with her liver-spotted one.

He answered her as I stepped towards her scant stall. I had a few notes in my pocket, I could buy some ribbons to send home to my mother. She would pass them on to my sister and niece. But before I could get close Al'Shani crossed back towards me, an arm out to shuffle me in the opposite direction, back towards the park and the station. I peered over his shoulder, the old woman eyed me curiously, but he was leading me away from her before I had the chance to express a desire to look over her vivid collection or purchase anything. Wary of the warmth of his touch and the way he had clenched his fist earlier after touching me, I avoided his arm and turned to follow his direction. We both walked silently now, filled with our own thoughts. When we crossed the open square to the opening of the Metro, he stopped at the stairs leading down.

He hesitated for a moment before pulling the bundle of ribbon from his pocket, removing one and returning the other.

'A gift for you.' He held the colourful swatch in hand and held it towards me.

'I can't,' I stammered.

'Why not? You brought me a gift.' He moved his wrist to show the carnelian beads wrapped around it.

'But they were yours, already.'

'And I am grateful for their return. Our women, our old women, are famous for their needlework. It is a piece of our country to take home with you.'

I hesitated. The ribbon itself was black, embroidered with a garden of flowers in greens and purples and yellows. I remembered the words the old woman had spoken.

'What did she say to you when she gave it to you?'

Al'Shani's eyes narrowed thoughtfully. 'Do you really want to know?'

I nodded.

'She said I chose well, that the ribbon would offset your beauty.'

To distract from the flush of heat to my face I admired the beautiful shades he had chosen and as much out of discomfort as avarice I nodded and held out a hand for the ribbon.

He pulled his hand back. 'No. Allow me.'

He stepped close. He draped the richly embroidered fabric over my head before stepping behind me, shifting my dark braid to tie the band at the nape of my neck, brushing against me with his fingers as he knotted it. Then he stood back, tugged a little here and there allowing the long ends to fall down over my shoulders and down my chest before tipping his head gently to the side and offering a smile, it triggered the dimple in his cheek.

'She was right. Beautiful.'

I told myself he was referring to the ribbon but the look in his dark eyes told me otherwise and left my cheeks flushed. Flattered and horrified by the surge of emotions I felt I forced my eyes to the beads about his wrist. The ones I had found on the remains I had processed. His gaze followed my own.

'Travel safely, Vittoria. And thank you for these.' He flicked his wrist. 'Call me when there is anything more you need to know.'

I would like to say I did not watch him walk away, but I cannot. He never looked back. I snatched my hand from the silken ribbon when I realised I was touching it, and pretended not to see my Chadian guards swap a smile. I did not realise until I boarded the train that he had never signed for the beads. Dr. Habermann was going to kill me. As I glanced at my phone to check the time a message vibrated in, crossing the screen while I watched.

Who is the beautiful man smiling at you? Mum

I frowned, tapped open my camera roll and did a two-fingered sweep to zoom into the photo. There, at the station we had just pulled away from, standing beside a marble pillar, a dark-haired man smiled at me from above his paper. Al'Shani. With a double tap, I deleted the image and settled in my seat, determined to ignore my mother's question.

Chapter Seventeen: A Taste of Freedom

Rome, AD 74

Titus spent little time finding him a position and with his few belongings, Alexartos soon found himself striding uphill towards the immense building overlooking Vespasian's new building project, a fighting arena, unlike anything the world had ever seen. The so-called Domus Aurea, once Nero's palace, put the modest Imperial palace on the Palatine to shame in both size and splendour and while the Empire's newest Praetorian could see why bluff Vespasian, the warrior emperor, would feel uncomfortable here. Alexartos could not help but wonder that he would permit another to reside there.

After identifying himself to the door slave he was drawn through to the atrium where the man he was to protect was presiding over the morning *salutatio* ritual. The immense hall was packed with supplicants waiting on the attention of their patron, one of the richest men in Rome, the same Lucius Valerius Catullus Messalinus he had noticed at the banquet. As he took a position at the rear of the hall, behind the queue of patricians, equestrians, merchants and debtors, in that order, Alexartos was surprised to find his Prefect, Titus, seated on the gilded couch beside the former consul, much as he had at the banquet. He was further surprised when the emperor's son caught his eye and gestured imperiously that he should move forward. When Alexartos hesitated, the Prefect leaned and spoke to a pretty slave boy by their side. Following the line of Titus' pointed finger, the boy slipped down into the crowd. Titus leaned his head closer to that of his friend and whispered in his ear. The man nodded and a second slave boy was sent scampering from the room in another direction.

In short time the pretty lad appeared beside him, a musical tinkling accompanied each step and Alexartos could see the fine chains of bells around both wrists and ankles, not an unexpected accessory for the slaves of a blind man.

'*Salve*, Praetorian. My master welcomes you and would have you present yourself to him. You must follow me.'

Alexartos nodded and followed the boy, the mass of waiting supplicants parting like a river around a boulder as they saw his new Praetorian uniform and the sword he was permitted to carry as a defender of the Emperor. A few gave scathing glances in his direction as he was brought immediately to the foot of the dais on which their patron's couch resided. Others measured him carefully to ascertain exactly where he fitted to be advanced so swiftly.

Alexartos stopped beside the boy, who bowed to Titus and Messalinus before slipping back into position as wine-bearer. He waited to be introduced. It was Titus who took the duty upon himself.

'Messalinus, allow me to present a sign of the Emperor's great regard. The Praetorian, Artos, lately come from the Judaean provinces. Artos served with me when we brought down the walls of Jerusalem, though he spent some time in the desert after that. He is a good man and a fearsome warrior.'

Messalinus' eyes gazed emptily over him. 'Welcome to my household, Praetorian Artos. I am honoured by this sign of the Emperor's favour.'

It was not a new sign. Alexartos had spotted no fewer than four other Praetorians beside entrances to the room, all near dozing with boredom, but still maintaining the alert position drilled into them. None of them were men who were known to him. This was not surprising, he knew few men in Rome. A fifth stood behind the Consul, one hand on the hilt of his gladius. Alexartos recognised the hooded eyes. Petronius, one of Titus' favoured henchmen. A brutal bull better known for his thuggish intimidation tactics than his prowess in battle, though he was infamous for both.

Alexartos inclined his head, not for the man who couldn't see but for those who could and might report. 'I am honoured to serve.'

'Excellent. One of Titus' men, from Jerusalem. We are fortunate indeed.'

Messalinus' urban drawl held a tone that suggested his actual feelings strayed far from his words. More tinkling of bells drew closer and the man's blind gaze fixed on the sound.

'Ah. There you are.' He sat up, making a small space on the couch beside him. Titus stood to make additional space, taking up position behind the couch as though he, like his Praetorians, were on guard duty.

A woman stepped up beside him, moving past him to take the steps to the dais, her silken stola and deep purple palla brushing him as she passed along with the scent of crocuses, a heady scent that reminded him immediately of the plain he had once called home and the delicate white blooms that pushed their way from the earth in spring each year. His wife had worn them in her hair. The woman took a seat beside the consul, close but not touching him, tucking her feet underneath her.

'Praetorian Artos, this is my wife, Arrecina Quartia.'

Alexartos did not miss the way her gaze dropped when he spoke her name and her mouth tightened. Like the Praetorian, Petronius, he had met her father, Marcus Arrecinus Clemens briefly in the Judaea, where they had fought together at Vespasian's side. He knew Clemens had served as one of Vespasian's two Prefects alongside Titus and that the older man had been honoured with a position as Consul alongside Messalinus and that in the following year, he would serve as Governor in Hispania, while rumour suggested Messalinus would take the more profitable governorship of Crete and Cyrenaica, or perhaps the still richer prize of Macedonia. The girl shared his mass of dark hair, which, in the father, was liberally shot with grey and worn in a warrior's cue rather than cut short in the Roman style. Other than that, there was little familial resemblance. Arrecinus was tall and lithe, skin dark from exposure and perhaps a hint of African descent, limbs tangled with hewn veins like an ancient grapevine. The man's frame had spoken of sparseness and endurance, the girl was on the short side of average and plump and soft in all the right places. Alexartos suspected she would barely come to his shoulder. Was she perhaps ashamed of her equestrian origin? Certainly, she was fortunate in her marriage.

When her eyes lifted she pinned him with a dark measuring gaze. It was the same girl he had noted at the General's feast, her plump lips pursed tightly, her eyes cold and dark and distant. Although tempted to label her haughty, he didn't miss the way she almost flinched when her husband's hand settled on her forearm, pulling her closer, to settle her hand on his forearm in the position of marital accord so often immortalised in sculpture. Alexartos had the fleeting impression of the consul's wife as an injured deer, frightened but too wounded to run and forced to face her hunter. He half expected her to stamp a foot in a defensive show. She didn't. She was not after all a wild creature, but a Roman matron.

'Quartia, this is Praetorian Artos, sent by the Emperor to join our deputation of Praetorians.'

The young woman nodded but said nothing. Being this close he became certain that the shadow near her eye was in fact the bruise he had suspected, skillfully covered with paints and powders but still a bruise. Despite Messalinus' apparently solicitous care, her responses suggested it was not her first bruise, of course, she was not the first wife to need to perfect paints for that reason.

'I have decided to set him as your personal detail.'

He did not miss the flair in her eyes as her husband spoke but since the announcement surprised him too he could barely suppress a frown. Her flash of anger was unmistakable.

'With respect, Senator, I am a procurator of the Praetorian guard; I was sent to lead the men who guard you, not play nursemaid.'

By Mars, he must be tired. Alexartos cursed internally and waited for the backlash for his unwise words and speaking without permission. But the former consul merely stared unflickering at a space to the left of his chin, a hint of a smile at one side of his lips.

'I have no doubt you would make a formidable deterrent to any attempts on my life, Praetorian, but as you see, I am already served by several of your colleagues. Petronius, here,' he gestured at the hulking figure beside and behind the curule chair the man sat on, 'is also a procurator and commands my guard, and I have your own Prefect by my side. Surely you do not doubt Titus Flavianus' ability to protect me?'

A few of Messalinus' lackeys tittered behind him. Alexartos considered Titus' stance and recalled the way the Prefect had slipped morsels of food gently between the man's lips at the banquet. Something told him the Emperor's son would not stray far from the blind man's side. There were already rumours that the Jewish Queen, Berenice, Titus' recent consort, had been instructed to return to the Jewish provinces, so he doubted 'protection' of the Consul was the intention foremost in the Prefect's mind. A practical man, and a soldier of many campaigns, Alexartos lacked the Roman disgust in men who loved other men, though he lacked the Roman taste for both men and boys.

Senator Lucius Valerius Messalinus gave him no time to protest. 'There have been threats made against my wife as a means of getting at me. I am often absent on business for the empire and forced to leave Quartia at home. It would reassure me to know that in my absence she was well guarded.' He smirked just a little. 'You can command her guard. And it would trouble me less to know that her every move was under watch, every word spoken in her presence was measured for threat.'

Messalinus placed a hand upon his wife's arm letting it settle there before making a stroking gesture. 'It would distress me greatly should any harm come to her in my absence.'

The woman did not move and she kept her eyes down as her husband spoke but something in her posture suggested she did not welcome this level of personal scrutiny and protection.

Alexartos nodded to acknowledge the man's words, pressing a fist to his chest in the Roman manner of accepting orders and showing respect. Titus lent to whisper in his lover's ear. The man smiled, patting his wife's arm.

'There you are, dearest. Is it not reassuring to know you will never be far from the watchful eye of the Emperor's man? That no word can be whispered against you without being scrutinised? How safe will you feel?'

Alexartos felt the question was rhetorical and the woman's lack of answer suggested she read it likewise. Her eyes had lifted now to stare at him, narrowed slightly and hostile.

'I am grateful for your consideration, Messalinus, but surely it is unnecessary. I so rarely leave the protection of the villa.'

Messalinus smiled. 'But my dear, don't you see? This will give you the protection to do so without concern. Think how the Praetorian's presence will free you from your little worries.' He caressed her cheek. It seemed a loving gesture. She held still under his touch. 'Go now, my dear. I would not like to keep you from your business or bore you with mine. Take your Praetorian with you. Keep him close.'

α

Thalia seethed.

In the month since she had inherited her Praetorian neither of them had spoken a word to each other beyond commands and their acknowledgment but there had not been a moment when she had been out of his sight. The man did not even appear to need sleep, for he stalked her even in her nightly wanders, a dark shadow in the periphery of her vision.

She glared at him now, standing beside the open doorway, arms across his chest. His head nearly at a height with the lintel, well beyond her reach. She guessed that the top of her head would barely reach his bare, bronzed shoulders. His hair was as dark as a raven's wing, as dark as her own, though without even the hint of a wave. He kept it tightly braided and bound with leather into a warrior's club, all but the wisps of hair that fell around his face, not quite long enough to reach the braid. They fell like strands of silk, doing little to soften the edges of his face, as sharp as the blade at his side. She had been startled to notice his eyes were blue. Not the grey-blue of Messalinus' light eyes, but the blue of a summer sky. And just as cold, she decided. He was not leaning against the wall as a normal person might, but always alert and poised though in the time that he had followed her surely he had noticed there was nothing that suggested she was actually under threat. Still, she imagined him reporting every word spoken in her presence. She wondered if he maintained that granite face when he spoke to her husband. Did he sleep with it?

Thalia considered the shadow in the doorway. It was clear that as her guard, he was also there to act as a spy, reporting on her to Titus and his lover. She resented his constant presence, his constant listening. This was not new, she had never been alone, not truly, there were always slaves around, slaves who were obliged to report on her, even if, like Kaeso, they did not want to. But a guard, like this, there was never a reason for him not to be at her side.

Why did it bother her so much that this one man followed? Why did his blue eyes watching her bother her so much? Why did it matter that he would be the one to report on her? *Was it his silence?*

She didn't think he had spoken more than a dozen words to her in the time he had been here. Several of those only to summon her to attend her husband. Thalia chewed her lip. What was it that Messalinus had said when he had set the man to guarding her? That he was to free her from her worries? Would that he could take the sword he carried and thrust it through Messalinus' chest. That would free her. No. There had been more to her husband's words. The Praetorian would give her protection to leave the villa without concern.

Since the women of Rome had determined her a spy, most casual invitations had dried up, they avoided 'seeing' or speaking to her in the baths or marketplace. She made do instead with Nero's glorious, and largely silent, bathhouse and the travelling merchants that attended the villa, bringing samples. It surprised Thalia to realise that she had done to herself what Messalinus had done early in their marriage, isolated herself. It occurred to Thalia that with the protection of the Praetorian, she could leave the villa. She could go to the markets, buy scrolls, attend a play, walk freely through the busy forum, go to the bathhouse... once the bruises had faded.

Did she dare?

'Kaeso.'

The boy looked up at her from where he had been reading Homer. He was learning quickly, following each word on the scroll with a finger, his mouth moving as she sounded out unfamiliar words in his head.

'I need you to dress my hair and then find my saffron palla, the one that goes so nicely with the amethyst stola.'

The boy blinked. 'Has the Domine summoned us? Are we going somewhere?

She smiled tightly. 'No, and yes.'

α

She did not order a litter. The morning was so fair and fresh that she chose instead to walk. Kaeso was fairly skipping as they made their way down the hill, past the palace and towards the forum. It had rained the night before so most of the cobbled roadways were free of waste and detritus. It had been so long since she had walked this far that Thalia soon found herself short of breath and desperately trying to hide it from the man that stalked along at her side. He would have preceded her had she been willing to reveal their destination, but she was not.

His expression was wary, eyes flicking about the busy streets, as though he actually believed that there had been threats against her.

Being *Nundinae* the market was seething with people. Food was always freshest on the eighth day, when, overnight, the city filled with wagons bringing fresh produce to sell and most households sent a flotilla of slaves to gather the freshest staples to supplement what they themselves grew or was sent in from private farms. Despite the crush, people stepped warily around Thalia, leaving a respectful distance between themselves and the armed Praetorian. No doubt his stormy expression contributed, along with his sheer size. It was even better than her usual accompaniment of two burly slave guards armed with clubs. Oddly, this made her smile.

She lingered at a stall selling cool drinks, slowly sipping a concoction of honey and ginger and freshly squeezed grapes as she waited for her breathing to settle and her heart to stop pounding. The silk of her stola clung damply between her shoulders. The Praetorian was clearly uncomfortable with guard duties of this kind; he would likely be far more contented stabbing an enemy in the throat. Nor did he seem entirely comfortable with the constant flow of questions Kaeso asked as the boy eyed the weapon at his hip. She found herself smiling for the second time that day.

Adjusting the light silk of the palla over her head to shade her against the angle of the sun, she stepped into the street. 'Come on then. I am told the scroll seller has a new shipment from Athens. Perhaps he will have a copy of Aeschylus' plays.'

She crossed the street, stepping lightly upon the raised stones placed carefully to ensure that the wealthy did not have to dirty their shoes in the muck that built up in the street. To stay beside her the Praetorian was forced to step into the gutter.

'Domina, you are most welcome!' The elderly scroll seller greeted her with a broad smile and ushered her into the shade of the overhead awning. Although she had not seen him in years now it had not stopped her from being one of his most valuable clients.

'Salve Manisto. How is your daughter?'

The man beamed even wider. 'Junia is well, Domina, she has married and is soon to have her first child.' He mimed patting a broad belly while holding his back.

Her smile faltered, she chided herself for her envy. 'I am pleased for her Manisto, though I am certain you miss her help about the stall.'

Junia was one of the few plebeian girls Thalia knew who could read, having grown up helping her father, an old scholar and freedman.

He shrugged. 'What are you seeking Domina? Perhaps I can help you?'

She looked up from where she was unravelling scroll after scroll, setting a few on a growing pile to her left. 'I have been seeking the works of Aeschylus.'

'Sadly, Domina, I have not seen a copy of that in some time. I do, however, have some new copies of plays by Aristophanes, the print work is exceptional. And I have an excellent copy of Euripides' *Iphigenia at Aulis*.'

She emerged into the sunlight feeling elated. Kaeso held nearly a dozen scrolls, tied into a bundle like firewood in front of him. They moved onwards, but not far and Thalia lingered at a perfumer's stall, sampling vial after vial until she lost all sense of smell and one gave off much the same aroma as another. She dabbed one on her wrist and held it towards her scowling protector.

'What do you think?'

His eyes narrowed but he made no move towards her. So she held her arm towards Kaeso who obediently stepped forward and promptly wrinkled his nose.

Thalia capped the bottle and placed it back to the despair of the stallholder.

She let her gaze linger on the Praetorian as the flow of humanity pressed between them. 'Why are you here?'

'Your husband is important to the Emperor.'

'To Titus,' she sneered, unable to help herself, and this far from Nero's house in the freedom of the moment unable to force herself to care.

The Praetorian shrugged. 'I don't speculate on politics.'

'How refreshing. Surely a man with your talent would be better guarding Messalinus?'

He looked at her, brow furrowed. 'Your husband wants you protected.'

She sniffed. 'Protection for me is the last thing on Messalinus' mind.'

'Doesn't every man seek to protect his wife?'

'If that were true, why are you skulking around following me rather than guarding your own woman?'

She didn't miss the way his expression faltered and the blue eyes darkened. Nor was she willing to let the matter rest when she had clearly made an impact. 'So you have a wife then? Did you leave her in some tent beside a battlefield, or is she holed away in some dank insulae in the Subura slums, while you eat and sleep in luxury on the Palatine.'

His eyes flashed dangerously. 'The Scythians killed my wife on the day I met your General Vespasian. I wasn't there to protect her, or my father.'

She was silent for a moment, the gaze measuring his words for their honesty and deciding the pain was real. 'Emperor Vespasian,' Thalia corrected softly, her expression chastened. She began to walk again, after a moment he kept pace. 'I can assure you, however, that Messalinus lacks your motives.'

'Perhaps your husband felt he was better served by having me carry your shopping.'

'Do it then.'

His stride faltered. 'Do what?'

She turned towards the slave boy and plucked the bundle from his arms, holding out to the Praetorian. 'Carry my shopping.' She pushed it at him and he had little choice but to grab it or allow it to fall. 'I am sure if someone attacks me you can beat them to death as easily with a scroll as you could bloody them with your sword.'

She raised an eyebrow challengingly. Behind her the slave boy surreptitiously stretched his arms, arching his neck, relieved to have been unburdened.

He glared at her murderously but he did not let them fall.

'Come, Praetorian, we have much left to do.'

α

She was careful not to overdo the 'freedom' she had been permitted herself. One outing a week she allowed. A walk through Livia's gardens. A play at the theatre of Pompey. A visit to the baths of Agrippa, though she found it disconcerting to know he was watching as the bath slaves rubbed in the fragrant oils, massaged her naked flesh and used the metal strigil to remove the excess oils before she dipped beneath the near-boiling water of the *caldarium*. Sometimes, for fun, she challenged him, meeting his eye in what she imagined to be a provocative manner, the way she had seen women do when flirting with someone from a social deficit. Or at least she tried, for it did not seem to bother him to meet her gaze, at times he even appeared amused by her. It irked her.

As punishment, each time they went out, she found some excuse to make a purchase. Often it was something ridiculous and frivolous. A bushel of ostrich feathers, a low-backed chair, inlaid with ivory and plumped with pillows, a basket of figs. Once, a thigh-high bronze depicting Priapus, with his engorged member proudly displayed. Each time she thrust her purchase at him to carry. Though on each occasion his eyes narrowed, like they had with the Priapus statue, making her smile, yet he had not refused.

Thalia selected a scroll from the armful he currently held.

'The rest can go on the shelf.' She turned to the couch by the window, with its conveniently close short table, currently laden with inks and quills, and unlooped the leather tie that held the selected closed, unravelling it carefully before her. The Praetorian moved with a dangerous grace and an efficiency of movement to place each of his burdens, with care, in the shelves. She found she enjoyed watching him but she found herself flushing as she noticed Kaeso watching her closely.

'Do you think it is something I might learn, Domina?'

His voice was so wistful that she was taken aback.

'To write plays? You are doing very well with your reading but you have some way to go before you can write well enough to write a play. But soon, Kaeso.' Thalia had not the heart to tell the boy that she doubted Messalinus would support a slave in such endeavours that he considered a waste of time.

The boy shook his head slowly, a slight smile forming. 'Thank you, Domina. But I didn't mean to write plays.'

Thalia frowned. 'What then.'

His eyes darted towards the Praetorian. 'That.'

'What? Being a guard?' The glance the guard shot her made her consider how condescending her tone had been and she looked away, unsettled by a twinge of guilt.

'No,' he spoke softly, licking his bottom lip nervously before he dared speak. 'I would learn to fight with a sword. My mother told me my father was a famous gladiator.'

Thalia suppressed a smile. What child growing up in a brothel would not want a famous father? 'Then perhaps you should be talking to our bold Praetorian warrior and asking him for lessons?' She raised her voice as she spoke, letting the words wash over her taciturn guardian. The warrior in question let his gaze drift across the boy's gangling and awkward limbs and the early spots of adolescence with a raised eyebrow.

Kaeso ducked his head.

The following morning, and each day after, she woke to the cracking of wooden practice swords.

Chapter Eighteen: Chutko, Vazhko and Bary

Lviv, 2023

'Think of it as a diplomatic mission.'

'I am a forensic anthropologist, not a diplomat.'

‘Then think of it as a cultural study into human behaviour. Look, Tori, you have already established a connection with Mr Al'Shani.' Habermann sounded aggrieved, she knew they were short on manpower.

'I really don't deal well with the living.'

'Learn, Doctor Benino. Consider it an educational experience. Sign over the remains, attend the funeral on behalf of the UN, and spend some time enjoying the city. Lviv is an architectural marvel and the Russian bombs have not fallen anywhere near there.'

Late last month the bombing near Izyum had recommenced as the Russian artillery pounded the region from the safety of their occupied zones in the Donbas region.

'Grads.' Habermann had commented, lifting his head to listen when the first rounds had begun to fall. 'This is just the Russians saying hello, telling us they are still there, just trying to create panic.' Grads, he had explained, were truck-mounted batteries. The Russians drove them in, launched waves of missiles, and then moved them back out. It had done little to reassure us. Since then the *'dum, dum, dum'* had become a regular fixture of our work and we had actually begun to adjust to the ground shaking as we carried out our investigation. Some had come close enough that they seemed to lift the skin off our bodies and suck the air from our lungs, sending us to the lower basement levels for a time. Most fell far from us, targeting the civic centre or moving military targets.

I had not mentioned this in any of my communications with home and I waited until they were silent to make any calls.

Habermann was right. Located on the northwestern edge of Ukraine, near Poland, Lviv was far from the active warzone. I struggled with the guilt of leaving the others behind. Although we had finished processing the bodies from the second mass grave outside Izyum and the number of exhumed bodies and remains we were brought or delivered to, carefully hidden by those who cared, had slowed, we were low on numbers. The bombings had seen several students and volunteers forced to return home. All the while our evidence continued to mount, as did our dossier on the war crimes that could be attributed to the Russian President, his commanding general in the offensive Igor Vlachenko, and the officers in charge of the pseudo-Russian invasion.

We had finished with the remains of the family, carefully recording every piece of evidence. It had been decided that the bones could be reburied. Al'Shani had refused permission to bury them in the local cemetery and I could not blame him given the ongoing conflict. Instead, the remains would be shipped to Lviv for burial in a cemetery there that had a Muslim section. Closer cemeteries with provisions for Islamic burials were all in areas under Russian control. The whole process had taken months of paperwork.

With the documentation complete, Habermann had arranged for all the remains to be contained within a single coffin for the journey. Samir could decide how they would be buried. As he brushed his cheek against mine Dr Habermann passed me a package wrapped in brown paper and tied simply with twine.

'Put it in your bag. Don't open it until you have arrived in Lviv. It's for the coffin.' His warning told me the item was likely the sky blue flag of the Crimean Tatars with its golden tamga, a reversed trident-like symbol, in the top left corner. It was a flag we found, not uncommonly, wrapped around victims who were buried secretly by friends or family. Although it would never be officially mentioned I had no doubt Habermann had provided it to drape the coffin on its arrival in Lviv.

In return, I handed him the tin containing what was left of the fruit cake Morag had sent me after returning to Scotland several weeks earlier, called by special request of Scotland Yard. The tea she had left in my care was hidden in a pair of my oldest socks in the bags that I would leave here until I returned. I was not really being generous. We lived in too close proximity for any real personal space to be developed and no matter how well hidden I doubted the cake would outlast my absence. The possessions of others not being particularly sacrosanct in our odd little international bubble.

Habermann handed me the train tickets and I scrutinised them briefly in the act of tucking them in my backpack when something caught my eye.

'The dates are wrong.'

Habermann frowned and held a hand out for them. I complied and he flicked over to the second ticket. 'No. That's correct.' He held them out to me.

I took them reluctantly. 'What am I to do in Lviv for two entire weeks? Bruce! I have work to do here, there are still remains...'

He shook his head. 'Victoria, stop. It's nearly Christmas. You have worked nearly every day for the past eight months, I haven't been able to get you out of the morgue even on your days off.'

I started to protest but he didn't let me speak a word. 'It is too much. You need a break. Do touristy things, sleep in, take long hot showers. See the beauty in Ukraine, not just the death. If you want to visit somewhere else, just arrange flights. Go home and sing carols with your family. Hit a beach in Hawaii. Anything. But I do not want to see you back here before the date on that ticket. Am I understood?'

He emphasised each word of 'I do not want to see you.' I frowned, flicking the edge of the ticket with my finger.

He ducked his head to look me squarely in the eye.

'I mean it, Victoria. Take a break. No one can deal with death every day like this and still focus on life.'

I nodded, but my expression must have been bleak. He laughed. 'Andrew told me I'd need to have you escorted to the train, that you work too hard. Is he right? Do you need an escort?'

I scowled at him but only to cover feelings of guilt that assailed me. I had not spoken to Holly or Dalton in months. My efforts to contact my family, even bleaker, using poor reception as an excuse to only share an occasional post on Facebook. Being chastened did not stop me from dragging my feet. I did, while waiting at the station, check out the varying tourist destinations in Lviv and check that my hotel did, in fact, have a private bathroom which I upgraded to a room with a bathtub.

First, I had to get through returning Al'Shani's family. I could not explain why the prospect of this venture made me so nervous.

Ω

I had not expected the assembly of people on the station when our train finally pulled in, escorted by an honour guard of Ukrainian soldiers. Despite my self-determined disinterest, I found it easy to identify Samir, even from a distance, even in the clump of sombre and respectful mourners and Islamic clerics. It was not simply his well-cut grey suit under which he wore a pale pink shirt, that made him stand out amongst a sea of black coats over white shirts all trimmed with embroidery, but something about his posture and the slant of his shoulders. I had clearly taken far more notice of them than I was comfortable with and I could not let myself forget; he was a grieving widow and I could never entertain the notion of a relationship. As I stepped onto the platform the woman beside him leaned over and fixed the smudge of embroidered pink fabric, a handkerchief, in his jacket pocket. Then she chucked his cheek in an affectionate and completely platonic gesture.

A small child, wearing a winter dress in a matching shade of deep fuschia tugged on his hand. In the child's arms was a familiar plush Blue Cattle Dog. I realised I was seeing the artist of the pictures on the fridge in Al'Shani's apartment. He reached down and picked her up, perching her comfortably on his hip, pointing solemnly at the coffin being carefully removed from the baggage compartment and placed on the wheeled trolley. The bright blue cloth with its golden tamga icon was almost cheerful in the pale mid-morning light.

Ω

The car ride between the mosque and the cemetery was a quiet one. Yamina, a cousin to Samir's wife, the one who had fixed his kerchief and pinched his cheek, smiled reassuringly at me over the head of five-year-old Melie, Al'Shani's daughter, who I learnt had somehow miraculously survived the attack on the farmhouse while just an infant. Yamina spoke softly in English, taking the relative calm of the car ride to inform me of funerary protocol and I was grateful for her willingness to act as my guide and shepherd. Yamina explained that, as women, we would be permitted at the cemetery but must remain standing in a designated spot. Al'Shani's mother, Amina, was riding in the car with us. She watched me like a curious crow, her eyes dark, not hostile, but sombre. The mother of a linguist and she spoke only Ukrainian. Her husband was already at the cemetery. The males of the family would be buried first, with Elirë's father interred first, then her brother-in-law and the sons. The twin boys would share a grave although their bodies would not be permitted to touch. Each would be laid to rest on their right side and facing in the direction of Mecca.

The women would then be likewise buried, from oldest, Elirë's grandmother, to youngest, Elirë's eight-year-old niece. Afterwards, the mourners would return to Samir's hotel rooms and share meals and stories about the deceased.

The cemetery was unlike any I had visited before. It covered several hillsides, burial sites blending with the bush, funeral monuments grew like wild plants, in haphazard arrays, all dusted with an unusually early snow. It was an odd mix of styles. We drove past a row of massive edifices the likes of the many Italian sepulchres I had seen, where generations shared their resting place. There were many graves indicated by crosses, and more with grey stone monuments and carved angels of the sort that graced older Australian cemeteries. There were sections of bare muddy earth where new graves, those of fallen soldiers were indicated by Ukrainian flags, bunches of irises and simple wooden crosses. The Islamic section of the cemetery was different again. There were no lines of carefully pruned roses or walls filled with niches, cremation being against Islamic law. Instead, the grave plots here were simple stone-edged plots or slabs, at each end rose graceful narrow pillars or columns, many topped with something that looked like the end of an old-fashioned clothes peg, some ornately shaped, others simple. Many of the pillars were gracefully carved with designs or etched with Kufic script, the preferred style of writing for the Koran and architecture. Its graceful curlesque-style far more ascetic than our own blockish text types.

I had little difficulty keeping my focus through the slow process of carefully interring the ten sets of remains, each carefully wrapped in a white shroud cloth called Kafan. Some bundles were pitifully small, a few bones at best. I had spent many hours in a small room off the mosque, instructing those who handled the remains on what order to place the bones, a complex task when so much was missing, and all to ensure that the remains would face the correct direction for their rest. The mullah had carefully marked each white bundle with a small figure to instruct those who laid them. I noticed that the men who handled them, Samir included, did so with the utmost respect. The anthropologist in me was fascinated both by the ritual and the surroundings. The bodies would not be permitted to touch the soil, nor were they interred in coffins. Instead, each carefully wrapped bundle was placed on wooden boards, with wooden sides and a wooden plank above before every man attending dropped three handfuls of dirt upon the top. Although there were over a hundred male mourners present each grave would still need filling once all mourners had departed. In time, I imagined, Samir and his family would ensure the tiny minaret-type markers were placed at each end of each burial. I resolved to tell Dr Habermann that he was correct in his surmise that I should view the trip as an educational experience, that from an anthropological perspective, there was much I had learned.

Midway through the ceremony, I found the small hand of Al'Shani's small daughter woven into mine. It was surprisingly warm.

There were few tears, these had long since been shed and though a solemn occasion there was an atmosphere of peace, even joy, at the return and permanent safe placement of their family members.

When the final handful of half-frozen soil had been dropped on the final plot the men turned and walked in a solemn procession that passed where the women were waiting and, without acknowledgment, continued to the waiting vehicles. The women followed in their wake, Melie pulling me along after her.

Despite their kindness and attempts at inclusion, few spoke English and it was difficult not to feel set apart. The food materialised in a profusion of dishes in colours and scents that reminded me of walking through the spice bazaar in Egypt and I was provided with a plate piled with foods whose names I could barely remember let alone pronounce, though they were both savoury and sweet and good. I watched conversations take place in gestures and laughter as the family drew together and I felt odd and isolated and alone. After as short a time as I considered polite, I shifted Melie, who had been glued to my side, and said goodbyes to Yamina and Al'Shani's mother. Melie's father was surrounded by a ring of men that I had no intention of breaching.

So, I was surprised to find Samir and his daughter waiting in the hotel lobby when I descended the next morning. It was Melie who spotted me first, darting from beneath his grip and gleefully dancing around me. Samir followed, reaching a restraining hand out to catch his daughter and pulling her to his side.

'I'm sorry. I hope you don't mind our intrusion. I never got a chance to thank you for bringing them home to me.'

I nodded, fiddling self-consciously with the straps of my knapsack. 'The United Nations were grateful to you, Mr Al'Shani, for your courage in bringing them to our attention. It was the least we could do to bring them home.'

'Please, call me Samir. I didn't get to speak with you yesterday, though Melie tells me she looked after you.'

'She was a wonderful host,' I replied, smiling at the child, her dark hair twined back in two plaits, woven with pink ribbon. I doubted the handiwork was her father's. The girl cocked her head, like a sparrow, to listen to her father's translation before beaming broadly and rattling off a series of words in Ukrainian that all tangled together. I waited for her father to translate.

'Melie suggested that we take you to the Teatre Lialok today. It is her favourite place to visit.'

I considered the unfamiliar words. 'I guess Teatre is theatre but my Ukrainian does not reach to Lialok?' I asked.

'Teatre Lialok, the puppet's theatre.'

'Lviv has a Puppet Theatre?' I asked. I had not noted it in my Google search.

He nodded, seriously. 'I told her you would probably prefer to see the Historical Museum or the Virmens'kyy Sobor.'

Reading my blank expression he corrected. 'The Armenian Cathedral.'

That was on my list.

He winked at Melie. 'Fortunately, they are all very close together, so I suggested that if she was patient and we gave you a personal tour of Rynok Square and the Cathedral we might visit the puppets afterwards. The girl nodded solemnly up at me.

'Melie love lialok,' she spoke, touching her own chest and saying the words in thickly accented English. 'Melie love Chutko, Vazhko and Bary.'

Perplexed, I looked at her father. 'Chutko?'

He smiled, 'Chutko, Vazhko and Bary are puppet dogs from the tale of the Iron Wolf.'

'I would like to see that.' I looked from father to daughter, both clad in identical hopeful expressions. 'How can I refuse?'

Ω

Samir and Melie had been excellent guides, their personalised tour of the famous domed building, built as an Armenian church in the 14th Century was comprehensive, though clearly informed by the guidebook printed in Ukrainian that Samir had picked up outside. Like Melie I was spellbound by the colours. The outside of the building was constructed of thick, massive sandstone bricks in the Romanesque style, while inside the Middle Eastern influence of the

Armenians was clear. As Melie spun about near the altar I gaped up at the ceiling, the hanging chandelier and the ornately painted dome, which reminded me of the patterns used in Ukrainian ribbon making and embroidery.

Then, when the child's restless shifting became too much, we found a food cart from which emanated delicious pastry scents and was introduced to *pampushki,* deep fried doughnuts, filled with sweet cherry preserve and frosted with icing sugar, resembling the snowy square we had wandered into. Clearly, a favourite with Melie. Samir and I both got a few pieces before the paper cone was emptied, well before the short walk brought us to the tall theatre building.

To Melie's great delight, the performance was her favourite tale, the Iron Wolf. The set was simple, a castle and a forest. The theatre itself was painted black. The floor was set with cushions and the children scrambled to take positions as adults took up the bench seats. Puppeteers in black, their eyes alone showing, wove through the simple set with their puppets walking, dancing and prancing beneath their clever fingers until the story grabbed the audience and they simply disappeared. Samir had explained the tale to me in low whispers, any words that were Ukrainian, until scowling neighbours shushed him. Following the tale without words was not hard, puppetry is a very visual medium so it was like watching a ballet and interpreting the scene.

The protagonist, a clever young man whose puppet features looked distinctly like President Volodymyr Zelenskyy made a deal with the Iron Wolf, a creature that looked very little like a wolf, instead presenting itself as a metallic bearlike creature, on its back in a turret was a very familiar bald and shirtless man.

The audience hissed when the wolf arrived, muttered when the young man made his deal and called encouragement when the man fled the punishment he had agreed to. Melie wriggled with joy when the character was joined first by Chutko, then Vazhko and finally

Bary. Each canine puppet wore a kerchief, the first in red and white, the second in red white and blue and the third in black, yellow and red. In the end, the young man fell into an exhausted sleep and when the Iron Wolf arrived the faithful hounds surrounded the beast, pinned it and tore out its throat. The audience roared approval and cheered as the young man, free of his pursuer, returned home to wed his bride, the three dogs by his side.

I was silent for some time after emerging, blinking, into the light. Melie made up the difference in conversation, prattling away in mixed Ukrainian and English, with a few words I suspected were Turkish thrown in.

'The show bothered you?'

I offered Samir an apologetic shrug. 'I was a little surprised by how thinly veiled the propaganda.'

He nodded slowly. 'Of course. You see the worst of the war in what you do but you do not really live it as we do. Since the war, the puppet theatre has doubled their performances in order to bring relief and joy, particularly to the children.'

I nodded, watching Melie frolic, hands held in front of herself like paws as she imitated the puppet dogs. 'I understand. I think what bothered me most was that the boy's allies got all the credit when what I see here is very different. Putin thought you easy meat, forgive the pun, but it is the people that have withstood him, not America, or Poland or Germany.'

I was grateful when Samir forebore responding immediately and allowed myself to get lost in the square. Its buildings were not old in the way that many buildings in Italy were old, but the youngest was older than anything in my country. I loved the way each building rubbed shoulders with its neighbour but kept its unique style. Without exception, they were all four stories high, with the bottom floor a shop or shops. Above them, windows looked out in uniform arrays into the square and the grand city council building. Each building was painted in a unique pastel shade. I wondered who chose the colours. They looked even more magical because of the fine layer of snow that had fallen the previous evening and the Christmas-sy lights strung across the square. I could hear people laughing from the ice rink that had been set up further along the square. Habermann had been correct. Here in Lviv, it was like the war did not exist.

Melie had begun to dance around one of the four fountains set around the square. I stepped closer. Snow had begun to fall and was dusting the head and shoulders of the statue. I peered closer and recognised the familiar features.

'Amphitrite.'

I was startled to see the goddess here. I had stared at her likeness many times in the mosaic in Herculaneum.

'What is it?' Samir stood by my side.

'The goddess Amphitrite. I didn't realise she was here. Amphitrite is a Nereid. She was chosen to marry Poseidon, god of the seas but she refused and ran away. Poseidon sent dolphins after her and they found her and dragged her back to him. There is a magnificent mosaic of her in a house in Herculaneum, the Ancient city I worked in before I came here. They call it the house of Amphitrite and Neptune, but they are incorrect because while Neptune is the Roman version of Poseidon, Amphitrite's Roman equivalent is——'

The word froze on my lips. I was grateful he could not see my face.

'You're shivering. Come back to my hotel. Stay for dinner with us. I will cook you a meal, you can tell Melie all about Amphitrite and the dolphins and I can explain why we value our allies, even though they have not set foot in our country..'

I shook my head, my hands were shaking, my shoulders had joined them but it had nothing to do with the cold. Amphitrite had been taken back by the dolphins, forcibly raped by and married to her husband, Poseidon. I could hardly tell Melie that story, even if her puppet shows were thinly veiled and graphic anti-Russian propaganda. Nor would the Roman name of Amphitrite pass my lips.

Salacia. Goddess of the Seas. The name of Massimo's yacht.

But as I turned from the fountain I was confronted by both a spinning and pleading child and her equally insistent father.

Ω

Samir had proved a more than adequate cook, even confronted with the limited utensils and appliances his hotel room offered and Melie and I served as willing apprentices, chopping and stirring as required, with greater or lesser precision. The child's chatter through dinner had kept the occasion from feeling uncomfortable, despite the fact that the previous day I had watched this man bury almost his entire family. After dinner, we played cards and I learnt numbers 1-12 in Ukrainian in order to play an excessive number of hands of *Porybalyty* or 'Go Fish.' The ordinariness of the situation slowly eased the memories evoked by the fountain in Rynok Square.

When the child started yawning, Samir took her to the bathroom to clean her teeth and get her ready for bed. Sweetly, she insisted on presenting me with a 'goodnight kiss' before being 'tucked in' on the lounge in front of the television.

I waited, restless, increasingly uncomfortable and determined to leave, while Samir read the girl a story before kissing her brow and returning to the kitchen. Presented with coffee and more of the amazing pastries the country offered, I found it increasingly difficult to speak words of farewell. I ran my hand over the picture the child had drawn for me of herself, her father, and the puppets and I, all suspended on strings.

'Melie seems very happy.'

A proud father, Samir smiled.

'I didn't know...' I began, then stopped uncertain how to proceed with my question, in the end I erred with directness. 'Will you tell me about her?'

He sipped his rich coffee in silence for a moment before nodding. He realised I did not mean about the child, but about her survival.

'Melie was a few months old when the twins had their birthday. It was late and she was tired and refused to settle, so I took her outside for a walk. It was a beautiful night, the stars were like diamonds in the sky, so bright in the cold air.'

I nodded.

'She liked it when I sang to her.'

He sang a few bars of a familiar song, his voice unsurprisingly rich.

'At first, I thought it was fireworks. Then, I knew better. We are accustomed to the sound of gunfire in Ukraine. I was torn. Melie was asleep, but there was gunfire, coming from the farmhouse...'

I heard the hitch in his voice and regretted my question.

'I hid Melie in the old Volvo, in the barn.'

I recalled seeing both the car and the ramshackle barn with its sagging roof and nodded.

'I had just placed her on the floor of the car when I heard the screams...'

His voice hitched and I reached out a hand. I meant to place it on his hand, to reassure, but as if by its own volition I found it pressed to his cheek. His eyes were liquid with sorrow. He placed a hand over mine, then pulled my hand away. For a moment I was ashamed. I had touched a Muslim man, a clear offence by their religious precepts. Then he pressed my hand to his lips and I trembled.

My hand had barely brushed his face, his touch and his kiss were both so light they had barely been felt but the force of it had burned. From the expression on his face, Samir had felt it too. That odd compelling pressure, the heat, the electricity. He had reached out again, his fingertips brushing my cheek, running along the line of my jaw, thumbs brushing my lips. When he leaned forward, I moved to meet him.

Chapter Nineteen: No Longer Necessary

Moesia, AD 75

Artos found he was scowling as he shifted aside to let the Imperial messenger into the room and Felix called out announcing his arrival. His shoulders tensed in irritation as he realised that his bad mood stemmed from her reaction when he had announced he could not escort her to the forum that morning. The way her frown had formed a wrinkle between her brows and her lips had pressed together had made him smile at the time. But now he was bored and frustrated, standing vigil at Messalinus' door, while Petronius shitted his guts out in the *latrina* after indulging unwisely in seafood at one of the Subura taverns the previous evening. Messsalinus' head turned at the announcement, blind eyes turned to the doorway, keen ears listening for the scuff of steps. Titus paced restlessly near the window. Artos understood the tenseness in the man's shoulders. Titus was a warrior and had been too long cooped up in Rome. He wanted to return to the East and finish squashing the ongoing rebellions in Judaea. Barracks gossip said the man had even sent Berenice back there to await him. Artos wondered how long the proud queen would wait, but it was none of his business.

At Messalinus' exaggerated cough, Titus strode across the room and snatched the scrolls from the hands of the messenger and dismissed the man. The messenger bowed low, one hand to his chest in acknowledgement of the Imperial heir. Felix followed him. No doubt to ensure that none of the priceless artworks went missing on the man's way back out.

'What is it?'

Titus grumbled. 'I don't read as well as you 'Linus. Give me a chance.'

It was a careless statement from a bluff soldier and Titus was so intent on the scroll he did not notice the way the former Consul's mouth tightened to be reminded that he could not even read his own messages anymore. Only Titus could get away with such a thing.

'It is from the Senate. Confirmation that Macedonia has been given to you. Congratulations, Proconsul.' Titus made a mocking bow, the gesture lost on the new Proconsul.

Messalinus grinned, as well he might. Macedonia was a rich region and Artos had no doubt, like every Roman governor before him, Messalinus would mine it diligently for every coin he could extort.

'There is another,' Titus said, frowning over the contents of the next scroll. His lip curled as he read. 'From your father.'

The Proconsul sat up straight. 'What does he want?' There was no mistaking the tension in his voice.

'You father sends his greetings. He speaks of your brother, Gaius' successes on the battlefield and his promotion to Legate. He asks about his investments in Rome.'

Messalinus grunted. 'What else. What are you not telling me?'

Titus hesitated. 'He asks about the state of your marriage. Reminds you that all of Arrecinus Clemens' daughters have so far proven fecund and wonders if you recall that the purpose of having a wife is for the creation of heirs.'

Messalinus was silent; even from a distance Artos could see the muscle in the man's jaw twitching as Titus scanned the rest of the missive.

'He makes some interesting suggestions on improving fertility, temples your wife should make offerings at, foods beneficial for fertility. Even an intriguing suggestion that you tie a knot around

your left testicle when serving her so that you can guarantee a son.'
Titus chuckled.

Messalinus scowled.

Titus fell silent.

'Tell me what he says.'

The warrior shuffled.

'Titus!'

'Your father says that if you cannot manage the duty of an heir
then Gaius might prove more adept at the challenge.' Titus hesitated.
'My friend, perhaps it is time to…'

Messalinus' mouth twisted. 'I can't… I won't.'

Titus crossed to him, tossing the letter on the brazier as he passed.
He rubbed Messalinus' shoulders with long firm motions until a little
of the tension seemed to slip away.

They had clearly forgotten that it was Artos and not Petronius on
duty this day. Hidden in the shadows of the doorway neither man paid
him heed. Artos could barely hear Titus' next words.

'I could do it for you.'

Embarrassed, Artos stepped further from the doorway.

'And you think she would allow that? Have you actually met my
wife?'

Silence held for a time.

'There is another solution. My daughter is of age to marry. She is
young yet though, not ready to bed. The connection would please your
father and with her youth you could put your father off for years.'

'And what do I do with the wife I have?'

'You are heading for Macedonia. Once you are there, send for her.
All sorts of misadventures happen on the road.'

Artos slipped even further down the hallway.

α

He felt uneasy. Despite the light that filtered, dappled, through the canopy and though there was ample space to weave between the trees, Artos could not feel secure. Born and raised in a sea of grass, with skies so broad they almost reached forever, he ached for open space. This was rather like weaving through dark reaches of the Subura, and in his overactive imagination threats lurked hidden behind each bough. His vision was hampered by beech and oak and fir. Sensing his rider's unease, the mount beneath him danced and wove, scattering last season's leaf fall. He loosened his grip on the reins and shifted his seat, the stallion settled somewhat but Artos did not.

He had been this way since overhearing the conversation between Messalinus and his lover in the tablinum last winter. For weeks he had considered telling her. But what could he say that she might believe? Snippets of an enigmatic conversation. He wasn't entirely certain what Titus had implied and whatever it was, it wasn't as though Messalinus had agreed. And what proof did he have of anything? He reined his horse in a circle and scanned the trees again. When he looked back towards her he could see she was staring at him. She must have asked him something. He searched his mind for it but came up blank.

'Perhaps you should bathe more often to clear the wax from your ears, Praetorian.'

Artos shrugged, unwilling to engage in banter he could not win. Travelling through this skyless place probably had her nervous too.

'What does Rome want with Macedonia, anyway?' she repeated.

'Other than to own that which was once Alexander's?'

The straightening of her lips expressed her displeasure with his answer. 'Surely your scrolls could tell you this," he replied, indicating several wooden boxes in the cart behind her.

Her answer was to narrow her eyes.

'Animals and crops are the wealth of Macedonia. But General Vespasian told me there was a wealth of minerals and metal in the ground. Iron and copper and gold. Timber and resin and pitch from Macedonia are important to the Roman fleet.'

She nodded.

'The Governorship of Macedonia will make your husband even more wealthy.'

She said nothing. Little wonder. He could have left her safely in Rome while he served his term as governor but for reasons known only to himself, Artos knew it was not love of his wife or desire for her company, he had insisted she travel to meet him. Messalinus himself had travelled ahead, with twelve lictors, half a legion, a caravan of wagons, his bevy of pretty catamites and his golden lover, Titus, who was returning to Judaea for a time. By contrast, their own caravan was modest. Two dozen wagons, mostly furniture and statuary, several dozen slaves and an escort of Praetorians, many of them green. It was something else that made Artos nervous. Some of these men could barely swing a sword, he could not imagine what use Titus thought them. Yet, Messalinus had sent Petronius with them. The surly, often drunken Praetorian served Messalinus by doing whatever cruel and dirty work his patron required, and in return he gradually accrued wealth and property. Petronius would retire a wealthy man. He did not like the man, but Artos could not deny Petronius' military prowess and welcomed his company with the raw recruits Titus had assigned. Artos shot a glance to where the man sat on the bench of a wagon, a cup and dice in hand, weighted no doubt. The wagoneer would no doubt learn it to his deficit.

'It's so quiet.' She observed.

She was right. Aside from the shuffling and low chatter of men and creaking of wagons there was no sound. Not even birds. His body tensed, and the stallion's reaction was immediate.

Artos dropped his hand to his sword and spun to call the alarm. As he faced Petronius, the wagoneer grew a feathered shaft straight through his right eye. He toppled, soundless from the wagon, into the leaf litter below. Petronius' reaction was sudden as he leapt from the wagon, into the saddle of his mount and wrenched the beast's mouth to spin him around. His eyes locked with Artos.

'Ambush!' He roared.

By this time the forest came alive with movement and the cries of injured and dying men. The green Praetorians fell as fast as the wagoneers.

Artos dug his heels into the stallion's side and leaned the reins across his neck, forcing the beast alongside the carriage that held the Governor's wife. He plucked her from the vehicle as an arrow brushed through her hair, embedding itself in the heavy wood. As if she were little more than a sack of beans or a deer carcass, he dragged her in front of him and heeled his stallion towards Petronius. The man had his sword out and had just hacked deeply into the neck of a ragged attacker, splitting the man deeply down towards his chest before dragging back on the sword. Artos drove the stallion alongside and nearly wore a sword through the gullet for his efforts. He pushed the woman towards the other Praetorian. For once, she was mercifully silent, in shock no doubt.

'Take her, get deeper in the woods. Keep her safe.'

The man looked startled, then grinned, a menacing leer. He nodded and, digging heels into his beast's sides, Petronius roared and angled for the deeper cover, away from the winding length of the Via Egnatia. One of the attackers, armed with a large recurved bow, stepped out to take aim at the disappearing Praetorian. Artos roared, leaning forward, his stallion leapt towards the man. Artos blow took off the man's arm at his shoulder. While he looked for his next enemy, the stallion lurched beneath him, throwing itself backward as the thick shaft of a spear embedded in its stomach.

Artos' leg was crushed against the trunk of a thick oak and his head crashed into a solid low-hanging limb. Darkness overtook him.

α

Fear and fury combined to pound in her ears, exacerbated by her downward position, held in place bowed over the horse's withers by the Praetorian's arms. The sounds of weapons clashing and men hollering and dying battled with the pounding in her ears and the thudding of the horse's hooves as they dug first into the cobbles of the old Roman road, and then into the loam and leaf litter of the forest.

Thalia closed her eyes to avoid the growing disorientation and nausea accompanied by her unnatural position. The sounds of battle slipped into the distance behind them.

After a while, she felt him ease back on the reins, and the beast's forward momentum slowed. Thalia risked opening her eyes, the horse's hooves spun, turning for a moment to face the direction they had come from, then shifted again, completing the circle to be pushed onwards, deeper into the forest.

Thalia wanted to cry out but she found the air had been forced from her lungs by the jostling. As they wove deeper into the trees she forced herself to focus on trying to regulate her breathing, slowly sucking in air that smelled like sweat, horse hide and leather, but still was sweet and welcome. In time she began to beat her fist against the Praetorian's legs. He ignored her until she dug fingernails into his flesh. His response was to kick at her.

'Let me down!' She hissed.

The solid blow of an open hand stung her backside, as offensive as it was painful.

'Shut up!' He snarled. 'Do you want them to find us?'

Did she? Thalia considered the matter while she hung, still face down. Discretion silenced her and she rested her head against the horse's shoulder, damp hair beneath her cheek. They went deeper still into the forest, further from the Via Egnatia. In time they headed down a steady embankment and into the clear water of a stream. Petronius turned the beast to follow the watercourse for some distance. Obscuring their tracks, she realised. After some distance they took the further bank, rising back into the leafy expanse of the forest.

She had lost track of time when Thalia realised he had reined in the beast and it stood, twitching beneath her cheek as he listened for any sound of pursuit. Caution silenced her. Finally, the weight of his hand lifted from her back, a fist hauling against the fabric of her stola pulled her upright and dumped her unceremoniously in the leaf litter. Her legs, long cramped from the awkward ride did nothing to collect her, instead crumpling beneath her.

Thalia glared up at the man, his face still turned, listening.

'You must go back and help them.' She kept her voice low, little more than a whisper.

His head turned, amber eyes glancing over her, an unpleasant grin quirking one side of his wide narrow mouth, his gaze dropped below her face. Her own followed. In the wild ride she had lost her palla and the shoulder of her stola had torn, exposing the creamy curve of her breast. Petronius' gaze was lascivious. Thalia recalled the way he had thrust himself against her while escorting her back to her rooms after she had endured a beating at his hands and the direction of her husband. She tugged at the material, tried to make it cover the flesh beneath then straightened her back and glared at him. Seated as she was unceremoniously in the dirt, she doubted its efficacy.

'If you go now, you could assist your men. I will remain here. Leave me your knife. I will protect myself.'

He leaned back in the saddle, lifted his left leg over the high pommel and slid with a thump to the earth.

'If you do not go now, I will tell my husband that you abandoned his men and belongings.'

It was an idle threat, and they both knew it.

The praetorian grinned, wider. Then to her surprise, he offered a hand.

She was shaking, Thalia realised, as she lifted the hand not holding her dress to place it in his. The man pulled her easily to her feet, the traitorous limbs still unsteady beneath her. She was grateful for the trunk of the tree he leaned her up against.

'Do you really think your husband cared at all for anything in those wagons?'

It was the longest speech she had ever heard from him. His voice was gravelly, like an avalanche of rocks subsiding.

'My husband does not give away his property, even to armed bandits.' She recalled her husband's words on the night she had received the chains about her wrists, when he had pressed his body into hers, his voice a whisper of warm air against her neck. *I do not relinquish what is mine.*

Petronius smiled, nodding a little. 'Unless he has other plans for it.'

Thalia considered all the discarded blonde boys. Of Kaeso, who had soundlessly disappeared from her life.

'He needs me,' she asserted. In an odd way she knew it to be true. Her existence kept his secrets safe and legitimised him.

The Praetorian's head took on a tilt as he considered her, his grin widening. 'He did, but you are no longer necessary.' The man agreed. 'Surely, you have noticed that Titus' daughter is much grown of late?'

Thalia blinked at him. *Titus' daughter?* In the months before their trip was planned Julia had been often to visit her, sometimes in her father's presence, sometimes alone. She had been grateful for the girl's company but known well enough not to spill secrets unwisely. For all that she hated Titus, her niece idolised her father and Thalia would say nothing to threaten that. As a result, Julia was much enamoured with Messalinus, watching him wide-eyed. It had amused Thalia to watch him play to her adoration, flattering her and flirting with the child. It had been safe to do so, Thalia knew. He had no interest, despite the curling locks of golden hair she had inherited from her father. At thirteen she was just entering her womanhood, shy and willowy.

'Now you see it, don't you?'

At thirteen, Thalia realised, Julia was old enough to be wed.

His smile did not reach his cold cat eyes.

'He has a wife.'

Petronius shrugged.

'Julia is like his little sister, his niece. He grew up with her father.' Thalia tried to deny her growing understanding. Petronius watched her like a cat watched a mouse.

'Yes, daughter of his brother, his lover.'

She was shocked he would voice those words. Messalinus would have had him killed for saying it aloud. Discretion was a trait he valued above all but beauty in his household.

'Why would he not want to marry the daughter of his lover, keep it all in the family to speak.'

Her hand had shot out, instinctively, aiming for his leering face. His reflexes were quick, capturing her wrist in a crushing grip.

'You are no longer necessary.'

His words were chilling.

'The death of the Proconsul's wife on the way to Macedonia will be considered a tragedy. Remarriage would be expected, and who better to marry than a maid so closely connected to the imperial family? A shame really. Such a tasty little thing to be wasted, as you were.'

Her wrist was still in his grip but in his taunting, his grip had grown lax. Thalia took a breath, and considered the lessons her father had once taught both his daughters. As she pulled frantically down with her arm, she lifted her knee, forcing it upwards, towards his centre. The blow was glancing, not as successful as she hoped, but in blocking her he had dropped her hand. Thalia spun and darted behind the tree, pushing off it both to give her momentum and because her legs still faltered below her. In her headlong flight she heard two things, the sound of his laughter and the crash of his footsteps following.

α

Someone was going through the dead horse's saddlebags. Despite his flickering consciousness, Artos forced himself to stillness, not daring to breathe. A hand brushed over his belt, his puteo dragged from its sheath. Someone tugged at his belt to free the sheath too, but the buckle was digging into his hip on the other side, the side where his leg was pinned beneath the weight of the dead stallion. The man cursed and spat, his sputum hitting the leaves near Artos' head. Then feet scraped and footsteps moved away. With his eyes still shut, the Praetorian listened, the sound of fighting had died away. Only when silence fell again did he allow himself to breathe. Eyes still shut he catalogued the extent of his injuries.

The head wound that had knocked him out hurt like Hades and would leave him with a roaring headache but he doubted it had even broken the skin of his scalp. The worst pain was in the leg that was pinned beneath the animal. He considered the likelihood of a break. If it was broken, stuck out here in the middle of the forest, he could only hope that someone would come and, seeing the remains of the caravan, would investigate. He wouldn't be far from the road. But if no one came, even if he could get his leg out from beneath the beast, then he would be prey to the attention of bears or wolves, even a lynx or boar would be more than he could handle, unarmed and injured.

Artos was not the kind to wallow in self-pity. Then, he remembered the girl and Petronius. The man would return, he knew. But he wouldn't wait to be found helpless. With one hand braced around a low branch, Artos braced himself. With a leather shod boot against the cooling flesh of the stallion, he pushed with all his might. Pain arched through his injured leg, the beast barely moved and darkness found him again.

α

She lurched to evade him, but his hand, reaching, caught in her hair and pulled her to a jerking halt, her forward momentum curtailed momentarily. Then he used it to his benefit swinging her violently up against a tree. The breath left Thalia's lungs with a whoosh and she found herself once more crumpled amongst the tree roots.

Not for long though. He wrapped a large hand around her ankle, dragging her towards him. Thalia scrambled to find something to grasp, damp tree roots slipped beneath her fingers. She hurled a handful of dirt and leaves at his face, the impact left a muddy smear but caused no damage. Petronius landed on her then, his knee in her stomach, his hands pinning her own over her head. Her heartbeat was a relentless pounding drumming in her ears.

'I like my women to have some fight in them.' He grinned, his breath reeked of rotten teeth. With both her hands secured in one massive palm, he freed his other, to flip the torn fabric of her now soiled gown and expose the plump white flesh of her breast. He twisted her nipple cruelly between his fingers as she fought to draw air back into her tortured lungs and darkness threatened the edges of her vision. Refusing to give into the darkness she writhed, and tried to get her knees up between them. Slowly her desperate lungs refilled with precious air as he used his own knees to part her legs and gave up his punishment of her breast to drag the frayed fabric of her dress upwards. One-handed he shoved aside his tunic, arranged himself and thrust into her, burning and searing her core.

He paused between thrusts to lean close, one hand now wrapped in her hair as his lips neared her ears.

'Do you know how long I have imagined this moment?'

A white fleck of spittle fell on her cheek, she turned her head and would have closed her eyes had something not caught her attention with its movement. And as his pounding rhythm against her hips drew towards a crescendo that was mercifully swift, his howl of release both ecstatic and almost pained, he collapsed against her, eyes shut. But not for long, his limp body dragged from off her own and shoved to one side. His eyes failed to open as Artos aimed a vicious kick into his ribs and discarded the thick branch he had used to knock out Thalia's attacker.

She wanted to act with dignity, but it was beyond her and instead, she pulled her knees towards her chest, wrapped her arms around them and began to cry in deep uneven shudders. Thalia felt rather than saw Artos crash to earth beside her, after a few minutes his hands reached for her. She did not fight him as he pulled her onto his lap and held her against his chest like a frightened child as she wept, all the while whispering requests for her forgiveness.

Chapter Twenty: A Message from Home

Lviv, 2023

I woke. The weight of Samir's arm held me beside him, the warmth of his body, nestled against my own. His breath, a steady exhalation of warmth against her neck. The morning was a pale rose blush that filtered through the wooden slats at the window and could be ignored. What could not be ignored was the urgent need pressing in my bladder, nor my awareness of the pink blur that shifted in the doorway. I internally cursed well-oiled door hinges while taking a moment to bless the foresight I had shown at some ungodly hour to writhe my way back into the singlet top that had been discarded the previous evening.

This had never been my intention.

I considered ignoring both the bladder and the blur and sinking back into the strength and comfort of Samir's chest but that the blur sharpened, stepping closer to the bed, revealing itself to be about the general size and shape of a five-year-old wearing a pair of fluffy pink pyjamas emblazoned with the smiling cartoon image of Dora the Explorer. It was very much like the ones I had once bought my niece when Kate had been enamoured with the animated South American explorer and her primate companion. The girl hovered, shifting from foot to foot, her hand clenched in front of her. Her lack of surprise at finding a woman in her father's bed made me wonder, briefly, how often this had happened. Nothing about Samir gave me the impression this was commonplace. For me it was an uncomfortable first and I was tempted to pull the covers over my head and pretend I could disappear. After a moment's hesitation,

Melie held the clenched hand out toward me. The words she lisped, in Ukrainian, were unintelligible but unnecessary. On the palm of her small hand a bloodied tooth, freshly pulled from the gum was proudly displayed.

I waited for Samir to stir but his breathing remained steady. It took some slow and careful wriggling, all of which amused the waiting child, but I managed to writhe my way out from under his arm without waking him. With his eyes closed and his face relaxed in sleep, the worries of the week had disappeared and he looked years younger. Aware that my legs were bare and my pants were not immediately evident I gratefully seized the fallen coverlet, wrapping it around my waist. Dignity preserved, I sat on the edge of the bed and cast my gaze around to locate my missing pants. *Ah, there, beside the open door to the ensuite.* The girl blinked at me owlishly before studying her sleeping father.

'Let's let Daddy sleep shall we?' I whispered.

I knew Melie had some English but no idea how much, so I pointed at Samir and mimed sleep. 'I have to go to the toilet first and then we'll go and take care of that tooth.' I pointed from myself and the ensuite door then to Melie making walking motions with my fingers.

Mercifully the child understood, echoing the shushing gesture I had used earlier that was globally recognised, it seemed. I pressed the girl's fingers closed around the offending tooth. Melie grinned, revealing the bloody gap in her smile, then slipped back out the door as silently as she had entered.

Thankfully, the ensuite door was as well-oiled as the bedroom one and a pair of plush hotel robes hung behind the door. I slipped one on over my pants and top since I had left my jacket over the chair on Samir's side of the bed.

When I emerged Samir still slumbered, his breath a relaxed hush as I slipped out the door and into the modest living room. The girl was waiting, her legs swinging from the high stool beside the kitchen bench, her tongue poking through the new gap as she peered intently at the screen of her father's phone, her thumb swinging over the glass as she played a game.

'Does your father let you play with his phone?' I asked.

It was a pointless question. Melie smiled up at me blankly before returning her attention to the screen. The girl's minimal English was not enough for a dialogue of this kind.

'Tooth?' I asked instead, pointing to my own.

The child grinned, revealing again the deep dimples in her cheeks; she held out the tooth, still cupped in one hand.

I turned to the cupboards, opening first one then another until I located glasses, taking two from where they sat and half filling both with water before turning back to the bench. I gestured to one of the glasses, making a gesture like dropping something into it. The girl complied and with a plink the tooth hit the water and dropped to the bottom, releasing a diffusion of pink into the water.

I hesitated standing there. I had never in my life woken up beside a man, with a child standing by the bedside. I had never dated a man with children. As charming as the child had seemed during our interactions the previous day, I was not nearly comfortable in the presence of small children and well aware that I had not once been alone with her. But there was blood smeared on her chin and her hand was likewise stained. I found myself running my tongue over the back of my teeth and recalling the strange sensation of the new gap and the metallic taste of blood in my mouth as a child.

'Melie?' I held my arms in an open-handed gesture and the girl took the hint and, setting her father's phone on the countertop, allowed herself to be lifted to sit beside the sink. She was heavier than she looked and I tried to recall how my niece Kate had felt at the same age. Had I ever actually picked her up? I took the second cup and mimed taking a sip, swishing it around in my mouth and spitting back into the sink.

'Do you think you can do that?' I asked, handing the glass to the girl, who did exactly as she was bid, I had her repeat until, at last, the water she spat in the sink ran without any pink.

'Melie, do that.'

'Good girl. Well done.'

Melie smiled. 'Good girl,' she parroted.

I dampened some paper towels under the tap and gently wiped her face and hands. Perhaps I was not as bad at the whole parenting skills thing as I had always imagined I would be. Not that I was enlisting for the job on a permanent basis. There was nothing in my life that would suit sharing with another, adult or child, I realised. But given I was here in Samir's rooms, cleaning blood off a five-year-old's hands it was not a line of thought I really wanted to pursue.

With my hands under her armpits, I lifted her from the benchtop and sat her back on the chair. I considered the tooth in its sea of water. At home, I would have wrapped it in a tissue and had her put it under her pillow but I had no idea if the tooth fairy even existed in Ukraine, let alone if a pillow and coins were the order of the day. My phone was in my bag upstairs so googling wouldn't help and I was hardly going to use Samir's phone, even if it seemed to not have a screen lock.

'Right. Shall we get breakfast? Something soft I think?'

Breakfast was clearly a word Melie knew for she nodded her head and grinned broadly. I turned to the cupboards of the small kitchenette. It was stocked with the ubiquitous collection of four cups, bowls, plates and glasses, a toaster and a kettle but nothing that could have passed for food. A couple of teabags, coffee and sugar sachets sat on the bench. In the fridge a small container of what I assumed was long-life milk.

'It's not looking good, Melie. Unless you have an instant coffee habit?'

She frowned at me, not understanding.

A shuffle in the doorway revealed a welcome form. Melie scrambled from the stool and threw herself at her father. He lifted her easily, pressing a kiss to Melie's forehead and looked across at me, smiling almost shyly. I felt a blush rise to my cheeks.

I was well out of practice at 'morning afters' and shifted my gaze to the empty bench. 'We were just contemplating breakfast.' I gestured at the open row of empty cupboards.

'I see.' He deposited the girl back on the stool, she promptly pointed at the glass of red tinged water.

'What is this?' He lifted the glass, peering at the tooth at the bottom.

Melie began to chatter in a rapid-fire manner, Samir listened intently as the girl spoke, ending up poking her tongue at her father through the now less bloody gap in her smile. He replied in their shared language and I observed the easy relationship they shared and wondered, not for the first time, what exactly I thought I was doing. What affairs I had were always fleeting things, crippled by my inability to forget my past and doomed by my reluctance to invest myself. What was I doing invading a family unit?

Samir's gaze lifted to mine and I realised I was chewing my bottom lip.

'Thank you.'

It took me a moment to realise he was referring to the tooth. I shrugged in acknowledgement. 'I was not certain if you have the Tooth Fairy in your country?'

'Tooth Fairy?'

'You know, lose a tooth, stick it under a pillow, and the tooth fairy comes in the night, takes the tooth and leaves a coin.'

He smiled, obviously bemused by the idea. 'What does a fairy do with a tooth?'

I found myself frowning, uncertain. 'I really don't know.' He laughed and I found myself smiling back. 'It is a tradition in Australia.'

'And did the tooth fairy give you a coin for your teeth?'

'Yes. And no. Sometimes she did. It was my mother of course, not an actual fairy. But sometimes she forgot and left it there. When that happened she told me that the Tooth Fairy had been very busy in the night and had run out of time and that she would surely come that night instead.'

'And did she?'

'Yes. But she only gave us a dollar coin and my friend Tracey's Tooth Fairy always left her a ten-dollar note. I couldn't work out why we were being ripped off. My teeth were as good as hers.' I hesitated, lost in the revery. 'It was my sister who explained that it was Mum that put the money there and took the tooth and that because our Mum wasn't as wealthy as my friend's, we only got a dollar.'

'So you told your mother that you knew?' he asked.

I sniffed. 'Of course not. But I stopped telling her when I lost teeth and I sold them to my friends instead.'

'Very entrepreneurial.'

I nodded.

'In Ukraine, it is tradition to hide the tooth in a dark place until the new tooth grows, but I rather like the Turkish tradition. It is believed in Turkiye, that if you bury the tooth where you want your child to be when they grow up it will help them achieve it. A bit like predicting the future.'

I found myself considering the tooth in the cup and the dark-haired, dark-eyed child. 'I like it. Where would you bury Melie's tooth?'

He glanced at his daughter, who had picked up her plate and begun licking off the last of the syrup. Samir took the plate from her with a flow of words that sounded like good-hearted chastisement. Melie grinned, poked her tongue at him through her teeth as she slipped down off the stool and ran to the lounge, using the remote with the ease of modern children and surfing channels until she found the Ukrainian version of Nickelodeon. Samir shook his head with a smile.

'I don't really know. I don't want to choose her life for her. I just want her to be safe and happy.'

I recalled the way he had hovered at the burial site when we had exhumed the remains of the rest of his family. 'Perhaps keep it for her, and when she knows what she wants, she can bury it for herself.'

His dark eyes crinkled at the edges. 'You are very wise, do you know that.'

'I should be. I am a doctor.'

'Now, breakfast? There is a lovely *pekarnya*; a bakery below in the street. They make *oladyi*; they are like pancakes. The coffee is good.' He glanced at my state of dishabille and grinned, the dimple flashing again. 'If you and Melie wait here, I can bring it up.'

Now he was speaking my language. 'Coffee sounds perfect.'

'Let me duck down, we'll have breakfast and then perhaps we can share a shower?'

The look he gave was both innocent and suggestive. I found myself smiling.

'You can watch cartoons,' Samir gestured at where Melie sat before the television, 'or take a shower.'

'I'll wait.' I offered with a smile, settling on a stool at the bench.

He smiled, and slipped out the door.

On the couch in front of the television Melie sang the theme from Bluey at the top of her voice; it was surreal listening to the familiar tune in another language. After a few minutes of unsuccessfully trying to translate the Ukrainian voice-over of the Australian cartoon, I was startled by the sharp vibration of Samir's phone. Melie had left it on the bench beside me. An incoming message flashed onto the screen. An attractive redhead, face in profile in the bubble beside it, the image caught mid-laugh, hair streaked with white blond, flashed onto the screen. The message was written in English.

> Flight arrives Sunday 6pm.
> I can't wait to get home.
> Don't be late! I love you!

The notification slipped away leaving me staring at the home screen, a photo of Samir with Melie on his shoulders both laughing at the camera, and it struck me that the image had to have been taken by someone. The jiggling of keys in the doorway heralded Samir's return. I found myself pushing the phone away from my reach, like a child confronted with a plate of brussel sprouts. The tightness in my chest was a warning. I pushed back from the centre bench, thoughts racing. I shoved away from the bench.

He had made no mention of a girlfriend, but then, neither had I asked. I slipped into the bedroom, the bed where we had made love still a tangle of sheets. My eyes slid over the bedside table where his wallet sat half covered by my bra, dangling from Samir's side of the bedhead. His bag was open against the wall. I ached to open the wallet or ransack his bags for evidence that yet again I had made a wrong choice. I schooled myself to stillness.

The words of the message burned themselves into my brain. I had never been the 'other woman', I didn't like how it felt now. I felt betrayed. An unfamiliar empty ache tugged at me.

Fool! I berated myself, snatching my errant bra. One night was not a relationship. He had made no offers and I had no claims. So why did this hurt? Distantly, I heard keys in the hotel room door. My small backpack was on the floor near the window; I crossed to it, collecting the clothes that had been scattered, pushing them back into the open mouth of the bag. I picked up my phone and went to slip it into the front pocket when it vibrated in my hand. I jumped.

'Joining us for breakfast?'

Samir's voice was warm and the tone light. In his hand he held out a paper cup that steamed slightly. The scent of coffee was intoxicating and sickening. A rectangular bulge in his pocket said he had retrieved his phone. Had he seen the message? Nothing in his face suggested he had.

I shook my head, unable to articulate the words. Last night he had pressed his lips to my hand but it had been my choice to kiss him. I had been drawn to him since the farmhouse. I had agreed to the invitation and I had let him slip the sleeve off my shoulder and kiss the tender hollow in my neck. He had been hesitant and gentle, waiting until I reciprocated before making the next move. I had never felt remotely threatened, only cherished. It was an adult decision and I was not looking for a relationship. I had spent my whole life avoiding them. So why did I feel so sick about this?

'Not hungry? We have time for a shower. I'll scrub your back if you'll scrub mine.' He offered.

I could simply ignore the text I had seen. Take advantage of the moment, enjoy the sensation of a human touch my body actually seemed to welcome and crave; and when my holiday was over, return to Izyum without another thought. People did this all the time. Why did it feel like such an abhorrent idea?

The phone in my hand vibrated again, the pulse notifying me of an incoming call. The word Mum flashed across the screen. Perfect timing. I dismissed the call with a flick, pushing the phone deep into my back pocket. He was still standing in the doorway, coffee still in hand, watching me.

'I … I have to go. Something has come up and…'

A line creased in the middle of his brow. I waited for some sign of guilt but there was only concern in his expression.

'I have to go,' I repeated, the words falling flat, even to my ears. I slipped past him, careful not to let any part of me brush against him, in case I weakened. I knew he had followed and was watching puzzled as I crossed the room to scoop my jacket off the chair and tie it around my hips rather than struggling with shaking hands to force it over my arms. Shoving my arm through one of the straps of my backpack I realised he was still standing in the middle of the doorway. Beneath the jacket, the phone vibrated against my backside.

Samir's face was clouded with confusion.

'What can I do? Let me help.' He reached for me, moving out of the doorway as he did so.

I recoiled from his touch, scared by the empty feeling in my chest, fearful of the chemistry his touch evoked. Knowing how easily I might step into his embrace and forget that on Sunday someone else would take that place, I forced my face to stillness. The same way I did when speaking to the family of a victim, or telling a student that their research proposal was flawed. 'You can't. I have to go.' I ducked past and out the door, trying to ignore the scent of him that filled my senses. He followed.

'At least let me call you a taxi.'

At the sight of the phone in his hand, I felt dizzy, like I was going to be sick. From the lounge Melie looked up at me, still poking her tongue into the new and unfamiliar gap in her smile. What sort of man brought someone home when his girlfriend was absent but his child wasn't. I caught a fleeting glimpse of my face in the hall mirror, hair still dishevelled from last night, face pale, eyes wide.

'No. Don't do that. I'll flag one.'

I reached for the door. I wanted to say something mature and worldly, to shrug off emotion the way I could in the field or the confines of the lab or morgue but nothing came to me. My fingers fumbled at the catch, it wouldn't give. I tugged at it wildly, aware that my breath was now coming in uneven gasps.

'Tori, what's wrong? Please tell me?' His face seemed so earnest.

'Let me out!' The words tumbled out louder, harsher than I expected as I swung to face him.

He stared at me for a moment, his expression puzzled and hurt, and then reached past, not brushing me, but reaching for the catch. I felt the door give way, swinging open behind me. I pressed the button to the elevator and when it made me wait, aware of Samir standing in the doorway, I took the stairs, refusing to look back.

It was fortunate that I had a good sense of direction because it was two blocks before I saw a taxi, and one more before I successfully hailed one. The driver's English was halted. 'Where to?'

For a moment my mind was blank, searching for the name of my hotel.

The man waited, watching me curiously in the revision mirror. The phone in my pocket buzzed again. I shifted and reached for it, determined to turn it off when I saw the name on the screen. My mother was persistent at times, but the benefit of distance was she rarely tried to call more than once before giving up and sending a text. A text I would often ignore. Swiping up before I could school my hand to stillness, I answered.

'What is it, Mum?' I knew my tone was sharp.

There was silence at the end of the line and for a moment I wondered if I had pressed accept too late and missed the call. Then there was a sobbing breath, as though someone was trying and failing at calming themselves. 'Mum?'

'You have to come home, Victoria.' Her voice was paper thin.

'What? Mum? Why?'

'There's been an accident. Your sister…' her mother's voice broke off. 'You need to come home.'

Chapter Twenty-One: In the Shadows of Vesuvius

Moesia, AD 75

The water was frigid from snow melt in the distant mountains and it raised bumps across she looked like a goose plucked by slaves and trussed ready to be roasted. Despite the rivulet's frozen temperatures Thalia didn't want to leave it, she had scrubbed at her flesh until it was red and raw, the part between her legs even more pained than it had been before, but she could not stop until she could erase the feel of him on her and inside her.

'Domina, please. Come out before you catch your death of cold.'

Could one catch death? Would death be a bad thing to catch? He stood on the edge of the stream in only his tunic, holding his dark-dyed cloak towards her. She was tempted to refuse him, say that death was a preferable companion but she knew deep down she was not a woman to easily surrender. Despite the hurts and the ache deep within her. She noticed his knee was badly swollen, a deep tear in the flesh oozed blood that was no longer bright, joining a smear that wound down his leg and dyed his ankle dark red. A leather strap wrapped tightly just above the injury stopped it from flowing more merrily. No wonder he had not attempted the steep bank.

'I have a fire started.'

She tipped her head considering his words, they could have been spoken in a foreign tongue. Perhaps they were, he must have had a language before he learnt Latin. None of it made sense really. Her body began to shiver and though she wrapped her arms around herself Thalia could not stop the shakes. The Praetorian limped forward, angling his body to attempt the incline.

'No. Stay there. I will come to you.' She was surprised her voice sounded so level. He looked surprised too. Still shaking, her limbs barely responsive she managed to reach the edge and step from the water's chill embrace. The cooling air of the forest wrapped around her and she realised, looking straight up that stars had begun to appear in the violet expanse above.

She stopped a pace away from him. He held out the cloak and she wanted to take it, really she did, but her limbs had stopped responding to her requests, and simply stayed wrapped around her, shaking with paroxysms of shock that she could neither control nor stop. His eyes never dropped from her face as he gently wrapped the cloak around her, securing it with a length of leather she vaguely recognised as Petronius' belt. When her legs refused to comply with an order to follow him, he gathered her, and with little more than a grunt to acknowledge the pain lifting even her slight weight caused him, carried her to the overhanging rock shelter where, as promised, a flickering golden fire danced merrily.

Neither of them looked at the trussed form of the other Praetorian, bound to a tree trunk and gagged, so neither knew whether he had awakened from the blow or not. Further back the Praetorian's horse, now hobbled, munched on the sparse grass of the modest clearing.

He let her find her feet and she felt them buckle, dropping her unceremoniously into the dry earth of the overhang. She immediately felt the warmth of the fire.

'Is it safe?' Thalia asked through chattering teeth, gesturing with her chin, the only responsive part of her, towards the fire.

'They won't be looking tonight. They will be eating and drinking and celebrating their success as any successful bandits might. And I've banked the fire so it can't be seen except from above.'

It was true, he had made a snug hollow for it, and a fallen log obscured its glow from the other side. She relaxed a little, allowing the warmth of fire and cloak to seep into her body.

'They weren't bandits,' she murmured. 'They were Titus' men.'

She felt his blue eyes on her, but the warmth of the fire had lulled her lids into falling and the shock of the day slipped her consciousness away.

At some point during the night, she felt him move beside her, pulling her gently shivering form against his warm chest. When the shivering subsided and she slipped back into restless dreams Thalia had the sense that though he shared his warmth with her, he would not sleep. It almost made her feel safe.

A trussed bird, plump and plucked, skin turning golden and leaking fatty fluid to hiss into the waiting embers was slung across last night's fire pit. A small mound of berries and a handful of mushrooms sat on the prone log beyond the fire. Petronius' water skin leaned against the log. Her mouth was dry and the savour of cooking fowl tempted. Of her companion, nothing could be seen. Thalia sat up, limbs aching. She ignored the other ache, the one inside her and reached to pluck a pair of berries between her fingers, sniffing them. They were small, plump red berries, like the raspberries of Rome and hunger overcame concern as she popped them between her lips. They were sweeter than they had any right to be and the rest of the small pile vanished swiftly.

Thalia was reaching for the water skin when she heard the very obvious scuff of footsteps approaching. She was surprised to recognise the footfalls as the Praetorian's. When had she become so aware of him? He was limping still, she could tell, from the hesitation every second step. He did not seem surprised to find her awake, simply stepped around her, deposited a fresh load of dry branches and a handful more berries and seated himself, swollen knee stretched out before him. The blood had dried and flaked. He watched her quietly as she untied the mouth of the waterskin and drank deeply. It was warm and slightly stale but it slaked her thirst. In time she held the skin towards him. He shook his head. When

Thalia picked up the berries he had brought and held them towards him, the Praetorian smiled.

'I ate many as I picked them.'

She nodded, hunger getting the better of her as she popped several in her mouth, letting them burst between her teeth and savouring the taste. It felt odd, almost guilty to enjoy such a simple thing after what she had been through. Artos leaned forward, ripped a leg and breast from the roasting bird and handed them to her. Ignoring the dripping grease and the scalding heat she ate quickly. He handed her a second leg. This she ate less ravenously before wiping her hands on the edge of his cloak.

'You were right. They were Romans.'

She glanced at him. 'You found them?'

He shook his head. 'But I tracked them and the footprints they left were standard military issue, no matter the clothing they wore. The Proconsul wants you dead.'

It was a statement, not a question, but she nodded in agreement anyway.

'I'm sorry.'

She knew from his tone that he did not mean for the fact her husband wanted her killed. She refused to think about the thing he was apologising for. Feet aching, she stretched her legs before her and tried, surreptitiously to massage her aching calves. In the light that spilled into the overhang, she could see the damage to her legs, angry scratches, slices and grazes, gained from fleeing from her pursuer. They were not bleeding, not now, but they blushed an angry red and some were hot to the touch as she ran her hands gently over them. When she noticed him looking she tucked her legs closer and pulled the ragged length of his cloak over them.

She shook her head to negate the need for an apology. 'Please don't be sorry. You saved my life. I should be thanking you.' She hesitated, 'Was there anyone else...?'

His expression was bleak so she didn't continue, staring instead at her battered hands and broken nails. She imagined the expression on Messalinus' face should he reach to hold her hand. Then she recalled the reason she was here.

He reached forward to pluck the bird from the spit, holding it out towards her. Thalia shook her head and watched as he began to pluck the dark flesh from the bird, chewing with evident appetite. When he was done and the bird no more than bones he bent to gather up the mushrooms, wincing when he did so. Again he offered her the mushrooms, only eating them when she refused. She let the flickering embers capture her attention as he ate until the silence between them lengthened. He stood, reaching and adding another branch to the fire, and the dry leaves erupted in flame. From the ground at his feet, she looked up at the man who had saved her.

He had lost his sword, probably in the battle and his long dagger was also missing, leaving the belt and sheath empty. His tunic was bloodspattered and torn so that it barely covered his torso, beneath it, naked flesh and chest hair. It was a startling reminder that no matter how civil, this man was no Roman, given to plucking and shaving. Around his neck, from a stained leather thong hung the pendant she had noticed on a few occasions now, surprised as always that a mere soldier, even a Praetorian favoured by the Emperor would have such a trinket as a golden pendant. It seemed incongruous on the hewn warrior before her; a beautifully worked female form, a voluptuous goddess and completely naked.

'Will you share your thoughts, Domina?'

Thalia could not help but blush as she was caught appreciating the form in front of her. How strange that despite the horrors she had just endured the sight of this man still moved her. The Praetorian was like a statue formed in bronze, but not of a god like Apollo or Eros. If the Praetorian was a god he was a god of war like Mars. His muscular torso narrowed at the hip, and his thighs and calves were powerful and well-defined. No. Not Mars. She took in the broad shoulders and hewn arms littered with scars and silvery marks she recognised as burns. If he was a god, he was Vulcan. God of the Smiths, forger of weapons. He was beautiful, but in a rough fashion, that of a man who fought and worked and did not rest in luxurious Olympus or flit around causing mischief or seducing maidens. He was nothing like Messalinus or the monster who did his bidding. Shocked she even considered such thoughts given what she had just been through, Thalia felt warmth infuse her face again and spoke to distract herself.

'My name is Thalia,' she said. 'I think you are entitled to use it.' Her gaze shifted to the swollen knee and the oozing wound. 'We are going to have to do something about that leg.'

He glanced at the offending limb and its injury.

The edges were jagged and raw, blood still welled in the deep crater that had been gouged into his flesh. She considered what she could do to fix it, here in the forest. Would they make it far enough to find somewhere safe, if she didn't?

'Your husband doesn't call you that.' His words disrupted her thoughts.

'What?'

'The Proconsul calls you Quartia.'

She shifted her gaze from his wound to his face. His dark eyes showed only curiosity.

'True. He insists on using the name my father gave me, Arrecina Quartia. The fourth Arrecina. I have three older sisters, you see?'

He shook his head. 'Romans,' he scoffed. 'You think you rule the world and you cannot even give your children true names.'

She shrugged. She could not argue. 'I chose my own name. I chose Thalia.'

'Thalia.' He repeated, the words gentle and strange with his foreign accent. 'What does it mean?'

Thalia smiled. 'It is the name of the youngest of the *Gratiae*.'

'*Gratiae*?'

'The Graces, a triad of goddesses. Daughters of Jupiter; they personified beauty and charm, music and song, dancing and laughter. The youngest was Thalia, she was wed to… the god, Vulcan.'

She blushed again. 'And you? I think of you as The Praetorian but I have heard them call you… Andos? Anthos? Is that the name of your birth or was it one you chose?

'My father named me Alexartos. My brother called me Artos.'

Thalia nodded, repeating the name silently in her head to force it into her memory. As she did she forced her gaze back to the injury. She reached forward, letting her fingertips drift gently across the clean flesh around it and was surprised when the smooth surface rippled with goose bumps. She forced her thoughts to the medical treatises she had read over the years and distant memories of her mother's medical garden and home cures. What could help that might still be available to her? She recalled moss on the trees, she could use that to clean and pack the wound. There were plenty of pines, if she could find something sharp she could access the inner bark and use some of that. She could use the edge of her cloak for bandaging if she could tear it.

'I cannot fix this the way I would at home but perhaps we can do something.'

He nodded, reached over the log and dropped a parcel of fabric in her lap. The fabric was fresh and clean and expensively woven, she recognised it as hers. As she opened it up to reveal a long dress, a palla and sandals. Only then did she notice that where before he had been wearing only one caligae, he now wore two leather sandals, though a little too small.

'You went back to the caravan.'

He nodded. 'They had taken almost everything but had no need for your woman's chest. I brought the simplest gown I could find. She considered the fabric in her hands, he was right, although seeded with pearls, it was probably the least adorned garment she owned. It was creamy-coloured and soft. If she plucked the pearls she could easily pass for an ordinary woman. The pearls and the semi-precious stones on the bracelets around her wrists could pay for passage to… *where?*

'I don't suppose you found—'

He dropped a pouch containing her sewing kits into her lap.

Thalia smiled. At least now she has something to mend the rent in his skin with. She opened it to remove a needle and thread.

'Let's see how brave Praetorians really are.'

α

He was brave. Beyond a flinch, he did not make a sound or move a muscle as she stuck the sharp needle through his flesh and drew the thread after it. She bound the injury in moss and astringent pine sap before wrapping it, and his twisted knee, in the palla he had found. When she was done they both examined her handy-work. If only she could mend her own wounds as easily. Though there was no outward sign of her trauma she knew she would carry it with her, she just hoped that would be all she would carry.

'What do we do now?' she asked.

He shook his head. 'You cannot return to Rome unless you want someone to deliver you back to your husband.'

She shook her head, aware there was no option for her to return. If she allowed him a next time, Messalinus might prove more adept. 'You need to kill him.' She glanced in the direction of the trussed Praetorian and was surprised when he shook his head.

'If we did and it was discovered we would be hunted across the empire. As murderers of one of the Emperor's guards, we would be killed on sight, crucified, or fed to the beasts in one of your arenas for the entertainment of the mob.'

'Not me.' She ventured a false half-smile. 'I am a Roman citizen.'

His brow raised. 'Right. A hot bath and a sharp knife, instead.'

Thalia shrugged but accepted his logic. She had wanted to put Petronius' blade through his heart but in truth, she could not look at him without the urge to throw up.

He raised his voice and deepened his tone, not loud, but enough that the sound would likely carry. 'We head East. If we make it through Dacia we will find the plains of my homeland. We can disappear into the grasslands. Rome has never really conquered there.'

'And what would I do on the grasslands, Praetorian?'

His eyes were serious when they fell on her. 'Live.'

In the end, Artos dealt with the matter in typical barbarian style, a solid fist to Petronius' scowling countenance gave him the satisfaction of spreading the man's nose across his face and breaking a few teeth, but left him alive and unconscious. His ropes were loosened but not untied.

Thalia followed in her rescuer's footsteps with precision, trusting that he knew how to avoid leaving a trail. It was only when they turned abruptly when they reached the Eastern hills that she realised she too had been deceived. Artos had no intention of making for the vast tundra. When they emerged on the coast a week later, a half-dozen pearls secured their passage on a trade vessel. By the time they climbed aboard, he was barely limping.

α

'Napoli?' she asked, as she stood at the fore of the vessel, the wind catching the sails behind and above their heads. The blue sky was interrupted by the ribbon of white shore and verdant hills, before reflecting in the water of the bay. She was grateful that the seasickness of the early parts of the journey that had seen her suspended over the rails, losing anything she had forced herself to eat or drink, had passed and she could enjoy the view. As they had then, still now, his strong arms rested on the rail on either side of her, she was nestled between them. Artos didn't actually touch her. He hadn't since carrying her back to their shelter, except at night, when she slept in the shelter of his body and shared his warmth. And if sometimes his arms wrapped around her when she woke sobbing from a dream, neither of them spoke of it. But his protection was evident to all who saw them and smiled to see a young couple so evidently in love.

He nodded, staring across the bay, to the east the immense cone of Mt Vesuvius cast its shadows across the bay and the seaside villages that nestled around it in the fertile reaches of Campania. It was a benevolent giant that made the land for miles around so rich and fertile that it was said the farmers of Campania harvest not once, but thrice, each year.

'It's not far from Rome.' She tendered the thought.

'No. Close enough that no one would dream of searching for us there.'

Thalia nodded, in the waves at the front of the vessel a pod of Neptune's dolphins leapt and frolicked, diving deep to leap above the white spray. Their antics made her smile, and she refused to feel guilty for it either. With a shake of her head, she turned to face the man who had saved her life, stepped closer, until she was touching, and reached up on tiptoes to press her lips against the stubble about his neck. Artos only stiffened for a moment before his hands wrapped around her, pulling her into the closeness and protection of his body. The golden goddess, the huntress, hung between them.

Chapter Twenty-Two: Admissions of Guilt

Melbourne, 2024

For someone who spends so much time in a morgue and surrounded by the clinical equipment and sterile smells of disinfectant, I hated hospitals. There was no rational explanation for it, no personal experiences that left me feeling hollow, I had never so much as broken a bone. But from my earliest childhood, hospitals reminded me of losing Clare. They were the great white sterile monsters who swallowed my sister for days, weeks or months, leaving me feeling like an only child, forgotten by my mother who spent her life worrying about Clare and not noticing that I worried too.

Clare had been in Kinder when my consul father had swept my mother off her feet, the proverbial Italian stallion. She had been seven when she was diagnosed with Type 1 diabetes and our family was poised to move to Italy, our lives already in boxes, tickets purchased, to follow my father home. Instead, my mother had stayed. Clare's health issues meant regular dialysis, the frantic search for a donor kidney and no chance for relocation to a foreign country our mother didn't know, even to follow her handsome foreign husband. His parting gift, a swelling belly. A child he would not meet for a further four years.

At eight years old Clare had her first transplant, a random donor, whose gift put a healthy blush back in her cheek and left her free to really play with the little sister who always left her exhausted. It failed months later. My mother had given her a kidney the following year. This gave Clare nine precious years and allowed her to finish high school, go to university and meet David Leibermann, the man she had married. The man who had given her her final gift, the kidney that resided in her to this day. David had been killed two years later, on tour in Afghanistan, leaving Clare as a sole parent to Kate. Kate had kept Clare sane and she threw her entire being into being the best mother anyone could imagine. David's kidney kept her alive.

My mother had been thrilled when I had announced that I wanted to be a doctor. I would find a cure for diabetes, she had declared, then was horrified to learn that I didn't mean that type of doctor. Unlike my mother's aspirations, I did most of my medical training in a morgue. Morgues didn't bother me the way hospitals did. Perhaps it was simply that the upper floors of the hospital—morgues were inevitably located in basements—were filled with people who were unable to keep emotions in check. Even those who managed not to express it through tears or shouting or pleading seemed to ooze emotion from every pore.

I hovered in the doorway of 3B. I had brushed my hair in the elevator, pulling it back into its customary ponytail. My clothes were creased from long hours spent sitting. I don't think I smelled bad but I was aware of the layer of fuzz on my teeth and silently ran my tongue over them, hoping it was not visible to the naked eye. Not that anyone was looking when I took that final breath and stepped into the room. It was larger than I expected, filled with light. Bunches of flowers lined the windowsill in a riot of colours and an assortment of plastic vases. A helium-filled balloon with brightly coloured writing spelled out the words 'Get Well.' Someone had strung cheerfully blinking Christmas lights across the window.

As always my mother was beside the bed, she had her back to me, an arm wrapped around Kate. I could not see their faces. I didn't really want to. I knew well the exact shade of pallor they would be. My mother would not have called me unless it was serious. Very serious. I also knew the expression of glazed despair that would inhabit their eyes. I had seen it too many times on the faces of the loved ones of the victims on my table.

The machines in the room made soft humming noises and were counterpointed by the steady beeping of monitors. My younger brother, Matt, and his father—my step-father—Phil, were in hushed conversation. A young man I didn't know sat uncomfortably in the hospital chair beside Matt, both hands clenched tight and resting on his knees.

It was Matt who saw me hovering and rose from the chair as fluidly as he did on a surfboard, his lanky frame well-tanned, making the blond hairs on his arms stand out. I found a smile for the blue-eyed world wanderer. He took me in his arms without waiting. It still felt wrong for my baby brother to dwarf me.

'Hey, you made it.'

'Where else would I be?' I was grateful that he chose not to answer.

'Come in. I'll introduce you to Bayani.'

And so, though I would happily have remained in the hallway, I was drawn into the bright space. As I was introduced to the handsome young Filipino man with eyes I imagined were more given to laughter than sadness. Still, like all of them his sorrow was evident. Phil squeezed my arm and pressed a whiskery kiss to my cheek. My mother, who had lost her first husband to cancer, her second to the lure of homeland, a wandering eye and a typically Italian attitude to the male need for companionship, had met Phil in the bed beside her when she woke up after giving Kate her kidney. He had donated his own to his sister. He was a kindly silver gentleman who adored her, and, in time, had gifted Clare and I a baby brother. I found myself gazing through the flickering Christmas lights, out the window, acutely aware that behind my back, away from the view overlooking the gardens of Royal Park, my sister lay unmoving beneath the sheets and my mother and niece sat perched at her side.

I forced myself to turn, to navigate the edge of the bed, and bring myself to my mother's side. She stood, wrapping me in a one-armed hug, that left her other hand free to hold Kate's hand. I let her cling to me and felt her trembling. When she drew back her face was worse than I expected and was surprised that despite the plumping, she looked old. Her make-up barely noticeable; dark rings circled her eyes. It was the dark rings that linked us, Mum, Matt, Clare and I shared Mum's blood but had little else in common, not even our appearance. While Matt towered over me, his blonde hair, faded to platinum from exposure to the sun, Clare was shorter than me again, and looked even smaller in the large hospital bed with all its fittings.

It was not as I had imagined. When my mother had said a car accident, I had imagined traction and broken limbs, miles of bandages and mangled features. Instead Clare lay on the bed perfectly intact. A small yellowing bruise was evident high on her right temple. If it wasn't for the honey blond hair I would not have recognised my sister at all. Her bottom length hair had been plaited into a long tail that hung over her shoulder but like all of her seemed leached of colour, more grey than blond. Her lips were cracked, forehead and cheeks were reddened and looked rough to the touch and swollen, oh so swollen. Her eyes were barely visible in the puffy flesh of her face. Her arms, resting on the covers were likewise bloated, though her hands looked like those of an old woman, all sinewy and clenched over her tiny fragile body. The machine I heard was drawing a constant stream of sluggish blood and returning something slightly brighter but it was clear the dialysis was not working.

'You said it was a car accident.'

My words sounded shrill and loud in the silent room. Kate stared up at me in horror.

My mother imposed her body between Kate and I, her hands out and up as though to ward off anything I might say.

'I know what this is.' I did. I knew end stage renal failure, I had looked it up in medical books as a child, morbid with curiosity about what was happening to my sister. 'Why didn't you tell me? Why didn't you call me back?' My voice pitched rough and low, tears streaming down my own flushed cheeks.

'We are a match. You knew we were a match!'

Matt and Phil had me by the arms and were pulling me out of the room and into the hallway, my mother followed, still waving her hands. Kate's stricken expression as she stood in the doorway stopped me dead. Even Bayani was gaping at me in wonder.

'You will stop that now, do you understand?' My mother's voice was ragged. 'This is not about you.'

'I told you to warn her,' Matt said.

I stopped fighting them. Let the wall I had been pushed up against hold me upright. After a time they released their grip.

'Go back to Clare. Kate needs you,' Phil murmured.

My mother obliged. My brother hovered, clearly torn between familial loyalty to his sister and the comforting presence of Bayani. I could not blame him for his choice. With an arm around my shoulder Phil pushed me down the hallway to a bank of connected chairs, forcing me to sit.

'It was a car accident. Clare had a head on with a small truck. Luckily Kate was not in the car. She was unconscious when the ambulance brought her here. The doctors said the neuropathy had become so bad that it had impacted on the nerves that control her movement but they also said her kidneys were at 5% functionality. They put her straight on the machines but, Tori, they said it was too late.'

I had known that just from seeing her. I understood what he was telling me.

'Clare knew it, Tori. She had been hiding it from us for months.'

He must have expected I would argue because he didn't wait for me to say anything.

'Your mother is right,' he said steadily but not without warmth. 'This isn't about you, Tori. Clare knows you are a match. She knows you would have come home, would have given her a kidney. But she didn't want that.'

I stared at him blankly. Then something Clare had said while we had spoken when I was in the airport lounge in Rome came back to me. *David is taking care of me.*

'It's not about me,' I echoed. 'It's about David.'

Phil considered me seriously, shared a brief but approving smile and nodded.

'She won't let David go.'

All she had left of the man she had loved and lost was the kidney that now failed her. For the second time in just days I found myself in the arms of a man I thought I could trust not to hurt me. This time, I hoped I was right. I wept, brokenly, great shuddering gasps that made my ribs ache and threatened to leave me without air, until even tears failed me. In time Phil offered me a crisply ironed and folded handkerchief from his pocket. I blew my nose noisily. Despite the damp he took it from me, folded it more carefully and tucked it away, rising to his feet.

'Bathrooms are that way.' He pointed. 'You know where we are when you are ready.'

I blinked at him, prepared to say I could not do it. I could not face them.

'You are not a coward, Tori. But when you do come back, remember Kate. This is hard enough on her without the rest of us falling apart.'

I did remember Kate, the expression of disgust and despair.

Phil patted my shoulder. 'Five minutes Tori. Or I will send your mother after you.'

When I entered the room the next time, they all pretended not to notice me. Although Bayani gave me a solemn wink, which made me love him instantly. I forced myself to study the form on the bed. Kate had undone her mother's braid and was studiously rebraiding it, twisting the strands of hair hand over hand. There was as I had noticed earlier a clearly visible tint of silver in Clare's hair. Unsurprising, as I recalled pulling her first grey hair when she was twenty-three and I sixteen and on our return flight from Italy. She had joked that she would be grey long before our mother and, in part, she was right, though the silvering would never now take over.

I studied her loose face. The damage from where her head had struck the steering wheel was minor. Someone, I suspected my mother, had applied moisturiser to her bright red cheeks. With her lids closed and her mouth relaxed she looked to be sleeping. There were tiny crow's feet at the corner of her eye that I hadn't noticed the last time I saw her. Tubes, tucked behind her ear, fed her oxygen. Smaller lines snaked out from bandaids that covered the inner part of both elbows, these were hooked to the dialysis machine which whirred steadily. Her left hand was held tightly by my mother, who didn't look up when I entered, nor even when I took position on the opposite side, holding Clare's limp but warm left hand.

Someone, Matt I think, asked about my flight, and I answered in a distracted tone. Over the hours to come, in hushed conversation so sporadic that it barely deserved the title, I was told about the accident that had brought her here. She had been Christmas shopping and was on her way to collect Kate from Cello lessons when she lost control of the vehicle and hit the oncoming truck. The driver had not been injured, no one had, not even Clare, not really. I watched Kate's face as I listened. Her gaze never left my sister's face and her expression barely altered, except for the silent flow of tears that would stream soundlessly down her cheeks before drying for a while. I could tell she blamed herself. Her mother had been coming to pick her up. I wanted to tell her it wasn't her fault but I had no credit to offer platitudes with.

'She waited for you,' I heard my mother say and found myself wishing that she hadn't.

'She wanted you here. You were so close.'

We had been inseparable, until our year in Italy. After that Clare had been so busy with her own life and raising a daughter and I had thrown myself so deeply into my studies that I had barely acknowledged the existence of my family. I had tried, sporadically, to be a good aunt, but aside from Dora the Explorer pyjamas, I lacked the instinct inherent in my sister. I had always felt uncomfortable with Kate, and with Mum and Clare both doting on her, I figured she had enough feminine influence in her life.

Mum spoke again, it took a moment for my brain to register the comment. She was staring at me intently.

'The doctors said she has a week at most. Days maybe. They have given her morphine. She signed a DNR when they first brought her in.'

Oh. I realised now what she was asking me to understand. My sister was sedated and on heavy pain blockers, these would increase with time. She might wake but she would not survive. Not without a kidney that she would not accept. My gaze wandered the bright coloured balloon with its callous message. I wondered why no one had moved it, stuck a pin in it, and shoved it in a waste basket. It seemed the ultimate in futile hope and bordered on cruelty. I ached to stomp on it.

Instead I met my mother's gaze and nodded, then shifted my eyes to Kate. I wanted to ask if she understood but I didn't dare.

As the hours progressed any conversation ended as we listened to the hum and buzz and beep of instruments and watched the erratic lines that represented heart rate.

First, Matt and Bayani left. I smiled to see the way their fingers interlocked. This was the first boy he had brought home. Matt promised he would return to do a late shift of watching over Clare.

Then, as if in obedience to some silent command of my mother's, Phil rose and put a hand on Kate's shoulder. He bent to kiss the top of her head. A single tear rolled off the tip of her nose. She let it.

'Come on, Kiddo. Let your Mum get some rest.'

She moved, reluctantly, but she moved. Squeezing Clare's hand with hers. She never looked at me or spoke to anyone.

My mother and Phil shared a glance.

'You go down and pay for parking. I'll speak to the doctors and be down shortly.' She looked at Kate. 'Get me a flat-white on almond-milk from the cafeteria?'

When the pair had slipped from the room her eyes met mine, they checked to see that I had understood. I did. My sister was dying; soon.

'Now is your chance to thank her.'

The words cut through to my soul, like a scalpel. My mother knew how to hurt.

I kept my expression carefully blank. My mother studied me critically for a long moment and then, with a single squeeze of my hand, followed her husband and grand-daughter.

A long strand of hair fell across Clare's round face, left out when Kate had loosed her hair. I reached forward, tucking it behind her ear, along with the tubes suspended there.

Now was a time for waiting. My mother would spend the time praying. I could have told her there was no point. If there was a god, he or she would only welcome Clare. Her sins would not need expiating, after all, she had already done all her suffering here on earth. So we would simply wait. After that the remains would be interred, her coffin settled beneath the ground under the same piece of lawn that had claimed her father and her husband, attended by the woman who had witnessed each burial. I felt a rush of pity for my mother. I found myself thinking about Samir and the losses he had undergone and the stoic courage he had shown as the bodies of his family were finally laid to rest and the way he had, afterwards, taken me in his arms, so many years after he had lost them. How dare I judge him for finding comfort after such trauma?

Thank her, my mother had said. Instead, I found myself spilling the words out to my sister, telling her all the things I had omitted about Massimo and my eviction from Ercolano, of Ukraine and the war dead, of my attraction to Samir and the guilt I now felt for acting on it, as well as the bitter disappointment I felt over my discovery that I was not the only one to share his bed. I even told her how angry I was that she was depriving her daughter of a mother. Finally, I found myself reassuring her that Kate would survive Mum's spoiling in the years to come. In my head I vowed that the idea of leaving a child without a mother was an excellent reason to never procreate. Even with the thought constrained to my mind, I heard Clare laughing at me. I found my cheeks wet but did not know exactly when I had started crying. I let them fall. I didn't even notice the nursing staff who came in to check the monitors before slipping silently away. Distantly I heard the pinging of messages to my phone but they were just one more electronic sound in a chorus of white noise.

I don't know how long it had been since I ran out of words when I felt the flicker of movement in the hand I still held. I lifted my head and felt her gaze. In the puffy tight flesh of her face, her eyes were narrow slits but they were open. Open and staring at me. The pain in them was clear and I reached for the buzzer to call the nurse.

'No.'

The word came out in a whispered exhalation.

I found myself staring at her, more uncertain than I had ever been in my life. Something in me wanted to run, not to face this. Her hand flickered under my own and I squeezed back, as we had when we were children, silently communicating in squeezes when we were supposed to be silent, sitting on the hard wooden pews in Church.

'Let me give you a kidney. Please, Clare?' The words I had promised myself I wouldn't say tumbled from my lips. They rang with desperation.

Her eyes closed, deliberately. I knew this was a no.

'What about Kate?' I hated myself for saying it. This time her eyes didn't close, but the corner of her mouth twitched. Her hand squeezed mine. Her lips moved with the next exhalation, words I could barely discern but knew instinctively.

'Your turn.'

I found myself shaking my head in refusal. I could not.

'I can't. I can't be you.'

Her eyes closed but she forced them back open. Where she found the strength I didn't know.

'Needs you.'

'No. She has Mum and Phil. They love her and will look after her.'

A minuscule shift of her head was a refusal of my words.

'Your turn.' Somehow, despite being barely audible the words were spoken with authority.

We were silent for a minute. I wanted to tell her I had missed her. I wanted to apologise for not being a better sister, a better aunt when David had died and left her as a single parent, even though I knew it was a lie. I had made myself so busy with my career that I had rarely had time to think of my sister or her child and when I did I made myself busier still. I wanted to apologise for sending messages and facetiming when I should have been there with her. I wanted to tell her I was sorry for abandoning her and leaving her to clean up my mess.

'I love you, Clare-bear.' That was all I could manage.

Her hazel eyes leaked tears. Tears she could not wipe away, so I did.

'Tell her… you are… her mother.'

They were the first words that she expressed clearly and they rang with imperative. The effort to enunciate them shifted her out of consciousness. She left me no opportunity to deny them or refuse them. I stared at her in horror.

Then I heard it, the shifting in the doorway. I had been so intent on Clare that I hadn't noticed we had company. I turned my head, expecting to see a nurse hovering.

Instead, two dark eyes, a mirror of my own met mine. They too seemed filled with horror.

'I came back for my cello.'

Her tone was expressionless. She pointed to the corner of the hospital room, beyond her mother's bed. I couldn't tell how much she'd heard or understood. I looked at the cello case, leaning against the wall. When I glanced back, she was gone. The cello remained.

In time, my phone pinged twice in close succession.

The first was a reminder that I had missed another call and message from Samir. I swiped to delete them, unheard. The second was from my mother. I didn't need to read it to know what it said.

Kate knew.

Ω

The ocean breeze washed over us as we sat on the verandah of my mother's unit at St Kilda. The chill down my spine had nothing to do with it, my mother's glare, however, did.

'What do you mean you leave in the morning?'

I frowned at her. 'I mean my flight leaves at 10 am. I have to get back to work, I have been here a week longer than I planned already. The war crimes tribunal in the Hague is in just a few months and there is so much we need to do to get ready.'

She said not a word, just stared at me. I stubbornly took a sip of wine and stared out over the water, as though the matter were decided.

And it was. There was nothing I could do. Below a tram rattled down the line, headed for Luna Park.

'You can't go. You know you can't. Kate needs you.'

I scoffed. The girl had not spoken a word to me in the two weeks since her mother's death. We had struggled through a Christmas no one could find enthusiasm for and a New Year no one celebrated. I knew she was back to school soon. To my knowledge, she had not cried since the day I arrived and to my surprise had even managed to make it through a short eulogy at Clare's memorial service. She had held her grandmother's hand and distributed tissues, but remained apart from it all. She had not looked at me. Not once.

'No,' I said shortly. 'What she needs is a series of visits to a counsellor. What she has is you. She has settled in here now.'

In truth, the girl had already had a bedroom in my mother's house, so it had just been a matter of collecting the rest of her things. Clare's furniture had been put into storage. The house would be sold, even Kate had agreed there was no point holding onto it until she had finished school and she had plans for University. The money would be held in trust until she was 25, with a proviso that allowed her to dip into it when the trustee, my mother, deemed it necessary. But if I knew my mother there would be no such need.

'I don't think you understand. She is not staying here.'

I was startled. 'Surely not boarding school?'

'No,' my mother said carefully, taking a sip from her own glass before placing it on the glass-top table between us. 'Kate is going to live with her mother.'

My jaw dropped. 'You can't be serious!'

My mother reached her perfectly manicured hand towards mine. I snatched my hand away. 'Clare's will was clear. It is time for you to step up to your responsibilities. Kate is to live with you.'

I shot from my seat, letting it crash to the floor. Since hearing my sister's words, the last she had spoken, I had willfully pretended it had never happened. Kate seemed happy to let me perpetuate the myth that neither of us had heard the pronouncement. Well, not happy, if I am truthful, but deliberate and determined to pretend they had never been spoken.

'No!'

My mother didn't reply, nor did she stop looking at me.

'No. I leave for Europe in the morning. I can't take a child into a war zone! What am I to do, let her play in the streets with the tanks? Have her help me with autopsies?'

'Enough, Victoria.' Her tone was implacable. 'You can both pretend as much as you like but it doesn't make it any less true. Call whoever you need, tell them you are not returning.'

My heart was beating so rapidly, my legs shook. Breath didn't seem to be finding its way into my lungs for all I was gasping it in. 'She is happy here, she loves you and Phil. How could you do that to her? She barely knows me, she doesn't even like me. My life has no room for a teenager.'

My mother glared at me. 'Then make room. I just lost my daughter. I won't let you throw yours away!'

She rose fluidly and, taking both our cups, slipped back into the house, shutting the screen door behind her.

I understood that I had just been given notice. My life as an academic vagrant was finished, after fifteen years of delay I was to finally take up my duties as a mother.

$$\Omega$$

The pier jutted out from the white sand of the beach like a humerus from the elbow of the coast. The sun had set, leaving both sky and ocean tinted with rose gold, edged with amethyst and silver, there seemed no line between sky and earth. The curved lamp posts already glowed and while always crowded, the press of people had grown fewer. Fishermen and women still dipped their lines out over the edge though nothing seemed to be biting. Small, one-masted wooden sailboats were anchored in the safe water beyond the breakwall, bobbing slightly. Beyond them, the lights of the Melbourne skyline, a jagged-toothed jaw in the distance, glowed warmly. The air was still warm but the breeze that touched my shoulders was cooling rapidly. I held Kate's jacket over my arms, a peace offering of sorts. Can a jacket undo rejection and 15 years of neglect and lies? I nearly turned there and then. In the pair of cute wooden shelters that edged the pier, facing each other, a pair of teens were lost in kissing and touching each other. I looked away, unsure if I was embarrassed for them or for me. I tried desperately to forget being that age. The age my daughter—I forced myself to use the words—was now. Further along, at the edge of the pier, where the rails traced their way out to sea, seagulls squabbled.

In the distance I saw her shape, legs dangling over the side, chin resting on hands resting on the horizontal rail, staring out into the distance. I edged closer, trying to look like any other tourist. A pair of joggers laughed as they bounced past in their activewear. A small dog raced at seagulls, barking wildly.

Gold faded to a brush of twilight blue and purple.

The girl on the edge of the pier shivered. I forced myself to walk forward, to stop beside her and drop the jacket over her shoulders. I counted myself lucky that she didn't push it away. I stood at the railing, looking out over the water, trying to find the elusive horizon. I had ever been a coward. My daughter, it turned out, was braver than I, almost.

'So. It's true then. You're really my m…'

It seemed she couldn't even speak the word.

'I am not——that.' Apparently, I couldn't say it either. 'That was Clare. She was the one who nursed you and washed you and dressed you. She made your birthday cakes and sang you to sleep at night, kissed your wounds, drove you to practices…'

The list, I realised a little too late, was exhaustive, so I stopped. She nodded, not looking at me, staring out across the ocean.

'But yes. You were mine first.'

More time painted the sky midnight blue and silver. A cargo ship, lit up like a Christmas tree made incremental movements in the darkness, another much further from shore seemed to be still.

'You didn't want me.' Her voice was flat.

I inhaled, slowly before letting the breath go again. It was an accusation I couldn't fairly deny. 'I was sixteen when I discovered I was pregnant. Seventeen, when you were born. I couldn't even look after myself.'

I tried out the excuse and found it wanting.

'Clare was twenty-five. She had been on anti-rejection drugs for well over a decade by then and spent the equivalent of months on dialysis. Your father had given her one of his kidneys a year earlier but he was back on tour and she was healthy for a time. So she came with me to Italy. The plan had been to put you up for adoption.' I paused to look at her, her expression was blank, but she was listening.

'Clare had three miscarriages in four years of marriage. The doctors told her that if she fell pregnant again it would kill her. David told her that he refused to lose her. When she took you in her arms the first time, you were crying. I couldn't stop you crying.' I could feel the jerk in my throat remembering that moment and the utter hopelessness I felt with the small creature in my arms that had grown beneath my ribs and the screaming that had seemed to drill its way unerringly into my brain. I had been beside myself. 'But the moment she held you, you stopped and looked at her. You stole her heart and she never got it back.'

I heard the hitch of a sob in her throat but dared not touch her. I knew I had given up any rights I may have had.

'She loved you, and David loved you. And you kept her going when David was killed in Afghanistan.'

I forced myself to ignore the mosquitos that had landed on my arms and were sharing their fluids with me as they ingested my blood. I noted the number that had landed on her legs.

'There are mosquitos.' I observed pointlessly.

'You should go back to Kosovo. I don't need you.'

'Ukraine,' I corrected. 'And I know you don't. But that's not what your mother wanted.' I hesitated. 'And I owe her.'

'I don't want to live with you. I can stay with Mammar and Pop.'

She used the childish word she had invented for her grandmother when she was just learning to speak and I was reminded how young she was.

'I don't know you and I don't want to. Please let me stay with Mammar.'

I knew she was trying to hurt me and I couldn't blame her for her success. What she said was true.

'I don't think we have a choice. The will…' I offered lamely.

I couldn't tell her that her Mammar was insisting.

She swung her legs back over the cement surface of the pier and pulled herself up to stand, waving off the whirr of mosquitos. 'I hate you.'

I watched her walk away, back towards the shore and the glowing skyline of the city. I let her have her distance and followed, rubbing my arms and wishing for repellent. She hadn't said the words harshly, her tone was empty. But I knew I deserved it.

Chapter Twenty-Three: A Quiet Seaside Village

Herculaneum, AD 79

The stairway was narrow and steep and the wooden stairs were worn. Thankfully a tall window set at the top of the stairway left it well-lit. Thalia shifted the heavy weight of the vase on her hip, balancing it carefully as she reached the door to their apartment. It still made her smile with a sense of accomplishment that she could carry the heavy water-filled container up the stairs and balance it for long enough to free her hands to unlatch the door. A shove from her hip pushed it past the tight jam of the door and she stepped into the modest space that was her own. When they had arrived and were finally able to secure an apartment Artos had needed to do the chore of making trips to the communal well and carrying the vases for she had not the strength or dexterity to do it herself, and soon the vast swelling of her centre obstructed any hope of carrying.

Once the child arrived, Thalia insisted on taking on the chore and freeing Artos to his work in the smith. She had dropped and smashed the earthen vessel several times, splattering herself in water and mud, before she learnt the knack of carrying it.

'Let me help, Domina.' Charis offered.

The slender child looked like a hollow reed, but Charis was far stronger than she looked. Thalia had been both grateful and embarrassed by her relief when Artos had brought the girl home one day, as a surprise. Barely ten-years-old, the child had been skinny and ragged, her hair shorn to prevent lice. Still, she was more capable than her mistress. She barely spoke a word for weeks until Thalia realised she spoke little Latin and could converse only in gutter Greek. Born a slave, the girl had been sold when her Greek merchant master's unwise investment had failed, leaving him bankrupt.

Artos often scolded her for her insistence on collecting the water herself, when the girl could do it, but Thalia found pleasure in knowing she could do this simple task and she enjoyed the sense of community that could be had in shared gossip between the women waiting to fill their own containers. It was an opportunity to learn who was ill or injured, who was with child or courting, which patricians had descended on their holiday homes along the bay to swell the winter population of the seaside town with hundreds of new faces and fresh business. For Thalia, it was the opportunity to make sure that those visiting the region were not known to her or to learn which parts of town she would need to avoid lest she somehow be recognised, as unlikely as she thought it. The rich holidaymakers rarely noticed the common people of the town and few would expect to see an ex-consul's wife bartering for fish near the boat sheds or waiting to fill a water container at the well that brought clean water from the Serino aqueduct.

Charis took the vessel from her mistress and leant it carefully against the wall in the corner of the space they used as a *culina*. The area amounted to little more than a bench, a drying rack for herbs and vegetables and a few large storage pots and an assortment of bowls and utensils. Using a ladle to scoop out some water she added it to the pot that bubbled over the modest but effective clay oven Artos had designed.

Thalia inhaled. The bubbling meal smelled far better than any of her poor efforts at cooking. Thalia blushed to consider her uselessness as a new bride and young mother. It was yet another reason to be grateful for the slave girl, whose mother had been a cook in her previous master's household.

'Where is Aglaea?' Thalia asked, the space was far too quiet for the rambunctious three-year-old to be present.

'She is playing downstairs with Sabatina's daughter.'

Thalia stifled a smile of pity for Sabatina, wife of the freedman baker Sextus Patulcius Felix, who owned and ran the *pistrinium* downstairs.

She noticed the open wooden tablet with its wax filling and the stylus on the bench where the girl had been sitting and moved to allow the light from the shuttered window behind her to illuminate the items. A carefully transcribed copy of one of Catulus's poems was etched into the wax. She had begun teaching Charis to read and write, as she had Kaeso so many years earlier. Artos had shaken his head but said nothing about her whim to educate slaves.

'Well done! You have scribed the *psi* perfectly.'

The girl blushed with the praise and busied herself scooping some of the stew into a wooden bowl for her mistress, breaking a segment from the large round loaf of bread bought fresh that morning. Thalia accepted the bowl, gesturing that Charis should serve some for herself, the girl shook her head. Breaking off a piece of bread Thalia dipped it in the stew, chewing slowly and enjoying the rich taste.

'Crab?' she asked.

'And whitefish,' Charis added with a nod.

Living beside the sea came with obvious benefits, besides the fresh sea breeze.

She had the girl recite the verse of the poem she had written between bites and praised her for her dictation. Running the last of the bread around the rim of the bowl to soak up what was left, Thalia savoured the last mouthful; the slave girl scooped a second helping into a deeper bowl, this one with a fitted lid, before wrapping a larger segment of bread in a clean cloth.

'Shall I take this down for the Domine?'

Thalia shook her head. 'I will take it. Perhaps I will give Sabatina a break from Aglaea's incessant chatter. She placed her bowl on the bench and tore off a segment of the wheel-shaped loaf her neighbour had baked that morning, smearing it with soft goat cheese. She balanced this on the parcels of food the slave handed her.

She found her daughter, covered in a fine dusting of flour, under the baker's counter, where a rat dog's whelps were wriggling and whining. The animals served an essential purpose in keeping the storerooms with their bags of grain vermin-free. Aglaea was seated with no less than three of the writhing furballs on her pudgy lap, climbing over her deeply dimpled knees, while the baker's daughter teased them with a collection of bright pheasant feathers on a piece of string. Both girls chortled at the puppies' attempts to capture the tempter as Aglaea tried to evade the wet tongue of the pup that had climbed her chest and was busily laving her chin with its pink tongue. She watched the children playing for a moment, emotion nearly choking her.

Despite the canine charms, the offer of bread and cheese and the opportunity to visit her Pater were enough to assuage Aglaea for the loss of her playmates, both canine and human. With one hand in her mother's and bread and cheese smeared around her mouth, the girl chattered almost incessantly all the way to the street of smiths. The smell of molten metal, vinegar and smoke made the purpose of the street unmistakable, as did the constant rhythm of metal ringing against metal as the smiths worked the stuff with heat and brute force. The street that divided the smith's shops from more commercial premises was broad, ensuring a healthy distance between the variety of forges and Herculaneum's more flammable buildings. People, no matter where they lived, had a healthy fear of fire. As they reached the dark stone building Thalia scooped her daughter up onto her hip. She smiled at the immense door guard employed to protect the merchandise, for Artos worked not with base metals but with precious silver and gold. The slave did not return the expression, but he did move his body ever so slightly aside to allow her to pass.

Artos was not at the forge, where a pair of slaveboys worked at keeping heat over the bellows under the watchful eye of their elderly master, all three dripping with sweat. A third slaveboy hovered nearby, charged with the constant supply of new fuel for the fire and water for those working near it.

The old Smith, Orestes, glanced up from his work. His smile revealed the gaps between his blackened teeth. 'You'll find him out the back. Keep hold of the child, so many hot things here.'

Thalia smiled her thanks, not attempting to reply over the roar of fire and bellows. It was the same warning issued each time she entered, as though she would not keep a close eye on Aglaea in this place of molten metal. As promised, she found her husband in a workshop space further in. Unlike the dark furnace room, this narrow space, dominated by a tall wooden bench, was filled with light that fell from a high window and illuminated the space. Artos had his back to her. He had clearly been working the forge earlier for he had removed his tunic and worked only in a leather apron and his loincloth. A fine dusting of soot clung to his broad shoulders and in places where sweat had run, made dark stripes down his back, like the striped African horses she had once seen slaughtered in the arena. Here and there older scars, reminders of battles long since fought marred his form. His dark hair was longer than it had been when they had lived in Rome. He wore it, loosely braided, tied back with a leather strap. There were flickers of silver threads in its darkness she had noticed as she had braided it that morning.

'How long do you plan to stare?' He spoke, not turning.

Thalia smiled. 'As long as I like.'

'Papi! We bringed you food.' Aglaea wiggled at her hip, longing to run to her father and be tossed in the air but her mother kept her grip moving to stand beside him.

A pair of gloves was discarded on the bench. This meant he was not dealing with anything hot. With a small hammer, Artos was gently tapping what looked like lumps of clay, rapping carefully at them until they cracked and crumbled, revealing the sheen of gold at their core then scrubbing at them with a wet, metal-bristle brush.

'Orses!' Squealed Aglaea with delight.

The child was correct. It was a herd of small golden horses, each in different positions, one standing, one pawing, one galloping, another rearing. Each was about the size of the golden goddess Thalia wore on a strap around her neck, the one Artos had given her when they had spoken vows before the priestess. The same one he had made, long before, for his wife, although she had never worn it. The horses were beautiful and detailed and clearly his own work.

'Have you a commission for them?' She asked running a finger across the flying mane of one, and letting Aglaea touch it gently.

'No. They are votive offerings for the Earthshaker. Orestes will sell them before the festivities begin tomorrow.'

'They will fetch a pretty price.'

He nodded, there was little doubt these masterpieces would only be sold to the richest of patricians. 'Rich people have more to lose when their villas shake.' He raised an eyebrow, smiling. 'All those pretty fragile statues. The horse is sacred to Neptunus Equester. That will make these more valuable as offerings, and the more valuable the offering the greater hope of the giver for mercy.'

Thalia thought it more likely these prancing metal ponies would make their way into the houses of the rich than offered as votives to the gods, but she had far less faith in deities than her husband did, and far less faith in people. Artos scooped Aglaea from her arms, tossed her in the air, and caught her deftly. Both smiled at her with matching grins and eyes the exact same shade of blue as Artos placed their daughter on the bench beside him, handing her a small hammer, not the one he had used, but an apprentice's tool. He pushed a lump of dried clay in front of her and let her beat it in joyful and enthusiastic mimicry of her father. Thalia frowned as she gathered up the small golden offerings, each one a heavy weight in her palm, and placed them well out of reach before handing him the woven bag she carried with the jar of stew and bread.

'Don't worry, there is nothing in that one. One of the boys left it out overnight. Once Aglaea has crushed it I will put it back in the slurry and we can start again.'

He opened the tight lid of the wooden bowl and tendrils of steam rose, laden with aroma. Artos inhaled. 'Mmmm. Charis fish stew?'

She nodded, not letting his tease affect her. Both knew domestic chores were not her strength.

α

The morning, which had started chill enough for Thalia to have hovered over the small glowing brazier, had turned warm. The cloak she had draped about Aglaea had long since been discarded and, along with her own, was bunched over Charis's left arm. Hooked over the slave girl's skinny right arm was the basket filled with their morning purchases.

The cooler weather had heralded the exodus of the seasonal holidaymakers, who descended on the seaside town in droves for the cooler climate and breezes during the hottest months of summer. Well did Thalia recall the sweltering season when all who owned or could rent villas on the coast left Rome en masse to escape the oppressive heat, scorching air and dire stench of the overpopulated city. With the return of the rich patricians to the capital, the population of Herculaneum was halved but the marketplace was still busy with the hum of trade and the buzz of buyers. For the first time in months, the permanent residents could stalk the stalls without having to fight for access against the servants of the pleasure villas that ran the length of the coastlines. Herculaneum's more common folk were revelling in the plentiful Autumn harvest of sea and mountain and the reduced prices that came from the decrease in competition.

Already Charis' basket held bunches of gold-green globes from the mountain vineyards, sweet yellow pears and a pair of blushing pomegranates. While Thalia found the fruit frustratingly fiddly to eat she knew Alexartos enjoyed bursting the gleaming ruby arils between his teeth. Thalia considered the stall before her, a pile of wrinkled walnuts formed a mountain much like the one that overshadowed the town and cast it into early shadows each afternoon. She selected a handful, shaking each in turn. Not all had sufficiently dried after picking so she discarded any that didn't rattle in their shells.

Thalia was in the process of handing over a coin when the pile of walnuts shifted, tumbling like a landslide from the table as the stones beneath their feet shifted with a roar that reminded her of the mob at the games in Rome. Her hand shot out to grab Aglaea and pull her close, the wriggling puppy in her arms pressed between them. Charis' dark eyes were wide but she stood with her legs braced until the tremor stopped. Like Thalia, the slave had quickly become accustomed to the movements in the earth that were typical of the region. A burst of laughter bubbled from Aglaea, the unnatural child, who rather than fear the shaking found it unaccountably exciting. Thalia held her tight, exchanging glances with Charis who was bemused by the child's evident joy in the unsettling event.

The townsfolk, most of whom had stepped into the streets at the first shudder to avoid falling roof tiles, were checking the skyline for damage before going about their business, sidestepping the shattered tiles that littered the streets like giant bird droppings. Before them the middle-aged stall holder was on hands and knees, scooping up the windfall of walnuts, some had rolled their way down the sloped road several paces and were being scooped up by opportunistic children or crushed underfoot by traffic.

'That was the third one this month,' Thalia murmured. 'More than in the entire first year we lived here.'

The store-holder straightened, letting a cavalcade of nuts tumble from her palla back into the low-sided baskets on the makeshift table.

'The priests of Neptune will be making a fortune this afternoon selling sacrifices to the Earthshaker,' the woman said with a dismissive shrug.

Thalia was certain she was correct. Being the god of both the seas and earth-shakes, Neptune was a popular deity in this place. The golden horse offerings Artos had created had sold out in record time at the festival of Neptunalia and more than a dozen bulls had been sacrificed but it seemed that the Earthshaker had not been propitiated and continued to show his displeasure.

'The priests have not been so popular since the Year of Marius and Afinius. The quake that year brought down half the forum and the Temple of the Four. It was even worse in Pompeii. Most of the Patricians sold up their villas and moved closer to Rome after that. Plenty of sacrifices to Neptune that year. Not so many in the years following, too many starved to death or moved away in the aftermath.'

Thalia nodded, certain that this latest shake would cause a bounty for the priests. While she agreed with the geographer, Strabo, that the shakes were an earthly phenomenon there were many who were of a more superstitious mindset. The woman leaned over the table a little and lowered her voice. 'They say Neptune was upset with Emperor Nero that year. I wonder what Emperor Titus has done to upset him?'

Thalia forced a smile and bent over to collect the coins that had spilled from her fingers. As she stood, Aglaea held another out to her. The coin caught the morning sun, showing the gleaming profile of

Rome's new Emperor. A shiver ran down the length of Thalia's spine. For all her good sense she could not discount the disturbing pounding of her heart as the head of Titus seemed to stare in her direction. She forced herself to smile at the child and to take it carefully rather than slap the offending coin from the child's fingers. The metal felt uncomfortably cold beneath her fingers. The inscription commemorated Titus' fifteenth commendation as imperator and heralded another successful military victory.

Thalia pushed the coin in the direction of the shopkeeper, and turned from the stall, not waiting for change. She didn't recall having such a coin in her possession and had been almost superstitious about avoiding any coins marked with that particular profile. Her skin crawled now at having touched it and the lingering feeling of being watched left the hairs standing on her forearms. Taking Aglaea's hand in hers she drew the child down the street to the public fountain, pulled the half-grown pup from her arms and placed it on the ground beside the fountain. Thalia picked her daughter up, holding her over the basalt edge so that Aglaea's short arms could reach the water.

'Wash your hands.'

The small face looked up at her with Artos' blue-eyed stare. The stubborn mouth set.

'Not dirty.' Aglaea held out her grubby palms to prove it.

Thalia raised an eyebrow. Both palms were dark with grime and the creases well embedded with dirt. 'You think not? I think they are as filthy as Ajax's paws.'

They both looked down at the dog, seated at their feet, stubby tail wagging in the dust. Ajax had been a gift from the baker's family and Thalia sometimes imagined that the child loved him more than both parents put together. He cocked his head charmingly to the side, his white paws were stained red-brown from the street. The creature yapped.

Aglaea giggled, wriggling in her arms nearly as much as the pup.

'Wash your hands and we will see if we can find some late-season blackberries.'

Aglaea's eyes lit up at the suggestion and she rubbed her hands beneath the water with some vigour but little effectiveness. Small rippling waves in the water's surface heralded a small aftershock, the likes of which would continue throughout the day.

Sometimes the unstable earth of the region made Thalia miss Rome and the earth that shook only in the arena.

'The aediles will need to send someone to clear the aqueduct,' spoke Charis from her side, gesturing at the comedic mask with its open mouth through which normally water poured, now barely trickling.

Thalia frowned. She hoped they would act quickly. Tempers frayed readily when water was in short supply and the entire town was dependent on the aqueduct.

'All clean Mammina; berries now?'

Thalia considered the girl's streaky palm. It was foolish to imagine that superstitious fear could be washed off with water. Still, she moved her knee to wedge it below the child's bottom, freeing her hands to help scrub the child's hands beneath the waterline. Was it her imagination that something in the water smelled foul? She shook her head, seeing Titus' image had merely unnerved her. It had nothing to do with the quake, the barely flowing water or the oddly acrid scent she now imagined on her hands. Drying the child's digits on the trailing edge of her palla, then drying her own as Aglaea displayed her clean hands for the dog to sniff at, Thalia forced herself to dismiss the portentous feeling of dread.

'Right. Let's find some blackberries. No. Leave Ajax down. He can follow us. That way you have your hands free for berries.'

Aglaea considered the dog, tail still wagging in the dirt, but the thought of handfuls of berries was clearly enough to motivate her. Finally, the child nodded and placed a hand in Thalia's.

'Come, Ajax.' Aglaea called, the dog stood, its entire rear end wiggling in tandem with its naturally short tail, and trotting happily in their wake.

Chapter Twenty-Four: Small Steps

Melbourne, 2024

I settled my laptop bag on my hip and juggled the two plastic bags full of groceries into my left hand, to scrounge through my pocket for the keys to the apartment. It was only when I slipped them into the lock that I realised it was already unlocked. Behind the door music was thumping, the volume increased drastically as I opened the door, pushing it shut behind me with a foot to spare the neighbours the atrocity my daughter thought was music.

I had slipped away early, bringing my laptop home to do marking, and had expected peace and quiet for some hours yet. Thursday was usually cello practice. Instead, Kate's door, usually a closed sanctuary, was wide open. The music blared from a barrel-like speaker that shifted in colour as I watched, a birthday gift from my mother. I swear it was revenge for forcing her to listen to my music as a teen. Kate's bed was non-existent, instead of her usual tidily ordered space where everything had its place, the room looked like sections of Ukraine we had entered only when escorted by UN soldiers for our safety. A shoe went flying across the room and landed near my feet. I wanted very much to shut the door and keep walking but I no longer had the luxury of forgoing parental responsibility.

'Is everything alright?'

I had to repeat the question three times before there was a semblance of response, an exasperated shriek from deep within her cupboard. Taking the risk I stepped over a pile of winter jumpers and towards the bedside table and its thumping speaker, finding the down arrow and pressing firmly to reduce the decibel level. This prompted a head to pop out beside the cupboard door. From the flush of her cheeks and the glassy quality of her eyes, I knew her distress but had no inkling of its cause.

'Do you mind?' Kate snapped.

A deep breath. 'Nope.'

Her eyes narrowed but she still looked on the verge of tears. 'I hate this place. I can't find any of my stuff!'

The look of her room would suggest otherwise but I chose to keep my mouth shut, wisely, I thought. I practised the eyebrow raise my mother had been an expert in. From the narrow glare Kate shot I guessed I had it right, my lip twitched involuntarily.

'What do you want?' She stood in the doorway, both hands on her hips.

Another breath. I sat on an uncluttered edge of the bed and tilted my head a little to peer up at her. 'To see if there is anything I can do to help.'

'I doubt it.'

I nodded and moved to settle myself a little more, for the first time appreciating the tactics my mother had used.

It didn't take long.

'We have an overnight hike next week. I was looking for my old backpack, the one that was Dad's... David's...' she self-corrected, 'but I can't find it.'

Her voice had a heightened tone and I realised that she had probably discovered that the desired item had likely been lodged in the storage garage where all of Clare's things had been packed along with anything Kate had not taken. We had not visited it in the three months since Clare had died and I doubted Kate felt up to facing it yet.

'I have something that might work.'

She rolled her eyes and muttered something that sounded like 'I doubt it' before disappearing back into the shelves.

I stood, stepping back over the mountain of wool and fleece-lined clothing in the doorway and went to my own cupboard. My travelling bag was stored there. Upending it casually on my bed and giving it a light shake, my passport fell out and an assortment of odds and ends I had picked up in my travels. I did a quick frisk of the many pockets and hidden zippered spots before patting off some accumulated dust and heading back for my daughter's room.

She had not turned the volume back up and sat with her back to the wall, her head on her knees. From the shake of her shoulders, I assumed she was crying. I stood, feeling helpless in the doorway.

'Go away.' The voice was almost missing its vehemence and she sounded much younger than her fifteen years.

I stepped across the fabric Alps and placed my offering on the bed. 'I used this when I travelled overseas. Plenty of pockets to stuff things in.'

She glanced up, eyes puffy and red, a streak of mascara smeared down her cheek. She studied the bag, considering it, and then nodded.

'Can I help you with all of this?' I gestured at the mess.

'No.'

Her lips were a tight line.

'Can I get you a drink or anything?'

'No.'

Another deep breath. I nodded to her. 'Let me know if you change your mind.'

I was through the doorway when I heard her parting words.

'Thanks.'

I paused, not game to look back.

'For the bag.'

I refrained from going near the room while she attempted to bring it back into order and in gratitude, she refrained from turning the volume back up. As I sat, nursing a gin and tonic, my laptop perched on my knees, I considered the encounter a win.

She emerged finally when the doorbell rang with a delivery of Chinese food from the takeaway around the corner.

Her eyes were still pink but the makeup had been wiped clean and not reapplied.

'Beef and black bean?' Kate asked hopefully.

'And sesame chicken, and special fried rice.'

She nodded with a glimmer of a smile. 'Prawn crackers?'

'Of course.'

She turned to the kitchen cabinets and rattled through the cutlery drawer for appropriate tools, handing me a fork and spoon in exchange for the entire plastic tub of the dark syrupy favourite.

We ate silently for a while, both sitting at the bench, neither of us had yet sat around the four-seater dining table, except when my mother and Phil joined us for a meal.

'I'll wash up?'

I found a smile, knowing washing up meant only tipping the cutlery into the dishwasher and placing the leftover containers in the fridge.

'Sure.'

She pushed the clear-sided container to one side and helped herself to another pale yellow prawn cracker, crunching it between her teeth. Then, as if remembering something shoved a hand in her pocket. 'What's this? It was in one of the pockets in your bag.'

Kate held up the leather strap from which dangled the tarnished but familiar heavy gold pendant.

I held out a hand and she reluctantly dropped it in my palm. I aimed at avoiding my 'teacher voice' as I explained how Roman children received protective amulets to keep them safe until they came of age to be considered an adult and passed into the protection of other gods. I ran my thumb over the familiar surface as I told how it had come to be in my rather dubious care.

Her eyes widened as she grinned. 'So you stole it.'

'Not intentionally.'

She sniffed, still smiling. 'Maybe not but you did. Steal it, I mean.'

I frowned. 'I suppose so. Except that, I will take it back. One day. Until then I just have to keep it safe.' I considered where 'safe' might be, given I had left it forgotten in my bag and I didn't really have anything that needed to be kept safe. Jewellery was not something I owned or wore. I would never own anything as beautiful as the string of unmatched pearls or the golden goddess pendant that had shared the grave with the child's moon-shaped lunula.

'Mum's jewellery box has a lock. You could keep it there,' Kate offered. 'I won't touch it.' She added after a moment.

I considered my daughter. The pink had faded from around her eyes and we had almost had a normal conversation. I nodded, handing her the charm and hoping it would keep her safer than it had the last child it adorned.

Ω

It was only when I was certain that Kate had fallen asleep to the thrumming noise emitted from her speaker that I had set on my laptop, balanced precariously on my knee, my study having been usurped by my daughter's mountains of clothing and material possessions.

I clicked away from the thesis application I was reading, and opened my emails, scrolling down to find the message I had received earlier in the day. I skimmed through the lengthy response, looking for the video file I was seeking. It was a CG recreation, a reconstruction based on the photos I had taken on my phone of the knife we had found with the bodies in the boathouse. I had reached out to some of the very clever minds in the ICT department and they had put me in touch with one of their most gifted. I had provided the scans and the photographs and he had used the dimensions to recreate the scenario I had imagined about on the same day I had been evicted from Herculaneum.

I spared a glance in the direction of Kate's room, feeling guilty about my continued obsession with the job I lost, even though I knew there was nothing I could do about it. I clicked play.

The screen showed the knife, a Roman pugio, as though enchanted it spun against a black background, shifting in angle and pitch, spinning until I was almost dizzy watching it, before it finally slowed. The ICT nerd was clearly a gifted artist, with a flair for design because he had sharpened the image, taken away the wear of time, and recast the handle. I was startled to see the scorpion figure etched into the hilt of the handle.

Then the scene changed, the knife became pixels and disappeared and a face came into view. It was one that made me shudder. It was a strong face with a hewn jawline, stubbled even by my clever artist. The hair, which I considered too long and reddish where I had envisaged salt and peppered brown, fell over the forehead but was unable to obscure the flattened mess of a nose. A pair of blue eyes stared from sockets I felt sure should have been an almost amber, catlike shade of brown. They lacked the proper level of malevolence.

I was startled when a disembodied hand appeared, grasping the red forelock and pulling it back. The knife had returned, held in the grip of a hand that drew it across the imagined throat of the red-haired Praetorian, sawing a little as it went, then the knife stuck. The face faded, disappearing into the blackness of the background, the hand also, leaving the grey-white bone of the scan. The clever graphics faded, leaving the original images which froze, then slowly rotated, showing the skull in profile, the knife's blade sitting just where the notch I had felt so clearly in the mastoid process.

I shivered. Words appeared, unfurling across the screen.

> Scans show the weapon and injury represent a potential match. 72% likely.

I knew age and wear would make decisive identification impossible. With a trembling hand, I pushed my mouse so the cursor hovered over the X in the corner of the screen. I clicked.

I didn't need the elaborate graphics. I didn't need the additional 28%.

I just couldn't work out how my murder weapon had moved from the lavatory in INSULA VII in an alleyway near the forum to the boathouses on the foreshore. I considered what I knew of the two male skeletons, both of whom had the telltale indicators of men known to warfare, neither of whom were longtime residents of Herculaneum. Had my boathouse warrior killed the Praetorian?

It didn't matter, I told myself. I wasn't going to be able to get my hands on the remains again. The screen closed with a final click, and I pushed it away from me and placed it on the coffee table beside the cold mug of instant coffee Kate had left me.

Chapter Twenty-Five: A Pine-shaped Cloud

Herculaneum, AD 79

Thalia dodged out of the way of the wagon, loaded with household goods that groaned as it made its slow trek over the cobbled roads, barely missing the stepping stones that allowed the people of Herculaneum to cross the road without stepping in the muck that was tossed there daily. A pair of women and three small children perched on the back of the load, their bodies jolting with the movement. A half-dozen slaves followed the vehicle. Another *familia* emigrating from the region. A few men, late for the *salutatio* ritual, faces shadowed with worry, hurried towards their patron's homes. Boys, the wealthier carrying scroll cases and wax tablets, or trailed by slaves who did so for them, bustled and shoved at each other, trying to tip the unwary off balance and push them into the street. Some loitered, reluctant to learn. Thalia adjusted the lighter weight of the empty water vase on her hip and crossed the street, stepping lightly on the stones. As usual, there was a small crowd around the fountain, like Thalia, each carrying earthen vessels to collect the day's water, mostly women whose homes were on the upper floors, unserviced by domestic water supply piped into ground floor houses. Today's crowd was larger than usual and from the furrowed brows and frustrated stances, it would be a long wait.

'Have the aediles not had the pipes cleared yet?' Thalia asked, observing the sluggish flow of water.

Frentia, who lived in an apartment up the street, rolled her eyes. 'The *curator aquarium* is in Pompeii, apparently, their need is greater than ours.'

Thalia nodded. Pompeii had a larger populace and relied on the same aqueduct as Herculaneum. She set the water jar on the ground, balancing it against her thigh and settled in to listen to the gossip.

'Claudia Pulcher is petitioning the *aedile* to do something about the water, the fuller's guild is up in arms...'

'The fullers guild is full of piss and whinge.' A few of the women tittered at this coarse jest. 'They would do better petitioning the magistrate. Arrius Ulpianus is a personal friend of Titus, if anyone can command action it is Ulpianus...'

Thalia shivered at the name of the Emperor, it seemed to her that his shade was stalking her, even this far from Rome, the man and his lover, her former husband. She shifted her concentration to a different group of women and a different conversation.

'Did you hear there were giants seen moving on the hillside?'

'Giants?' a voice scoffed. 'I bet that was started by Actius after one too many cups of wine.'

'No. It's true.' Another voice. 'And someone found a whole flock of sheep, and the shepherd, dead, in one of the valleys.'

'Wolves most likely.'

'No, they say there wasn't a mark on them.'

'Well, perhaps that will drive the price of mutton down.'

α

She was not sure in what order it happened, the roar so loud it set her ears ringing and filled her head with stuffing, the shudder that lifted and dropped the ground beneath her or the wave of force that knocked her from her feet and set her on the pavement, staring up at the mountain beyond the rooftops. Roof tiles fell like hail, striking a number of the women. One, blood streaming between the fingers pressed to her head was pointing at the mountain, her lips spoke words that Thalia's ears couldn't seem to decipher, sound seemed to

321

be muffled. She shook her head, pushed herself up from the ground and followed the many moving into the centre street, uncaring of the mess beneath their feet, desperate only to evade the clay shower. Blood oozed through cuts on her hands, she wiped them on her tunic as she gazed upwards in horror.

Above them, Vesuvius spewed like a fountain, a mass of shuddering grey that, as the ground stabilised, began to drift, like snowflakes, in gentle spirals around them.

Somewhere a child cried.

Without a thought for the water jar she had carried and heedless of the panicked people spilling from doorways into the streets, she ran, heart pounding, towards home, towards Artos and Aglaea. By now, the populace had shifted from shock to panic, they flooded the streets, staring up towards the mountain. Some, loaded with belongings, were already pushing and shoving their way towards either the port, in hope of securing a vessel or towards one of the city gates to escape by foot or cart or the back of mules. She pushed her way through the crowd, and was less than surprised when reaching the bakery to find the hulking shape of Artos also shoving his way towards her. Falling into the reassuring space of his arms she allowed him to hold her, squeezing her fiercely.

'What is happening?'

Artos shook his head. 'Perhaps the Gods, perhaps something else. Grab your little pot and any clothes and we can carry them. We will take Aglaea and Charis and leave the city.'

'How?' Thalia asked, looking upwards, the mountain was hidden by grey haze and it was impossible to know what was happening above them.

'We will go to the harbour, perhaps hire a fishing boat, or by road if we must. Maybe Felix will sell us one of the mules that drive the mill. We'll come back when the mountain quiets again.'

She nodded, relieved, as they slipped into the even darker stairwell that led to their apartment. Artos took the stairs three at a time, his long stride devouring the space. Thalia hurried behind him. The door to their apartment was ajar and jammed tightly against the floorboards from the unsettled shifts in the ground. It took Artos a sharp charge with his shoulder to move it.

The oven had toppled during the quake, spilling charcoal across the floor. A woven mat had been charred but now only smouldered weakly. Charis had done well to smother the fires under armfuls of cloth and what water had been left in the basin. Thank the Gods she had been vigilant. Thalia scanned the silent room for the slave and their daughter. The slave girl was on the floor, knees tucked to her chest. In the poor light of the sputtering oil lamps the slave had lit as the sky fell into a premature twilight, Thalia could see Charis' chest heaving with panic, the tear-smudged face looked up at her in a pathetic mix of horror, hope and gratitude.

'The door was stuck, I couldn't move it.'

'Where is Aglaea?'

Charis took a shuddering breath and looked ready to burst into tears once more. 'Where is my daughter?' Thalia repeated, she could feel Artos step up behind her, and place calming palms upon her shoulders.

'I was mending your stola, Domina.' She glanced at the ashen, damp cloth that had been used to smother the fire on the mat, Thalia recognised her best dress but without concern for its fate. 'Aglaea was chattering about playing with the horses. I thought she was speaking of the toys the Domine had carved.' Thalia nodded, Artos had carved over a dozen wooden horses for the girl. 'After the earth shake and the fire, I looked for her. She was gone!' The final three words were more wail than elocution.

Thalia glanced at the now open door, recalling the gap that had greeted them, wide enough for a small child to fit through. When she turned to face Artos, she knew her face was bloodless. He gripped her arms and dropped his head to hers.

'Horses, Thalia. Aglaea went to visit the horses. We'll find her.' He turned to the shaken slave, giving orders for her to pack quickly and wait there for them to return.

Thalia considered the possibilities. Each day when they walked Aglaea paid homage and left offerings of grass, wildflowers, feathers or even pebbles at the feet of horses all across the town, from the narrow stalls below in the bakery where the two mules used to grind the grain slept to the livery stables near Artos' workplace where the well-to-do kept their beasts or hired them when in need. Then there were the statues. The horses in the temple of the earthshaker, the ones in the fountain in the great palaestra and the statues of the theatre, then there were the four bronze horses pulling a quadriga and the marble equestrian statue of Marcus Nonius Balbus, both located in the forum.

Artos too had clearly been making the same list. He squeezed her shoulders. 'I will check the stables, then the palaestra and the Temple of Poseidon. You check to see if she is with Felix's mules, then check the theatre and head for the forum.'

His eyes were filled with resolve and concern. 'If you find her, bring her to the statue of Marcus Nonius Balbus, the one in the Forum. I will do the same. Wait there for me.'

He could feel her shaking beneath his hands and he pressed a kiss to her brow. 'We will find her.' His voice was fierce. 'We will bring her home and collect Charis and then we will leave.'

He pulled her down the stairs behind him, as though reluctant to release her hand. They parted in the street, he admonished her to be careful and reminded her to meet him in the forum.

She slipped inside the bakery, where Felix and Sabatina were gathering their goods. Sabatina had a child in each arm, afraid to let them go, when she saw the worry on Thalia's face her own echoed concern.

'What is it, Thalia?'

'Aglaea, we cannot find her. She went to visit the horses.'

Sabatina nodded, 'I don't think she is there but you can check. Felix has Balius harnessed and hitched to the cart, but we are leaving Xanthus, she is lame and cannot move quickly enough.' Seeing the concern painted on her friend's face, she attempted a reassuring smile. 'I am sure all will be well, and we will return in a few days. We have left hay and water for the beast, she will be fine.'

Thalia nodded, not in the least concerned for the animal, but disappointed that they would not be able to hire the beast to aid their own retreat from the city. She slipped past the harried woman and out into the rear of the bakery, where Felix was loading the small cart. The tall grinding stones with their protruding struts, to which the couple usually fixed the mules, which turned the stones and ground the grains, were still and silent. Thalia slipped into the stall, where the one placid mule rested a forefoot and watched the happenings with curiosity. There was no sign of Aglaea.

With a quick wave to Felix, she slipped back into the shop and out into the street. Sabatina called out to her.

'We are leaving as soon as we are packed, you are welcome to join us when we do.'

Thalia smiled her acknowledgment of the offer and stepped into the busy street. Already, Artos was lost to sight. Already, the ash was ankle-deep on the ground. Weaving her way through the worried masses, each with their own agenda, Thalia paused to scan each small face as a child appeared in the dusty grey fog. At one point she was knocked into a wall, at another, she was knocked to the ground in the street and nearly trampled. Bruised but determined she shouldered her way into the theatre precinct. The building was dark and empty and this was a blessing for as she traipsed her way up to the second tier, breathing was becoming difficult, the air was so filled with ash. She paused to wrap her palla around her head more securely, covering her mouth and nose to allow her to breathe more freely. She checked the shadows around the bases of the three equestrian statues, even sifting the ash for signs of Aglaea's offerings.

She was about to continue when a sound caught her attention, sharp yapping barks. There, huddled between the plinth and the wall was a small ash-coated figure, defended by a half-grown rat dog. Thalia scooped her snuffling daughter, the dog squeezed between them and pressed her cheek against Aglaea's small, wet soot-stained one. The child shook in her arms.

'The mountain is angry, Mammina.' The child whispered in her ear.

'It is, but we are going to find Papi now and then we will get away from the mountain. Now, let's put Ajax down. He is big enough to walk and we will find Papi in the forum.'

The ashen cloud seemed thicker as Thalia strode towards the forum and Artos.

α

The grey cloud was definitely growing thicker, clouding his view and shortening his breath, not unlike the dust storms he had experienced on occasion in the land of his birth. Artos considered covering his head and mouth with the rough woollen cloak he had grabbed before leaving their apartment, but he feared it would make him unrecognisable to his daughter.

He had hurried to the stables near the smith and checked each stall with no luck, slipped through the near empty palaestra, its pools already choked with grey ash, the horses at the fountain reared and pawed over a pond of grey sludge, but Aglaea was not there either. He had hurried to the Temple precinct and the temple of Neptune, god of the seas, causer of earthquakes and lover of horses. But his daughter was neither in the streets on the way or at the pawing feet of any of the statues. That left only the forum, with its bronze horse-drawn quadriga and the equestrian statue of Marcus Nonius Balbus.

After the initial upheaval and roar from the mountain and the fear and chaos it had caused in the streets things were growing quiet. With no further damage beyond the survivable shifts in the ground and the billowing grey clouds, those who had not fled almost immediately had largely returned to their homes to await the passing of the strange but apparently harmless phenomenon, lighting lamps to brighten the darkness and making offerings at the household shrine and to their favoured icons to propitiate the angry gods. This made it far easier to spot small bodies in the street. The forum, however, was busy, fearful and angry citizens were mobbing outside the Praetor's house, which opened near the Collegium Augustalium. Artos almost pitied the man, unlucky enough to be in residence at this time. Did the noisy crowd actually believe that the Roman magistrate could stop the sky from falling? As he checked around the plinth that held the bronze horses, even climbing up to check inside the chariot, Artos had once found his daughter perched there, he was aware that Praetorians, in service to the magistrate had appeared from the direction of the Temple of Mercury and the town treasury, and were forcing their way through the frustrated crowd, using their bodies, heavy wooden batons and at times the hilts of their swords, to crack down on limbs and heads until a wary space formed around the Praetor's residence. A convoy of slaves carrying heavy chests and toting bulging sacks slipped through and into the domus.

The buffer of open space went as far as Artos' next destination, the equestrian statue of Marcus Nonius Balbus the elder, who according to inscriptions had wisely chosen to support Octavian at the end of the republic. Distracted, Artos failed to notice the attention he had garnered. With his head and shoulders uncovered, his face and form clearly visible he had drawn the attention of one of the Praetorians, a man with burly shoulders, a middle—once chiselled—now given to corpulence and a crooked nose that matched the twisted pull of his sour lips. Pushing his way through the remnants of the crowd, Artos missed the gestures the man made to the Praetorians he clearly led, nor did he notice the way they spread out to slowly surround him.

Pulling himself up onto the plinth, Artos wrapped an arm around the waist of the town's benefactors, scanning the forum for any sign of a small child and her dog.

'Oy. Get down from there!' One of the Praetorians demanded.

With a distracted nod, Artos complied, as he did so something caught his attention, a woman, with what looked like a child on her hip, both of them shrouded in her palla which was liberally dusted with ash. Was that a small dog at her heels?

Reaching his arm up to clamber back onto the plinth, to see and be seen, Artos nearly missed the swing of the short baton the Praetorian carried, noticing only in time to pull his hand and receive a glancing blow, rather than the crunching action that may well have broken his arm. He swung to face the man, scanning his features in case the guard was known to him. He wasn't.

Artos raised both hands in a placating gesture. His right arm smarted from the blow but it wasn't lasting damage. He simply needed to assure the man he was not up to harm and get back to finding Aglaea.

'I mean no harm, I was looking for someone.'

'Aren't we all. You need to come with me.'

Annoyance was building. The Praetorian was shorter than him by half a head, and lighter. But he was one of several and Artos had no desire to gain further attention. He twisted his head in the direction he had seen the pair but the crowd had blocked his view. When he turned back he saw that the attention he dreaded had been drawn. Four men in ash-coated Praetorian cloaks, the reddish-purple so vivid that it stood out despite the poor light and grey turmoil that drifted around them. Two of them, weapons drawn, had moved closer. They were the faces of strangers but they were studying his movements as though he were quarry they had driven to ground and were waiting on a signal to bring down. Artos considered his options. Even four he could fight but not without drawing more attention.

The sound of barking drew his attention, he turned his head and caught sight of the small ratdog, with the patch that covered half his face. Behind the dog; a woman and a child. Thalia caught his eye across the distance between them.

'Well, well. If it isn't Vespasian's favourite barbarian.'

Recognising the voice though not the odd nasal intonation, Artos shifted stance, trying to move his shoulders to block the man whose voice came from behind the equestrian statue and the woman and child across the square.

'RUN!' he mouthed, hoping she would see, as the owner of the voice stepped around him.

As the speaker's head turned in the direction of the barking, Thalia shifted, stooping to grab the dog, the fabric of her palla hiding them all from view.

Slowly, Artos turned to face the man he had not seen in years now and had no desire to ever face again. It was with some gratitude he noticed the mangled mess that centred the soldier's face, recalling the blood that had dripped from it after Artos himself had crushed it years earlier in the forests of Moesia. He imagined it made breathing difficult and the thought made him smile.

'Yes, it is you, isn't it Alexartos. Admiring your handiwork are you?'

Artos shrugged.

Beneath a crooked nose, the man's lips formed an unpleasant smile. 'I thought I'd meet you again in Hades, and look, here we are.' The man swung a beefy arm to gesture vaguely at the space and the ash that fell, deeper and darker now around them. Something bounced off the man's leather breastplate and fell into the ash at their feet. Both men looked at it. Another struck Artos on the top of the head, his hand shot out to grab it as it fell. A rock, about the size of a child's marble, so light he could barely feel the weight of it though it was warm to the touch. Both Artos and Petronius stared at it. Pumice. Artos recognised the substance, the same material widely used in the baths.

Yet another piece fell between them. And then another. The Praetorians around him squinted up at the sky, shielding their eyes from the ash, trying to identify the strange new experience.

Artos knew at that moment he could run, but he doubted he could outdistance all of them, *and where would he draw them?* He took the momentary distraction to glance behind him. Relief flooded through him, there was no sign of Thalia or Aglaea. He prayed to all the gods who might listen that she would take his advice and run, while she still could.

With one hand shielding his head from the increasing number of small lightweight projectiles, Petronius, once Praetorian guard to Consul Messalinus gestured to the men. 'Disarm him and bring him with you. The Praetor is going to want to see who we found.'

'What about the crowd?'

'Forget them, the man snarled. 'They are sheep, we have caught ourselves a wolf.'

α

'What is this?'

Praetor Ulpianus frowned at the group before him.

'Praetor, in securing the treasury we discovered this one, he was about to make off with a chest full of coins.'

'Liar!' Artos spat. His reward was a sharp thud beneath his ribs with the hilt of a Praetorian's gladius which knocked the wind from him. Only their grip on his arms kept him standing.

'When my men apprehended him, I recognised him.'

'Recognised him?'

'Yes. I knew this man in Jerusalem and Rome. He was a Praetorian.'

'*Was* a Praetorian?' Ulpianus' attention peaked.

'Perhaps you recognise him? He served with Emperor Titus and was assigned with me to protect the Proconsul Lucius Valerius Messalinus.'

Artos wasn't sure if he imagined the twist of distaste on Ulpianus's lips. The Praetor stepped closer and scrutinised him as he tried, air whistling through gritted teeth, to refill his lungs.

'Ah yes, the barbarian horseman. Alexander.'

'Alexartos, Praetor.

The praetor nodded, his foppish curls bobbing beside his cheeks. 'Well, let him go then. I am sure he has a reason to account for what you saw.'

Petronius shook his head and took a move to position his body between his captive and the praetor.

'No, Praetor. With respect. The man was sentenced to death for betraying his master. He disappeared while we were travelling through Moesia with a fortune in jewels and...' Petronius dropped his voice to a lower pitch as though reluctant to speak. 'And the former Consul's wife.'

Ulpianus stepped closer, peering at Artos, over the Praetorian's shoulder.

'I remember some scandal. I thought the woman had been murdered by marauding tribesmen.'

Artos noticed Petronius' flinch and wondered what price he had paid for reporting the loss, but not the death, of Messalinus' wife. He prayed Thalia had the sense to take their daughter and find a way to escape the city. The ground shifted under his feet with another of the aftershocks.

'Perhaps she was,' said Petronius gruffly. 'Praetor, he must be questioned and the sentence given him fulfilled.'

'That is hardly possible at this moment, Petronius. You may have noticed that the sky is falling?'

'He is a very dangerous man, Praetor.'

Ulpianus studied Artos again before shaking his head and swinging to face the Praetorian, his eyes far more astute than his foppish appearance suggested. His mouth opened to speak. As he did so the earth gave a resounding crack that sent every man in the room flying. Ceramics that had been saved from earlier blasts shattered as they struck the marble tiles. Sculptures that had not yet been packed or were too unwieldy or heavy teetered and crashed to the floor, one slave was crushed beneath a large marble depicting the town's patron demigod, Hercules. His screams were shut off quickly as the roar of a shuddering earth continued. A slab of heated rock the size of a wagon slammed in through the compluvium to crash in the empty pool beneath, more rocked the roof above, crushing tiles into powder. An intense wave of heat washed across the space.

Artos discovered himself on the floor, two Praetorians struggling to rise beside him. He might have run but for the ringing in his ears and the disorientation that clearly affected several others. Pushing himself to his knees, he shook his head.

The Praetor was brushing ash off his toga and considering the mess around him. He turned to the captain of the Praetorians but his eyes were already on the doorway.

'You may stay and interrogate him, if what you say is true you have my permission to carry out the sentence, but do so quickly and join us on the road, we head for Neapolis.' The man let his eyes flick fleetingly over the Praetorians. 'You may have one man to help you.'

Petronius' fist made a thud on his leather breastplate as the Praetor fled the room. Those capable of doing so rushed after him. Only the Praetorians awaited instructions.

'Drusus Vibius, remain. The rest of you are to accompany the Praetor.'

The soldiers hurried after the Praetor, though one man hesitated, he stopped several times, looking back towards them before slipping out the door.

α

As the lash cut down on the flesh of his back Artos bit the inside of his lip, refusing to make a sound. Petronius was not so inclined.

'Enjoy that,' the man spat out between cuts. 'I was flogged because of you, you know.'

Another cut.

'For letting you escape.'

A third. Artos focused on the man's words to keep from groaning.

'I was sent back to Rome in disgrace.'

Another. Petronius was gasping heavily now. He was not as fit as he had been when they had served together in Jerusalem as younger men, or even as in Rome. It was so easy for a Praetorian, on light guard duties, to lose condition. Artos noticed his breath reeked of wine.

The money belt at the man's side jingled with each new movement. One more lash and he halted, panting. Unable to continue to raise his arm, the praetorian kicked out at him instead, knocking Artos' feet from under him. The rope around his wrist held him suspended from the rafter above his head. The rope burned as he pulled on it to stand once more, shifting around to face his persecutor.

The man's nose sat at an uncomfortable angle, the sight made Artos smile, earning himself the butt of the whip across his face, crushing the flesh against his teeth and busting his lip.

'Where is the woman?'

Artos spat bright blood but didn't answer.

'Did she run away with you? Did you convince her to marry you now she was ruined?'

Artos was surprised by the man's perception. He had never rated Petronius as anything but a bully and a thug. Exactly the type of soldier Vespasian's son liked to keep near him.

'She's here somewhere, isn't she? That was her across the square wasn't it. Maybe I'll find her and take her back to Rome with me. That ought to ensure my welcome. I imagine Titus and Messalinus would pay handsomely for that.'

Artos' answer was a glob of blood and sputum spat into the man's face.

He saw the effect clearly because white light invaded the room, lightning from the mountain. It was at that moment that he saw her, a shape in the doorway, a rounded shape cradled in her arms. He recognised it. It was the rounded terracotta jug he had bought for her in the marketplace when they first arrived in Herculaneum. She had been drawn to it because of the glazed design of the Goddess Artemis on the side. The jug was where she hid their meagre wealth, what coin they had, the pearls that had been her mother's, and if she was not wearing it about her neck, the gold pendant of Artemis. Artos groaned, not for the pain of the fist that ploughed into his belly, but for his despair that she had found him and not run as he had hoped.

Petronius must have seen the movement in his gaze, or the despair on his face for at that moment he turned and faced the doorway. Artos lost sight of her as he tried to drag air back into his lungs, hanging by his arms it was almost impossible to do so. He forced his legs to support him, forced his mind past the black-red haze, forced his lungs to relax, there would be air he knew, it would just take time. The doorway was empty when he looked back at it.

Petronius handed the whip to the Praetorian in the shadows.

'Watch him. Don't go anywhere. I'll be back soon.'

If he had been able to, Artos would have thrown himself after Petronius, tearing the man's throat out with his teeth if he had to. But the haze was only now clearing his eyes as the air slowly returned to his lungs. He hung there, helpless to save her.

Chapter Twenty-Six: Face to Face

The Hague, 2024

I had not seen Samir since I had brushed past him and out onto the streets in Lviv. I hadn't read any of his messages or answered any phone calls. After four months he had stopped trying. It had taken far longer than I had expected. So to see him now was… I didn't have the words.

The feathering of silver at his temples had spread a little. It suited him, made him look wiser, more academic. They had dressed him in a dark suit, well-tailored to show off his strong shoulders and lean limbs. His face was serious, and his dark eyes were grieving as he gave his statement and answered their questions. For the second time, I heard how he had been outside, up in the leafy hills that looked down on the now destroyed farmhouse, how the night had been cold and the baby had not stopped crying. How he had heard the shots and wanted to run to them but had to keep his baby girl safe and how he had hidden the sleeping infant in the Volvo parked in the barn.

When he spoke of hearing a scream and racing into the building unarmed I thought I saw the trail of tears that slipped down alongside his nose. I hadn't realised there had been an older daughter as well. My stomach rebelled at his recount of her treatment by the men who had invaded her home.

'Dr Benino?' A voice whispered at my side, I shifted my head to see one of the suit-clad Chambers clerks, interns who worked at the Hague, leaning forward from the seat behind me.

'Yes, that's me,' I whispered.

'Dr Benino, a Dr Habermann sent me to retrieve you.'

I cursed Bruce under my breath. No doubt he wanted to run over my testimony one more time. I shook my head, I was missing Samir's words. I shifted my gaze back to him. His voice cracked a little as he spoke of attacking the man who had held his daughter, of a gun with no bullets and of the rifle butt to his face which explained the silvered scar that split his brow and traced a fine trail across his left cheek. With a shake of my head, I recalled tracing it with my fingers while we had lain together in bed. I had wondered at its cause but not asked.

'Dr Benino. Dr Habermann was quite insistent.'

So, as Samir spoke of his daughter being taken by the green men, I ached for him, knowing the fate of young women who were taken by the Russians. I had exhumed and examined too many of them. I removed the headset and placed it on the receptacle in front of me. As I stood, a movement in a sea of still and attentive bodies, Samir's eyes met mine, widening for a second. I gave what I hoped was an apologetic wave and slipped through the audience and after the clerk.

Ω

'Dr Benino?'

I knew the voice immediately and let my attention shift from the glare of reflected light from the countless windows that made up the cubed buildings of the Hague. I forced a smile.

'It's Victoria, or Tori if you are a friend.' I offered for the second time now.

Samir stared at me, eyes tracing my face, a muscle twitched in his jaw. After a moment he spoke. 'I thought I was, but in honesty, I am now uncertain.'

My smile wavered and I shifted muscles to reinforce it, telling myself that it was not hurt I heard in his voice, perhaps pique at the way I had left. I forced myself to be an adult and meet his gaze, suddenly more aware of the thickening at the bridge of his nose and imagining I could see tiny lines of silvered scar tissue. Closer now, I could see he had lost weight, and looked a little drawn, I blamed the court case. All of a sudden I wanted to ask how he had survived, I needed to understand the cost, but he had already given exhaustive testimony and I doubted he wanted to go there again.

'I wanted to thank you for your testimony and again for what you did for my family.'

I nodded. 'I just hope it all helps in finding some justice.'

He shrugged, rolling his shoulders. 'It will or it won't.'

I badly wanted to make a joke about philosophy but knew neither levity nor philosophy were my strong suit. Instead, I tried to reassure him. 'You got to tell their story, Samir. That is important. It was heard.'

'You had to leave.'

'Yes, I'm sorry, I was being summoned.'

He nodded. 'I want to introduce you to someone.'

It was then I noticed them, standing outside the courthouse by the sign with its wreath of olive branches around a set of scales. The woman with the streaks of bright red and platinum hair, unhidden by a headscarf. She wasn't laughing and facing me I noticed she was much younger than I had first thought, her face free of the makeup that had defined it in the avatar on his phone. She wore a pencil-line dress that hugged her slender shape. Her hand was stretched out as Melie skipped about beside her, leaping the pavement tiles from one to another over the crack that divided them. The woman was looking at me, studying me intensely and I had the distinct and uncomfortable feeling she knew both who I was and what I had done. The thought brought back a flush of memories that I had forbidden myself, the touch of his hand on my body, the press of his lips on my neck, the warmth and strength of his arms. Desperately, I cast a look at my watch.

'I'm sorry, Samir, it was lovely to see you again.' My words sounded lame, even to me. 'Perhaps another time?' I deflected. 'I have an appointment with…'

'Vittoria!'

They had not waited. The child, free of the restraining hand that held her, had rocketed into my side, wrapping her arms about my thighs. Her dark hair, still a riot of curls, had been somewhat tamed into two plaits beside her head, tied with red ribbons. She stepped back and grinned at me, pointing to the well-grown tooth that she had lost during my brief stay.

'It grew back!' She pointed out using English words.

'Yes, but you seem to have misplaced another.'

The words were too many, too quick, and the child looked to the young woman with the red and white hair, who translated. Melie grinned, then poked her tongue through the newer gap.

So close now, the young woman looked at me curiously, but in an expression that was without open hostility. Samir pulled her to him, settling her under his arm, beneath the protection of his body. I felt a frisson of envy, and shame.

'Tori, I would like you to meet Mara,' He paused. 'My eldest daughter, Samara. She was still studying in England when you visited us. Samara, this is Dr Victoria Benino, the woman from the UN I told you about.'

All the air in my chest seemed to vanish in an exhalation as I tried to process the words. He had said that the Russians had held a gun to his daughter's head, that they had taken her. There had been no mention of her in the paperwork we received in Izyum, and no remains that I had unearthed and processed. I knew my gaze tracked the similarities in their faces and though there was some cultural likeness there was little that said family. Clearly, the young woman, who faced me so confidently, was more like her mother. In the midst of this I found myself shaking her hand, her grip was firm in my own.

'Thank you for what you did for my family.' She spoke the English words well, with a British lilt meshed with her own accent.

She met my gaze with her, her dark eyes steady and curious.

'It was not just me. My team was instrumental in the work with your family.'

She nodded. 'Yes, but you were the one in charge, and you were the one who brought my mother's *misbaha* home.' She shifted her wrist to show the beads wrapping her wrist. They looked fitting there. Her eyes were serious as she pinned me in her gaze. 'You were the one who brought my mother and brothers home and gave my father closure.'

I wondered just how much she was saying, but it occurred to me then that it didn't really matter. My mother and daughter had just emerged from around the corner and were crossing the road towards us. Kate was wearing a new jacket, clearly they had found somewhere to shop. Her eyes were bright and full of curiosity, she had enjoyed the trip, the experience of a new country. Clare had been such a homebody, never leaving Australian soil once she landed, with her daughter in her arms, to greet her handsome young husband at the airport. I sensed that for Kate this trip was a beginning of claiming the world she would want to know. Perhaps she was not so unlike me after all. I found myself smiling at the thought. To my surprise she smiled back, waving her arm.

I shifted my gaze back to Samir. I had felt him watching my reactions intently and forced myself not to imagine it was more than curiosity. But when I caught his eye his dark gaze held mine.

'I'll just take Melie for a hot chocolate, she has been begging me all day,' Mara offered.

'No, wait.' I held out a hand as if that could stay them. 'I would like to introduce you to some people.' I glanced back at Samir. 'My mother and my daughter travelled with me.'

I refused to look at his face in case it betrayed the surprise I expected, turning to wave to the pair crossing the plaza.

If any reaction was evident it was gone when I turned to introduce him to my mother and then to Kate. His smile was warm and expression unflappable as he shook first my mother's hand, then took my daughter's. In turn, he introduced both to Samara and Melie. I caught Kate's expression of delight at the colourful arrangement of Samara's hair, and deliberately ignored the speculative expression on my mother's face as she took in the shape of the man beside me.

'So, you work with the United Nations, Samir? Are you an anthropologist too?'

Samir shook his head. 'No. I am a Ukrainian National, I met your daughter when she was working with the United Nations to exhume and return the remains of my family.'

It was gratifying to watch my mother's mouth drop open and to see her, for a moment, speechless. I watched the expressions chase over her face as she took on the news and discounted a relationship behind us. I suppressed a smile to see it.

'Perhaps you would like to join us for lunch?' He offered.

'We just had lunch.' My daughter cut in before my mother could reply.

Samir nodded.

It was Samara who proposed a solution, inviting my mother and Kate to join her and Melie in search of hot chocolate. 'I am sure you two have plenty to catch up on.' She let her gaze drift between us.

Following the girl's hint, my mother's gaze flicked from Samir's face to mine, a speculative expression back in situ. 'That sounds lovely. Kate and I were eyeing off a patisserie down the block, I am sure they have hot chocolate.'

To my surprise, Samara turned then to her father. 'Why don't you take Tori to lunch, you were both in there so long you must be starving.' Her eyes gestured at the building with its flicking flags. His glance at me offered an explanation for the daughter I had not known about and a curiosity about the one he had not known. He raised an eyebrow in question.

I nodded.

'I have my phone, message me when you are finished,' my mother offered. 'Perhaps we can explore some of the shops together after we indulge.' Her smile took in Kate and Samir's two daughters. I had little doubt that she would be wrangling for information. But with Melie's few words of English and having never met Mara I felt I was safe to agree with an easy smile.

We found our way to a small tavern where, unsurprisingly, Samir was able to express our desire for a table and translate the menu, guiding my choices away from anything containing pickled fish, a popular addition to so many dishes here at the Hague.

As we waited for our meal Samir continued his story. He took up from where I had left the courtroom. When the Green Men had knocked him out they had taken both he and Samara back to their encampment in the hills. He believed they had kept him for his talent for languages and guessed that had he not managed to escape, he would have been forced to act as translator as the men captured and interrogated and tortured his countrymen, those who opposed the 'peaceful' occupation of their country. When he had woken he had no knowledge that Samara had survived and been taken also.

'I was fortunate that they were lax in their security. They had left me, unconscious in the back of the truck, while they reported to their superior. I bound my wound with rags, I had no time to consider it. One of them had left a jacket on the backseat and I put it on. I guessed that if I looked like I was supposed to be there I would have a better chance of getting away. I was right.

I overheard the officer in charge berating the men who had taken us for not being tidier about the operation and insisting they returned to clean up the site.'

He stopped as our meals arrived and only resumed speaking when he had finished a good portion of his plate, and then, spoke around mouthfuls.

'I knew I had to get back to the farmhouse. If I didn't they would return and I would never know what had become of my family, nor would there be any way to prove it.'

I nodded. The Russians had been very good at hiding most of their crimes and knew burning bodies effectively destroyed evidence. Only the quick action of the Ukrainians had resulted in bodies hidden where we could eventually find them and investigate, often based on anonymous reports. I could only account for the two mass graves in Izyum as the Russians assuming they would maintain control of the region and had too little time to 'sanitise' as they were driven back.

'I had found a motorcycle that had keys dangling from the ignition and was about to liberate it when I heard a scream.'

He pushed his plate away from him then. I glanced down at my own barely touched one and forced a fork into my mouth, chewing slowly as he resumed his tale, not looking at me but at the hands held in clenched fists on the tabletop.

'I knew the voice. You cannot imagine my joy and the horror of hearing it.'

While I did lack the imagination I could understand the juxtaposition of emotions so I nodded him on.

'It took some time to find her. In that time the alarm had been raised that the man they had brought in was missing. I simply joined the search party and tried not to limp. It helped that I spoke fluent Russian. It was dark and they could only see that I was one of them. One of them even shoved a Kalashnikov at me, just in case the intruder was armed.'

His grin was short and bittersweet.

'While I was looking, I found the building where they were holding her.'

He paused as a waiter took his plate, I waved them away from mine, despite my interest in his story, I was in fact starving.

'I walked in the front door and told them I had been sent for the girl. They had beaten her badly, and both her eyes were swollen shut which was a mercy. Had she seen me I don't know if I would have pulled it off. She still wore the dress my wife had made for her to wear to the party but it was torn… and her underwear was missing.'

I nodded slowly, not taking my eyes from his, never wondering if he might see the empathy I had for the child who was a victim of rape.

When he continued after a few moments his voice was thick. 'I forced myself to drag her by the arm, out the door with my gun by her side. I put her on the front of the bike. She was shaking so badly I thought she might tip us. And when I started the engine I was afraid she would throw herself off the bike and kill us both.'

I found my hand on his fist. When he looked at me his expression was agonised, but he opened his hand and wrapped his fingers around mine, as though it were the most natural thing to do.

'We rode straight past the sentries who guarded an entry, not an exit. I had to ride one armed because Samara fainted and I had to hold her on the bike.'

I had seen those winding roads on our trip to the farmhouse and marvelled that he managed to navigate them on an unfamiliar bike, one-handed.

'I took her to some caves I knew in the mountains. I left her there.'

He looked at me then. 'I knew they had raped her, I wanted to go back and kill them all but I had left Melie in the car at the farmhouse and we had been gone now most of the night, dawn was already lighting the horizon. I knew at first light they would return to clean up the mess they had left, whether or not they found me.'

I knew what he wanted from me. 'You had no choice.' I said, and meant it.

He considered my face, weighing my words, then nodded. 'The farmhouse was silent when I arrived; I was afraid for Melie. I cannot tell you my relief when I found her still in the car, asleep. I had to decide then what to do. While she slept I made my way into the farmhouse. They had clearly thrown a grenade or two in when they left but the house is old and solid and it hadn't fallen. Some of the furniture had burned. The effect on the bodies was worse…'

He broke off then.

I knew he must have told the entire story to the court and I had no desire to make him suffer twice. 'I know.' I squeezed his hand. 'I saw. How did you get them to the forest?'

After a minute he returned the squeeze. 'I took blankets off the beds, I gathered what I could, but the day was breaking and I knew I couldn't stay. I think I made eight trips across the meadow. With each trip, I was sure they would arrive and I would not make the next. I couldn't drag them, I knew it would leave traces and I could only hope they wouldn't look too closely at the ground.

I had only just grabbed a shovel when I heard the vehicles. I had enough time to hide the motorcycle, grab Melie and make it to the forest when they arrived.'

I was grateful when the waiter arrived to collect my plate and offer, in halting English, the choice of dessert or coffee. I ordered two coffees, and smiled at the waiter, asking him to repeat the dessert options, drawing his attention away from Samir as he tried to contain overspilling emotions.

We sat in silence while waiting for the coffee. It was nothing like the coffee he had made us in his apartment in Kharkiv, but it was something to distract us. I stirred in sugar while checking the message from my mother. She had taken all three girls to the Madurodam. We had spoken of visiting it yesterday but Kate had had little interest in miniature villages when shopping was on offer. I composed a short, grateful reply and shared the information with Samir, who nodded his acceptance of my mother's running interference.

'They never saw you,' I said, knowing this was true.

'No. Their investigation of the house caused some upset but I suspect they were not willing to return to base and admit they had lost a dozen bodies. They used gasoline to soak the outside of the house, set a fire and left.

I am not much of a believer but Allah must have been with us because although she was soaked and dirty and starving Melie never made a sound. I buried my family, waited over an hour to see if they might return, and then reclaimed the bike.

They had left the old barn standing and I was fortunate that Elirë had left one of the baby bags in the car so I had a small supply of nappies, bottles and formula and a change of clothing for Melie. Nothing for Samara and I.'

He stopped talking for a while, nursing the cup in one hand. It shook ever so slightly. When he continued he met my eyes directly. He made no comment on the moisture on my cheeks.

'It was a week before Samara would let me touch her. She just sat in the cave rocking Melie and crying.

I could have gone to the neighbours but I suspected that one of them had identified us to begin with. So at night, I would raid the closest farms taking anything that might be useful. Clothes that were left on lines at night. Fruit from trees, eggs from coops, even the odd chicken.'

He smiled deprecatingly at that memory. 'I was mostly a town boy. I had never learnt how to kill or pluck a chicken, let alone gut it and cook it. It was not something I would like to repeat.

And then I stole the goat.'

He said it so matter of factly that I nearly inhaled the foam on my coffee and despite the tears that had tracked my face to that point

I looked at the man sitting across from me, in his immaculate court attire and tried to imagine him plucking and gutting a chicken, or climbing a mountainside with a bleating goat hanging over his shoulders. The image in my head made me laugh.

I was rewarded with a smile of such gentle sincerity it touched me.

'A goat?' I prompted.

'Of course. Melie needed milk. I was terrible at milking it. In the end, Mara took the job from me. I think it was the animal that brought her back to me. She tended it as gently as she did the baby and it followed her around the caves like a dog at her feet. She cried when we had to leave it behind.

It took weeks before the injuries to Mara's face faded enough that we could risk being seen in public and even then, travelling to Kharkiv was terrifying. My parents were alive and safe, but I couldn't stay in Ukraine, I needed to feel my family, what little I had left of it, was safe. So, for a time we lived in Türkiye, where Elirë had distant family. They were at the funerals.' He reminded me.

I nodded, recalling the gathering of people swathed in black and the mountains of food they had prepared for the wake. But I didn't want to dwell on the memories of that day or what followed, or the way I had fled his home with no explanation.

'It was months before Mara spoke again. Still, in the end, she went back to school and did well enough to win a scholarship to University in England. My father became ill, so Melie and I returned to Ukraine and I got a job at the University in Kharkiv. It was through them that I learnt about the UN mission. I took leave, left Melie with her grandparents and sought out Bruce Habermann. I knew the region was still occupied in places and an active war zone in others, and I still don't know if Mara gave them my name, so I travelled on my cousin's passport just in case. We look a little similar.' He shrugged.

'Demir Benici,' I said, recalling the name.

Samir smiled.

'Then I met you. The rest is history, as they say.'

I wanted to tell him it would all be alright now. That the ICC would admit the mountain of evidence we had submitted as proof of war crimes and act to sanction the Russians or demand their withdrawal from the parts of Ukraine they continued to occupy. But I knew the best I could hope for was the opening of a tribunal that would allow further investigation and in time, some ability to prosecute the Russians for their crimes.

I realised Samir still held my hand and was startled by how comfortable it felt. When I met his gaze his lips tipped up in the smile that showed the dimple in his cheek and I found myself smiling back. Then his smile faltered.

'You left, so suddenly. And you didn't respond to my calls.'

I wanted to tell him the truth, admit seeing Samara's message and the misconception I had run with but when I opened my mouth only a half-truth came out. 'My mother rang. She told me that my sister had been in a car accident. I wasn't thinking clearly.'

The concern on his face was clear and honest.

'Is she alright?'

I pursed my lips and shook my head. 'She died. My daughter, Kate, had been living with her and we had to learn to be a family again. We are still learning. I am afraid I am not much of a mother,' I admitted without explanation, feeling guilty that after such open honesty, I treated him to half-truths, but I was not ready to give more.

'And your mother, she helps you?'

'With Kate? Yes, they have always been very close.'

'I am sorry for your loss.'

I nodded, as always feeling the futility of responding to the sentiment. What could I do or say that could possibly be an appropriate response to that? Especially in the face of his own losses.

'So you have returned to Australia.'

I nodded again. 'Yes. I could hardly take a teenager into a war zone.' Belatedly, I realised what I had said and met his eye apologetically. He flicked me half a rueful smile. 'Kate encouraged me to return to Ukraine but it didn't seem right. She lost so much when Clare died. Clare was more of a mother to her than I ever was.'

What a master I was at skirting the real truth. 'I took a job lecturing at the University in Melbourne.'

'And how are you finding that?'

I exhaled, looked at my fingernails, perfectly manicured and growing in length, the hands of someone who was not digging around in the field or dealing daily with mortuary chemicals. 'Dull. Terribly, terribly dull.'

His smile woke mine in response.

Chapter Twenty-Seven: Second Chances

Melbourne 2024

I sat with my knees on the coffee table, the laptop perched on the incline. I had still not come to a satisfactory arrangement with regards to an office, though Kate and I had been unit shopping for the past two weekends to find something more accommodating for both of us. Within reach, on the edge of the lounge, was a steaming cup of coffee made using my newest acquisition, an Italian coffee machine. Beside it on a saucer were a pair of Anzac biscuits, golden and crunchy on top with the base more than just a little burnt in places, the product of Kate's growing interest in destroying my kitchen appliances. On the screen, the spinning icon my daughter had reliably informed me was called a 'throbber' circled as I waited for a call connection. When the screen did open the background gave me a disconcerting feeling of familiarity and nostalgia. The computer I was connecting to was seated on the desk Andrew Dalton kept relatively clear, something that could not be said of the rest of the space which was cluttered with the debris of decades of research and fieldwork.

Dalton's face lit up and he began talking immediately. No sound was forthcoming.

'Andrew, you are on mute. You'll need to unmute.'

He frowned, I could read his lips as he muttered imprecations about 'unmuting', his eyes scanning the screen and his fingers poised to strike whichever key he thought might help with this. I feared he would disconnect the call when Holly invaded my view, reaching over Dalton's shoulder to touch the screen and activate the microphone. Andrew was still muttering about technology as she grinned and waved and settled herself on a stool behind him, in case further assistance was needed.

While Dalton offered awkward greetings and pleasantries I took a sip of my coffee and settled myself deeper into the lounge. After some minutes, when he seemed no closer to whatever he had requested the meeting for and even Holly was darting glances at her watch, I put my coffee down.

'What is it that you wanted?'

His mouth opened and closed a few times and he scowled at me through the screen.

'How are things with you and Kate?'

I permitted myself a small smile. 'We are growing on each other.'

In the background, through the open door of the bedroom, I heard her sniff. The kind of disparaging sound teens are excessively fond of making. She must have been curious because I could barely hear the burr of her music.

'And her education? How is she doing at school?'

Trust the Professor to be concerned for her academic well-being. 'She is a good student, she works hard and gets good grades.' Very good grades. I had just not adjusted to being a bragging parent, yet.

'Have you considered boarding school?'

In the bedroom, there was absolute silence.

I frowned, where was this going? 'No.'

Dalton took a sip of the tea Holly had placed beside him. A golden pastry I recognised as a bombolini, his favourite, sat at the front of my view. I knew it had come from the bakery just across from the apartment I had lived in for a time. It had been my habit to bring them to work with me some mornings. I picked up one of the ANZAC biscuits and bit down. They were sweet and good despite the charring. I wondered how long it would take him to get to the point. For once, he did not leave me guessing.

'Now, Victoria… I received a call from the team at *National Geographic*.'

My mouth dried out instantly, making it hard to swallow. My thoughts slipped to the lunula safely cushioned in Kate's jewellery box. Had they finally realised it was missing? I waited for whatever came next.

Andrew leaned forward, placing his cup and saucer back beside the keyboard. His face moved so close to the screen that his head took up nearly the entire space, his eyebrows, wild as ever twitched as he scowled at the screen, his eyes darting.

'Holly, how do I do that sharing screen thinga-me-bobby? I can't find the button.'

Behind him Holly rolled her eyes, flashed me a grin and leaned over his shoulder. Abruptly my view changed. A stack of folders filled the homepage, in front of a photo of the English countryside and a collection of what I assumed were grandchildren. The cursor moved across the screen to hover over one, before clicking.

Taking up the screen were the faces of the four bodies I had worked most closely on in Herculaneum, the boat shed family and the latrine man, their 'reconstructed' faces staring placidly at me from across the globe and a couple of millennia. It was not the first time I had seen them. When I had first received them the technicians had made the young woman's hair straight and the nose of the latrine warrior undamaged, I had insisted they redo the work and now the young woman's almost black hair was naturally curled and the man had a jagged scar across his nose which had veered across his face, making him look even more malign. His hair was no longer red, eyes no longer blue. Sometimes when I slept I saw these faces.

Andrew muttered, a few more clicks changed the screen and he selected another folder, another file. In the small, side-camera view he leaned forward a little, eyes skipping across the words, scrolling down through the document. It was the paper I had written, late at night, while listening to the burr of Kate's music, the hushed whisper of her late-night conversations and felt the long silence between us. It set out my theory about the death of the Praetorian and the connection between him and the weapons I had found in the boat house family's possession, both the jug and the pugio. The document included all the photos I had taken on my phone the night before I had been evicted from the premises. It read more like a historical fiction novel than a thesis but I had found myself compelled to leave it that way.

'I shared this with my friends at *National Geographic.*'

For a moment I just stared at him, unable to conceive the betrayal I felt. The document was not meant to be shared, I had shared it with Dalton only to get him to check my theory and only because I felt an odd sense of dissonance each time I considered my time in Italy. I had left a job unfinished and it bothered me.

'They would like you back.'

My head shake was instinctive.

Rather than pressing, Dalton picked up the cup and saucer beside the keyboard. He raised the cup to his lips and took a slow sip. He watched me process. It was a technique regularly used by academics. Let the silence run and nervous students rushed to fill it. I wanted to resist.

'Doing what?'

He smiled behind the cup and set it carefully back in the saucer. 'In Ercolano. They were taken with your theory and the response they have had from the pieces they shot while you were there rated very highly. With the push to reopen more investigations, they would like to finish the documentary. There was even talk of a new series.' Andrew hesitated before pressing on. 'You did sign a contract.'

I had, but that was before I was removed from the site. 'I can't.' I pointed out. 'I can hardly present for them when I am not allowed on site.'

He sniffed. 'You could, you know. You don't think David Attenborough was always on site.'

I didn't. I had once seen an entire program on the elephant caves of Kenya, then seen identical footage interspersed with shots of Attenborough, as though the original footage was actually his, and he was truly there. 'I'm not David Attenborough.'

'You underestimate your appeal. But they don't want you to do it from a distance. They want you here. Back in Ercolano.'

I shook my head. 'I am not allowed on site. You know this. I told you what happened.' And I had. Holly and Dalton were the only people who knew the truth and although both argued that I should have pressed charges against Massimo, I had been adamant in my refusal. Besides, so much had changed.

Andrew smiled. 'Actually, you are. You don't watch Italian news I am sure, but a certain Minister for Tourism has been dumped over numerous allegations of sexual misconduct against women. Apparently, there is some kind of worldwide social movement going on that he was caught up in.'

Despite my surprise, I couldn't help a smirk. Dalton might know everything there was to know about anthropology but modern social movements more or less eluded him, especially if they took place using hashtags.

'Massimo is no longer minister?'

'Massimo will be lucky to stay out of jail.'

I let this digest for a while, chewing thoughtfully on my biscuit.

'It doesn't really change anything. I doubt the ban will be lifted. Cyrano would be happy to never see my face again. Surely he would be thrilled to do the piece. Or, if they prefer, there are dozens of other anthropologists who would sacrifice a limb for the opportunity.'

'True. But both Franko and I insisted it was your discovery. They want to do a full documentary on the murder mystery, the ultimate 'cold case' file, and they want you to be the face of it. And they are right. I've read your work, it's not as thorough as your doctoral thesis but what you have discovered is extraordinary. The folks at *Nat Geo* have worked with the Italian government and its new Minister to recall your ban. They want to start as soon as possible.' He paused to let this sink in before smiling. 'Close your mouth, Victoria.'

I did as instructed.

Ω

The view from the unit was outstanding, it looked out over the Shrine of Remembrance and the Botanical Gardens, in the distance you could even see a hint of ocean. It was three bedrooms, enough for a room each and a study for me. Best of all it had two bathrooms so I wouldn't have to try to find a surface free of make-up products and canisters of body sprays. It had been three days since the Italian call.

'Well, what do you think? It's pricey and I know it's further from your school but it's closer to Grandma and Pop.'

Her expression was opaque as she looked at me. 'Why are we doing this?'

I frowned. 'We need more space.'

'But the offer from Italy…'

I shook my head. I turned back to the view. The realtor saved me by striding back into the room.

'There's only one car space but it is very close to the tram line.' He continued the sell, not seeming to take a breath as he launched into the rest of a pre-prepared speech on the benefits of the apartment.

'You have to take it, Tori.' Kate's expression was so earnest that I turned.

'Really? I thought the wardrobe space was smaller than you liked.'

She exhaled, blowing a strand of hair from her face. 'Not the apartment. The job.'

In the weeks we had been back in Australia much had changed. She didn't call me Mum, and that was fine with me, she had, however, dropped the 'aunt' and we had settled to almost roommate status. Kate cooked a lot of our meals, having quickly learned that culinary skills were not in my arsenal of talents. In return, I hassled her about her homework and assignments, corrected her grammar, made disparaging comments about her wardrobe, and ignored the late nights when I could still hear her talking on the phone. How could I not? Sometimes I even heard her laugh.

Once a week we ate dinner with her grandmother and Phil and when we did the conversation flowed naturally and freely. Although my mother and I had never actually discussed the changed arrangement of my life I did occasionally catch her looking at me, and smiling. Matt had recently informed them that they would be grandparents again, although they would have to travel to the Philippines to visit their impending grandchild. I believed she and Phil had already begun to make plans for a three-month sabbatical to Asia. This only made matters worse. With how far we had come I was not willing to shunt Kate into a boarding school just so I could forward my career.

'I can't, Kate. You know I can't.'

'I spoke to my school, they will let me board. It would mean you wouldn't have to hassle me about homework, and our phones are locked away at night, so no more all-night conversations. That should make you happy.' She dimpled at me.

The realtor frowned from Kate to me, envisioning the loss of commission.

'The answer is still, no.'

He perked up.

She stood opposite me, her gaze intense. 'I know that Grandma forced you to take me and that you would have gone back to

Ukraine otherwise. I know you hate marking papers and giving lectures.'

I couldn't argue these points.

'Grandma was right. We had to get to know each other.' She actually reached out towards me, her hand an open invitation. I took it. She squeezed once, I squeezed back. Kate smiled. 'I am lucky you know. Not everyone gets to have two mothers. But we know each other now and you shouldn't have to give up everything for my sake. I want you to take the job.'

My vision had blurred. I took a steadying breath, my world condensed to our hands, my daughter's hand in mine. I squeezed again, not surprised when she squeezed back, she was, after all, Clare's daughter as well as mine.

The realtor cleared his throat. I had no doubt he had other appointments.

'Kate, I am really glad you feel like that, and I appreciate it. I do. But for the first time in my life I am not running away. I am not leaving you behind while I traipse across the globe.'

I was surprised when she beamed. She slipped her hand from mine and pulled a wad of papers from the school bag she carried on one shoulder, holding them out to me and topping the pile with a pen. 'Great, I'll need your signature then.'

I scanned the top page, an application for a passport, below, sheets already filled in, were applications to study by distance.

'You know I have never been to Italy. It'll be an adventure.'

My daughter stared at me, daring me to refuse her.

'Turn around.'

She looked at me quizzically then obliged. I rested the paperwork on her back and clicked the pen. 'You have you know. A flight from Italy to Australia. You were just a tiny baby.'

I signed the top page, filling in the boxed spaces with my full name in block capitals and held it over her shoulder.

She spun around and smiled. 'I guess I am just going home then.' She pulled something out of her pocket. I should have been furious to see the now-gleaming gold lunula. 'This too.'

The realtor sighed.

Chapter Twenty-Eight: Friends and Enemies

Herculaneum, AD 79

Thalia had little time to consider her options. The man had seen her, she knew he would be coming. The sky was so dark it might well have been night, but a film of dim light emanated from an opening to her left. The next door was far too distant to be of use and the end of the alley as far again.

Heart erratic with turmoil she ducked into the open doorway, her hand clipped the edge, an arrow of pain shooting up her arm. In the reflex that opened her fingers, the jar containing their meagre wealth was knocked from her hand and struck the tile floor. Remarkably, it did not break, but rolled across the floor. It no longer mattered, anyway. She had seen the man who held her husband and it left her cold and shaking. A bribe would never work. A heavy, acrid scent assailed her and she recognised where she was. A series of stone-topped benches were carved with circular cutouts, in the centre of the room a large heavy vase was filled with sticks, like a dying pot plant that had lost all its leaves. Thalia knew that on the other end, submerged in water, she would find the sponges. The rich aroma of human waste assailed her senses. A lavatorium. She was stuck in a lavatorium, with only one exit, the door she had come through. As she considered escape a shadow fell across the doorway. Thalia felt for her belt, and the small slender all-purpose knife she kept there. It was hardly a weapon to use on an armed Praetorian.

Petronius stepped through the doorway, one hand on the hilt of his gladius. The pallid light of the lamps burning each side of the doorway revealed a smirk on the severe planes of his face. It sat below a nose that jutted at odd angles with his face, the last time she had seen that face the nose had been swollen and bloody and the amber eyes blackened. It was Artos who had smashed his nose. She had no doubt now that her impression had been correct and this ghost from the past was flesh and blood.

'Arrecina Quartia.' He spoke with a not-quite smile.

'Thalia.' The response was instinctual, slipping from her lips as her thoughts raced.

'Imagine finding you here, and now. I wonder whether your husband will be pleased or disappointed to discover that you are, in fact, alive.'

'Messalinus is alive?'

In the shadowy flickering light the man smiled once more, the effect was chilling. The thud of large rocks on the roof seemed to be getting heavier and more regular, the air more stifling. The earth shifted once more and both of them adjusted their stance almost automatically as it rolled beneath their feet. The pot, in the centre of the room, with its forest of sticks, rocked but did not topple.

'He is.'

'Then you must take me back to him.' Her voice sounded breathless and she wondered whether it would help or hinder the fiction she had decided to paint. She had considered the knife at her side, measured it against the one at his belt and only hoped that she could get close enough.

'I don't think he'd want to see you.'

She forced a frown. 'But I am his wife.'

'He has a new wife now, one Junia Claudia.'

Her thoughts raced, so he had not married Julia after all. Relief flooded through her, she would not wish Messalinus on anyone, least of all her niece.

'No… please, you must bring me back to him. He is my husband. You don't imagine I chose to live here, in this backwater, no better than a slave? A barbarian's whore?'

'You chose to run away.'

'Chose?' her voice was pitched and sounded almost to panic, her heart beat in time with the rocks that pummelling the roof, or so it seemed as he stepped closer. 'I did not choose! You raped me and that beast abducted me.'

Another step closer. Thalia stepped unconsciously backwards, shrinking from his presence, suddenly aware of how large the man was.

'Did he indeed?' Petronius spoke softly. 'Messalinus sent me to kill you, you know. But I rather like to think I would have refused. I still remember the feel of you beneath me. Sometimes I wondered if our time together left you with our child?'

For a moment she was startled. *Had he seen Aglaea?* No. She shook her head in denial.

Thalia dropped her head as though shaken by the recollection, when instead she sought to hide her eyes as she measured her chances of grabbing the knife and stabbing him. The chances were slim. Another shock shifted beneath her. Petronius stumbled. She propelled herself forward and in a moment of luck managed to get her hand on the knife but as she tugged on it, it caught in his belt. Petronius' hand closed on her own, his grip crushing. Thalia let out a whimper.

'Stole you, did he?' He snorted, his right hand pinning her arm painfully behind her back, pressing her against his leather breastplate as he did so, the hilt of his gladius digging against her hip. 'I don't think so. I think you are right though, you are a barbarian's whore. I think you enjoyed our time so much it turned you.'

His breath was hot and reeked of sour wine.

Deftly forcing her second arm behind her back and pinning both with one hand, he freed his left hand to grab her face, tilting it in the pale light, his fingers digging into her jaw.

Abruptly, she was no longer afraid. Her death was here, as was Artos'. She could only hope that Charis was clever enough not to wait too long to escape with Aglaea. A crash and the sound of shattered tiles heralded a piece of flying rock large enough to crush a cart, hitting the roof. Petronius jumped at the impact but did not release her. A shadow flickered in the dubious light of the doorway, stooping to pick up the jug that held all their money and her jewellery. An opportunistic thief.

'So long without your husband's touch you must have been aching for me. Not really his sort were you?'

He tipped her head the other way, as he did so she found another hardness pressed against her. She let him move her as he pleased.

'His new wife, mousy little thing that she is, does not look to have any more luck being bedded by him than you did. I wonder if he would welcome the return of his first wife.'

Unbidden, a moan escaped her lips. 'Perhaps, once I have dealt with Alexartos as he deserves, I will take you with me. By the time we reach Rome, maybe I'll have planted a bastard in your belly and if Messalinus doesn't want you back, perhaps I'll keep you. Either way, I am sure I will be well compensated.'

He shifted to push her in front of him, towards the doorway when he stumbled. Had there been another ground shift she had not noticed? No. The ground was steady. His grip dropped away from her arms as he crashed to his knees and then buckled over to land face first on the ground, toppling the jar full of toilet sponges.

A shadow in a praetorian cloak leant down, dropped the small heavy jug that he had used to indent his superior's head, and turned to face her.

Thalia threw herself towards the doorway.

It was the man's voice that halted her.

'Domina, wait… Thalia.'

There was a rich musical quality to the voice, though it was far deeper than she recalled. The shifting light of the lamp revealed her saviour's face as he stood beside the body. The young man smiled, in his tanned face dark almond-shaped eyes twinkled. His hair, darkened somewhat, though still fair was in tight curls.

'Kaeso?' She flew into his arms, sobbing.

After a moment he pushed her from him. The once effeminate youth had grown, his bare arms were solid with muscle, and he stood almost as tall as Artos now.

The body on the ground, moaned softly, the fingers, on one hand, scratched feebly at the floor. Thalia considered him for a moment, narrowed eyes betraying her fury. She stepped from Kaeso's embrace and stooped over the body. Despite the blood that ran in narrow rivulets from some point in his hair, leaving veinlike red tendrils around his ear and down his face, the fine layer of ash that had dusted the floor was disturbed by the breath from the Praetorian's nose. His eyes made rapid flickering movements between narrow slits. Thalia knelt beside the body, one knee in the ash, the other on the man's back below the shoulder blades. Her hand was wrapped around Petronius' pugio. This time it pulled freely from his belt. Her left hand gripped the thick dark hair on his head and pulled back, his head was heavier than she anticipated. Kaeso may have made a noise when she did what happened next, perhaps shocked at the violence of her action. She pushed herself to her feet, the bloodied dagger still in her fist, staring down at the patterns made in the ash by the rhythmically spurting arterial blood.

Thalia froze.

'Domina, there is no time.' He looked at the body and the room, then strode across the narrow space and with Herculean effort managed to shift one of the heavy granite slabs with the key-shaped cutouts suspended above the sewer pit. 'Help me?' Kaeso asked, 'Take his legs?'

And so, the Prefect's daughter, the former Consul's wife and the barbarian's lover thrust the knife, still slick with blood into her belt, took the Praetorian by his sandalled feet and helped dump his body in the lavatory, though not before Kaeso had rifled through his clothes to snatch the keys tied to his belt. As the stone slab was returned Thalia stooped to collect the jar she had brought with her and tucked it beneath her arm, it might still be useful in paying for passage from the hell that surrounded them. Kaeso removed his cloak, folded it several times and handed it to her.

'Hold it over your head to cushion yourself from falling rocks.'

She obeyed, following him with the makeshift cushion over her head, out into the street, following his bare head as he strode, with all the confidence of a Praetorian and towards the carcer.

Chapter Twenty-Nine: You Are My Home

Herculaneum, AD 79

Thalia stepped around the second body, well aware that Kaeso had deliberately positioned himself so that, if she had seemed intent on slitting another throat, he might be in a position to stop her. She was too intent on the cell door before her to explain that the second unconscious man was no threat to her or her family. The key Kaeso passed her fitted easily into the latch and when the cell door opened, leaving an arch of clear space on the ashen floor, Artos blinked at her in surprise before his features rearranged themselves into a smile. Kaeso slipped through the door after her, using his own knife to saw at the hempen threads that held his arms out of Thalia's reach.

He stumbled, and nearly fell, but Thalia steadied him, taking his weight while he found his feet and the blood returned to his hands. These he tangled in her hair, his head bent to hers, his lips pressed against hers. It was fleeting but they had little time. 'You found Aglaea?'

'Yes, I left her with Charis.'

'Kaeso.' Artos nodded his thanks, not releasing his grip on her. 'I wondered if it was really you. I owe you my life.'

The younger man nodded seriously.

The ground shuddered again beneath their feet. Artos tensed.

'You need to hurry. I must return to my troop and to the plaza, the Praetor will be ready to leave. I would ask you to join us, but Artos is too easily recognised. I know Ulpianus sent to Misenum for help, by now Admiral Pliny will surely have the fleet at sea, perhaps heading to the shore was a faster way to escape than laden with goods as we will be.'

Thalia nodded, she had seen them gathering the wagons, crawling with slaves, loaded with possessions and weighted with smaller more portable sculptures and treasures. By now the Praetor and his family would be loaded in the covered wagon and ready to leave.

Artos shifted his gaze from the tall Praetorian to his small wife and when she shrugged, back again. He held out an arm and the younger man gripped it firmly. 'I thank you for your help Kaeso. We will retrieve our daughter and head for the sea. May the gods keep you.'

The former catamite, now Praetorian, nodded as a large piece of rock hit the roof with an accompanying cracking of tiles. 'Hurry. Keep your head covered. I don't think we have long.'

Kaeso bent down to kiss Thalia on the top of her forehead. 'Be careful who you stab with that.' He said with a glance at the dagger she had tucked beneath her belt.'

'Take care, Kaeso. And thank you.'

She hugged him fiercely as Artos plucked the dagger from her side and tucked it in his own belt.

Having refused to take back his cloak her former slave and saviour slipped out the door.

It was terrifying to step out into the darkness, the only hint of light came from the west although at times they thought they could see flames, flickering walls of them, on the distant mountainside. The three figures walked together to the end of the alleyway before turning in opposite directions.

The constant rain of particles and heavier crash of larger rocks made Thalia wonder if perhaps the rumours of giants on the hillside were correct, some of the chunks of rock that fell from the sky were too large for a man to lift and were surely hurled by some supernatural force. They struggled through shin-deep deposits of ash and pumice, their cloaks pulled over their heads and wrapped about their faces to save breathing in the acrid-smelling filth. Artos grunted and swore as one of the smaller rocks struck his shoulder but refused to slow his pace, dragging Thalia past half-buried statues in a surreal landscape. Roofs groaned ominously under the weight of the accumulated rock. Sometimes they passed others, struggling likewise. No words were shared, everyone seemed intent on some goal. Once, Thalia stumbled over what turned out to be a corpse, buried in ash, head crushed by falling rock. Soundless, Artos tugged her to her feet and onwards.

Thalia had barely entered the dark stairwell, lit by the muted light of a half dozen oil lamps sputtering in the thick air when a child's body struck hers.

'Mammina! You founded Papi.'

In the insipid light, over the dark tousled hair of the child pressed between them, Thalia considered the frazzled-looking slave and felt gratitude wash through her. Not only had the girl remained to care for the child, but she had packed small bundles of belongings for each of them to carry.

'Should we stay here? Is it safe to take Aglaea out into that?' Her voice was barely a whisper as she considered carrying her small daughter back out into the hail of rock and rain of ash and pebbles.

Above them, the building creaked and groaned.

Artos' eyes met hers. 'It is no safer here and as Kaeso said, the fleet will pull in at the beach. I agree with him, I don't think we have much time.'

Thalia compressed her lips keeping her worry to herself. At her feet, Ajax whimpered. She passed her daughter into Artos' strong arms, handing up the dog so that her husband held both child and beast and crossed to take the slave's hand and with a squeeze, thanked her. A fleeting smile tilted Charis' lips.

'We make for the shore,' she said as she bunched up Artos' thickest cloak and arranged it over him and his burdens. Thalia handed a bundle of clothing to the slave, 'Hold them over your head, move quickly, don't lose sight of us, it is near dark as night out there.'

She took up another of the bundles, tucking it over her head to hang off one hip before holding Kaeso's thick cloak over her head, she tucked one hand into her husband's belt before sending a short prayer out to any god who might be listening.

'Ready?' Artos asked.

With a reassuring smile for Charis, she nodded and without letting go of her husband they climbed out into the rubble, now almost half her height and into the thickening choking blackness struggling as the earth shifted again beneath their feet and the air shuddered with its roar.

It was like travelling through a storm, the air was filled with ash that threatened to choke them and a hail of rocks pelted down on their heads. Only reminding herself that reaching the beach was their best hope of escape kept her from seeking shelter each time Thalia was struck by a sizeable piece of scalding rock or tephra. The light had become non-existent, except for the red glow on the mountain behind them that seemed to flow in arcs on the distant peak. She was startled when she nearly walked into a man standing, one arm lifted to the sky, but then relief flooded through her. They had reached the beachfront. The man was the statue of Nonius Balbus that overlooked the plaza above the boatsheds, where the wealthiest of the town's fisherman stored their boats and equipment. He stood buried ankle-deep, a considerable achievement given the plinth on which the marble stood was very nearly half her height.

There was considerable movement below. People holding wads of cloth or board over their heads to ward off the pumice huddled in miserable clumps on the shore staring out towards the sea. More huddled around the shed openings, a few, using oars to clear the ash and pumice that had built up before the opening, left cave-like depressions in the darkness of the wall. As they reached the foot of the stairs Artos exchanged greetings and hushed conversation with a few who were known to him before pulling her close and dropping his head to her ear.

'The fishing families took their boats as soon as the ground began to shake, with the exception of that one.' He indicated the keel of a small boat that had been upturned and nearly buried.

'A few tried to take it out earlier but the pumice was so thick on the sea that it was impossible to row.'

Thalia squinted at the scene before her. Beyond the handful of hopefuls looking out to sea, it appeared that a carpet of undulating pebbles that lifted and fell like a great breathing creature lay before her. The floating pumice was so thick that the water could not be seen.

'What does that mean?' she asked, even knowing the answer.

He exhaled slowly, tightening his one-armed hold on her, Aglaea nestled squirming between them. 'It means that even if the fleet were on its way they will never get near the shore.'

She let the words settle in her mind.

'There is no hope then.'

'I didn't say that.' His tone rumbled like the mountain overhead. 'This all may stop, and when it does the fleet may get through, or we might be able to make our way to Napoli along the coast road.'

Thalia nodded as though accepting his words. A roar along the foreshore suggested the weight on the roof had overcome another building and it had collapsed in on itself. There was little point to wondering if the residents had escaped.

'Come, let's see if we can find some space inside. Get Aglaea out of this.'

The sheds were crowded with families, mostly women and children who had taken up spaces and claimed them as their own. A dozen or more lamps threw pallid light that went some way to illuminating the space, at least enough to avoid stepping on anyone. It was not until the third opening that Artos was able to push his way through, all the way to the back, where a niche in the rear wall gave enough space for a handful of bodies. The floor was filled with rope and nets which Thalia shuffled until there was a nest. She settled in amongst the coils, pulling Aglaea and the pup onto her lap. Charis took up position on a mound of netting and began rustling through the bundle she carried, emerging with a lamp, a half circle of Felix's bread and a jug.

The slave exchanged a segment of their loaf with near neighbours for the use of their wick to light the lamp. In the amber haze, they shared out the bread and sour, watered wine. Even Ajax got a few crumbs before the slave wrapped what was left in cloth and tucked it away for later. Eternally hopeful, Ajax whimpered but the slave was not forthcoming and the pup settled instead for the warmth and reassurance of his child master's lap.

Artos stood, stooped under the low roof of the niche.

'What are you doing?'

He cleared his throat. 'I will wait outside, with the men.'

Thalia considered the refugees around them. It was true, many of the men had chosen to wait outside, but many more huddled, by themselves, with a huddle of other men, or with their families.

She reached to grasp his hand, wrapping her fingers through his. 'I'm not ready to lose you again.'

'Thalia, if I wait outside, others can use the space, women, children.'

'Are there more?' She studied the darkness of the boatshed opening. In truth, none had arrived since they had, it seemed they were the last of the stragglers. Perhaps others were huddled in their own houses unwilling to risk the falling skies, hoping and praying that their roof might prove more solid than those nearby. Crushed under the weight of sky debris.

'Don't go Papi.' Their daughter's quavering voice proved the decider, Thalia shifted to give the man who had saved her from her life as a wealthy patrician wife and brought her to this place. She found that despite her fear she could not regret her choices. Artos slipped his arm behind her and she leaned her head against his shoulder. Like hail, the staccato beat of rock, softened now by the piles of debris it landed on but still a steady susurrus continued. A few children cried fitfully, hushed now and then by adult voices. Some sobbed quietly in the darkness.

'Story, Papi?' Aglaea curled in her lap, her head resting on her father's thigh.

Normally it was Thalia who told the stories, drawing on the poems and plays and stories she had read. Artos' stories were of battlefields and hunting, of bloodshed and death, yet this seemed appropriate and she listened, sheltered by his strong right arm as he told of the siege of a city on a mountain in Judaea, a place called Masada. Unlike when he had told the same story to the Emperor, this time Artos' story was of the bravery of the people who continued to fight the Romans despite being held, under siege for months, while they starved as the Roman army feasted about their campfires. Who threw rocks, while the Romans hurled boulders and fiery arrows, until, unwilling to concede defeat and to permit their people to be taken as slaves, the men drew lots and set about quietly bringing death until, when the Romans finally pounded down the gates all they won was a city of ghosts.

α

Thalia was uncertain what had woken her. From the steady but light breathing of the man beside her, she knew he was not asleep. Around

371

her the boatshed had fallen into silence, punctuated by the night noises of dozens of sleeping forms.

'What time is it?' she whispered. She had lost all sense of time.

He seemed to consider for a moment before answering. 'Close to the sixth hour. I think.'

Charis shuffled on her net bed.

'Does it seem quieter? Has it stopped?' Thalia looked towards the shed entrance. Along the shore, she could make out the silhouettes of men, huddled around a fire. The falling debris must have ceased for that to be possible.

'A little while ago, yes. Go back to sleep. We will leave in the morning. For now, rest. At least we know this roof will not collapse.'

She was quiet for a time, listening to the exhalations of her daughter's breath and the soft suckling sounds she made, her thumb tucked in her mouth. The golden crescent shape of the child's lunula, which had fallen out of her tunic and lay gleaming like the real thing in the light of the lamp beside her cheek. Like the golden Artemis pendant that hung between her breasts, Artos had made the amulet with his own hands and placed it around the child's neck on the eighth day after her birth, when they made sacrifices to the goddess Juno and spoke her name aloud for the first time. The amulet was to protect her until she was old enough for marriage. A marriage that Aglaea would choose to a man she could love. She and Artos had agreed on that. She remembered the expression on his face as he held the tiny sleeping infant in his arms, he could wrap both hands around her and cover her completely. The only time he came close to showing equal joy was when he looked on her. Thalia nestled closer into Artos' shoulder.

Charis fidgeted restlessly. 'Domina, I must go outside. I need to find a place to relieve myself.'

Thalia nodded, her own bladder was full, but with Aglaea lying on her lap, the small tousled head tucked between her breasts, a trickle of drool slinking its way down towards her navel, she dared not.

'Don't go far. Stay clear of the men on the beach.' She warned in a whisper as the slave girl slipped, like a shadow between the prone bodies and out of the arched opening.

Artos stretched his legs, grateful for the additional space one less body afforded.

'Where will we go?'

Artos frowned. 'Anywhere away from here. In case the Praetor returns or worse, reports my miraculous appearance in Herculaneum to Rome.'

'What about your home? Will you show me your homeland? Show me your golden plains where the horses run.'

He wanted to tell her, no. That between the Roman occupiers and the unpredictable tribesmen it was not a safe place for them, then he imagined standing with his arms around her, bathed in sunlight, a westerly wind playing with her dark hair and rippling the gleaming seedheads of the grasses. He imagined Aglaea running, giggling through grasses taller than her head, chasing after wild horses. He could almost hear the thunder of their hooves. Only the thunder, getting closer, getting louder, was not merely in his imagination.

The men around the fire on the beach had turned and in the flickering firelight their faces reflected open-mouthed horror. By his knee, Ajax let out a low threatening growl. Aglaea twitched in her sleep.

Artos pressed his head against the dark one beside him, the woman he loved, pulling her closer against him, forming a protective huddle around the child as if together they could keep away the coming danger.

Thalia turned her head towards the beach as Artos whispered in her ear, his breath warm on her cheek.

'You are my home. Home is wherever you are.'

Epilogue

Ercolano, 2024

Holly had thrown herself into my arms when I walked through the door, nearly knocking the bag of pastries from my hand.

'Bombolini?' Dalton asked hopefully.

I handed him the bag.

From behind his desk and an open door Direttore Franko Cyrano nodded but did not emerge. I found I could forgive his treatment, knowing how confused he must be to have my return celebrated after the ignoble nature of my exit less than two years earlier.

'My turn, Holly, before you smother her.' Andrew Dalton smiled over her shoulder having glanced up from inspecting the paper bag's contents.

Chastened, Holly stepped back, allowing her mentor to step forward and envelop me in a fatherly hug. 'Welcome back. We knew we would see you again. Filming starts next week I hear?'

I nodded, but stepped back to usher Kate forward, she stood, looking both pleased and self-conscious.

'My daughter, Kate.'

Holly cooed as she crushed my daughter into a hug. Kate held out her hand to Dalton. 'I am pleased to meet you. My class watched your documentary on the sewers of Herculaneum in Ancient History last term. It was fascinating.'

'Did you indeed?' Dalton smiled as he puffed up like a proud peacock.

Ω

I closed the door to my lab behind us, allowing Kate a moment to breathe deeply in relief. She had handled the flight with aplomb, had marvelled during the three days we spent in Rome doing all the touristy things, but had been pleased to claim a bed in the small apartment we now shared in Ercolano. From Kate's window she could even catch a glimpse of the bay of Naples, my own faced the mountain. Kate had already put up the Christmas tree, decorated with shiny baubles bought in Rome. Beneath it, carefully wrapped, were the presents my mother had sent for us both for our first Christmas together.

'You're doing well,' I murmured and she shared a grin.

'*Molto bene,*' she said, practising her textbook Italian.

'This is where I work.' I gestured, encompassing the two brand new benches with their gleaming stainless steel tops, the outer ring of cupboards and the piles of boxed skeletons stacked on them, the printer, microscope and two stools beside the benches. I pulled my laptop out and placed it beside the printer in its usual space.

Someone, Holly I guessed, had managed to return the space to its original condition. I had little doubt it had been re-occupied before last week.

'Take a seat.'

She did, assuming possession of one of the two wobbly stools.

I moved to the plastic boxes, pulling three from the stack and placing them on the bench before Kate. I had not even needed to read the numbers labelled on the front. I opened his first, then hers and then the child.

'This is them?' Kate asked.

I nodded and proceeded to point out the differences between the male and female skulls and pelvises. Kate listened intently. The bones still felt comfortingly warm when I touched them.

'She was so tiny.' Kate stared at the remains of the child.

I nodded. She slipped a hand into her pocket and drew out a handkerchief. I recognised it as Clare's by the careful embroidery, a talent my sister had had, along with a will to make things beautiful. I hoped it was something she had passed on to our daughter. Peeling open the white fabric she exposed the golden lunula and looked up at me.

I nodded again.

Hesitantly, my daughter reached out and let the golden pendant dangle over, then slip between the tiny rib bones, beneath the tiny skull.

'There you go, little one.' She said softly. 'You are safe now.'

THE END

AUTHOR'S NOTES

What Remains is a fictional story inspired by my study of the Cities of Vesuvius and the investigation of human remains there, including the recent discovery of what is thought to be a praetorian guard (though this one not found in a toilet). But it was also inspired by my fascination with forensic anthropology and the stories told by Dame Sue Black, a forensic anthropologist who has worked with the identification of victims of mass disasters, including war crimes on behalf of the United Nations. Samir's story is inspired both by one of her stories and by articles written about UN documented War Crimes in Crimea and Ukraine.

Prefect Marcus Arrecinus Clemens, his daughter Tertia (Clementia), the child Julia, Lucius Valerius Catullus Messalinus, Emperor Vespasian and Titus Flavius are all true figures from history, and perhaps I should apologise to Titus who history records as a 'Golden' Emperor though glosses over suggestions of a dark and violent past. To Messalinus, I make no such apologies, history records him as a violent and much-hated informer, his blindness and his consulship are recorded facts. At present, there is no historical record that tells us of Messalinus' fate.

Currently recorded history tells us that Vesuvius erupted a little after midday on the 24th of August in AD79, sending most residents fleeing. Not all escaped, however, and shortly after midnight a pyroclastic flow of superheated volcanic gas and tephra engulfed the city, burying it in up to 20 meters of volcanic material that would have killed any remaining inhabitants of the town almost instantly. Of the human remains discovered in Herculaneum, most were found to have sheltered in the 'boat houses' along the shoreline, no doubt in hope of rescue from the sea.

I have chosen to work with more recent and disputed dates for the eruption, setting in in late October, a theory based on the presence of braziers, graffiti, coins and the presence of season fruit that would be too early for the established August date.

After all that, while heavily researched, there are many times (too many to note) where I have altered settings, descriptions, events and attitudes to suit a modern audience. This is after all historical fiction and artistic license is necessary.

The eruption of Mount Vesuvius and its catastrophic effects on the region were an early test of Titus capacity as Emperor and one that saw him shine. Records tell us that he immediately dispensed aid to the region and generously opened not only Rome's but his own personal coffers to assist the refugees. He even visited the area, twice.

While there are presently no accounts of survivors (aside from the belatedly written account of a teenage Pliny the Younger, who at Misenum, many miles away, could not have actually seen much) recent studies have traced the names of residents of Pompeii and Herculaneum and found post eruption records of them in other places, so many did survive, relocate and thrive, though they never returned to the towns which were buried beyond trace.

The entire modern timeline is purely fictive although Australian experts of all kinds, like the wonderful forensic archaeologist Dr Estelle Laser who is responsible for much of the research conducted on the human remains in Pompeii, have and still do actively work in the region and provide new insights into our ever-evolving understanding of the past. The reopening of the region to excavation (post COVID) has, however meant that there are many exciting new finds being exposed every week and these are regularly released to the media. Who knows what else will be uncovered!

ACKNOWLEDGMENTS

Although writing is very much a solitary business, getting that book into readers' hands is never a solo venture and there are many to thank.

Firstly, to Peter, my most stalwart supporter who never doubted I could do it, even when I did. Thank you for believing, and for encouraging me to hone my craft even when it meant days and nights and weeks away at writing retreats, conferences and workshops, and all the expenses that come with this expensive and time-consuming vocation. Thank you for keeping our lives running while I wrote, and wrote, and wrote. I couldn't have done this without you.

To my mum, who encouraged me to write stories as a child and read to me every night in my childhood. You helped me grow my love for words.

To Fiona McIntosh, who first made me believe being a writer (for real) was both possible and plausible.

To Kate Forsyth, my mentor, who encouraged my early ideas and drove me wisely and ruthlessly to make it better.

To Dr Samantha Tipper who read the forensics and helped me get it right, or as close as could be to suit the needs of the story.

To Jo Mackay, who found my sample chapter and made contact, and to Johanna Baker (also from HC) who made me rewrite it three times and made it better each time, thank you for making me believe the story had a shot and polishing it in the process.

To Dee and Historium Press who quickly scooped up the lost and homeless manuscript, gave it a home, and put the Historium imprint on it. Thank you for believing in my story and making this dream a reality.

To Kathy Servian and Emma who made my pen and ink characters into living breathing people.

And to my future readers, whoever you are, for taking the time to hear my stories, I have many more to tell so the more you read, like, share, and review the better chance you'll get to read more!

ABOUT THE AUTHOR

Erryn Lee has spent most of her life between the covers of books, her love for historical fiction drew her to a career as an English and History teacher, where she enjoys sharing her passion for both language and the past with young adults (at least until she needs to give it up to write full time).

When not teaching or writing she is deeply immersed in research and studying her Masters in History. Erryn lives with her husband, a fluctuating number of horses and three bossy cavoodles on a horse farm in the picturesque central west of NSW, Australia.

Follow the author at
www.errynleeauthor.com
www.historiumpress.com/erryn-lee

REVIEWS ARE APPRECIATED

www.historiumpress.com